*Ye shall know the truth
and the truth shall make you mad.*

Aldous Huxley

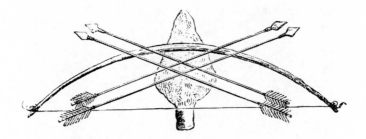

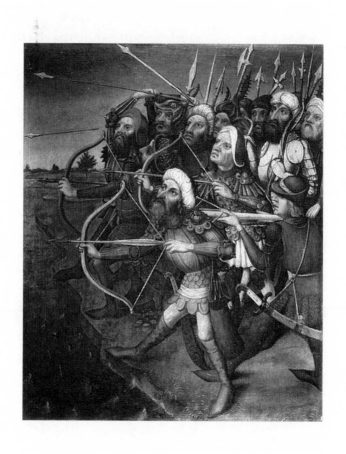

Thomas M. Meine

ARCHERY THROUGH THE AGES

In the Twilight of Truth

Manufactured and published by
Books on Demand GmbH, Norderstedt

Copyright © Thomas M. Meine
5th Edition November 2016

ISBN 9 783732 293063

CONTENTS

PREFACE

Myths, folktales, legends, they have been poured upon us from a seemingly inexhaustible horn of plenty since the days of the ancient.

We are burdened with far too many of these wacky stories and whopping lies, and the very least we must do is to critically evaluate the content of these commonly senseless concoctions by using our common sense.

Non the less, many people firmly believe in most of this crap, and the primary reasons for this behavior are:

1. They do not know better.
2. They like it or they just accept it this way.
3. Others told them to believe it.

Seldom enough can we trust it, because it is true.

But even if we are aware of the fact that this yarn should not to be taken seriously, like most of the content of the myths, folktales or legends, we must also question the value of such 'works' and must honestly ask ourselves: What is it good for?

Fairy tales are good. Santa Claus and Snow White are good. On the other hand, many stories we consider to be of cultural value are not good. If we treat them like fairy tales – fine! If we try to find a hidden message or a deeper sense – a waste of time!

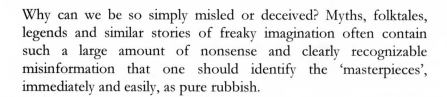

Why can we be so simply misled or deceived? Myths, folktales, legends and similar stories of freaky imagination often contain such a large amount of nonsense and clearly recognizable misinformation that one should identify the 'masterpieces', immediately and easily, as pure rubbish.

We are simply taken for a ride when we read some of the famous legends. If we want to increase this foolishness, we must reach for the Greek or Roman myths, whereby the latter are nothing else but cheaply cribbed versions of the Greek literary applesauce. The Romans just bothered to change the names of the characters.

Myths, folktales, legends – they are so deeply engraved in the memory of people that they will find it extremely difficult to separate themselves again from this intellectual dung, and often they will not succeed at all.

But then, they do not differ anymore from the North Koreans who believe, after long years of intense exposure to the propaganda, that the everlasting leader Kim-Jong-il was born on the Paektu-San (the white-headed mountain). See what happens when you tell them that his birthplace was in fact at the arse end of nowhere, a tiny fishing village in Russia, called Wjatskoje.

Bow and arrow often play a leading role in these crazy stories, which are quite often only shoddy efforts of intentional misinformation. Therefore, and for the sake of my beloved archery sport, I have decided to go to the bottom of all this in a forthright way.

I will try to shed light on some issues and point out things where clarification is urgently needed, but I must warn you beforehand: When I did my research for this book project, it soon became clear to me – and you will make this experience your own – that things appear to be worse than one could have ever imagined.

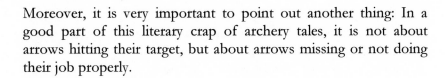

Moreover, it is very important to point out another thing: In a good part of this literary crap of archery tales, it is not about arrows hitting their target, but about arrows missing or not doing their job properly.

In other words, no bow and arrow in the hands of brave men, using this weapon in an effective way, have influenced the history of humanity. To the contrary, many of these cheap novelettes of the past try to make us believe that history has moved forward through a series of badly shot arrows.

But not only the stories itself have a penetrating odor of deception. We must strongly assume that occasionally some of the works have not even been written by the person who is famous for them.

One writer, celebrated for the efforts of other people, is the famous William Shakespeare. In great likelihood, he was just the front man for a plagiarist behind him, who did not want to put his own credibility and reputation at risk.

Was it Francis Bacon, son of the Lord Keeper of the Great Seal under Queen Elizabeth I? Was it Edward DeVere, the Earl of Oxford, who might even have invented the person of William Shakespeare or Walter Raleigh or Christopher Marlowe?

The only significant document Shakespeare had definitively written himself (if he existed at all), was his last will.

He left his widow with nothing but 'the second best bed' in the house. And I ask you, is this characteristic of a man, hailed for some of the greatest plays and poems known?

But that's not all. He whoever Shakespeare really was, had not only written out of hiding, but had even stolen famous pieces of literature in best 'legend style'. This is plagiarism at its best by William 'the copycat' Shakespeare.

Let us just take 'Romeo and Juliet': We know the worn out pattern of this work from Hero and Leander, Pyramus and Thisbe, Tristan and Isolde (with or without music from Wagner), Flore and Blanscheflur or Troilus and Cressida. These stories are of Oriental, Greek, Germanic or Celtic origin or had been cribbed from many other sources.

Geoffrey Chaucer, an English writer of the 14th century, was the first one to use the rather oafishly woven basics of this theme in his epos 'Troilus and Criseyde'. It was copied by Arthur Brookes in his 'Tragic History of Romeus and Juliet' of 1562 and by his fellow Englishman William Painter, who wrote 'Rhomeo and Julietta' in the year 1567. The latter two had copied their 'works' from the French version of Pierre Boaistuau of the year 1559.

Pierre Boaistuau himself had stolen the idea from Matteo Bandellos and his 'Romeo e Giulietta' of the year 1554. Believe it or not, also Matteo Bandelos had pilfered his drama, namely from the version of Luigi da Portos of the year 1530.

The 'original first copy' by Luigi da Portos came out with the title 'Giuletta e Romeo' (Juliet and Romeo). What a brilliant idea of distinction by the later literary pirates to turn the names of the main characters the other way around: 'Romeo and Juliet'.

Shakespeare, or the counterfeiter behind him, had stolen complete sentences – word for word! – from the 'work' of Arthur Brookes and other material from William Painter, but these writers had themselves already massively stolen intellectual property from others, who in turn had repeatedly and systematically transferred those possessions for their own use...

Sad, but true: Romeo and Juliet by William Shakespeare is nothing but a 'summary of highlights' of other Romeo and Juliet or Juliet and Romeo stories.

Moreover, Shakespeare's dramas 'Troilus and Cressida' (another screwed up love affair), as well as 'The Two Noble Kinsmen', had been copied from Geoffrey Chaucer's works.

Even 'The Knight's Tale' by Geoffrey Chaucer – the template for Shakespeare's 'The Two Noble Kinsmen' – was not original. It had been stolen from Giovanni Boccaccio's 'Teseida', whose heroes are named Palemone and Arcita.

This, in turn, gave Richard Edwards the 'inspiration' to write a play called 'Palamon and Arcite', whereby he not just 'borrowed' the name, but also the plot.

The stage collapsed, when the play was performed in Oxford before Elizabeth I. Three people died and five were injured in this accident. In the year 1566 that was no reason for a longer interruption; the show continued to play that night.

'A Midsummer Night's Dream', one of Shakespeare's most 'original' plays, is nothing but a pirate copy, sucking honey from several sources.

So much for that part of classic literature…

Shakespeare's academic contribution to literature is – openly spoken – of highly doubtful quality. Who cares? What concerns bow and arrow, there is apparently nothing of importance in his literary patchworks we must criticize. However, there are other 'productions' we archers must be worried about.

With all this in mind and mainly concentrating on the investigation of the misuse of bow and arrow or the role of archers in other shoddy outpourings, called myths, legends or folktales, I dedicate this book to all my comrades of archery. And those who have not yet shot an arrow from a bow will make their own exciting discoveries, as we walk together through the twilight of truth.

You are all cordially invited to follow me into this strange land, lying in the shadows of madness, drug inebriation and other mind dulling, paranoid excesses that must have inspired those 'great works of culture', whether or not you believe in the myths, folk tales or legends or if you just love them as they are.

In this book, you will also find some stories of newer date, noteworthy or trivial, somber or rather amusing. They have been included to let the reader relax once in a while from the horrible discoveries related to these myths, legends and folktales.

However, if you see your picture of our so-called cultural heritage damaged, try to take it with humor, even if it might occasionally prove to be difficult.

The potatoes and the humor have one thing in common: You must dig them out first. But then, good or bad is often just a matter of opinion.

MYTHS, FOLKTALES, LEGENDS AND OTHER RUBBISH

At first, I will try to differentiate the terms, although the borderlines are somewhat fluent. One thing should be common: These stories are not about historical facts or true events. If that would be different, they would not be myths, folktales or legends.

Storytelling is a common feature in all cultures. Most people enjoy stories, true or untrue. Consequently, this has created the storytellers and they have balanced the demand and supply from the beginning of civilization.

The myths have a religious or occult background with a focus on prehistoric times, along with the inventing of mythical creatures and demons. They try to explain to us the origin of the earth. On top of that, the poets have dreamed up all kinds of gods.

The folktales, very similar to the myths, are said to have a central message. They are dealing to a lesser extend with the gods, but tend to refer more to heroes of flesh and blood. Based on oral transmission, they sell us incredible events, yet after all, with a claim to truth slightly above the fairy tales.

Legends pretend to be more factual reports. They have been communicated over the centuries and adapted or changed to the spirit of the time, whenever they were passed on in their more befitting style.

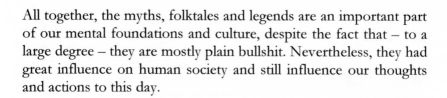

All together, the myths, folktales and legends are an important part of our mental foundations and culture, despite the fact that – to a large degree – they are mostly plain bullshit. Nevertheless, they had great influence on human society and still influence our thoughts and actions to this day.

Facts are facts, but unfortunately often twisted. When the facts are twisted – we call it 'spinning' in the political arena – it becomes an art, as the spider has created an intricate web. We sell our product to people as a tablet of truth, and shysters follow a fascinating procedure that allows them to twist not only the facts, but also the entire law. That way, they can convince us all and, by repetition, even themselves.

Statistics – only for the sake of completeness – are all too often not a reflection of the truth and are habitually falsified, embellished or made relative by shrinking or dragging either the value- or the time axis, according to the needs.

Only the *fairy tales* are good and honest (with some exceptions). Fairy tales tell us beautiful and exciting stories. Fairy tales are not true – and we know that. Fairy tales have the decisive advantage of presenting stories to us, openly showing what they really are: They are fairy tales and, when written down, they are found in books where the cover correctly says what you get inside: *fairy tales*.

Now, there is an exception: the *political fairy tales*. They are only recognized as such after the elections, because they have not been called fairy tales before.

There are myths that are short-lived and others that have been a phenomenon through history. Many of them appear in variations, yet with essentially the same content in different cultures. Others go through time with constant changes, like the myth of Prometheus.

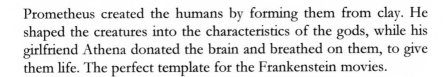

Prometheus created the humans by forming them from clay. He shaped the creatures into the characteristics of the gods, while his girlfriend Athena donated the brain and breathed on them, to give them life. The perfect template for the Frankenstein movies.

The folktales, like religions and ideologies, can take dangerous courses or may even be subject to misuse, especially if Wagner accentuates the stories with opera music. Hence, they became destined for malicious exploitation, although he was not to blame.

There is no point to contemplate the extent of truth or fiction contained in the myths, folktales and legends, considering the mostly moronic content.

Some may believe that there is a hidden truth, not accessible by pure rationality or that the storyline has a deeper sense. On the other hand, there is a lack of any usable clue what the meaning could be, besides 'non-sense'.

I suppose that many of these pipe dreams show us only the backward state of science and the limited intellectual capabilities at a certain point of time in the past, combined with inability to find enlightenment for the inexplicable.

Similar to the Greek myths, humans have chosen complete satisfaction to express their fantasies in all kinds of stories when the mind could not reach further.

At the time, one was simply overwhelmed. Today, a halfway intelligent human being should be nothing but amused about this rubbish or – even better – appropriately disgusted.

Does it describe it all? No, I am also of the opinion that all this nonsense represents not only the weird understanding of the world by the storytellers, while the rest of the population believed in their fantasies. I am sure that some of the 'philosophers' and 'poets' came up with their baloney, fully aware that they would take the piss out of people, notwithstanding the fact that some of the writers probably just wanted to entertain.

Of course, there is also the scheme of providing moral guidance. Some of this bunkum been produced to teach people how to behave and to avoid the consequences of misbehavior.

Myths and legends usually include hurt and embarrassment. All is then blamed on the stupidity, dishonesty, negligence or greed of people. If none of that applies, it is attributed to the power of destiny.

If the public would be remotely aware, they would realize that much hurt also comes from the exposure to these stories or paying attention to this garbage.

Admittedly, it is nothing else than what is too often presented to us today in the area of pseudo-information or propagandistic reporting by whatever news network. We do not call it myth or legend, we call it television, but I am sure, future generations will not base their wisdom on the 'Misfits' or the 'X-files'.

The old Greeks, especially, have put so much hogwash into their stories that, even in the old days, one should have recognized the merciless stupidity in its full dimension. We cannot explain the weird fantasy-monsters, the disgusting incest-relationship within the families of the gods – usually in worst-case combinations – the absurd and bizarre imaginations of constellations in the sky or the mysterious islands, solely with a mental confusion of the poets.

Whilst some of the storytellers have certainly recognized the value of entertainment of myths, folktales and legends in a world that did not know radio, television or the Internet, many of these stories have been used or even been made up by the ruling class for their own purposes.

The Catholic Church in particular, had employed a large number of manipulating 'pen pushers' and spin doctors to bolster its image and power. During earlier periods, everything was written in Latin and at the same time, the masses were kept ignorant, prompting their inability to read this fudged material. Instead, they had been frequently exposed to verbal mass stultifications from the pulpit.

Humans need both, facts and myths, as well as rationality and spirituality to cope with the incomprehensible questions pertaining to our existence and future in the universe. The myths are a refuge from the mysterious and sometimes even from reality. Nevertheless, the ability to create myths and fantasy stories are part of the difference between vegetating and living. Deception, irony, sarcasm, lies – man has brought his abilities to communicate on a higher level, but is harming only its own species with it.

Our modern and illuminated society should however be in a position to evaluate the miniscule amount of truth or the distressful quality of information contained in the various myths, folktales and legends.

It is long overdue to shed some light on the true value of the 'best sellers' of the myths, those with ancient Greek origin, supplying us with most chaotic, contradictory and completely illogical stories. Historians or scribes may suck their honey from it to understand the past or in connection with philological-cultural studies, but as an alleged source of sober information, we must throw them into the closest garbage can. If there is still some room left, the Roman copies of the Greek myths and most of the folktales and legends should follow the same journey.

To present these weird Greek or Roman myths to children and young adults, might still be marginally acceptable, but to sell them as 'particularly valuable and important' in schools and universities, might as well be treated as a criminal offense. I feel a great need to express this in such full openness!

Myths, folktales and legends provide a rich source of material for school lessons. There is an old saying: *"Some teachers are just one lesson ahead of the class."* In that case, this discombobulating stuff comes in handy to get a breather and to keep the kids distracted.

We can also use the wide variety of myths, folktales and legends in different ways and at all levels. Many of these stories are already suitable for Kindergarten, because they are so similar and predictable. Their predictability makes it easy for kids – ages 3 years and up – to guess what is coming next and thus facilitates the understanding, despite largely unknown vocabulary.

We all must fathom out and be concerned about one thing: If we are feeding our own species with such intellectual trivia, thereby neglecting to comment and criticize the dissolute lifestyle of the Greek gods or if we continue to look for Platon's pipe dream of 'Atlantis', we do not need to wonder about the consequences.

Rap music did not just come by accident. Something must have gone severely wrong before.

Some future date, we might wait in vain for our pension checks.

If no money reaches the pension pot, because it has been spent by misguided future generations on dope, binge drinking or bungee jumping, it will be too late to think about what we should have done differently with their education during the most important phase of their intellectual development.

18

However, if you realize the simple truth and question the horrible outpourings, or if you clear up things in a blunt and unsparing way, you will – even today – not always find general acceptance.

The Earth is a disc. It was not long ago that this was an assumption. Ships did not dare to go out too far, afraid to fall down behind the horizon. How can the Earth be a globe? The water would flow away and the Australians would walk around with their heads upside down.

He, who once claimed that the Earth would be a globe, could soon feel the position of the Australians by hanging head down on the next city wall. No, it is the same gravity that holds back the water and pulls down our arrows when we have shot them from our bows, and the Australians from 'down under' are really – well, almost – walking around heads down.

People once thought that the Sun circles the Earth. Under the threat of severe penalty, it was forbidden to suggest that the opposite is true and that the Sun, and not the Earth, is the center of our galaxy. Why does the Sun rise and set if it is not turning around us? Very simple: The Earth circles the Sun and simultaneously turns around its own axis.

Then came the theories of Darwin, the entire genesis was thrown to the wind. We are descendants of the apes and they – like all other stages of evolution – offspring of primitive forms of life, down to small organic molecules.

Many, among them the former US President George W. Bush, flatly refuse to accept this history of origin. This is not compatible with the doctrine of the ultraconservative religious fanatics, self-declared itinerant preachers and religious con artists of the bogus churches in the USA. Well, what do you expect from an institution that has no inhibition threshold towards Elvis-weddings in Las Vegas. Hallelujah!

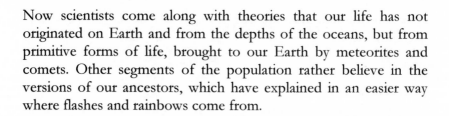

Now scientists come along with theories that our life has not originated on Earth and from the depths of the oceans, but from primitive forms of life, brought to our Earth by meteorites and comets. Other segments of the population rather believe in the versions of our ancestors, which have explained in an easier way where flashes and rainbows come from.

We want to know what has happened about 4 billion years ago, when life on Earth has developed, and a simple 'I don't know' is not accepted. There must always be a distinct explanation and if there is none, we are making it up, but are we even remotely aware what we do to one another with some of that pseudo-scientific mumbo jumbo?

There is an old Egyptian saying that among all sorts of grass, the papyrus plant is growing the highest. In the early days, it wanted to run away and avoid to be inscribed with ancient Egyptian myths, and as it has no legs, it shot upwards.

'Literature' comes from the Latin word 'litterae' (plural for letter). In the case of Greek or Roman myths, we should better spell it 'litterature'– deriving from the word 'litter' – rubbish carelessly dropped or left about, especially in public places.

BOW AND ARROW – THE LONG-DISTANCE EFFECT

Since primeval times, people have been fascinated by bow and arrow. This combination was the first machine functioning an 'extended arm' of man, right after the throwing of stones or the spear. It is the epitome for the early beginnings of a more sophisticated 'long-distance effect'.

Bow and arrow improved this long-distance effect, have mechanized it and made it more efficient. Now, the extended arm could reach farther and the distance to the target became larger and more secure. From the beginning, man has used this weapon not only for hunting, but also for armed conflict, murder and raids.

The system and technique of supplying an arrow with kinetic energy through the tension of limbs has been improved with the crossbow. Long before, catapults took up once again the principle of throwing stones. It all changed with the invention of the gunpowder. Cannons, guns and handheld weapons assumed the role of bow and arrow. Now, the warlike intention behind the long-distance effect went even more into the foreground.

Bombs and shells changed the scenery again. Missiles, so far generating their destructive forces solely from their momentum of mass and velocity, now carried destructive material to the target. The old flaming arrows already followed this principle.

Subsequently, this kind of the long-distance effect had to occur more and more away from the position of launching to prevent self-damage. Therefore, the fulfillment of a long dream of the human race, to be able to fly, came in handy also for this purpose – just bring it up and let it fall.

At the end of this development, we find the missiles. They now unite all features and we can even guide them to their target.

Today, if we follow the impact of remote-controlled missiles when watching TV and the news on the latest wars, we are – while far away from the events – scared and spellbound by the long-distance effect, whatever has been hit – or should not have been hit.

Many people and cultures who met during armed conflicts, have often fought with weapons from different stages of development. For the technical inferior side, this was mostly a conflict that, in the end, they could not win anymore.

However, if one looks at the history of humanity, the modern weapons have been around only for a relatively short time in comparison to the long period of bow and arrow.

All population flows, even those caused by the great World Wars, are like minor border corrections within a garden plot, compared to the immense movements of people and cultures on this planet accompanied by bow and arrow.

A larger aggregation of English longbows is often called 'the atomic bomb of the Middle Ages', although their real power and effectiveness is commonly overestimated.

If one holds a bow in his hand today and allows an arrow to fly, one can feel – often unconsciously – the fascination that still emanates from this first machine invented in the Stone Age.

It is a good thing that some weapons will disappear some day, especially in view of their martial use. Today, bow and arrow are

predominantly sporting gear and in countries that allow it, hunting instruments. But let us be honest, we would still fight each other with bow and arrow, if no new weapons had been invented.

The arrow, as a sign of orientation, is the most important and most used symbol of humanity, one that is understood throughout all languages and cultures. For us, it simply means 'direction', 'go there!', 'there it is!' We are automatically guided, whether on the highway or in the halls of the tax office, voting booths or even the morgue. No matter what individual shape the arrow has, we immediately recognize which course we have to take.

The sign of a one-way street tells us that this is not only a street we must use just in one direction; the arrow also tells us immediately which way to go.

Nothing has bullied people more than the diversion sign. We follow the command of the arrow in our cars in a well-behaved fashion. There are only a few exceptions to this rule, in countries commonly situated further south in Europe or across the Rio Grande, south of Texas. But occasionally even there, people can all move in one direction when the illegal immigrants run across the shallow river and follow the signs that point to America.

The arrow is the embodiment of speed. 'Fast as an arrow' is a generally known term. Mercedes called their racing cars 'Silberpfeile' (silver arrows).

Bow and arrow belong to the oldest weapons of man since at least ten-thousand, if not twenty- or perhaps even fifty-thousand years. The ongoing development and improvement of weapons was vitally necessary for humans since primeval times, not only battles and hunting, but also in defense against predators.

The characteristics of the humans were inferior to the physical and sensual capabilities of most animals. Power, speed, mobility, sense of smell, sight and hearing were developed to a much lesser extent, and they had no natural weapons like teeth, horns or claws. With their growth in intelligence and the changes in mobility of their hands, humans were able to make bow and arrow – and thus, our ancestors changed from prey to hunters.

The invention of bow and arrow, the first machine, in the same rank as the invention of the wheel or the development of language, converted the 'homo sapiens' to a 'homo technicus'.

When the basic principle of the bow was discovered, it did not only become a weapon. There are two other offspring from the bow – tools and musical instruments.

The bow drill improved the wood-on-wood technique of the fire drill. Enough friction is needed to generate heat, and instead of using both hands to twist the upper piece, a string was looped around it, kept tight by the bow. The bow drill then became the basis for the hand drill and the precursor of the turning lathe or, in another form of application, the coping saw.

Very soon, the bow emerged as a musical instrument from which our stringed instruments descend.

When Anne-Sophie Mutter enchants us with her Stradivari violin, we should remember that it was once an early man with a first musical aptitude who discovered that one could not only throw an arrow with the bow, but also create a tone when plucking the string.

This discovery was certainly demonstrated immediately to other 'stone-agers' and picked up by them, and suddenly, they were all plucking the strings of their bows. Soon, it had been noticed that the plucked tones differed from each other and that they could even be altered. The variation of the sound led to the first melody and 'mutual plucking' to the first orchestral performance.

After an uninterrupted sophistication of music up to the level of Bach, Beethoven or Mozart, we are today moving backwards to the initial starting point with some musical styles and presentations.

Jazz roars through New Orleans. Rap music comes from the speakers of 'Ghetto blasters', carried on the shoulders of our brothers, tap dancing through the South Bronx and cranking up the volume, so as to scare away mammoths and rhinos.

There are modern opera performances that often manage the balancing act to keep the music as close as possible to the original and then, they destroy the substance down to the Stone Age level, solely by the type of stage production. On the 250th Birthday of Mozart, in the year 2006, people have managed to do this, of all places in Salzburg – his city of birth.

Unfortunately, this sort of cultural derailment happens all over the world. If you think you are on the lowest level of opera performances, look for a staircase somewhere that leads down even further. Follow it, and you might find, way below, a simulcast of a modern performance by the 'Met', the New York Metropolitan Opera and their mise-en-scène experiments with musical underscore. I am afraid, as long as this type of staging is not made punishable by law and even supported by public funds, we just have to live with it.

Queens and Kings practiced with bow and arrow and goddesses and gods (even so they never existed) wandered around with this equipment. Bow and arrow are mystic and religious and stimulate the imagination. They are a magical combination and appear in myths, folktales, legends and stories all over the world, accompanied by their archery heroes.

The medieval archers can be distinguished from the normal mortals by their skeletons. The bowmen had to handle large draw weights in the past, because the performance of the bow came – more than today – primarily from the powers of their muscles.

On July 19, 1545, the Mary Rose, flagship of Henry VIII, sank before the harbor of Portsmouth, whereby almost the entire crew (415 men) drowned. Muster roll, Anthony-roll (illustrated fleet-register) and comprehensive archaeological finds gave proof of the presence of archers who had been on board the ship.

Comparative studies of the secured skeletons made it possible to identify the archers. They have shown obvious asymmetries in the left part of the shoulder (the left arm is usually the arm holding the bow). The strong pressure on the left shoulder resulted in an enlargement of the humeral head and the greater tubercle and in some cases in the formation of an 'os acromiale', normally a rather rare anatomical variant.

The sinking of this ship in 1545 was in the same year when Roger Ascham had published his book 'Toxophilus'.

The word Toxophilus (archer) is composed of the Greek words 'toxos' (bow), which is also the word for the poisonous yew (toxic, poisonous), from which bows were made, and 'philos' (friend) – a friend of archery.

Roger Ascham's work, which he dedicated to Henry VIII (picture on the left), was the first book on archery published in the English language. It was written as a dialog between two characters, Philologus (a lover of study) and Toxophilus (a lover of bow and arrow). Toxophilus is a scientist and a supporter of archery as a noble sport.

This book was also important in another respect: It demonstrated that one could write books or instructions in English, in a clear and generally understandable fashion.

In these days, even when the books had been published in English, the writers had used strange words from the Latin-, French- or Italian language to make things dark and mysterious.

Roger Ascham avoided neologisms and 'flowery' terms and contributed to the success of the English language as a vehicle of wider communication. Some descriptions of the environment, like the way in which the wind influences the flight path of an arrow, were vivid and unparalleled in English writing before.

TRANSITION

If you want to put the history of bow and arrow in the Western World in a nutshell, just sum up things in a simple way:

The Germans (at least their Angles and Saxons) fashioned England and Britain, the English created the longbow, the Americans have perfected it and became the main driving force behind many new technical developments in archery – with a few others that deserve credit.

So, once upon a time, there was no English language. The Germanic tribes of the Angles and Saxons, who conquered this remote place, brought the basics to Britannia and gave it the seven Kingdoms of North Umbria, Mercia, East Anglia, Kent, Sussex and Wessex – the Anglo-Saxon Heptarchy.

To us archers, England is important. It is the home country of the longbow (with some credit we can give to the Welsh), this powerful, yet largely overestimated weapon of medieval times. It was a feared weapon during the Hundred Years' War between England and France.

Modern archery – for hunting purposes and as a sport – had its comeback in the USA, and from there it spread around the world. A major push came from hunting with bow and arrow at the end of the US Civil War, as the possession of guns had been temporarily forbidden in the former Confederate States.

The 'mother' and starting point of modern archery was undoubtedly the book 'The Witchery of Archery' by Maurice Thompson, a noted American novelist, born in Indiana in 1844 and raised on a Georgia plantation.

Published in the year 1878/79, it was the first important English book about archery since Rodger Ascham's work Toxophilius (1545), and it had as much effect on archery as 'Uncle Tom's Cabin' on the US Civil War. Morris Thompson, who himself took part in the battles (1861 - 1865) on the side of the South, became the first president of the National Archery Association of the USA. I recently had the privilege to translate this book into German and it was published in the year 2012 under the title 'Der Zauber des Bogenschiessens'.

Maurice Thompson calls England 'the great mother of archers', but 'mom' did not do much anymore to move archery away from old traditions, medieval equipment and an almost forgotten field sport for the elite.

Once the flame of modern archery was ignited, we first saw the flat longbow, then all new types of recurve bows. Finally, the compound bow was invented and produced in the USA.

Cedar wood from the Port Orford cedar in Oregon and the northern part of California remains the prime material for wooden arrow shafts, and thanks to the innovations of Easton Archery, modern arrow shafts fly through the air, made from alloy and carbon or a combination of both.

And what about our feathers on the arrows, if we do not use different types of plastic fletching, which was likewise invented in the USA?

There is a long tradition in the USA called 'Thanksgiving'. With over 45 million birds killed every year – except one bird,

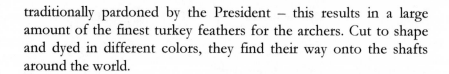

traditionally pardoned by the President – this results in a large amount of the finest turkey feathers for the archers. Cut to shape and dyed in different colors, they find their way onto the shafts around the world.

Turkeys are not always acquired as slaughtered animals. Once in a while, they are stolen from a pen, where they often live around the house as pets. On Thanksgiving, November 22, 2012, two teenage archers from the neighborhood of Santa Rosa County, Florida, were arrested on their way to the butcher and put in jail on $57,000 bail, for shooting such a family pet with bow and arrow.

Now back to good old England: A new language developed on the 'island of the longbows', with a little 'pep', added from the French influence. English, a West Germanic Language, also became a big success around the globe. It is still spoken by a shrinking majority of the Americans, struggling to hold Spanish in second place.

German did not become the official language of the USA, missing out by *a single vote*, because one of the guys favoring German sat on the toilet, just as the votes were cast in the Independence Hall in Philadelphia, Pennsylvania, in the year 1776.

English, back then, extended and spread over the former colonies of the long gone British Empire, brought in by adventurers and a great number of evildoers, banished to these places. This way, Australia did not only get the language, but also a criminal pre-disposition in their heredity, unequaled anywhere else.

Meanwhile, racy Yankee slang strongly invaded Victorian English, thanks to Hollywood, Computers and the Internet.

And honestly: If you go to London and listen to the musical absurdity called 'Proms in the Park' – an attempt to bring classical music to the masses at affordable prices outside fixed buildings – do you want to 'skedaddle' or simply escape?

If you panicky run away from Hyde Park when they feed the crazy mob with Verdi's Aida to satisfy the horde's yearning for cheap opera, there is one thing to remember before you jump into your car: You must drive on the left side of the road.

The next traffic circle is a roundabout and watch out for pedestrians; they are not coming from the sidewalk, but from the pavement. Walkers are not hurled onto your windshield, but onto your windscreen, after they bounce off the bonnet and not the hood.

Don't be confused when you get dressed: The British wear pants *under* their trousers, while the Americans wear their pants *over* their shorts, and Scots may or may not have underwear under their kilts.

Back to the German origin: The monarchs of Great Britain, often maliciously labeled as 'Royal Sauerkraut', all have undeniably German roots and are descendants of the House of Hanover or the House of Saxe-Coburg and Gotha.

George V. was the first of the monarchs who spoke without a German accent – perhaps a too radical change, which might have been the cause that his youngest son, the later King Georg VI, suffered with a bad stammer in his speech.

George V., the grandfather of Queen Elizabeth II., was married to Mary of Teck, who is of German extraction and 'technically' a princess of Teck, in the Kingdom of Wuerttemberg.

While George V. could not deny his Teutonic roots, he at least wanted to get rid of his German family name and renamed the Royal family the 'Windsors', after the Windsor Castle. Good thing they were not living in Sandal Castle in Yorkshire and luckily, the Windsors have avoided becoming the 'Sandals'. It was a bit easier with the name Battenberg. 'Berg' is the German name for 'mountain'. Cleverly, they flipped it to Mountbatten.

31

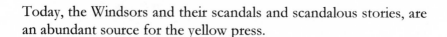

Today, the Windsors and their scandals and scandalous stories, are an abundant source for the yellow press.

It all started to break apart in 1936 when King Edward VIII., the eldest son of George V., trashed the crown and moved away with the elegant and twice-divorced American Wallis Simpson.

Before that, the Secret Service unit MI5 had even tried to attempt an assassination, just because Edward had asked for an official permission from the Yugoslav government to take a bath in the nude, together with Wallis, in the bay of Kandarola on the island of Rab (now part of Croatia).

During the reign of the German-blooded Queen Victoria, the Royal German breeding club was mostly a closed event. Victoria made it even closer – and married her first cousin, Prince Albert of Saxe Coburg and Gotha.

Queen Victoria, the mother ship of hemophilia within European royalty, had nine children and her 'dinghies' wedded into noble families across the continent. Her daughter Victoria ('Vicky') later became the German Empress and Queen of Prussia.

The daughter of the present monarch Elizabeth II., Princess Anne, who meanwhile plunged from second place and out of the top ten in the line of succession to the throne, marched to a different drummer and married an English horseman.

"Ein Griff in's Klo" (a grab into the loo), as her German relatives would say. He left her for an American horsewoman and then jumped horses again to join yet another American equestrienne.

Let us therefore begin with the stories of the book in the heart of the motherland of all that became English and British, at the Rhine River and pick it up from there.

"Ich weiß nicht, was soll es bedeuten, dass ich so traurig bin, ein Maerchen aus uralten Zeiten, das kommt mir nicht aus dem Sinn." These are the first words of a poem by the German poet Heinrich Heine, written in the year 1823. He tries to get us acquainted with the oddly constructed story about the beautiful blonde Lorelei.

A pleasant English translation of these lines (1978) comes from Tr. Frank, keeping up the rhyme of the lines: *"I cannot determine the meaning, of sorrow that fills my breast: A fable of old, through it streaming, allows my mind no rest."*

Not a German folktale, as one might initially think, provides the intellectual basis of this garbage, but a ballad of Clemens Brentano.

He in turn was getting the inspiration for his work from a variation of the ancient myth about the nymph Echo, and it was in fact the 'echo' of the trilling Lorelei that had caused a lot of problems.

Miss Lorelei combed her long blond hair, high up on a rock at the shores of the Rhine River, thereby warbling a seductive song that has irritated many skippers. They did not pay attention to their course anymore and shattered their ships in great numbers against the rocky reefs.

Though the story of the Lorelei is merely a silly fable, it lures many tourists from near and far to the Rhine. After a visit to one of the numerous wine bars, they are generally unable to keep their proper course – even without Blondie's songs.

In Japan, to this day, people believe that the Lorelei is as real as the rhythm of the tides or the effects of gravitation. She is amongst the three Germans every Japanese knows: Beethoven, Goethe and the Lorelei.

The well-organized tourists from the 'land of smiles' come in flocks and in busses into the region around the Lorely Rock, and the clicks of their cameras mingle with the melodious sound of the rushing river Rhine and the less melodious chants in the wine bars.

The yearning for their true inner Germanic homeland is deeply engraved in the soul of the English. Tourism on the Rhine River emerged after the Napoleonic wars. In these days, practically all of the visitors came from England, and as the word 'tourist' was not yet part of the German language (which it later became in the original form), every stranger was called an Englishman.

The Loreley, this figment of imagination, honored by the poem of Heinrich Heine, does certainly not raise any special interest by the archers, except to think of practicing with bow and arrow to shoot the blond pain in the neck from her rock.

On the other hand, we know many other 'works', where archers or bow and arrow are put into the center of events in an often obnoxious way, which shall now be relentlessly investigated.

The worst is yet to come! For this reason, we will begin with a rather harmless story and besides that, probably the most famous archery tale of all times. In order to 'jazz up' that meanwhile worn out legend, this chapter includes a few anecdotes about Howard Hill, seen by many as the best longbow-archer ever.

In this sense, let us now go over to England and step right into the Sherwood Forest to meet the mother of all twaddle around bow and arrow: The legend of Robin Hood.

THE LEGEND OF ROBIN HOOD

The best-known feature of the legend of Robin Hood is the so-called 'Robin Hood shot'.

Robin is said to have been able to shoot an arrow at another one already sticking in the target, which he thereby split in half.

A shot like this has definitively never occurred, simply because Robin Hood never existed.

This does not mean that such a shot is not possible. To the contrary, this can be seen quite often and usually happens just by accident. Therefore, a 'Robin Hood shot' only makes an impression if it has been done intentionally and the archer announces it beforehand.

If I spread around several arrows in the target area and another one subsequently hits and splits one of them, the result is also called a Robin Hood shot, although this was not done on purpose. In fact, it is rather a nuisance, because of the inevitable damage to the arrows.

The figure of Robin Hood is pure fiction. It has evolved over time, originating with a *Common Highwayman*, from there to acquire the title of *Noble Patriot* and finally became an early *Advocate for Social Justice* – 'take it from the rich and give it to the poor'. Frequently reworked versions, which have been adapted over time, and additionally invented ballads, made him become a legend.

Owing to an entry in an administrative file, which was effected in the year 1225, the 'authentic' Robin Hood was just a simple good-

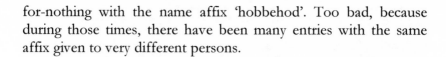

for-nothing with the name affix 'hobbehod'. Too bad, because during those times, there have been many entries with the same affix given to very different persons.

It is a well-known fact that 'hobbehod' is merely an old English synonym for a lawbreaker. The figure of Robin Hood would therefore only derive from a generally used medieval term for a thief or robber.

Then, there are historians who have – 'beyond any doubt' – identified Robert Fitzooth, the Earl of Huntington (1160-1247) as the 'genuine' Robin Hood.

Some 'authorities' are even more convinced that it must have been the Anglo-Saxon Robert de Kyme (1210-1285), who was banned in the year 1226 for thievery and breach of the King's peace. As a result, he has fled into the Sherwood Forest.

Roger Godberd is another candidate for the 'real' Robin Hood. He has terrorized the counties of Nottinghamshire, Derbyshire and Leicestershire in the years following the Montford Rebellion (1265) as the leader of a group of outlaws.

And finally, there would yet be Robert Hood (1290-1347), who was supposedly involved in a rebellion against King Edward II. He was expelled and fled into the Barnsdale Forest.

The oldest written evidence of the existence of a Robin Hood ballad originates from a collection of folksy poems composed by William Langland around the year 1377 with the title 'The Vision of Piers Plowman'.

In one of the poems a certain Mr. Sloth flatters himself that he can barely remember the Lord's Prayer, but knows the rhymes of Robin Hood by heart: *"I kan nought parfitly my Paternoster as the preest it singeth, but I kan rhymes of Robyn Hood and Randolf Earl of Chestre."*

This Sloth was seldom in a sober state, and therefore it can be assumed that the stories about Robin Hood which he recited and spread around, became more and more adventurous, and some anecdotes contained therein have originated solely in his souse.

The Robin Hood shot was even topped as the stories went around from mouth to mouth. When Robin Hood was about to die, he was said to have shot a last arrow from his bed to mark the exact spot of his grave.

On the very top of it, some Hollywood movies about Robin Hood have aided to conserve this hogwash into present time, and we always find his unsurpassed skills in handling bow and arrow in the focus of the fascination.

Hollywood did not want to stay behind and therefore contributed its own material to the 'completion' of the legend through the addition of further archery tricks and adventurous episodes.

After many silent Robin Hood films, a sound movie about the heroic outlaw was produced in the year 1938 with Errol Flynn and Olivia de Havilland in the lead roles.

Nowadays, it is possible to simulate the arrow-splitting Robin Hood shot and other show elements on a computer. Back then, everything had to be played out in reality. But how could this be done when nobody has the precise shooting accuracy to accomplish this task deliberately or over a longer distance?

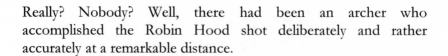

Really? Nobody? Well, there had been an archer who accomplished the Robin Hood shot deliberately and rather accurately at a remarkable distance.

The famous archer Howard Hill – perhaps the best archer of all times – was hired. They were certain that he would just have to shoot long enough and a Robin Hood shot would come up sooner or later.

Several hundred feet of celluloid and a lot of overtime for the camera operator had been reserved to capture such a scene, but the skills of Howard Hill were totally underestimated. The shot was repeated eleven times and – to the surprise of everyone – Howard Hill succeeded to split nine arrows at his first attempt.

Based on this impressive accuracy of his shooting, they could spontaneously incorporate other effects that would be done today with the help of computer technology.

The script required that some of the performers had to be hit by arrows. The producers took a few stunt men and simply strapped suitably dimensioned boards to their chests, which could be discretely hidden under their clothes. The courageous fellows were targeted with real arrows by Howard Hill, but remained unscathed.

Howard Hill, famous for numerous other incredible trick shots, received his first bow at the age of four.

He hit a swimming duck at a distance of approximately 160 yards (146.3 meters) or an apple on a human head (the famous William Tell shot) at a distance of 60 yards (54.9 meters), whereby the head of the brave fellow was protected by a bulletproof plastic cover.

When he shot cigarettes from the mouth of live subjects, he had chosen a somewhat shorter distance in exchange for the omission of such a protective cover for his assistants.

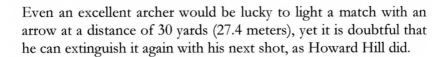

Even an excellent archer would be lucky to light a match with an arrow at a distance of 30 yards (27.4 meters), yet it is doubtful that he can extinguish it again with his next shot, as Howard Hill did.

Another unusual feat was to hit a swimming elk at a distance of approximately 180 yards (164.6 meters). This is quite a gap for a bow, but how fast does an elk swim?

It was highly unfortunate that, over time, he converted from a hunter to a primitive slayer of animals, driven by an insane obsession for new records, killing far more than 2000 of them.

He loved to go the Africa, because here he could claim one record after another, like the first killing of an elephant, although everything had already been done before. He just needed to be the first *white* man' to do it and this was a prerequisite in those days that an achievement would count as a record set by man.

What a strange world: This was just at the time when Jesse Owens was so openly received and celebrated for his triumphs at the 1936 Olympic Games in Berlin. 'Yesseh Oh-fens', as the Germans called him, was – like any other athlete – allowed to travel with and stay in the same hotels in Germany as whites, while at the time in many parts of the United States, Afro-Americans had to stay in segregated hotels when traveling. Jesse Owens even had to use the freight elevator at the Waldorf-Astoria Hotel in New York, to reach a reception honoring him.

Although many people know better, the myth of Hitler's snub of Jesse Owens is held persistent. Fact is, however, that honors were not bestowed upon Jesse Owens back in the USA. Both, Franklin D. Roosevelt and his successor, Harry S. Truman, refused to appropriately acknowledge his accomplishments. Since 1936 was a presidential election year, Roosevelt was afraid that he would lose votes in the South, if he played 'Kowtow' to an Afro-American man. He did not even bother to send a telegraph.

His German counterpart behaved very differently. Adolf had not only waved at Jesse after his victory in the 100-meter run, he even let him have an inscribed cabinet photograph of himself. Too bad for Jesse – that proofed to be not the best of souvenirs after all.

Back to Howard Hill: He shot arrows into the air and had eight of them flying before the first one came down again. He fired an arrow straight up and hit it with a second one when it came back.

When he had killed almost everything on the ground and in the air and these activities did no longer satisfy him, Howard Hill went to the water shores and shot fishes 3 yards (2.74 meters) deep and 50 yards (45.7 meters) away.

Finally, he had been shooting in every environment, until he realized that he had not been *under* water yet. With a special bow, capable of firing arrows 50 yards (45.7 meters) through the water, he went below the surface, aiming at sharks.

Complex technical studies in recent times have shown that one can split a wooden arrow with another, but that it will become stuck in the first shaft, seems nearly impossible. Nowadays, this would be an 'honor' more likely for archers who are using tubular shafts made of aluminum or carbon.

Contrary to Howard Hill, we can say about Robin Hood that he is only a fictional character and his famous adventures are just wild stories, made up by medieval rhymesters and exaggerated over time by traveling artists and modern Hollywood studios.

Nevertheless, I shall not fail to quote Robin Hood's last words:

"Now raise me on my dying-bed,
Bring here my trusty bow,
And ere I join the silent dead,
My arm that spot shall show."

CUPID AND HIS FAMOUS ARROW SHOTS

Here we have a first example of Greek bunkum that better belongs six feet under rather than on our bookshelves or in our libraries.

We know Cupid as a delightful little fellow, who makes people fall in love by striking them with his arrows.

Cupid, also known as Cupido, Cupidus or Amor, is the Roman clone of the Greek figure Eros and the god of love, or better yet, the god of uncontrollably falling in love, because he has no control over what comes thereafter.

This story was at first constructed by the Greeks and the Romans – as they always did – have copied it from them. In order to limit the confusion, we will stick to the Greek original story, but will call the chief character by his Roman name Cupid and not by his Greek name Eros, because this label is more familiar to us.

According to Homer, Cupid (Eros in his Greek version) was one of the five earliest gods (the god of desire), who emerged through time from gaping emptiness and chaos together with his god-colleagues 'Gaia' (Earth), 'Nyx' (Night), 'Tartaros' (Underworld) and 'Erebos' (Darkness).

As time passed, he sank to the level of a handsome, but still godlike young man, up until the time of the Greek classic. Later, in the Hellenistic period, he became the figure that we know today –

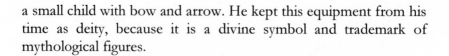

a small child with bow and arrow. He kept this equipment from his time as deity, because it is a divine symbol and trademark of mythological figures.

Bow and arrow served him well for his long-distance transfer of love. The gods had flash and thunder and this little fellow used the most powerful hand weapon of its time. There was also this contrast between the harmless little lad and the power he was able to exercise with the help of his archery equipment.

Cupid did not only come along with the Big Bang, he owes a further existence to his mother Aphrodite and her lover Ares (Venus and the god Mars in the Roman version). His mother was married to Hephaestus, the brother of her lover and the god of the art of forging.

This is the point where the mythological nonsense really starts. How can one who belongs to the first beings on this Earth and who has originated from nothing be fathered and born again some millenniums later?

Cupid had a major problem when he shot around with his arrows: He must have been one of the worst shooters ever. Accidentally, the little winged archer hit his own mother, who then promptly fell in love with Adonis.

He even topped that disaster when he ham-handedly injured himself with one of his arrows and subsequently fell in love with the lovely Psyche, the most beautiful girl of the time.

This was indeed a highly explosive story, because Aphrodite, the mother of Cupid, had actually influenced the little rascal to direct his arrows to Psyche, who should then fall in love with an ugly man, as Aphrodite was furiously jealous of the human girl with her breathtaking beauty.

Cupid, who had now himself fallen in love with Psyche, was in a complicated situation. He had to hide his identity under all circumstances and therefore sneaked out to meet his sweetheart only in the deepest darkness and disguised as a mysterious lover.

At some stage of the affair, Psyche could not hold back her curiosity, also because her sisters had persuaded her to reveal the secret about her mysterious lover. One night, she held up a lamp and looked at the face of the sleeping Cupid. Delighted about the handsome boy, the lamp fell from her hand and Cupid woke up. Now he had no choice but to leave Psyche.

Fortunately, both of them had a patron in the heaven of the gods. Zeus (Roman name Jupiter), the father of all gods, arranged for a good ending of the love story and both came together again.

Cupid made his way into the heart of Zeus, because – following the blood relationship – he is twice (!) his grandfather. Zeus did not have this twofold honor through his son Hephaestus, god of the art of forging and the husband of Cupid's mother Aphrodite, because Hephaestus is not the biological father of the little scoundrel.

He is double-grandpa, because the producers of Cupid are both children of Zeus. Aphrodite, the mother of Cupid, is an illegitimate daughter, and Ares, the biological father and lover of Cupid's mother, is a legitimate child of Zeus.

43

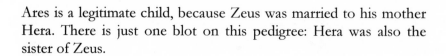

Ares is a legitimate child, because Zeus was married to his mother Hera. There is just one blot on this pedigree: Hera was also the sister of Zeus.

Those who are still able to follow along and are prepared to muddle through this incestuous, grimy clutter of sexual relations, will acknowledge the fact that the parents of Cupid, Aphrodite and Ares, have the same father, namely Zeus, but at least different mothers, and are therefore half-brother and half-sister.

The biological father of Cupid is even the product of a 'genuine' brother-sister marriage and continues in this style of reproduction with his half-sister.

Even worse, the grandparents Zeus and Hera, who tied the knot as brother and sister, are themselves descendants from a brother-sister mélange between Rhea and her brother Kronos.

"Almost heaven, West Virginia... ♪ ♫ ♪ ♫"

Aphrodite is the daughter of Zeus in the chaotic transcript of Homer. According to Hesiod, she is the daughter of Uranus. The story of her origin *('the one born in the foam')* is so repulsive and pornographic that I cannot put my pen to the paper and write it down, not even with my best intentions.

Following the antique hack writers Nonnos and Pausanias, Aphrodite is only a non-blood-related stepdaughter of Zeus.

Zeus particularly valued his grandson Cupid for seducing so many willing beauties, who then landed in the bed of Zeus, like the goddesses Leto, Dione and Leda, many nymphs, numerous pretty mortals and several demi-goddesses. The latter characters are the result of the many love affairs of gods with mortals, both his own and those of his god-colleagues.

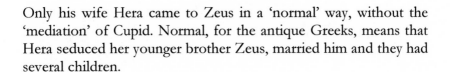

Only his wife Hera came to Zeus in a 'normal' way, without the 'mediation' of Cupid. Normal, for the antique Greeks, means that Hera seduced her younger brother Zeus, married him and they had several children.

Cupid could not shoot at Hera to make her a willing sister for grandpa, because at this time, he did not yet have this special ability. It was only after his second birth that he became the god of love, who could spread around love with his arrows.

To sum it up as one can get easily lost in this puddle of smut:

Cupid was re-born, after Zeus had fathered Ares, his biological father, with his sister Hera. Grandpa also fathered his mother Aphrodite, as an illegitimate child with Dione.

Ares and Aphrodite, half-brother and half-sister, then produced him, Cupid – the god of love.

Ares did not just impregnate his half-sister Aphrodite, but simultaneously his sister-in-law, as Aphrodite was married to his brother Hephaestus.

Therefore, it is no wonder that Zeus did this little winged archer a favor by rescuing the relationship to Psyche.

Can you take more of this? If yes, read on!

The love affairs of Zeus were often only short-lived, mostly because of the jealousy of his sister-wife Hera. Zeus, however, always took good care of the children emerging from his productive interludes, like Helena, Aphrodite, Iris, Dionysus, Hermes or Heracles, just to name a few.

It is no secret that Zeus had maintained a passionate homosexual relationship – parallel to this deep sexual abyss – with Ganymede, son of a King and the most handsome boy of all mortals. Moreover, this was the only long-lasting liaison he had outside the marriage with his sister Hera.

At the beginning, Zeus was able to hide this affair, as he had kidnapped and abducted the young man to the Mount Olympus.

In one variation of the story, Zeus had sent an eagle to grab the boy and to give him a free airlift. Another version of this twaddle tells us that the boy himself was transformed into an eagle, and he was brought up to the top in a cage.

A closer look into the family tree of Cupid reveals very clearly, and for an additional reason, that the entire story is a sham.

Cupid – as we remember – was delivered into our world with the big bang. After that, he was born again as the son of Aphrodite and Ares.

Cupid is the father of Uranus, who in turn is the great grandfather of Ares, the biological father of Cupid. He is therefore his own great-great-grandfather and his own great-great-grandson, all in one person.

When the contradictions had finally been noticed, the stories should have been consequently thrown into the next trashcan. To the contrary, the paradox was explained by the fact that there is a circulation and a reincarnation of the gods – thus creating the baseline for even more mystical humbug.

By all means, this is even more mindless as a justification than some reasoning and excuses you can occasionally find when people reply to questions in connection with traffic violations.

If one, however, wants to stick to a particular version, there will always be some explanations for illogicalities.

According to this abnormal piece of a myth, all three of them, the father Hephaestus, the mother Aphrodite and Ares, mom's lover and Cupid's biological father, were involved in the upbringing of the little winged archer.

Aphrodite is mostly described as being over-strained with the education of the child.

Therefore, one does not have to wonder – especially owing to this scruffy family background – that Cupid turned into a good-for-nothing, with all kinds of mischief on his mind.

It can be assumed that Cupid was only a fictional character in fictional stories. He was invented with the intention to palliate the immoral life of the gods, especially the piggish behavior of the Godfather Zeus and to conserve respect of the mortals. One is simply helpless against the arrows of Cupid and their effects, even as the father of all gods, and not responsible for the consequences.

Have the old Greeks already consumed hashish? We know that Opium was around by this time and used not only in the area of medicine. The main drug was the alcohol, which the old Greeks had drunken in alarming amounts and what has probably led to such a befuddlement.

No, wrong idea! In fact, you cannot drink enough to produce such baloney as the Greek myths.

The Bavarians have found an ideal place for Cupid – or Amor, as he is called in Germany with his Roman/Latin name – along with the perfect way of displaying this product of weird fantasies.

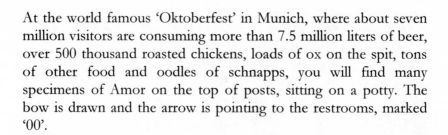

At the world famous 'Oktoberfest' in Munich, where about seven million visitors are consuming more than 7.5 million liters of beer, over 500 thousand roasted chickens, loads of ox on the spit, tons of other food and oodles of schnapps, you will find many specimens of Amor on the top of posts, sitting on a potty. The bow is drawn and the arrow is pointing to the restrooms, marked '00'.

The standard indication you usually find on the doors of restrooms is the 'WC'-sign for water closet. The '00' in turn is the sign you often see on doors of lower level toilets behind beer tents and similar locations.

Like many words in the domain of hygiene, the word 'toilet' comes from the French language and likewise the indication '00'.

In the old days, the large hotels in France already had the toilets inside the building, but usually just one on each floor, close to the elevators and the stairways. As the numbering of the rooms started from there, the toilets had been given the number '00'.

Could we not follow the Oktoberfest-example – in a slightly modified fashion – and put antique Greek gods on posts, with a book of Greek myths in their hand, pointing the way to waste disposal sites?

THE LEGENDARY SHOT OF ODYSSEUS

The Greek mythology is – and always was – a synonym for incredibly silly gossip.

Here is such a pathetic effort from the bottom drawer of the storage cabinet that houses antique junk. As a special annoyance to us archers, bow and arrow have been misused in the plot for a silly trick shot, as we learn from that insane story.

The myth called 'Odyssey' is the second epic besides the 'Iliad' that is attributed to the poet Homer. Written down in the late 8th century, the Odyssey belongs to the oldest and most influential works of the cultural heritage of literature in the Occident. This gives the part of bow and arrow, contained in this grotesque and shoddy tale, an elevated level of importance.

Odysseus was ruling over Ithaca, an island in the Ionian Sea, which is part of the Mediterranean Sea. He was married to Penelope and they had a son named Telemachus. The long lasting war against Troy kept him away from home, wife and child, for many years.

The Greeks were not able to reach inside the town of Troy, yet they finally succeeded through cunning and trickery. Some of their soldiers cramped themselves in a wooden horse, which was constructed in just three days with the help of the goddess Athena.

They placed the oversized nag before the city gate and feigned their withdrawal. The Trojans thought that it was a farewell gift from the Greeks to their god Poseidon, who had supported them in the battle.

The Troy soldiers neglected the warning calls of Cassandra and pulled the horse into the town, perhaps with the intention to insult Poseidon, who was not very well respected in Troy.

At night, the hidden soldiers crept from the horse, opened the town gates and the Greek troops stormed in. Odysseus thought that this was his own brilliant idea and he had been victorious without the help of the gods. This insult, along with the haughty self-adulation, had cost him another ten years of absence from home, as a punishment by the gods and in addition to the ten years, this war had already lasted. During that extended period, he was supposed to be aimlessly wandering around in the Mediterranean Sea.

My goodness! Was he so incapable to navigate in this small body of water? Was that the reason, why he could not find his way home for so long? Certainly not!

All kinds of other explanations were given, for example the acquaintance with the giant 'Polyphemos', the distraction by the

'Sirens' or the trouble with the monster 'Charybdis'; yet the delay in finding his way home was mainly caused by the magician 'Circe', who had intensely 'bewitched' him.

When he finally came home after twenty years of absence, his spouse was surrounded by many suitors (some sources speak of more than one hundred), who all believed that the king had been dead for a long time. The large crowd of men had already agreed on a competition that should decide who of them would win the rich Penelope for his wife, and Odysseus arrived just in time to prevent the renewed wedding.

It can be assumed that Penelope had also given up hope to ever see her husband again, and – most likely – there must have been more than just courtship by her admirers in all these twenty years.

When Odysseus had arrived, he was not recognized by anyone – not even by his spouse. Only his dog Argos made an exception and spontaneously identified him after twenty (!) years. However, with the exception of joyful and intense barking and tail wagging, it could not contribute much to Odysseus' recognition.

At the end of this weird story, bow and arrow had to serve as props for the final act. The competition was organized in such a way that the suitors had to draw the mighty bow of Odysseus and shoot an arrow through twelve axes (the holes that take the ax handles), lined up one behind the other.

None of the suitors succeeded in drawing that strong bow, much less shooting an arrow with it. Odysseus drew the bow with ease, and of course, the arrow went through the twelve holes. Now, everyone and not only the dog knew who he was and above all, his spouse Penelope had understood.

Well, if one can draw such a strong bow and shoot an arrow with it through twelve axes, one will certainly have the power and

51

accuracy of shooting to settle such a displeasing and infuriating matter in a huntsman's fashion, especially with so many men around courting his wife.

His son Telemachus joined in to help and Odysseus, in full fury, created a bloodbath and shot all of them. This in turn led to new conflicts with the families of the killed suitors until the goddess Athena finally made peace. However, on his bloody settlement of accounts, Odysseus did not want to shoot at women with bow and arrow. As an alternative, twelve disloyal maidens were hung on a rope straight across the court.

However, the joy of their reunion did not last long. There were frequent quarrels between Odysseus and Penelope. He did not believe her claim of twenty-year abstinence, given the presence of more than one hundred suitors upon his return.

Penelope in turn got knowledge of the fact that Odysseus, on his long wandering that followed the ten years of war against Troy, did more than just navigate throughout this trip. After all, he had fathered two children with Circe during this period.

Finally, the information leaked through that he was also killing time, for full seven years, in a cave with the nymph 'Calypso'.

Nymphs are divinities of lower rank. There are, sorted by their habitual whereabouts, sea nymphs, freshwater nymphs, forest- and tree nymphs, rain nymphs, meadow nymphs, valley nymphs, mountain nymphs and grotto- and cave nymphs – a lot of nymphs indeed when we consider that they did not exist at all.

If Odysseus had holed up in a cave with Calypso, the two really had serious reasons to stay out of sight, because Calypso is a sea nymph. The nymphs who usually live in grottoes and caves are the oreads.

The most famous of the oreads is Echo. The goddess Hera deprived her of her voice, but left her the ability to repeat the last words that are addressed to her. You can guess it now: That is the background of the word 'echo'.

Just as the word 'echo' comes from Echo, the word 'nymphomaniac' derives from the word nymph. Calypso was trying to persuade Odysseus to stay with her for good. In return, she would make him immortal. I think that at some stage, everyone will be fed up with endless repetitions, even when participating in a nymph's favorite pastime, and Odysseus left.

According to Homer, this wild lifestyle remained childless. After the time of Homer, this was somewhat corrected and children were added, resulting from this seven-year-long party in the cave.

Apollodorus, one of the archetypes of a rainbow press journalist, had named Latinus as a son of Odysseus and Calypso and totally ignored that he was already the son of Kirke.

Hesiod, another one who prefers gossip over facts, is blustering about two sons, Nausithoos and Nausinoos. This was probably the version that came to the ears of Penelope.

In summary: This is one of the stories, constructed in a totally confused fashion, as we know them in great numbers from the Greek mythology; an antique myth-hoax, including the famous (and simply impossible) arrow shot contained therein.

THE TREACHEROUS MURDER OF FROZEN FRITZ

Frozen Fritz, Iceman, Oetzi the Iceman or just Oetzi (so called after the Oetztal Alps, the place Fritz was found), whatever his name is, the 'findings' surrounding the mummy Fritz are occasionally so bizarre that I am always reminded of the wise sentence of Orson Welles: *"Many would never speak with a full mouth, but do it with an empty head."*

If they had found common objects next to the mummy, one would have given somewhat less thought to the death of the man from the ice. But when bow and arrow appear, myths and legends are automatically generated.

Moreover, they do not find an end to the wild speculations about Fritz, who walked around in the border region between North- and South Tyrol some 5000 years ago.

His well-preserved mummy was discovered on September 19, 1991, by the German couple and mountain hikers Erika and Helmut Simon.

Four days later, on September 23, 1991, his body was retrieved. When it came to light that this was a scientific world sensation, many other people appeared on the scene. All claimed to have found him first and wanted to become part of world history as first discoverers.

A woman from Slovenia and another one from Switzerland had been among those who have forwarded such a claim. They wanted to make people believe that they had discovered a dead body and left it lie around without ever breathing a word about it, and only after the entire matter proved to be a scientific sensation did they come up with their story.

The court of Bolzano, South Tyrol, found this completely implausible and awarded the first discovery to the German couple.

The Slovenian-Swiss alpine-girls had actually been very lucky. Fritz was found in such a good condition that they could have been sued for non-rendering of assistance or not having tried mouth-to-mouth resuscitation.

The 5000-year-old mummy was uncovered at the Tisenjoch (Tisen Ridge) near the Hauslabjoch (Hauslab Ridge) in the Oetztal Alps, above the Niederjochferner (a glacier), in an altitude of 3210 meters (10531 feet). The Institute for Forensic Medicine of the University of Innsbruck, Austria, carried out the recovery.

Soon, the bickering and wrangling continued. Now Austria and Italy were disputing the property rights relating to Fritz. As he was found in the border region between North Tyrol (Austria) and South Tyrol (autonomous region of Italy), both countries laid claim to the discovered body.

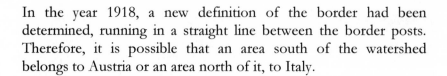

In the year 1918, a new definition of the border had been determined, running in a straight line between the border posts. Therefore, it is possible that an area south of the watershed belongs to Austria or an area north of it, to Italy.

Although the place where Fritz was discovered was already north of the watershed towards Austria, it was still part of Italy according to the regulations of the demarcation.

Since 2006, there is a new state treaty in force between Austria and Italy. It confirms the watershed as the borderline, but they have again made some exceptions, especially in the region around the Tisenjoch, which still places the discovery into Italian territory.

It is all a little confusing up there. For their own sake, Erika and Helmut should have pulled Fritz and his belongings a little more into Austria before announcing their discovery.

In the year 2003, upon the ruling of the district court of Bolzano, the government of South Tyrol had thrown stones into the machinery of justice and appealed against the judgment in favor of Erika and Helmut Simon. Among other things, they referred to other claims of 'first discoveries'. With the official determination of the original finders, a finder's fee had to be paid.

One can easily see that the administration of South Tyrol is strongly influenced by the lifestyle further south, despite all attempts of distinction and not working in line with the 'Habsburg efficiency' of Austria. This is demonstrated by the fact that the legal dispute went on until the year of 2009 when an out-of-court settlement was finally reached with regard to the finder's fee.

Not much was left after the legal fees that had to be borne by Erika and Helmut, but at least a little more than the paltry few thousand Euros, which the stingy State Government of South Tyrol was originally willing to give away.

As the predominantly German speaking autonomous region South Tyrol, formerly part of the Austrian-Hungarian Monarchy, is now embedded in a country where legal cases from the times of the Roman Emperor Nero are still waiting for a decision, one did not even then come to a final result.

It was uncertain at this point of time that the original discoverers will now be correctly acknowledged, which was really the main concern of the finders.

Putting a new map over the trail of Fritz, he was apparently on his way from North Tyrol to South Tyrol and presumably living in North Tyrol and therefore, he belongs to the North Tyrolians. As a former citizen of that area, he should subsequently be transferred back to his home region, regardless where he was found. That follows a simple logic, as the Italians also do not claim the right to keep the bodies of foreign vacationers who drowned in the Adriatic Sea or have been run over by a bus in Milan.

Be it like it is, instead of giving Fritz a decent funeral at long last, he is now displayed in Italy, or more precisely in Bolzano, South Tyrol, at minus 6 degrees and 98% humidity.

Next to the dead body, many important things had been found. Parts of the clothing, numerous articles of daily use and a very fashionable and in a smart way optically combined jacket with vertical streaks of brown and white goatskin.

The pants had been just leg warmers, as we know them from the native Indians in the USA. They also found a belt, made from calf leather and a loincloth, reaching down to the knees. The shoes of Fritz consist of different materials. The soles are made from bearskin and the upper material from deer hide. The shoe's interior is some kind of bast work with material from the linden tree and padding- and isolating layers from grass fiber. That must have been the Prada Shoe of the Stone Age.

Fritz wore a bearskin cap as headgear. Furthermore, a piece of grass of about 10 square inches (64.1 square centimeters), plaited from pipe-grass, was found next to the body. This was projected to the size of a rain protection; others believe that this is a part of a cape or a sleeping mattress.

The copper hatchet he carried with him was completely preserved. The blade consists of 99% copper, which, according to the analysis, originates from the country around Salzburg. Is this another hint to the Austrian origin of the iceman?

Well, that one is a bit difficult. Salzburg was an independent state for a long time, often shifted around between Bavaria (now a Free State in Germany) and Austria. The major slice of it finally became a part of Austria after the Battle of Nations against Napoleon, where the Bavarians unfortunately fought on the wrong side.

When the reshuffling of regions in Europe was in its final stage, at the Congress of Vienna in the year 1815, Prince Metternich of Austria, and others responsible, must have lost their concentration, and they forgot a large piece of the land of Salzburg, which had remained in Bavaria, with the main part going to Austria. Actually, Metternich was just impatient as some of his numerous love affairs were awaiting action and to all abundance, Lord Castlereagh, the British Foreign Secretary, was rushing around, intriguing in every nook and corner. Therefore, any speculations about where Fritz has bought his expensive hatchet do not bring us any further.

Fritz must have been a wealthy and well-respected person, as stated by some scientists, because copper is a precious material, not only in our time. The term 'rich' seems to be logical, but why are they so sure that he was also 'well-respected'? The same scientists came out with the statement that Fritz was treacherously murdered, presumably only for personal reasons and not because of greed.

Initially, the cause of death was identified as an arrow-shot from an ambush, whereby the projectile had penetrated the left shoulder blade in the back. Fritz was the victim of robbers.

But this theory soon began to totter, because many valuable items were still lying around the mummy. These would have been a logical reason for the cowardly assault and the robbers would have taken them away as spoil.

They also found a dagger of Fritz, which had a blade made of flint stone and a handle made from ash wood. Tiny fossils are enclosed in this flint stone, which appear in this combination only in a pit in the 'Monti Lessini' (Lessini Mountains) at the Lake Garda. This in turn speaks for Italy, or did Fritz just carry with him imported goods from that region?

Much more could be collected: A tool for shaping flint stones, a spike of lime wood with an inserted, a hardened splinter of deer antlers, the remains of a basket and two vessels made of birch wood, one of which presumably served as a container for amber.

And so it goes on, with a belt bag, with a blade scraper, a drill, the fragment of a blade and an awl about 3 inches (7.6 centimeters) long, as well as tinder with traces of pyrite – ingredients of a lighter commonly used in these days – and a perforated disk of stone, which could have had several functions.

But that's not all: They found arthritis in his bones and intestinal worms and all kinds of things in his stomach. Based on the mineral composition of the iceman's teeth, the scientists believe that this allows defining his place of birth, pointing towards two places in South Tyrol, the Eisack Valley and the Vinschgau.

That is enough now – we should think. One could hardly find more exciting things if the Titanic would be brought up to surface. Far from it! When the mummy was X-rayed, the presence of a

broken off arrowhead was revealed in the left shoulder of Fritz. We know the rest. When bow and arrow are involved, the legends are not far away.

The scientists were only certain about one thing: There had been an arrow coming from behind, but they desperately wanted to cling to an ambush attack – and if not in predatory intention, then for personal reasons.

I am honestly asking myself how one can hide on a glacier? One can surely hide in a glacial crevice, but not for a short time, because once in there, one would most likely be trapped forever.

Following this theory, people from his own tribe were after him and a robbery and the taking away of the findings would have unmasked them as the culprits. This is a very strange idea. If Fritz was killed for personal reasons, it should have been done the other way around and they would have staged a robbery and later disposed of the goods taken along, to hide the real motive.

There were speculations that someone wanted to remove the arrow as a piece of evidence pointing to the offenders, and it broke off behind the arrowhead. No! If possible, archers always try to recover their arrows to use them again.

I am inclined to doubt that people 5000 years ago were able to come up with any of these conclusions, when primitive greed and hunger for raw meat were determining thinking and acting.

Anyway, in most of the different theories, the shaft of the arrow was removed and the prey was left behind. The discovery of the arrowhead, thanks to the invention of x-ray some millenniums later, was – back then – certainly not part of people's imagination.

Was it jealousy, tribal feuds, a quarrel? Nobody knows. Soon, other researchers have emerged and as you can only arouse interest when you come up with a new theory and not with a confirmation of old wisdom, Fritz was now attacked from the front.

In addition to the wound from the arrow and an injury of the hand, they have identified a craniocerebral trauma, allegedly originating from a blow to the head, while many scientists are still almost fanatically pig-headed with their theory of the cowardly attack with bow and arrow.

Besides the arrow from behind, we now have an additional blow from the front that had caused the death. At first, an arrow from North Tyrol shot by his own people. Then, a blow to the head by strange robbers, coming from South Tyrol, followed by a half turn of Fritz in the longitudinal axis between North- and South Tyrol. But why has the aggressor or have the aggressors, coming from the front, not taken the prey? Was he, or were they, also from his own tribe or was it the same murderer, at first the arrow and then the final blow with the club?

As the theories became contradictory, the scientists have brought forward the – non-fatal – attack with the club by 24 hours and protected their story about a deadly arrow shot from behind. They 'determined' that Fritz stood upright and was looking in the direction of South Tyrol. He did not turn around to North Tyrol when he was hit, which would have been a likely reaction, after an injury of the shoulder by an arrow, coming from that direction. He must have been still alive, if the club was used 24 hours before – and the arrow shot was certainly not causing an immediate death.

Once more, they have been at their wit's end. No traces of blood had been found that could be associated with a fight.

Forensic experts are coming in flocks to the topic of the iceman Fritz. I only hope they are doing this in their spare time. Who is interested to know whether someone had intentionally or by accident shot at Fritz a few thousand years ago?

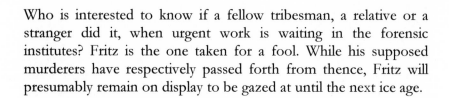

Who is interested to know if a fellow tribesman, a relative or a stranger did it, when urgent work is waiting in the forensic institutes? Fritz is the one taken for a fool. While his supposed murderers have respectively passed forth from thence, Fritz will presumably remain on display to be gazed at until the next ice age.

The truth is a different one: In reality, there have been neither robbers nor bad fellow tribesmen and certainly not a deceitful assault with bow and arrow.

There is a logic explanation why the rest of the arrow (the shaft) is missing. Fritz had an injury from an arrow shot, which occurred *before* his march through the Alps, and he was on his way to get the arrowhead in his shoulder professionally removed somewhere, or he had hoped that everything would fairly heal over time.

In the end, Scottish scientists disproved all theories about a deceitful assault. The University of Glasgow has continued to work in a sober fashion (as far as one can be sober in Whiskyland) and has not immediately committed itself, like all the others, when the arrowhead in the shoulder of Fritz has pushed serious research into the background in favor of wild stories.

According to the findings of the University of Glasgow, Fritz had carried with him antibacterial moss, which was undoubtedly used for the dressing of wounds. This means that the wound and the arrowhead in the shoulder were already there.

We have learned from an article by the Scottish archaeobotanist James Dickinson, published in the professional magazine 'Vegetation History', that six different kinds of moss had been found in the stomach of the iceman. Traces of moss had remained on his hands, and as he was eating the food with his fingers, some of that moss was getting into his stomach. It is important to note that one type of that moss does not grow in the border area between Austria and Italy, the region Fritz was found.

This obviously speaks for the assumption that Fritz was on his way through the mountains with moss from his tribal pharmacy, and he was treating his *existing* wound with it. The researchers had already discovered earlier some birch polypore which Fritz carried along, and what they indeed had defined as remedies, but they simply did not put that into the right context.

Most likely, Fritz was simply stumbling out of weakness caused by the wound in his shoulder, or perhaps due to carelessness, and haplessly fell on his head. He was not able to get up or to turn around and had remained in this position, on his stomach and lying across his left arm.

In recent times, experts are taking up the issue again and want to bring back the excitement to the meanwhile worn-out story.

In another version, Fritz was not able to string his bow fast enough and therefore became a defenseless victim. One fact is however undisputed across all the silliness brought up: The bow of the iceman was not at all ready for use and he had still tinkered with it along his way.

Poor Fritz, it appears to be inevitable to assume that some of the scientific theories have been developed over a good bottle of wine, which could be another reason for a staggering Iceman.

Many of those experts might not know how far the consumption of alcohol goes back in human history. We can today be certain that the production of alcohol had already begun at the time of the Middle Stone Age, 10000 to 5000 BC, along with the transformation of people to farmers and stockbreeders. Perhaps, Fritz had just been drunk and stumbled. I have my sincere doubts that he had been shot with an arrow from behind – on the spot where he was found. With all the precious items lying around Fritz, at the limit of what a man can carry through the Alps, I am even inclined to say that no one was even near when Fritz died.

The story of Fritz receives no rest and they continue to stir around in the world's oldest 'cold case'. 'By coincidence', they recently found 19 living relatives of Fritz in North Tyrol through an analysis of the DNA of 3700 men who had donated blood. The tests had actually been carried out in connection with a research project dealing with the settlement of North Tyrol.

Just by coincidence? Come on! The starting point was most likely the DNA of Fritz and the regional blood samples, available in great quantities, came in handy to satisfy the curiosity of scientists. They did not personally inform the newly found 'relatives' of Fritz, but want to extend their research and are now looking for cooperation partners in other countries, firstly in Switzerland and South Tyrol.

This will leave a lot more people guessing about who could be among the ones, identified as related to Fritz – perhaps even you and I. As far as I am concerned, the scientists can keep the results and also the bacteria collected from Fritz. For some of them, it's the only 'culture' they have.

THE STOLEN SKULL OF GERONIMO

Can you identify some famous Americans by a few words or sentences? If not, you will find the solutions at the end of the chapter.

(1): *"All I am, or hope to be, I owe to my angel mother."*

(2) *"That's one small step for a man, a giant leap for mankind."*

(3) *"I think war is a dangerous place."*

(4) *"I want you back; I want you back in my life baby! And on the way back, can you pick up some donuts please?"*

Or this one: *"Bring me a couple of large Paws (Burgers). No, make it three, no six, double cheese!"*

No clue? I make it a bit easier: *"The warden threw a party in the county jail, the prison band was there and they began to wail."*

(5) *"I would call my colleagues' attention to the fine paper that the United Kingdom distributed."*

But there is one famous person, a Native American and the most famous besides Elvis Presley, whom you will recognize by a single word: *"Geronimoooooooooo!"*

Actually, Geronimo did not have much to do with bow and arrow, as he had lived in a time when they had already become obsolete. Yet, in our minds, he represents the typical picture of an Indian, wildly riding on his horse and shooting around with bow and arrow. But in reality, he is only linked to this weapon, because he had signed numerous 'original' Apache bows up to his death in the year 1906. Besides that, he gave autographs and repeatedly sold copies of his hat – certified originals of course – along with two hundred thousand (!) personal items, like the buttons of his jacket.

During the last years of his life, he transported himself around in a car. It was not a Cadillac, as many believe due to a famous photo of the year 1905, but a vehicle of the long gone brand Locomobile.

Another photograph of the same day shows him standing in front of a dead buffalo, which he claimed to have killed – still showing several arrows stuck in the animal. That particular scene was sold as the 'last buffalo killed by Geronimo'. In fact, the animal had been shot before with rifles.

Although he was never a chief, he gained fame forever as the leader of the last Indian warrior troops who had surrendered to their overwhelming enemy.

'Geronimo captured – the end of the Apache War'. This was the headline on September 5, 1886, in all newspapers in the USA. Geronimo had been taken prisoner the day before. Five thousand American soldiers and three thousand from Mexico, as well as many Indian scouts, had chased him, but he managed to escape for six months.

Geronimo had already been captured some years before. On April 21, 1877, Major John Clum, who was best friends with the famous Wyatt Earp, arrested him – without the firing of a single shot.

John Clum was the first mayor of Tombstone, Arizona. On October 26, 1881, he witnessed the most famous gunfight of all times, at the O.K. Corral, where Wyatt Earp, Doc Holliday, Virgil Earp and Morgan Earp fought the Clantons and McLaurys.

After his internment, Geronimo spent some time in a reservation, which was partly assigned to the Apache by the Kiowa and the Comanche, and grew watermelons.

Later, as he aged, he became a welcomed 'VIP guest' on exhibitions, trade fairs and rodeo events, always with bodyguards around him. If Geronimo would be still alive, we could most likely meet him at the opening of a do-it-yourself store or together with Ronald McDonald under a big yellow 'M'.

His unwarlike end came on a cold winter night. He was drunk and on his way back to the reservation when he fell off his horse and lay helplessly on the ground for several hours. He did not survive the subsequent pneumonia and died on February 17, 1909. Geronimo was buried on the Apache cemetery at Fort Sill.

"Geronimooooooooo!" – a piercing scream that still penetrates into every limb of our body when we watch an old Western movie and the Apache warriors attack white settlers, seeking revenge.

"Geronimooooooooo!" was also the outcry of the US parachutists in WWII when they jumped from their planes, and people everywhere use it when they run about and seek attention.

The original name of Geronimo was not Geronimo. He was born sometime between 1823 and 1825 in New Mexico and was given the name 'Goyathlay', which simply means 'the one who yawns'.

In the year 1850 his mother, his wife and children, were killed by Mexican troops. This tragedy gave Goyathlay, alias Geronimo, superior power and strength, like the life force of the Universe, the gift of premonition and a walk without leaving footprints. He was able to hold back darkness and had the power to let bullets bounce off his body.

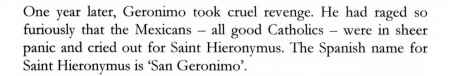

One year later, Geronimo took cruel revenge. He had raged so furiously that the Mexicans – all good Catholics – were in sheer panic and cried out for Saint Hieronymus. The Spanish name for Saint Hieronymus is 'San Geronimo'.

So, *"Geronimooooooooooo!"* *was* originally not an outcry during an attack, but a whiny and terrifying call for help. The fame of Geronimo, peppered with lots of excitement and adventures, had undoubtedly caught people's imagination.

We often hear the anecdote of 'the stolen skull of Geronimo' in connection with the Secret Society of Yale University. Every University or College in the USA has its own secret society. Well, almost all. I spend some time at the Northern Community College near Falls Church, Virginia, and we certainly did *not* have a secret society, but we told everyone that we have one; it was just so secret that only a few knew about it.

The most famous of the *real* secret societies are the 'Skull and Bones' of Yale University in New Haven, Connecticut. The two Presidents, George H.W. Bush (41st President), his son George W. Bush (43rd President), as well as their father respectively grandfather, Prescott Bush, had been – or still are – members of the Skull and Bones, like other famous people, for example William Howard Taft (27th President).

The members of that club call themselves the 'Bonesmen' and their clubhouse is named the 'Tomb'.

It is not disputed that this secret society has profound German roots. One of the founders, William Huntington Russell, had studied in Berlin. Originally, they were (and are still today) most likely an offshoot of a German secret society. The founding of the order in the year 1832 was financed by a cousin of W.H. Russell with money that came from an illegal opium trade.

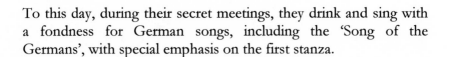

To this day, during their secret meetings, they drink and sing with a fondness for German songs, including the 'Song of the Germans', with special emphasis on the first stanza.

The third stanza of the National Anthem of Germany has meanwhile replaced the unpopular first one, but thanks to the Skull and Bones, the old traditions are still kept alive in the Tomb at Yale University.

The melody had been written by no one less than Joseph Haydn, originally for a song that was dedicated to Francis (Franz) II./I. As Franz II., he was the last Emperor of the Holy Roman Empire of the German Nation and later as Franz I. (first Franz in the local order), Emperor of Austria. At a later stage, the melody was adopted for the National Anthem of Germany.

It is also the tune of a popular chant of Protestant churches in the USA, which gives the singing from the throats of the Bonesmen a decent and peaceful touch when someone walks by the house and listens to the song without understanding the words.

The Skull and Bones Society is said to have stolen the skull of Geronimo from his grave and it is now kept in their clubhouse at Yale University and (mis-) used in ritual meetings.

One of the tomb raiders was Prescott Bush. The behavior of this controversial figure was even more unscrupulous than what we know from his offspring George H.W. Bush and George W. Bush.

Prescott Bush was a hard-baked personality and well known for his entanglements of all sorts and not only as a manager of Adolf Hitler's house bank in the USA.

During World War I, Prescott Bush served as a volunteer at Fort Sill. Together with five other members of the Skull and Bones Society, he is said to have stolen the skull of Geronimo, along with some bones and a silver saddle horn, from his grave at the prisoner of war cemetery at Fort Sill.

There are periodic attempts to get back at least the mortal remains from the Skull and Bones Society, especially as the Indians think that the soul has its seat in these human remnants; yet, they seem to forget that this would be the main reason why they had been stolen by the Skull and Bones.

In the year 2009, descendants of Geronimo have sued President Obama, Defense Secretary Robert Gates and Yale University in Federal Court in Washington D.C. and requested the return of the mortal remains of Geronimo. The case was however dismissed on August 10, 2010. What can we expect? The US legal system is a puppet theater of Yale University.

Secret letters and documents make the entire topic more than a conspiracy theory. A letter has been discovered as corroborating evidence. It was written in the year 1918 from one Bonesman to another and announced that the remains, dug up at Fort Sill by a group of Bonesmen, had been deposited in the 'Tomb'.

"The skull of the worthy Geronimo the Terrible, exhumed from his tomb at Fort Sill by our club and the Knight Haffner, is now safe inside the Tomb, together with his well-worn femurs, bit and saddle horn."

Today, the Skull and Bones Society does not deny that they have a skull in their possession, called Geronimo. It is kept behind glass near the entrance, but they leave open the question whose it is and where it comes from.

It can well be assumed that Prescott Bush and the bandits from the Skull and Bones have really robbed a grave. This would not be something unusual in this highly crazy secret society.

However, many people think that they might not have found the right skull at the Indian cemetery at Fort Sill, as all the graves were unmarked and overgrown. In any case, the mortal remains should go back to where they belong.

The Skull and Bone Society is believed to be associated with almost everything: Watergate, the CIA, sexism, occultism or the assassination of Kennedy.

Besides the skull of Geronimo, they are said to have stolen the skulls of Martin van Buren and Pancho Villa. All is kept within the collection of the artifacts in the tomb, which – according to the rumors – is adorned with many items like Nazi memorabilia or less exciting, decorative tchotchkes and strange objects like coffins, Tibetan bowls or innards which are displayed on Hitler's personal silverware.

Not to forget: They are also in possession of some bones belonging to Madame Pompadour, the mistress of Louis XV and at one time, the most influential woman in France.

The only full-time resident in the tomb is the 'bones whore', who helps that the Bonesmen leave the tomb 'more mature than when they entered'. As she (it?) is always eaten at the end of the year, and the bones are added to the collection, one has to wonder what kind of a whore this, a missing prostitute or a goat?

Perhaps the best kept secret of the Skull and Bones Society is the fact that they do not have the skull of Geronimo, but a lot of attention instead – very much enjoyed by them.

Solutions: (1) Abraham Lincoln, (2) Neil Armstrong on the moon, (3) Georg W. Bush, (4) Elvis – loosely quoted from the 'Elvis Tapes', secret recordings of Elvis' last telephone conversations, American Comedy Network and Elvis – Jailhouse Rock, (5) Colin Luther Powell.

NOBLE ARCHERS – CHINESE BELIEFS

Whenever 'special wisdom' is produced, the Asian tinkerers of mottoes are forcing their way into the first row.

But at first, one must consider the complexity of the Chinese language, which has a much more multifaceted structure compared to what we are familiar with in our part of the world.

Nevertheless, Chinese sayings are usually quoted one-to-one and brought among the audience in the West as a special source of deeper insights into our Universe.

The famous dictionary of the Emperor Kanghi, written (or rather hand-painted) in the year 1716, contains 47000 characters. The directory issued in the year 1994 had already 87000 characters, and meanwhile 92000 signs are registered. This is the reason why the Chinese continue to learn their written language over a lifetime.

Under these circumstances, it is somewhat more complicated to construct a sentence with world-shattering thoughts, than with our system of writing. What concerns modern text, 3000 Chinese characters are enough to have a rudimentary understanding of what is written. In the 'belles lettres', one needs 1000 signs more.

Have you ever watched a Chinese reading the newspaper? They often turn it around when they have realized they are holding it upside down, mostly recognizing that the headline is on the bottom. On top of this, you have all the confusion with the direction of the writing. Nowadays, and under the Western influence, they also write from left to right, but also the other way around. Some text is still written (painted) in a vertical mode, with the columns going from left to right or from right to left. Vertical columns for left to right facilitated writing with the right hand, which is also continually unrolling the coiled sheet of paper, whilst the left hand holds it in the upper left corner.

When it comes to the first names of children, the Chinese must reach deeply into the box of symbols to make them distinguishable from the rest of the Chinese mega crowd. There are only a few family names available, which are usually put up front.

About 85% of the population is sharing 100 names. 'Wang', 'Li' or 'Zhang' are the family names of 275 million Chinese. No wonder that the name for the Chinese population is derived from the term 'laobaixing', which means something like 'the one hundred names'. In the ethnic diversity of the USA, for example, 85% of the population shares 70000 family names.

Identity cards are mandatory and are issued partly hand written. A changeover to chip cards failed repeatedly, because the government's computer software was only able to recognize 32000 Chinese characters.

Officials, annoyed with the system, often advise people to change their name, because they are unable to record it onto the document. Irritated by the inability to conclude the transactions, they threaten to recall the applicants every three months and subject them to complete a new application, if the family name is not altered.

Back to the Chinese wisdom: There are numerous old sayings and despite being intellectually rather weak, they are much adored in the Western world. Earth-shattering cognitions are drawn from the phrase *"when the rain comes, your way will get wet"*. Or this one here: *"A content person, even if poor, can be happy; a discontent person, even if rich, can be unhappy."* No kidding?

Now, where all the 'wisdom' is written in short lines, archery is not excluded. Confucius, also known as Zhongni, Kongzi, Kong Qui or Kong Fuzi, is for sure the most famous of the Chinese tinkerers of jingles, although it has to be mentioned that most of the outpourings do not originate from him. In lack of anyone else to claim the prize – the credit was given to Confucius.

Lao (the venerable) Tse, also spelled Laotze, Lao Tu, Lao-Tsu, Lao Tzu, Laosi or Laocius, is another one of these tattlers who came up with empty phrases like *"a journey of a thousand miles start with a single step"*. Yes, venerable Mr. Tse, every distance you walk, and which is longer than a step, starts with a single step.

Just imagine, you watch a hillbilly painting his fence; you stop and say: *"Every painting of a fence starts with the first picket."* I guess you would soon run away from a loaded shotgun with a paint bucket upside down over your head – a good answer to Chinese wisdom!

How about the saying *"when too tightly drawn, the bow is cracking"*? One could lean to an authorship of Confucius or Lao Tse. However, neither of them is responsible for this slogan – it comes from Friedrich Schiller.

When Confucius was not busy constructing empty phrases like *"the drunkard is responsible for the befuddlement, not the wine"* or *"education is outside all class distinction"*, he took pleasure to occupy himself with noble qualities, which he then attributed to one or another.

'Master Kong' did not wish to miss out archery and came up with this twaddle: *"In archery, we will find a parable for the way of the nobleman. When the archer misses his target, he is turning around and is seeking the reason for his failure within himself."*

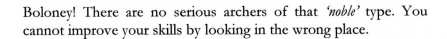

Boloney! There are no serious archers of that *'noble'* type. You cannot improve your skills by looking in the wrong place.

If an archer misses the target, he does not search within himself, but looks for the lost arrow. Thereafter, a great number of more important items have to be accounted for, which could be the cause of the missing shot. One must investigate about twisted limbs, a wrongly placed nock-point, the brace height of the string, loose feathers on the arrow, bumps at the shooting line – just to name a few.

Then we still have the wind and plenty of distractions and disturbances.

Especially the archers with modern and highly technical bows need a long checklist to evaluate all factors of influence and the effect they have on the flight of their arrows.

If he wants to improve his skills and find the reasons for a deviation from the ideal ballistic curve, a good archer has to explore the *external* issues and causes at hand to minimize the number of his missed shots.

If the archer searches inside himself, this might beg the question why he has given up bowling or figure skating in favor of archery, but will never provide a useful solution what concerns the improvement of his shooting.

Occasional imperfections of the archers, like a poor posture or a bad release, will more or less automatically disappear over time.

屁话 On the left: Chinese symbols for shit, nonsense, just in case you might want to clearly express your opinion on some Chinese wise sayings to local non-English speakers.

GESCHNETZELTES À L' ARCHER

Every year, around autumn time, a group of gourmets met in a hotel-restaurant in a small village in Central Switzerland.

On this day, the restaurant was closed for the public and exclusively used for this private event. They wanted to stay among themselves to enjoy a very special creation that was served to them every year: 'Geschnetzeltes (a typical Swiss dish, meat cut into strips or small pieces) – à l' Archer' (archer style).

They did not know much about each other and they just came together once a year on this special occasion. It was a mutual pleasure to savor a very special dish, always served in new and surprising creations, and also the wine and the other courses were presented in different variations.

The group of food lovers became aware of this rare opportunity through an advertisement in a supra-regional newspaper. The guests always slept in the same rooms, located above the restaurant and there were no other visitors during these days.

Over the years, the group steadily diminished in numbers. Nothing was said about those who no longer attended, yet the guests may have speculated as to their fate, but they were certain about one thing: There must have been serious circumstances that prevented their attendance and to miss such an opportunity.

Often asked, why he did not invite new guests into the circle, the innkeeper replied: *"I am running my little restaurant only occasionally, more as a hobby, after many years of hard working. When this group does not exist anymore, I will definitively retire for good."*

Victor Pavlovski, a native of Macedonia, came to Switzerland many years ago. After working his way up in the noble restaurants of the country, he had purchased a former tavern in a small village, which he had renamed 'Hôtel-Restaurant Victor'.

A beautiful longbow hung on the wall of the restaurant and, next to it, a quiver with arrows, graced with feathers in the Swiss national colors, red and white. Whenever somebody asked Victor about this bow, he steadily repeated: *"Some time ago, I often shoot this bow in my spare time, but today I do not have the strength anymore."*

Every year, when the guests were about to depart, he secretly gave one of them a small envelope. Inside this envelope was a message that asked the recipient to come a day earlier next year, to help and select the wine, but under the condition of complete secrecy.

Again, that year, the special guest punctually arrived one day before the meal. He certainly did not want to miss this honorable task to taste and select some precious drops for the banquet.

As usual, there had been a day of rest in the hotel and the restaurant. The special guest did not mind. He now could give his undivided attention to the important preparations and, perhaps, Victor would tell him a few secrets about his 'Geschnetzeltes à l' Archer'.

After unpacking his suitcase, he came down to the restaurant, full of anticipation for the wine tasting and in particular for the forthcoming events on the next day. He immediately recognized that the bow was not hanging in its place on the wall and he asked Victor about it. He responded: *"Oh, the bow, it fell down while I was dusting and I have given it away to be repaired!"*

Victor and his guest went to the door that leads to the wine cellar. *"Please!"* said Victor and the excited guest moved ahead and down the stairs.

It was dark and the guest felt his way along the handrail. When he had arrived at the bottom, he turned around. Victor was still on top of the stairs and switched on the light. The guest looked up to Victor. The blood was running cold in his veins. Victor stood there with the bow fully drawn and was aiming at him.

"What are you doing?" said the terrified guest. Victor, undisturbed and composed, replied: *"I am going to kill you now!"*

The guest laughed out and thought of a bad joke, but he immediately choked on his own laughter when he looked into the serious face of Victor. *"Why?"* asked the guest, almost paralyzed by his fear.

Now Victor was laughing and said: *"Have you never wondered why every year one of you was missing? You have eaten each other, one by one!"*

The guest was still hoping that this was just a bad joke, until Victor added: *"I could have become the Swiss archery champion some years ago, but some arrogant gourmets had repeatedly returned my 'Geschnetzeltes' with always new complaints. Time was running out for me and I therefore had arrived late for the competition."*

And into the silence, Victor added: *"You are the last one from your group. For that reason, I will this time not have a closed party. Tomorrow, I will put the Geschnetzeltes à l' Archer on the menu of the day".*

The last thing the guest could possibly hear was the sharp hiss from the feathers as the arrow flew through the air – a final fleeting moment, followed by silence, as he fell over on the stairs.

This was much in contrast to the lively atmosphere the next evening, when guests were drinking their wine and asking for a second helping of the 'Geschnetzeltes'.

SAGITTARIUS – INVENTOR OF BOW AND ARROW

This is another piece of mythical poppycock that someone must have excavated from the bottom of a rubbish pit. Once again, we are supplied with utterly idiotic material, especially by the statement, that a patched up monster has invented bow and arrow.

We can even localize the most important source of this wild flight of fantasy: The metamorphoses of the Roman poet Ovid, an eager collector of Greek myths. 'Sagittarius' is the Latin word for archer (Greek 'toxotes').

For us, in the Northern Hemisphere, the constellation Sagittarius is not visible all year round. The best time when it can be seen is in August. How much of it is visible depends on the latitude of the point of observation, between +55 and -90 degrees.

The Sagittarius is one of the twelve signs of the zodiac. The ecliptic transits this constellation, which means that the sun, the moon and the planets are wandering across, at least from our perspective.

It is the most southern sign of the zodiac and lies between the Scorpion and the Capricorn, the area richest of stars in the milky way, exactly in the direction to the center of our galaxy.

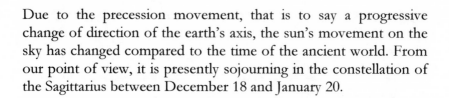

Due to the precession movement, that is to say a progressive change of direction of the earth's axis, the sun's movement on the sky has changed compared to the time of the ancient world. From our point of view, it is presently sojourning in the constellation of the Sagittarius between December 18 and January 20.

Many cultures have recognized the most diverse motives in this sign of the zodiac. For the Babylonians, it was an effigy of Pabilsang, a god with a lion's head and wings. Indians and Egyptians also saw an archer or a horseman.

This already shows how spongy the contours are – and to a great extend subject to all kinds of speculations. In modern times, sky-watchers from the Northern Hemisphere had come to the conclusion that it looks more like a teapot and a teaspoon, but no one dares to rename this star cluster, which could let us forget about the weird stories of its origin.

Whatever, in the insane fantasies of the Greeks, a rider and an archer were put together into a single creature and made the 'inventor' of bow and arrow.

With hoofs on forelegs and hind legs, Sagittarius would not have been able to make bows, arrows or bowstrings, so they gave this defaced beast a pair of human arms, in addition to the four legs.

As if that was not enough, the Greeks came up with several variations. One of it was the previously mentioned Centaur, a horseman, a human head and human upper body, combined with the lower body of a horse, allegedly the centaur Chiron, who was a perfect archer. But that cannot be correct, because the Centaur Chiron is already present in another place in the sky.

Others hallucinated with a figure called Krotos, one of the alleged 'inventors' of bow and arrow. Krotos was the son of Pan and Eupheme. He was a patient listener and passionate admirer of the

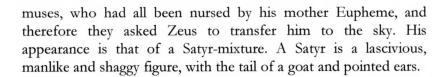

muses, who had all been nursed by his mother Eupheme, and therefore they asked Zeus to transfer him to the sky. His appearance is that of a Satyr-mixture. A Satyr is a lascivious, manlike and shaggy figure, with the tail of a goat and pointed ears.

Zeus wanted to mix in other characteristics and gave him the flanks of a horse. He had to combine and add so many things to ensure that all would fit into the *already existing* constellation.

Come on! There are so many stars up there, giving you the chance to connect them with lines, just as you please, resulting in the contours of about anything you like, from a chamber pot to a fancy hat of Camilla Mountbatten-Windsor.

Nevertheless, people born in the sign of the Sagittarius are cheerful, honest and candid. They believe in the future, the progress and like to travel; they love animals and walks in the fresh air. There is no evidence that they tend to be above average archers.

Suitable occupations for the versatile people born in the sign of the Sagittarius are judge, lawyer, cowboy, discoverer and adventurer, priest, missionary, religious instructor, forester, farmer, investment consultant, politician, cabaret artist, entertainer, comedian, inventor, administration employee, manager, philosopher, writer, journalist, author, poet, scientist, tour guide and tourist manager.

In the year 1932, the American physicist Karl Jansky discovered a big black hole in the constellation Sagittarius, 3.7 times larger than the sun. Is that the place where all our lost arrows are hidden that we have shot wide off target and which we could not find anymore, even after an intensive search? If I would be an antique Greek or Roman poet, I would tell you that this is the place where Krotos gets his supply of arrows, free of charge, by collecting the lost feathered friends of the mortal archers.

Perhaps I could come up with such rubbish after consuming a few bottles of Lesbian wine. No, that is not what you are probably thinking of. This wine is simply a wine coming from the island of Lesbos in the Aegean Sea, which has a long history of winemaking, dating back to the 6th or 7th century.

A lot of our modern day vernacular comes from the old Greek and Latin languages, like Aphrodisiacs – substances meant to increase sexual arouse and desire, named after the Greek goddess Aphrodite or Nymphomaniac – comparing women to nymphs who were spirits that would tempt men into sex and sensuality.

Lesbian – in its basic meaning – is simply someone who hails from the isle of Lesbos. The 'poetess' Sappho, whose home was on this island, wrote love poetry from woman to other women and is responsible for common use of the term 'lesbian'.

A few things must be taken into account when dating a lesbian born in the sign of the Sagittarius.

She embodies the lone huntress in accordance with her sign of the archer and values her independence; so do not try to rope her into a relationship after just a couple of dates. Do not send 'miss-you-messages' to her smartphone bordering on despair, she does not like that. She is very straight forward, hates beating around the bush and when it comes to pillow talk, she usually switches to philosophy.

RECORDS IN ARCHERY

 **O**nce upon a time, there was an archer...

In the year 1798, a long-distance bow-shooting competition was held in Turkey. The winner was Sultan Selim. He shot an arrow to a point 972 yards (888.8 meters) away.

How Sultan Selim has tricked people is often told on the quiet. The competition took place in Istanbul. One of the Sultan's cousins stood – well hidden – along the route and is said to have shot a second arrow when the first one got out of sight. The 972 yards (888.8 meters) would therefore be shared between two shooters, but not so bad after all. Today, a monument marks the spot where the last arrow went down.

The attending British ambassador, who had testified to this event, was supposedly in that permanent state of inebriation, characteristic for British ambassadors, especially during colonial times.

This record was meanwhile broken many times. In the year 1992, the American Kevin Strother shot through the air with a high-tech bow. The arrow needed ten seconds before it hit the ground at a distance of 1320 yards (1207 meters).

But this is all surpassed by the distances achieved with a so-called 'foot-bow', something similar to a crossbow.

To shoot this strange device, the archer has to lie on his back and pushes the bow forward with his feet while holding back the string with his arms.

Harry Drake, born in Kansas, USA, on May 7, 1915, has set several records with such a foot-bow. In the year 1971, he had shot an arrow to a distance of 2028 yards (1854 meters). The bow he used had a draw weight of 200 lbs.

The initial velocity of the arrow was 442 mph (711 km/h) and when it went down, it still had a speed of 231 mph (371.8 km/h). The total length of the flight (full ballistic curve) was 1.36 miles (2.19 kilometers), and its duration was 20.2 seconds.

In the year 1988, the same Harry Drake, by then seventy-three (!) years old, has lain down on his back again and made the arrow fly over a distance of 2047 yards (1872 meters).

This all is no longer part of the usual outdoor shooting. For that kind of exercise, one needs to go to a place like a dry lake in the high desert of California.

Many archers of this world will always remember Harry Drake, not only for his fantastic achievements, but also for the tragic way he died. In July of the year 1997, at the age of 84, he fell off his motorbike when he returned from an archery flight tournament.

In the year 1696, the Japanese archery-champion Wada Daihachi is said to have set an incredible record.

He was shooting an arrow every 12 seconds for 27 hours, without interruption, at a roofed shooting-range, thereby hitting the target at the end of the range 8133 times – a rate of almost 100%.

I think I have to change the batteries of my calculator. I figured out that this would add up to exactly 8100 arrows 'of which' 8133, *almost* 100% (?), hit the target.

In looking somewhat deeper, I think this was just a matter of bad translation. Wada Daihachi had shot an arrow approximately every

12 seconds, at a stand with was completely (100%) roofed, for 27 hours and had reached 8,133 times the end of the range.

In the year 1924, General Thord-Gray claimed an unusual record while competing against twelve pistol shooters. The target was placed 80 yards (73.2 meters) away and had a size of 26 by 26 inches (66 by 66 centimeters). Thord-Gray had 72 arrows. The 'Pistoleros' had six bullets each. The archer had nevertheless reached the same number of points as his opponents together.

What is the unusual part of this story I do not understand?

By all means, 80 yards (73.2 meters) were a respectable distance for bow and arrow in those days – but not world-shaking. At today's official tournaments, 70 meters (76 yards) are the standard distance. For small arms however, this target stands quite far away – if not too far – in view of an expected accuracy in hitting.

When I am shooting 72 arrows and my 12 opponents shoot 6 bullets each, then they also have, all combined, only 72 shots and on top of it with a shooting gear that – in this specific case - is inferior. If you want to bring this to a head: I can even easily compete with 72 arrows against 72 opponents, if each of them has only one shot.

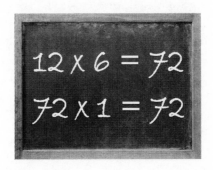

THE PAIUTE MYTH OF THE CREATION OF BOW AND ARROW

When the Earth was still young, three monsters controlled the world. They destroyed the harvest, drove away the game and killed the people.

The Paiute, an Indian tribe, were too weak and too unpracticed in warfare to challenge the monsters or to protect themselves against the evil of these beasts, but their God 'Shinob' saved his people.

He made a big bow from a rainbow and arrows from uprooted, mature trees. Equipped with these weapons, he chased away the monsters and brought peace to Earth.

The Paiute Indians are separated into a southern tribe, primarily living in Utah, Northwest Arizona, South Nevada and South California and a northern tribe, who settled mainly in East California, West Nevada and East Oregon.

Most of them were pushed into reservations. They have not become extinct and it is estimated that the population is about seventeen thousand today, with five thousand of them who live in these reservations.

The Paiute Indians were always poor and so they remained. Today, they make efforts to improve their standards of living with the help of the government.

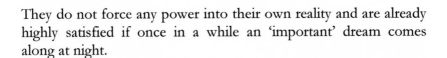

They do not force any power into their own reality and are already highly satisfied if once in a while an 'important' dream comes along at night.

This particular Indian tribe came in contact with the white man very late in time. He came into their land, mainly because of the rush for gold and ores or the emerging property speculation.

The destruction of their food plants, especially by new kinds of cattle brought into the area, forced the Paiute into assimilation. This fortunately took place quietly, because the initial penetration into their territory occurred only very selectively.

Their myth of the creation of bow and arrow is of course pipe-dream poetry, even if it is – in this particular case – of a rather kindhearted nature. It is more a fairy tale for their grandchildren and they do not try to take adults for a ride, like the Greek poets or let them search for a deeper sense.

The story is clearly based on the mentality of the Paiute and their usual handling of problems, especially if something cannot be immediately answered or explained.

They always have a repertoire of all kinds of stories at hand and are highly creative with their excuses, especially when things are urging for settlement or request concrete explanations.

Once, an old Paiute was confronted with piercing questions from his grandson. It really got on his nerves when he was asked where bow and arrow came from.

What would he say? And what about the time when bow and arrow had been invented? How could he possibly come up with an answer, when even today the experts do not agree among themselves whether bow and arrow have been in existence since ten-thousand, twenty-thousand or perhaps fifty-thousand years?

Had he made a statement like *"I don't know"*, it would have undermined his authority. So, he gave the version with their God Shinob to his grandson, who passed it on to his own grandson – when asked – and then on to his grandson and all following grandsons of the Paiute who were curious about bow and arrow.

The Mandan Indians are another interesting tribe. They are Native Americans who live in North Dakota. Half of their population still resides in the area of their reservation. The main weapons, used by them in the past for hunting and in hostile conflicts, were bow and arrow, knives and clubs.

The language of the Mandan had received much attention, partly because they have a much lighter skin than the average Indians in North America, and some believe that they even are of European origin.

Reports from the 18th Century about their housing, religion or physical features (including blue eyes and lighter colored hair), contributed to the speculation that they are descendants of Welsh settlers who sailed from Wales in the year 1170, together with Prince Medoc, and discovered America many years before Columbus.

Strange Welsh-style stone buildings, unlike any other American Indian structure, have been found in the regions of the Mandan tribe. Indeed, one of the constructions closely resembles Dolwyddelan Castle in Wales, the birthplace of Prince Medoc.

Prince Alexander Philipp Maximilian zu Wied-Neuwied, a German explorer, spent a lot of time studying the Mandan language and prepared a comparison list of Mandan and Welsh words and came up with the theory that the Mandan language is nothing else but displaced Welsh, also referred to as 'Cymraeg' or 'y Gymraeg'.

To me, it often sounds the other way around, like the Welsh language would be displaced Mandan. For example: Microwave heating is as new to the Mandan as it is to the Welsh. However, there is one difference: The Mandan call a microwave oven a microwave oven. The Welsh, occasionally struggling with new terms, call it a 'popty ping'.

A what? Well, 'popty' is a Welsh word for oven and 'ping' is the sound a microwave oven makes when the job is done.

The language of the Welsh-Indians in the New World has meanwhile developed to a more sophisticated stage. The Mandan named that new type of heating in accordance with the technique applied.

The Welsh at home — after all the alleged co-inventors of the longbow — are mentally still with an old oven and added the 'ping' to the name, to make it different from other ovens. They probably did not realize that the 'ping' is not a sound that comes when things are ready, but is simply an alarm when the preset timer has run out — with the food ready or not.

Not too long ago, the Indians had their own struggle with new words and called a locomotive a 'steel horse' to make it distinguishable from other horses.

Back to the Mandan: The bison was once the key to their livelihood before it was supplemented by agriculture and trade.

The Mandan Indians are famous for their Bison Dance. When they still depended on the hunt for bison and no bison had been around, they started their Bison Dance to bring the animals back into their territory. It was a critical part of their survival, as they not only ate the meat, but found uses for the entire bison, so not to waste any part.

During the Bison Dance, every man wore a bison mask with leather strips that hung from it, as well as the tail of the animal. Accompanied by music, drums and rattles, they danced in front of the cottage of the medicine man with their bows and arrows.

If one of the dancers was exhausted, he would lean forward and was symbolically killed with a blunt arrow. He then let himself drop to the ground and was replaced by another dancer. The spectators carried him away and – fortunately only in mime – cut him into pieces.

The dance always led to success and at the end of it, the bison came back. This was not, however, because of the magic of the dance; it just happened this way, because the Mandan did not stop dancing – for several weeks if necessary – until some bison were coincidentally passing by.

**Welsh-Mandan folklore: 'Plucked from the Fairy Circle'.
A man saves his friend from the grip of a fairy ring.**

BOW AND ARROWS – LOST IN THE LOTTERY

When you gamble, you can normally lose everything, including your bow and your arrows, but this is not true everywhere.

The 'Hadzapi' are a tribe of hunters and gatherers who live in Tanzania.

They hunt with a bow, similar to a longbow. It has a thickness in the middle of about 1 inch (2.54 centimeters) and roughly 1/2 inch (1.3 centimeters) at the tips. The string of the bow is made of tendons from the giraffe or the zebra.

When the Hadzapi hunt for birds and small animals, they use arrows with wooden heads. For the hunting of larger animals, the heads are poisoned and made of iron. This type of poison, produced from the rare kadar-shrub, is so strong,
that it can kill a rhinoceros.

The shafts of the poisoned arrows are also used for starting fires, as their heads can be changed. The front part is replaced by a special wooden attachment, which is then pressed against another piece of wood and rolled between the palms of the hand. This way, one can produce enough friction and heat to make the glow for the start of a fire.

The Hadzapi have a strong addiction to gambling. Their lottery is called 'lococuco'. Small, marked pieces of bark are thrown against the trunk of a tree, and the position of the pieces determines the winner.

91

In virtually hundreds of daily game rounds, they wager their entire possessions, which can change hands several times throughout the day.

There are only two things which they are not allowed to gamble away: Their bow and their non-poisonous arrows, because they are of vital importance for their survival.

The poisoned arrows can be wagered. If they are lost, like everything else, then the poor losers have to be temporarily satisfied with the hunt for small animals – with the non-poisonous arrows.

They can furthermore collect berries, fruits, roots or herbs or can feed on carrion. All cold dishes of course, because they have no more tools for starting a fire.

Speaking of carrion and cold dishes: Would that not be a good treatment for investment bankers, after they have lost our money in the financial lottery?

For a time, they would collect savings, work with it in a descent and responsible manner and no more bonuses and expensive business lunches.

WILLIAM TELL – THE APPLE-SHOT STORY

Many Nordic cultures have worked on this hokum, before the story finally came to Switzerland.

Here, in lonely places on the hills and remote spots in hidden valleys, the legend really started to flourish; yet something was still missing: The icing on the cake to move it up to the highest level that any literary hogwash can be elevated – a national epic.

It needed someone of the magnitude of the greatest poets of all times from the famous land of poets and thinkers: Johann Wolfgang von Goethe and Friedrich Schiller. If historians argue about who is the greater of the two, there is a point speaking for Goethe: He had the crazy idea with the William Tell story, but decided to let Schiller come out with it; but there is something that honors both of them: They have left the action in Switzerland.

The crossbow is the direct successor of bow and arrow. The smaller arrows that are used in a crossbow are called bolts. Whatever, there is a bothersome issue bow and crossbow have in common: Many legends that are dulling the mind.

William Tell, like Robin Hood, has never existed. The story with the apple-shot is an old hat of mystical origin. It comes from a Germanic folktale and variations can be found in Persian, Norwegian, Danish and Icelandic legends. The Norwegians have the old 'Thidrekssaga' (legend of Thidrek) and the Icelanders the 'Edda-legend'. The trick shooter, in their version, is called 'Orentel', whose name was probably converted into William Tell.

In the Danish adaption, the shooter is named 'Toko', a boastful soldier in the service of the Danish King. It is told that Toko was forced by the King to shoot an apple from the head of his son. Toko mastered the shot, but took revenge at a later stage and shot the King during an amorous adventure.

In Switzerland, a copy of the apple-shot tearjerker was used by the Helvetic scribblers to decorate their legend of liberation. It had never reached an outstanding importance, until a certain Mr. Schiller devoted some of his time to the subject in his later working period. The plot of the drama by Schiller, in line with the term 'freedom' – very fashionable in those days – was attractive, and, based on the Swiss pattern, the world-famous theatrical work 'William Tell' was created.

This drama of Schiller was the German certificate of authenticity for the Swiss national epic, and the Swiss liked it so much that the image of William Tell, as the national hero, was sustainably strengthened. Sometime during the 19th century, William Tell was officially confirmed in this function.

As outlined before, it was Goethe, who originally had the idea for a classical theatrical work, dedicated to William Tell. Contrary to Schiller, he had visited Switzerland on several occasions. He wrote a letter to Schiller about his plans: *"I am almost convinced, that the story of Tell could be treated in epic form, and if I were to succeed in my undertaking, in such a way as I am planning, it might come to the peculiar case, that the fairy tale would attain its absolute truth by means of poetry, instead of making the story a fable, like one otherwise has to do."*

What a sensational discovery is this letter from Goethe to Schiller!

It tells us, in an explicit and open way what some of the poets thought of the intelligence of their readers. Too bad, we do not have letters from Homer or Hesiod to their Greek writing colleagues about their projects!

That is like tapping the phone when 'Bush Senior' calls 'Bush Junior' on weapons of mass destruction in Iraq and the version to be given to their British henchman Tony Blair.

Actually, what followed that conspiratorial telephone conversation became internally known in the White House and the Pentagon as 'The Secret Operation William Tell'.

President W. 'Dubya' Bush had given the green light, by saying: *"My dad has an idea. We need to find someone from outside, someone who will give the story to Powell."*

Secretary of State Colin Luther Powell firstly refused to believe the horror stories about weapons of mass destruction in Iraq and subsequently refused to go to the UN with these weird accusations. Powell was under persistent pressure from the Pentagon and the White House to include doubtful intelligence in his report on Iraq's weapons of mass destruction. The first draft contained so much questionable material that Powell lost his temper. He threw several pages of this report up in the air and shouted: *"I'm not reading this, this is bullshit!"*

As Powell did not trust the Bush administration, they had to find someone else to give the 'facts' to him. Vice-President Dick Cheney and Defense Secretary Donald Rumsfeld came up with the idea to pass it through Britain and Tony Blair – personal cover name: 'Poodle'. Rumsfeld: *"Yes, he 'will tell' that story, he wants to be important!"* And Cheney added: *"Sure, Bambi* (political nickname for the inexperienced, saucer-eyed Blair) *is from Scotland, they like us, and moreover, he will drag the UK into this as well."*

America is not only the dreamland of adventurers, actors or poor peasants from Sicily, but occasionally even a British Prime Minister would rush over the pond and bow and scrape to be recognized as an important ally for this powerful country. From Downing Street to the White House – from rags to riches. When Tony Blair talked about Bush, Cheney, Rumsfeld & Co., he used to say to friends: *"I wish I were in their gang!"*

Not only Tony is longing for Wonderland. The strings of the royal purse are getting looser and allow bigger spending when there is an occasion for HM the Queen to visit the horse farms in Kentucky.

Anyway, Anthony Charles 'Lienton' Blair was so convinced and impressed by the preliminary work of the Pentagon that he not only gave credence to the story, but added his own anecdotal details. Tony Blair, the former guitarist and lead singer of the student band 'Ugly Rumours' (the name says it all), had written the lyrics to this guileful cock and bull ballad extremely well. When all went back to the United States, it captivated US State Secretary Colin Luther Powell so much that he became unwittingly one of the biggest liars ever before the UN, benignly referring to the 'fine paper' that the United Kingdom has distributed.

Blair gave a splendid example as to how legends develop. He had absolutely no evidence in support of the story that the Americans had sold him. When he replayed the version, he not only gave non-existing weapons of mass destruction a real existence, but these imaginary weapons of mass destruction became a frightening threat *"second to nought"*, as Tony, the worst export ever from Scotland to England, put it. But that's not all. Tony Blair made another scary point to the world about these *non-existent* weapons of mass destruction: *"They can be ready in 45 minutes!"* This had even impressed some of the skeptics among the American public.

The transformation of this story, created by and around Tony Blair, was a matter of weeks, compared to the centuries needed when the old legends had been developed and at those times, the storytellers could have very well invented a man-eating dragon, but even the worst of the bards would not have emptied the market square from a scared audience by saying *"it can be here in 45 minutes!"*

What the US administration did not envision: Tony Blair and the bunch of amateurs from HM's Secret Intelligence Service (SIS), commonly known as MI6, were not only naive enough to swallow this nonsense, but in fact, their silliness reached far beyond this point. Instead of simply repeating what he had been told, Tony wanted to produce some 'fine papers' of his own and made British Intelligence become a loony bin, drowning in shame and laughter.

When everything came to the open, the SIS had not only shown that the word 'intelligence' in their trademark is not necessarily linked to intelligent thinking and acting, they did not even have the guts and character to simply admit a dreadful mistake. The UK's 'erroneous assessments' had been blamed on cutbacks in the defense budget, accompanied by other paltry excuses. And what concerns Tony Blair, he has put the entry-level-IQ for a post in 10 Downing Street into the lower double figure range.

To turn absolutely nothing into *'a threat second to nought'* is not only an erroneous assessment of quantities in the justification of a war, it is simply utterly false and undoubtedly a criminal act. And if you think that the spinning of legends is a relic of the past – this proofs you wrong. And the result of this gaga action? Everything much worse than before and the terror has intensified. Well done, Tony!

But things are much worse! Old legends had been handwritten or passed on orally. The 'experts' around Blair used a popular word processing software from Microsoft. They were unaware of the fact that the documents carry forward hidden data and personal information – so-called meta data – everybody can read, if not deleted, like the original source from which the dossier was plagiarized and the names of all who contributed thereafter.

But also the CIA people must ask themselves: Why did they pass on a template for a legend through sophisticated secret service channels and then, they let Tony, an inexperienced parody of a leader, and the MI6 produce everything with the help of a standard software product that they have bought in a store around the corner? They were left alone and without adequate training when it came to handling sensible data. Was it a mistake to overburden everyone so rapidly and ruthlessly with soft- and hardware and American-English terms, especially in the IT-world, without sufficient sensitivity and understanding in a delicate case of secret service cooperation – especially when it comes to HM's Intelligence staff, suffering from frequently reduced budgets?

Just imagine, we could follow the traces of old myths and legends in such an easy way. Our cultural foundations would be doomed to collapse. But I am absolutely certain that the old Greek and Romans, and for that matter all plagiarizers of so many myths and legends, would have been able to better hide their sources, if modern word processing would have been around in those days.

When the full truth had finally become too obvious, Tony – after having left Downing Street – rushed out of the Anglican Church and into the arms of the Catholics, where the individual confession and – more important – the full forgiveness on unlimited occasions, is more effectively organized and not so much subject to the uncertainties of common- prayers and absolutions.

This makes it the ideal place for hypocrites, where one can get rid of a lifelong feeling of guilt, just in exchange for a few prayers of the rosary. With some practice, one can do a full round in 20 to 30 minutes. Records are held at 15 minutes, only a few seconds shy of the prayers becoming a mere 'lip service'. So it is often just a matter of timing, rather than understanding and regretting, and occasionally not worth more than the outcry *"Oh, my God!"* when a housewife has discovered that the sale of the 5-piece tea set at Wal-Mart was discontinued.

We should not assume that Blair's delayed decision to officially convert his religion has something to do with the people's sensitivity about the place of Catholics in British public life. That would otherwise mean that a closet Catholic had sneaked into the London government and – by all means – this is not something we want to presume.

Since the Act of Settlement that followed the Glorious Revolution of 1688 and the deposition of the last Catholic monarch, James II, there has never been a Catholic prime minister, besides the fact that Catholics are barred from marriage to the sovereign or the heir to the throne, not to speak of being barred from the sovereignty themselves.

And those who are Scottish thoroughbreds can relax. Tony Blair's father, once Secretary of the Scottish Young Communist League, had been adopted by a Scottish couple. His father's biological parents were two English middle class traveling entertainers (stage names Jimmy Lynton and Celia Ridgway). His mother was of Irish ancestry on the paternal side. Her father, another split personality, was an Irishman from Catholic Ireland and simultaneously a member of a Protestant sectarian organization.

Back to the original William Tell: The story now does not seem too weird after all, considering what had been done with the original American novel about weapons of mass destruction, when the 'revised' version re-appeared in those 'fine papers' from London.

Schiller himself recognized the sparse substance of this legend and called it the *"fairy-tale with the hat and the apple"*. However, like Goethe said, this pattern could not only be exploited from a literary point of view, but when properly tackled, it could be brought to perfect truth. In the end, Goethe did not want to do the dirty work himself and decided to pass it on to Schiller.

Goethe was lucky and able to rope his writing colleague into this, because it was an opportune time during a period where Schiller had no other pending projects.

At first, Schiller familiarized himself with the story and studied the 'Chronicum Helveticum' (Swiss Chronicle) by the chronicler 'Aegidius Tschudi' from the city of Glarus. In that legend, William Tell is a famous freedom fighter and an opponent of tyranny, who has lived at the turn of the 13th century.

The Habsburg bailiff 'Gessler from Altdorf' had put one of his hats on a post and ordered his Swiss subjects to greet the hat whenever they walked by. William Tell, an expert with the crossbow, refused the greeting. As a result of his disobedience, the bailiff ordered him to shoot an apple from the head of his son 'Walter', as punishment and deterrence to others.

Tell reluctantly followed the order and hits the apple on his son's head. The boy remained unharmed, and while people watched the scene, they noticed that Tell had carried a second arrow (bolt). Asked why he had another arrow, he responded: *"The other one is for the bailiff, in case I would have hit my child."* The bailiff became aware of the answer and gave orders that Tell should be tied up and brought to his castle in Kuessnacht.

The shackled Tell was brought aboard a ship and when it came into a storm on the Vierwaldstaetter Lake, he was freed from his bonds to assist in the rescue of the boat. Tell cleverly steered it against a riverbank where the steep face of the Axen-hill is rising up and jumped out on a protruding rock plate, which today still carries the name 'Tell's-Plate'.

William Tell quickly rushed over the mountains to Kuessnacht, waited for the bailiff at a narrow pass ('die hohle Gasse') and shot him dead with his crossbow from a secure hiding place.

"Durch diese hohle Gasse muss er kommen" (through this narrow pass he must come), are the famous words from Schiller's drama, like the 'Ruetlischwur' (Swiss Rütli Oath), *"wir wollen sein ein einzig Volk von Brüdern"* (we want to be a single people of brethren).

Summarizing the origination of the story, it might be exaggerated to say that the Swiss people owe their William Tell only to Schiller's efforts (and Goethe's ideas), but it sure got a lot of tailwind from it.

You might think that something like the legend of William Tell and its conversion into a national epic is not so important after all and that my remarks are perhaps exaggerated. In this case, just try to imagine that George Washington and the American War of Independence would be pure fiction, based on a novel by Samuel Langhorn Clemens, better known as Mark Twain.

And certainly, we do not want George Washington, the American hero and freedom fighter, to be just a fiction and a simple crossbowman who is mainly famous for having shot an arrow through a watermelon on the head of his son, after he had refused to greet the hat of a 'Lobster', a redcoat soldier or officer of the British colonial army.

ARCANE ARCHERS

Arcane archers are legendary archers and the elite fighters of the elves.

This short sentence contains two major errors: Elves do not exist – and never have – and therefore, there are no elite fighters of the elves, the Arcane archers.

In order not to leave all intellectual absurdities to the old Greeks and Romans or to the many folktales from other parts of the world, the Nordic mythology makes it very own contributions when crazy stories are circulated.

The elves in these tales are luminous figures and a group of natural spirits. The non-existing Arcane archers, who live among the non-existing elves, train their combat strength mainly through magic. Arcane archers have distinguished and supernatural abilities, related to bow and arrow.

All this is achieved by constant training of their magical powers. They also try very hard to improve the effects over longer distances. When the Arcane archers fight in a group, they become even more unpredictable and dangerous. Magical capabilities, combined with group dynamics, allow them to spread even more horror and fear among their enemies.

The arrows of the 'A-archers' are endowed with supernatural forces. So it happens, that a simple arrow comes flying along, which suddenly transforms itself into a bird and finally into a fireball.

Arcane archers can send out spotting arrows which fly around corners, overcome obstacles and penetrate fixed barriers.

Every elf can become an Arcane archer. Also half-elves can exceptionally slip into this role, if we leave aside the fact that also the half-elves do not exist.

Furthermore, the doors are open for warriors, rangers, barbarians or paladins. All they must do is to add magic to their fighting skills.

Vice versa, all of those who have already mastered the magic, like wizards, magicians or sorcerers, can become an Arcane archer, if they work on decreasing their deficit of fighting skills.

Monks, clergymen, druids, villains or singing bards usually fall between the cracks. The probability that one of them becomes an Arcane archer is extremely rare.

Several hours of daily target practice, individually crafted arrows – which must be in harmonic balance with the bow – and unlocking the inner-self to the art of magic, helps to ensure that the enemy will not only be injured, but his spirit is also captured.

Now, if you are interested in becoming an Arcane archer, I must remind you again that they do not exist. Therefore, the rules are merely quoted for the sake of completeness.

An experienced Arcane archer supervises the training, until the candidates have reached the stage of perfection. Then, a license is granted (or the blessing is given) in the name of 'Corellon', the creator, patron and god of all elves, in a fixed ritual in the presence of Corellon priests. The moon has to be in a specific position and this occurs only once in a decade, sometimes only once every twelve years.

THE ARROW SHOTS AT SAINT SEBASTIAN

Saint Sebastian is the Patron Saint of hunters and archers. Of all the saints around, this must be the worst possible choice, and if the saint would have a say himself about whom to protect, Sebastian – the other way around – would have never chosen the archers.

Depending on the country, he is the Patron Saint of so many people, cities and professions that one can easily lose the plot. Just to name a few: iron merchants, porters, cloth makers, gardeners, upholsterers, tanners, tinsmiths, soldiers and hunters, gunsmiths, stonemasons or pallbearers. He protects the city of Rio de Janeiro in Brazil, Palma de Mallorca in Spain, the Police in Munich, Bavaria, or the urban police in Italy.

Saint Sebastian became also the Patron Saint of the brush makers. The connection to this profession is highly horrid. When they saw the picture of the holy Sebastian with his naked body full of arrows, they felt reminded of their brushes.

In the USA, we know the Saint Sebastian River, a tributary of the Indian River Lagoon, which is part of the boundary between Indian River County and Brevard County in Florida, where the city of Sebastian is located nearby.

Saint Sebastian's date of birth is unknown. What concerns his birthplace, it was either Milan, Italy, or Narbonne, France, but we know for sure that he died in the year 228 in Rome, Italy – and the circumstances marked on of the lowest points in the history of the archers.

The admiration for the Saint was spread over the entire church during the time of Pope Sixtus II (432-440). As a protector from the bubonic plague, he was one of the fourteen Holy Helpers. In the year 680, Saint Sebastian freed the city of Rome from a raging pestilence (the Vatican's version).

Furthermore, Saint Sebastian is commonly referred to as a gay male icon. Unlike the others whom he protects, the gay community has intentionally chosen him themselves. Many hunters and sports shooters have a medallion of their Patron Saint Sebastian gracing the hunting room. As it is also a symbol of the gays, you would never know how to evaluate a good hug from your hunting friend.

The legend around Saint Sebastian is a very strange one – to say the least – but moreover, it is an insult to archers and archery as a whole. In the end, he was just a simple and faithful servant of early Christianity and had to die for it – as did many fellow sufferers.

The Catholic Church was in desperate need of more martyrs and saints, and therefore the Vatican heavily supported the story. The gruesome tale was very much embellished and unfortunately, bow and arrow play an important, yet highly ridiculous role.

Who really was that Holy Sebastian? Sometimes he was a simple soldier, sometimes an elite soldier or even a commander of the Praetorians, the much-feared guard of the Roman Emperor Diocletian.

Emperor Diocletian was born in Split, Dalmatia (now part of Croatia) and had a palace there that he later used as a retirement residence. This was also the place where he was buried. The interior area of the palace belongs to the World Heritage Sites. His sarcophagus is still there, but his mortal remains have disappeared. The Christians, heavily persecuted by Diocletian, took late revenge. They converted the mausoleum of Diocletian into a cathedral and put the bones of the Holy Domnius of Split, once beheaded by Diocletian, into his last resting place.

Diocletian was a man of drastic decisions. He was the one who divided the Roman Empire and the powers that presided over it. It had reached its largest expansion by then and he thought that it was no longer governable and could no longer be effectively protected against outside enemies. He was the only Emperor in Roman history who voluntarily resigned from office.

Diocletian wanted to eliminate Christianity because he considered himself to be a god. When it had been discovered that the simple soldier, or the elite soldier, or even the commander Sebastian was an advocate of Christianity, Diocletian immediately issued the order to shoot and kill him with bow and arrows.

In some variations of this story, Sebastian was first tied to a tree for that purpose. The Numidian archers obeyed and afterwards just left him there. Another version tells us that the body was thrown into the 'Cloaca Maxima', the ditch transporting the effluents out of Rome.

In any case, Sebastian was not yet dead. In one of the stories, a friend was supposed to have found him and in another one, it was the pious widow Irene, who wanted to bury him. He was however nursed back to health and instead of accepting things as they were, he – just halfway recovered – was heading straight to Diocletian and confirmed himself to Christianity again.

In the end, the Emperor, ruler over the giant empire of Rome and occupied with important state affairs, made it short: Disappointed and displeased with the great inefficiency and dreadful performance of his Numidian archers, he ordered that Sebastian should be brought to the 'Circus' (an event arena for gruesome public entertainment) and promptly clubbed to death.

In other adaptations of this saga, many more Christians were cruelly and methodically slaughtered at this occasion. All these incidents have been used as a warning by the Catholic Church: Whatever happens, hold on to your faith, even if we have to raise Church taxes a second time this year. It could become worse.

But I honestly have to ask myself: How could the Holy Sebastian become the Patron Saint of the archers? Should it not be the other way around and Sebastian would better be the patron of those chased by the archers, after the men with bow and arrow had participated in his failed execution, along with such a horrible presentation of archery by a bunch of incompetent warriors?

Anyway, Sebastian was finally clubbed to death in the Circus, but again, it was not determined what they had done with his body afterwards.

Once more, we have contradictory statements: They either left him lying in the Circus or he had been – again – thrown in the Cloaca Maxima. Whatever, when his friends found him, he was dead and they buried him 'ad catacumbas' (in the hollers of the catacombs).

And as if that was not enough of a wild story, another 'body-finder' came up. Sebastian appeared in a dream of the Christian woman Lucina. She took the body of Sebastian from the Circus and buried him – also 'ad catacumbas' – at the Church of the Apostles, whose foundation is today below the Church of San Sebastiano, on the Via Appia.

The Church of San Sebastiano is one of the seven early Christian pilgrimage houses of worship in Rome and the Via Appia is the most legendary of the Roman roads and one of the most famous in the world. Its construction had begun by the Roman Consul Appinus Claudius Caecus, and the street leads to finish some 336 miles away in Brindisi.

A walk along the Via Appia Antica (the old part) is a refreshing outing after time spent in the city of Rome, with many things to see and enjoy. The many historical buildings and monuments along the road make it 'the longest museum in the world'. Towards dusk, the place gets somewhat seedy. Armies of prostitutes, mainly from Africa, appear from nowhere, and you have to watch out not to be run over by a car, cruising up and down, with a leering old man behind the steering wheel. Unaccompanied female tourists should better stick to daylight for their excursion in this area.

Yet, not all the confusion ends here. Another variation of the story is set into a single event: Perforated by arrows, tortured, struck dead and thrown into the Cloaca Maxima, without intermittent recovery. This would at least place the effectiveness of the archers in a somewhat better light.

However, one thing is common to all stories: They all agree that he died on the 20th of January and of course, this day is named after him.

It is an old tradition since the Middle Ages that the first bottles of new wine, called 'Arrow of Sebastian', will be opened on that day.

The ordeal of the Holy Sebastian became a popular theme in the art of the Renaissance and the unclothed martyr, standing at the tree, became a favorite template for the early fetish of nude paintings.

In lack of truthful facts, the Catholic Church had instructed the Dominican friar Jacobus Voragine with the creation of a legend that he embellished with his own fantasies. Between the years 1263 and 1273 Jacobus wrote the 'Legenda aurea'. He erroneously took Mauritanian archers (never mind, they come from the same corner as the Numedian archery-failures) and described their shooting with the following words: *"They have shot so many arrows into him that he stood there like a hedgehog."*

Lastly, we have a totally different interpretation, without any reference to early Christianity, which appears to be the more credible and plausible version. The beautiful Sebastian is said to have awakened the desires of the Emperor and was killed because he had fought against the obvious advances. In this case, however, he should have been named the Patron Saint of the heterosexuals and not the homosexuals.

The desires of Diocletian became part of the work of gay writers like Tennessee Williams or Thomas Mann. The latter was even known to walk around with a Sebastian. He showed his widely known homoerotic enthusiasm by misusing (the name of) his dog, which he called 'Bauschan'. In the lower German language, Bauschan stands for Sebastian.

In summary: Contradictions and inconsistencies in every nook and corner. The spectacular death of Sebastian and the alleged circumstances have certainly been a good pattern for a martyr story.

ARCHERY TRADITIONS

 **A**rchers always stick to their traditions. Always?

This is certainly not true for all of them. For example, someone came up with the idea of a 'bow and arrow biathlon'. To switch the rifle for a bow is not exactly ground breaking original, but this could add a new dimension to outside archery in the winter.

One could even throw knives at the shooting ranges on the cross-country course, or the event could move on to the water, with water skies and harpoons.

Too crazy? No, it can become even more bizarre!

I do not have in mind shooting with bow and arrow at nudist camps. In fact, it is the strange idea to combine archery with golf. Yes, such tournaments really take place! There is also a name for it: 'Clout X-trail', a term, partly borrowed from the word 'clout-shooting', which is the shooting at a very distant target, marked by a pole with a flag.

Many farmers with a large meadow, the owners of abandoned airfields or the managers of golf clubs, frequently have requests for such venues. At the same time, the sport should become more elitist, the appearance more classy and preppy.

Sure, go shooting in a fashionable X-trail outfit, take twenty-five thousand Dollars for admission to the club, two-thousand five hundred Dollars annual membership fee and do not forget the two-year period on the waiting list for new memberships!

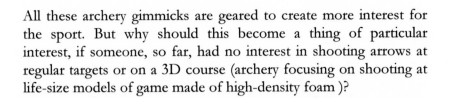

All these archery gimmicks are geared to create more interest for the sport. But why should this become a thing of particular interest, if someone, so far, had no interest in shooting arrows at regular targets or on a 3D course (archery focusing on shooting at life-size models of game made of high-density foam)?

One the other hand, if one is already engaged in the use of bow and arrow and finds the usual targets to be a bore, this could be an excellent outlet for frustration, possibly saving the world from something worse, as we will learn in the next chapter.

In case someone should be interested, here are the rules:

At the start, the archer stands at a marker and shoots his arrow. The first great distances are bridged with long shots. Before every new shot, the foot is placed at the spot where the first arrow has come down. This goes on until you come close enough to the flag. Be sure to carry along a solid rag to clean the arrows pulled out from the ground. The occasionally used fancy 'archer's tassel' might prove to be insufficient for such a heavy-duty job.

By the way: The archer's tassel does not only function as an ordinary arrow cleaner, but often as a club-identifier. The more tassels they have, the worse their shooting.

At the end, the archer does not aim into a hole, but at a small ball, mostly made of foamed material. Occasionally, you would see the use of a regular tennis ball. If the latter is badly hit and the arrow bounces off, a little more excitement for the audience that stands around the final target is guaranteed.

The archer is allowed to step back from the last marker when the foot is too close to the ball. This helps to avoid a shot straight through the toes, which would otherwise give another implication to the word 'handicap'. Of course, here too, the winner is the one who has needed the least amount of shots.

WE SHOULD NOT SHOOT ARROWS AT HUMANS ANYMORE

If we disregard primitive tribes that hunt humans with the intention to shrink and collect their heads, in some remote spots of the deepest jungles, the desire to shoot at humans with bow and arrow should meanwhile have faded into oblivion. However, people with bizarre behavior when using this shooting gear, still exist.

Out of the estimated four million modern bow hunters worldwide, three million are living – where else – in the USA. Many of the famous and traditional producers of bow equipment – and the material that comes along with it – have their headquarters in the USA and, of course, the compound bow, the last step of the technical development, was invented there.

Some peculiar folks get a special kick from 'aerial hunting', the comfortable way of hunting with a rifle. Equipped with a telescopic sight, they shoot out of a helicopter where they are mostly after wolves, bears and elks in Alaska.

Strange habits are nothing unusual, also in the USA *"that force for good in the world, the beacon of light and hope for those seeking democratic values and tolerance and freedom"* (Ronald Reagan) – *"and a place for damn good Hamburgers"* (my own supplement).

Now, what happens, if some archers, who are condemned by the rules of civilization to shoot at dead targets or are bored to hunt for normal game, feel that they must satisfy an unquenchable innate urge that asks for more. Where does the 'kick' come from?

Teressa Groenewald-Hagerman, a light blond American female, born in Texas, has been the first woman to kill an elephant with a bow, just because of a bet – a deranged act. She had crept into a herd of seventy-three elephants and fired an arrow at the unsuspecting animal.

A fellow hunter had told her that no woman had ever killed an elephant with a bow. In her own words: *"I couldn't turn down the challenge. I couldn't wait to get my elephant."*

One thing comes to my mind immediately: Can she have a two-digit IQ in charge of her brain and still be able to handle a bow? And the other thing that now puzzles me: What if the fellow hunter would have told her that no woman ever jumped off the top of the Empire State Building, gliding down with a pink sunshade? We might have had one more 'smashing' Blondie joke.

Blondie, a 'happily divorced' woman (she probably talks about her ex-husbands feelings), had subsequently taken a lot of 'beatings' on several Internet platforms from 'A' like America to the people of 'Z' like Zimbabwe, where the Elephant lived a peaceful life and was shot.

They named her 'Texan tosspot', disgusting, sickening. Besides comments like *"stalk her, skin her, salt her"* or *"I apologize for calling this disgusting two legged thing an animal, because it's an insult to real animals"*, there have been numerous suggestions that she should seek therapy.

She had 'worked out' four hours a day to be able to properly handle her bow. I think she should have better worked out on the step machine in a fitness studio or spend that time at the hairdresser.

The injured animal staggered 500 yards (457.2 meters) and had left a bloody trail before it crashed to the ground. Blondie spent the

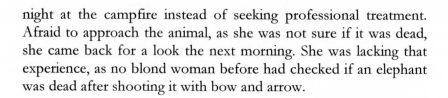

night at the campfire instead of seeking professional treatment. Afraid to approach the animal, as she was not sure if it was dead, she came back for a look the next morning. She was lacking that experience, as no blond woman before had checked if an elephant was dead after shooting it with bow and arrow.

The funny part of it (if one can still laugh at such utterly insane and cruel behavior) is the fact that there have been several women in the past that have killed large animals or have achieved other 'great things'.

These achievements have never been put on record and tell you why, if you think about history and sexism. Men were unwilling to acknowledge and record such accomplishments. They left pen and paper aside and waited for the right moment to document such a female record with a suitable background to make people become disgusted or to make the story a laughing stock.

But even that can be topped. What happens if shooting an elephant from 12 yards (11 meters) away does not satisfy the 'archer' in you?

Another American woman got the ultimate archery kick. This time the 'adventure' did not take place in Africa, but right in the state of Texas.

The 'Texan Lady Longhorn', named Julie, walked into a business park in Houston, equipped with a bow and arrow. Employees tried to stop her and during the confrontation, a man was shot and wounded by her. Two other employees counter-fired at her with their guns, but could not stop her.

When police finally arrived, she held up her compound bow and was obviously prepared to duel with an officer. Instead of putting the bow down as requested, she pulled the string and aimed at him. He had no choice but to mow her down and shot at her.

Julie's father had been working at this place, but it was not clear that she was looking for him.

At first, they were not able to get her victim into an ambulance and had to saw through the arrow to make things fit. In a rescue related sense, one was not prepared for something like this – even in the USA.

Members of her family stated that they were in fear of something like that happening for a long time and always tried to prevent it. According to them, Julie is very bright and has worked as a photographer and artist. She wanted to be a neurosurgeon or an architect, said her mother. Yes Ma'am, and perhaps Mary Poppins, Snow White or Lara Croft.

Despite she was hit several times, Julie survived, and the man she had wounded fortunately recovered from the arrow shot.

Although the police officer had done a good job by not hitting any vital organs of the impeded neurosurgeon Julie, the family blamed the police for shooting a mentally ill woman and stated that the law enforcement policies need to be revised.

Of course! Perhaps the police officers should play 'sitting ducks' until she was running out of arrows?

They went on with their blame in a more sensible way, saying that the State of Texas needs to allocate more funds for the cure of mental illness and after-hospital treatment. Preventative treatment is not in the dictionary in Texas.

What concerns the byname 'Texan Lady Longhorn' which I have attached to Julie: My apologies to all other Lady Longhorns, a name often given to women's sports-teams in Texas, inspired by the official State animal, the Texas longhorn (a breed of cattle).

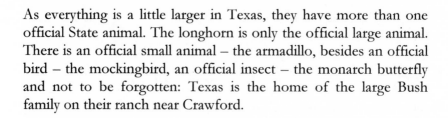

As everything is a little larger in Texas, they have more than one official State animal. The longhorn is only the official large animal. There is an official small animal – the armadillo, besides an official bird – the mockingbird, an official insect – the monarch butterfly and not to be forgotten: Texas is the home of the large Bush family on their ranch near Crawford.

This all leads me to a suggestion that should really satisfy the craziest and profoundest Stone Age instincts: a duel between Elephant-Blondie and the Texan Lady Longhorn with bow and arrow.

Saving the honor of the USA, which, by mere size and total population, must statistically come up with a greater number of crazy things compared to countries like Liechtenstein or San Marino, it has to be mentioned that also elsewhere in the civilized world arrows occasionally target humans.

In May 2008, a man in Germany had shot and killed his estranged wife with a hunting arrow from a compound bow. The arrow, which had been shot in the back of the women, had a razor-sharp broadhead tip.

The judge and even the female state attorney were not able to find particular maliciousness in the act. They ruled and pleaded only for manslaughter. The defense attorney even meant that this had just been negligent. It appeared that in the 21st century a murder using bow and arrow, even with a compound bow and a hunting arrow – shot in the back from a short distance – was outside the powers of imagination of a criminal court.

The arguments of the accessory private prosecution, pleading for murder, were totally ignored. Even the Supreme Court had to deal with this matter, because the defense had filed for appeal. The sentence of twelve years imprisonment, however, remained.

In the year 2009, an archer from New Zealand shot an arrow between the eyes of a woman, but this should not be counted in this respect, as it was an accident. His next-door neighbor was engaged to pick flowers, when he tried out his new crossbow and shot at loudspeaker cabinets (yes, you are reading correctly, loudspeaker cabinets). He did not hit the boxes, but his neighbor instead. Fortunately, and with a lot of luck, the woman survived.

In many countries, in particular in Europe, archers are afraid of stricter laws for bow and arrow shooting, after someone has gone wild with his (her) equipment, especially in view of the ever-growing success of the highly effective compound bows. There are already some limitations on crossbows.

The worst that can happen today in the world of archery, would be a ban on the free use of bow and arrow and that they would fall under the restrictions of the weapons law. So far, all is widely treated as sports gear.

However, a high school shooting with bow and arrow would be a real nightmare and could immediately lead to serious consequences. If you think this is a bit farfetched, you might not know how close this had come to reality.

The American archers can be more relaxed in this case as long as rifles, machine guns or rapid fire pistols are available for everyone at the sporting goods store.

Nevertheless, on November 30, 2012, we almost had such a disaster in Casper, Wyoming. 'Bow and arrow type attack on the college campus' were the headlines of that day.

There was a lot of confusion about the weapon and how it had been used, until it proved to be a compound bow. But this was more an internal family drama with three people dead: The assassin (suicide) and the father died inside the school. The girlfriend of the father was killed before at her home. The father just happened to be a teacher and was at work in his job, which could have been anywhere else. Whew! *"Take away this cup from me!"* – Mark 14, 36. That was close!

Before anyone had the chance to get silly ideas about bow and arrow used in school shootings, things came back to 'normal' within a few hours.

On the very same day, there was a shooting at the Morgan State University in Baltimore, Maryland. Fortunately, nobody was killed and the weapon – in proper style – was a semi-automatic handgun.

This shooting came on the heels of several other school-linked shootings in the area and less than three months after the last shooting at this particular place, dating back to September 12, 2012. Here too, the weapon was a handgun.

If worse comes to worse, Charlton Heston, the former frontrunner for the gun lobby in the USA, cannot come to the rescue of bow and arrow anymore, as he passed away a few years ago. He allowed his gun to be taken only 'from his cold, dead hand'. Too bad, he once had another hand free for a bow.

Charlton Heston did not get tired to bring forward his repetitious arguments in favor of a wider spread of firearms and to make them accessible to a greater number of people, with larger calibers and faster shot rates and perhaps an increase of the number of guns per person.

This has often reminded people of the movie Ben Hur. In the role of Judah, Charlton Heston participated in a chariot race in the circus of Jerusalem and won the competition against Messala. When trying to understand his arguments, one may get the impression that, during the filming, the chariot perhaps lost balance, and he wore only a decoration helmet when he was hurled upside down into the stands. Possibly, this has happened even more than once.

When he realized the first signs of Alzheimer's, he warned his fans, who would most likely soon become aware of his illness: *"When I am telling you a funny story for the second time, please laugh anyway!"*

It did not take very long and he even forgot that he just feared to repeat jokes. He lived in a state of permanent concern that his guns are taken away from him and always came up with his favorite sentence: *"Only from my cold, dead hand!"*

True or not: We should also forgive him his late idea to issue trading stamps at gas stations that could be redeemed for mortars and hand grenades.

'Murder in Berlin with bow and arrow'. However, this headline did not refer to the German Capital, but to one of the many Berlins in the USA. It was in Berlin, in the south of New Jersey, where a man had been accused of using a bow and arrow in a murder in January 2013. His lawyer said it was in self-defense.

The next incident of arrow shooting at humans, in February 2013, brings us to New South Wales in Australia. The offender had fired the arrow at his brother and his 93-year-old grandfather, but narrowly missed.

Now, we move on to May 2013, Little Rock, Arkansas, in the USA. Two men carried a bow and some arrows during a burglary attempt. When the owner came home and walked into his house, one of them shot at him. Fortunately, they had forgotten to put a tip on the arrow, so the victim was not seriously wounded. One of the 'bow-and-arrow-burglars' was stupid enough to come back to the house the same night and was promptly arrested. Later on, the other burglar was caught too.

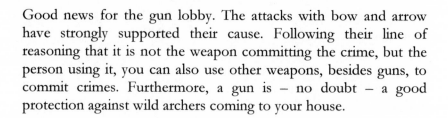

Good news for the gun lobby. The attacks with bow and arrow have strongly supported their cause. Following their line of reasoning that it is not the weapon committing the crime, but the person using it, you can also use other weapons, besides guns, to commit crimes. Furthermore, a gun is – no doubt – a good protection against wild archers coming to your house.

The first term Governor of Connecticut, Scott Walker, took it even a step further. He *invented* a murder with bow and arrow in support of the gun lobby.

At a news conference, held on Jan. 10, 2013, where even the Wall Street Journal was present, he responded to questions regarding gun control in connection with the killing of 20 children and 6 adults with a semi-automatic weapon at the Sandy Hook Elementary School in Newtown, Connecticut.

Walker argued that too much attention is paid to the weapon in such shootings and cited a recent case as an example: *"We just had someone last week in Neenah, near a school, kill someone with a bow and arrow."* Walker had considerable support from the National Rifle Association. However, there was only one problem with Walker's statement about the bow and arrow homicide: *it never happened!*

Walker's spokesman responded in an email: The Governor misspoke when he pointed out that someone was killed.

Walker was even wrong about the shooting in general. It had nothing to do with a school. The next one was more than 2.5 miles (4 kilometers) away. The police was called as a suspect was holed up inside the house and had potential access to *guns*. Pants on fire for Scotty!

But there is more that should interest you: If you give your son or daughter a bow and arrows for Christmas, think twice if you ever consider disciplining them. A 15-year-old girl from Washington

State, USA, did not take kindly to being grounded while also her mobile phone was taken away. She shot her dad with an arrow from a hunting bow and fled into the woods. Police surrounded and arrested her for investigation of first-degree assault.

The press called her behavior primeval. What? They call it primeval, when she was so badly treated and grounded *without* a mobile phone? The bow as a gift is OK, but once your child knows how to use it, never ground it and leave it without a mobile phone!

Fortunately, the 'penned up' daughter had used a practice arrow, not tipped with a broadhead and dad survived.

Holy crap! Immediately, calls were voiced in Europe to ban bow and arrow as free weapons. How long will it take that these shootings spill over into Europe?

On April 30, 2013, a 5-year-old boy from Cumberland County, Kentucky, shot his 2-year-old sister *with his own gun*, which he got at the age of four.

Local newspapers frequently feature photos of children who proudly display their kills, including turkey and deer. A company, specializing in guns for children, sells them under the slogan 'my first rifle' in colors like hot pink, orange, royal blue or in multicolor versions, thus respecting the taste of the Kindergarten-shooters.

Dad was away and mom was out on the front porch when it happened, and the kid did not notice that the gun was loaded. Authorities said that the shooting would be ruled accidental.

Let me understand this: It is not the fault of the gun, because it is always the person using it. It is not the fault of that young boy (using it), and it is not the fault of the parents, because they have

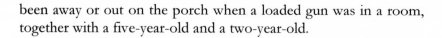

been away or out on the porch when a loaded gun was in a room, together with a five-year-old and a two-year-old.

How often must you be hurled into the stands in a chariot race, head first with a decoration helmet, to come up with such a line of argument?

There were no reports that also the two-year-old sister had a gun. This would be nothing unusual in Southern Kentucky, where children mostly get their first gun before they start first grade. Parents occasionally even bribe nurses to lay a loaded gun into incubators, as a first gift for the newborn redneck.

In April 2013, a four-year-old boy killed the wife of the Sheriff's deputy in Lebanon with a gun he picked up at a family cookout. He not only made a single shot, but fired a full round. No, we are not moving on to the Middle East, it happened in Lebanon, Tennessee.

A few days later, another 4-year-old boy killed a 6-year-old boy with a gun in New Jersey. When the parents heard the shot, they instantly called 911 and reported a shooting in the neighborhood, but had no clue that it was their own kid shooting around with a .22-caliber rifle and killed his neighbor-friend.

Sad, but true: The killing of a 5-year-old girl by her 8-year-old brother, alone at home with loaded guns in a remote community in Alaska (April 29, 2013), does not seem to be something unusual anymore.

For plenty more of such shootings after the printing of this book, please refer to your favorite news network or your local newspaper. Archers cross your fingers that they do not involve bow and arrow, especially in a high school shooting!

REDHEADS IN ARCHERY

Some archers may not notice or think about the hair color of someone standing next to them at the shooting line. Others react very differently. They may immediately engage lots of tricks just to move to a different spot or another target when a redheaded person is standing beside them.

The reason for their fear comes from an old superstition that the redheads will bring bad luck and poor results. The story has its roots way back and to one of the many anecdotes around Robin Hood. Although it is just another legend and complete baloney, some archers nevertheless take it very seriously.

At the request of Prince John, the Sheriff of Nottingham repeatedly attempted to catch Robin Hood. He never succeeded, so Prince John tried it himself with a cunning trick. He announced a bow tournament, offering a challenging first prize – a kiss from the redheaded Lady Marian Fitzwater of Leaford, a niece of King Richard and better known as 'Maid Marian'.

Robin Hood left his hiding place and joined the tournament in disguise. He was not only attracted by the prize, but more so, he was driven by his vanity to see himself as the winner of an archery tournament again. This made him forget all caution.

After he had beaten the Sheriff of Nottingham, everyone present knew that he could only be Robin Hood. Prince John, however, was already aware that Robin was among the competitors. His spies had been well spread throughout the spectators.

Mellie, the girlfriend and chambermaid of Maid Marian, was among the crowd – likewise with red hair widely visible. She, herself, was an excellent, but wild archer. So wild indeed, that she took great pleasure in hunting for mice in the castle with bow and arrow, and this was not always good for the furniture. She, of course, followed the tournament with great curiosity.

Mellie knew Robin Hood very well and after a successful shot of him, a *"well done Robin!"* spontaneously slipped from her tongue. Despite her swallowing further words, the spies of Prince John had heard enough.

Instead of running away quickly at the end of the tournament, Robin Hood increased his cockiness. He collected his kiss from the redheaded Maid Marian and was swiftly arrested.

Maid Marian unsuccessfully pleaded for his life, yet both were able to escape during the emerging turmoil. The chambermaid Mellie also managed to flee amidst the friends and companions of Robin Hood, who all had mingled with the crowd.

Now the people had to pay dearly. Prince John raised taxes fourfold. A great misfortune came over the land and soon the prisons were filled with poor people not able to pay the new levies.

Maid Marian, who was once played by Audrey Hepburn in the movie 'Robin and Marian' (with the wrong hair color), had temporarily moved into a monastery and Robin Hood was again hiding in the forest.

Because of these old fables, some superstitious archers do not want to stand next to redheads in a tournament, afraid that this will negatively influence their results.

ARTEMIS – GODDESS OF HUNTING

Artemis is the goddess of hunting, the woods and the guardian of women and children. Her well-known gear is the arrow and a silver bow, which were given to her by the Cyclopes. Despite her divine duties, she had often used this weapon to bring illness to humans. She also fired her arrows against the Giants when they attacked the Olympic gods and shot down the giant Gration, but did not kill him. Heracles had to come to her assistance and gave him another arrow, which finally ended the life of Gration.

Other attributes of Artemis are the vermouth herb and the cypress.

Now if you think, *"I know her – that must be Diana!"* you are not mistaken. The Romans, obviously too lazy to write their own novels, have repeatedly copied the weird stories of the Greek mythology, imitating the world of their gods.

In the Roman reproduction of this boloney, she is indeed called Diana. In the beginning, the gods of the Romans did not have the same importance as in the Greek myths. The Romans, however, were enamored with the Greek tales and simply 'borrowed' the basic storyline.

In earlier times, the Romans had their own gods with rather trivial duties. There had been divinities for every little thing and for each occasion. Quarters of the town, streets or even single houses, all had their own gods. They had minor gods and major gods for all life situations, opportunities and objects. On a single door alone, they had the god of the threshold, the frame, the hinges, the keys and the lock, the handles, the door panel and, of course, for the door as a whole.

What could have been more appropriate as to simply abandon this fragmented landscape of gods and to substitute these with the gods of Greek origin? The Greek gods like Zeus – who ruled over all the gods, Ares – the god of war, Artemis – the goddess of hunting, Hades – the god of the underworld or Poseidon – the god of the sea and the earthquakes – that was something sturdy! They have simply been renamed to: Jupiter, Mars, Diana, Pluto or Neptune.

We call Baron Munchhausen the lie-baron, because we find most of his stories hard to believe. He once told us that his troops had besieged a town, but so much time had passed during this siege, that they had forgotten which city it was. He decided to have a look inside and posted himself next to a cannon.

When it was fired, he jumped on the cannonball and flew towards the city. While he was airborne, he thought that he had indeed found an easy way into the city; but how could he manage to get out again? He gave up his plan, and when a cannonball, fired from the city by the Turks, came towards him, he jumped on it and flew straight back to his troops.

This is certainly crazy stuff, but compared to what the Greeks have patched together in their absurd stories, the adventures of Baron Munchhausen must emerge as the mother of truth.

Artemis, or Diana if you like, one of the twelve Olympic goddesses, was born together with her twin brother Apollo.

The Greek poets have seldom been able to write a few normal sentences before they have started with a silly story, not even for one or two introductory paragraphs. Therefore, the newborn Artemis – immediately after she had opened her eyes – engaged herself to help her mother with the birth of her twin brother.

Leto, the mother of the twins, was impregnated and of course, the incessantly lusting Zeus was responsible for it. Hera, the sister-wife of Zeus, was extremely jealous, but once again, she did not direct her rage at her brother-husband, but against the innocent victim Leto, who subsequently had to take flight.

To all abundance, Hera is also the guard over the marital sexuality. Nonetheless, this appointment did not cause her to refrain from sexual engagement with her own brother – married of course, to show a minimum of decency.

Hera, in revenge, put a spell on Leto to ensure that no place on Earth would be secure for her to give birth to the child of Zeus.

Subsequently, a safe spot had to be found for Leto. In this particular case of a pulp-inspired story, the ancient Greeks just invented an island that was floating about by the name 'Delos'. As it constantly changed its course, it could not be hit by the imposed curse. The Greeks then fabricated a mountain on this island, named 'Kynthos', where the twins were born. This gave Artemis the epithet 'Kynthia' (the one coming from the mountain). She therefore comes from an imaginary mountain on a floating island that never existed.

Artemis was a virgin hunter, who wandered through the woods alone, and – unless escorted by maiden nymphs – only dogs were allowed as her companions. She was said to never have been married and to be in dispute with men.

Her reputation was that of a cruel and severe goddess. As she was also the goddess of fertility, one can assume that there must be something fishy about her innocence and men-repelling behavior. Before dealing with this more delicate matter, let us look at the true characteristics of the 'well-behaved' Artemis and her twin-brother.

Leto, their mother, incited the twins to kill the children of Niobe, the daughter of Tantalus, ruler of the city of Sipylus. Leto was infuriated, because Niobe had boasted about the fact that she has fourteen children and therefore seven times more than Leto.

Sipylus (a city at the foot of the mountain Sipylus) has nothing to do with Syphilis, although the word as well as the malady is of ancient Greek origin. The name was coined by the Italian physician and poet Girolamo Fracastoro in his poem 'syphilis, sive morbus gallicus' (Syphilis, the 'French disease'). The main character of the poem is a shepherd named Sýphilos (Latin – Syphilus), which can be translated as 'in love with pigs'. He was the first man to contract the disease, sent by the God Apollo as a punishment.

Despite this undisputed Greek origin, it is called French disease in many countries around the world, while the French themselves call it Italian disease.

The Tahitians call it British disease. They have good reasons, as the Brits were the ones – along with the Bounty mutineers – who brought the infection to the island in exchange for stealing the breadfruit from Tahiti. The term remained in the South Seas, despite all efforts by the British to tell the natives that they themselves got it from the French.

Back to archery: As their mother had told them, Artemis and her brother Apollo took their bows and enough arrows and killed all the children of Niobe. She killed the girls, and he killed the boys.

On another occasion, Artemis herself felt insulted, because Meleager, son of King Oeneus of Calydon and Althaea, forgot to make a sacrifice to her, while thinking of all the other gods. Artemis sent the gigantic and frightful Caledonian Boar, a descendant of the mighty sow Phaia, which devastated the growing fields of Meleager.

Callisto, the best girlfriend of Artemis, was seduced and had her innocence destroyed. Of course, it was Zeus again, this masher, who was responsible. Artemis was disappointed and expelled Callisto, although she herself was once seduced by Zeus. As a result of this affair, Callisto became pregnant and later on gave birth to Arkas. Hera, of course, was jealous again and immediately retaliated. Instead of chastising her brother-husband for his countless love affairs, she directed her rage again at the seduced girl and transformed her into a female bear.

Fifteen years had passed when, by chance, Callisto – now a bear – saw her son Arkas while he was out hunting. She ran towards him with great passion, but he did not understand who she was and wanted to kill the animal.

It was Zeus, who saved Callisto. He transformed also her son Arkas into a bear and sent both of them up as a new constellation in the sky. Very ingenious! Instead of restoring Callisto back to human form, he brought mother and son to an equal level – as bears. The 'Big Bear' and 'Little Bear', as we know them as constellations, are therefore 'Mamma-Bear' and 'Baby-Bear'.

In order to come up with a plausible story, the encounter of Arkas and his mother was placed at a suitable point of time, fifteen years after his birth. Here, the old Greeks have at least provided some attention to obvious facts: The boy had to be grown up enough to wander through the forest, hunting with bow and arrow. At the same time, he had to be smaller than his mother, as all that had to fit into the 'new constellation' which they had cobbled together.

If one gazes up into the sky, one can see a part within the constellation of the Big Bear called the Great Wagon. The Little Bear looks very similar to the Great Wagon and that is why the Little Bear is often called the Little Wagon. If one looks even closer, one will recognize that the Little Wagon or Little Bear has an upwardly curved shaft, in contrast to the Big Wagon in the Big Bear.

At the end of the shaft of the Little Bear or the Little Wagon, one can find the fixed star Polaris, usually called the North Star or Pole Star. If one draws a vertical line from the North Star down to the horizon, one visualizes the northern direction.

One can also locate the North Star by extending the bright stars in the rear of the Big Wagon as an imaginary line. After about five times the initial distance, one is passing closely by the North Star.

The fact that Zeus had so openly displayed his paramour and their common bastard in the sky, made Hera even angrier. She asked Thetis, the goddess of the sea, to ensure that both of them shall never be allowed to dive down into the cool sea. This subsequently made them circumpolar constellations, which means constellations that never disappear from visibility in the sky.

What do they put into the Greek wine? Something like this can only be written down if one is totally hammered or has inhaled a substantial amount of cocaine.

In summary of this complete nonsense: Zeus impregnates Callisto, the girlfriend of his illegitimate daughter, who gives birth to a son. His sister-wife is furious and transforms the piteous girl into a bear, which is then almost shot and killed by her son. Then, Zeus rescues the bear, as he gives also her son a permanent fur coat and sends both of them up into the sky as new constellations. The jealous sister-wife of Zeus becomes even more furious and ensures that both stellar bears are not allowed to take a bath anymore.

In the year 1998, Professor Fishel Liberman, from the South Bronx in New York City, has made a scientific experiment, trying to find out how much the frequent use of drugs can influence the human brain.

Some drug addicted literature students, before starting with their detoxification treatment in a closed institution, were given – under strict medical supervision – a final maximum dose of their habitually consumed drugs or drug mixtures.

They were then asked to write a short story about a subject they felt interesting and important. They came up with everything: Mickey Mouse – first President of the USA, Elvis – his reincarnation as Buddha, Jumping Jack – first baseman of the New York Yankees, you name it. But nothing – a b s o l u t e l y nothing – came close to the profound mental deficiencies characterizing the Greek mythology.

Let us get on with it: Artemis had a well know encounter of a more intimate nature with men when she was taking a bath. Aktaion – a passionate archer and hunter – looked for a shady place at a cool location. He arrived in a valley and had reached a grotto where he saw Artemis swimming in the nude.

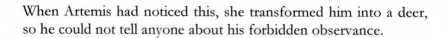

When Artemis had noticed this, she transformed him into a deer, so he could not tell anyone about his forbidden observance.

Aktaion now had four legs and two horns. When he saw his dogs, he immediately and unsuspectingly ran towards them – already secure in full gallop – and was quickly mangled.

The Artemis-priestesses had often reconstructed this scene with a lot of fun and passion. They all put dog masks over their heads and chased after a colleague, disguised as a deer.

Yet, the fake story about the virginal Artemis was unmasked at last. Her twin brother caught Artemis in an obvious embrace with Orion, who was also an enthusiastic hunter and archer.

Now, it was her own twin brother who was jealous and enraged. He challenged Artemis to a competition with bow and arrow. Artemis was to hit an indistinct target, very far out on the sea.

It was an easy task for her, but she did him the favor, hoping that he would calm down again. Naturally, she did not miss her target, but noticed too late that it was Orion, who was swimming out there. She had aimed at his head and perforated it with her arrow.

What are the old Greek gods or goddesses doing on the occasion of such a mishap? Correct, they are sending a new constellation up into the sky!

Too bad: Artemis was not able to completely assemble Orion again. While the Betelgeuse, the shoulder-star of the Orion, glistens in luminous splendor (Orion's blood from the head), it is difficult to recognize the head star 'Heka'.

Here we cannot only debunk the Greek mythology once more as total gobbledygook, but we are even able to systematically reveal the method how to cook up such senseless gossip.

A Greek goddess accidentally shoots an arrow into the head of her lover, and when she transforms him into a constellation in the sky, she is not able to reassemble him correctly. Really? Nonsense!

This is how the scripts for Greek constellation-myths are developed: You start from the end, with an *existing* assembly of stars in the sky. Take a few of them, draw some lines and create a character.

- In a constellation of stars, you see someone with a head injury.
- Who is not yet up there? Let us take Orion!
- Orion was shot in the head with an arrow.
- The arrow was erroneously shot by his paramour.
- The lady-love was Artemis.
- Reason for the shot: a competition, because the brother was jealous.

The entire sequence is now written down – specifically embellished – in reverse order.

There are other variations of this Greek myth from the penny-arcade. In another version of the story, Apollo had only asked Artemis to practice archery. Yes, that makes a lot of sense! The goddess of hunting cannot shoot well enough with bow and arrow and still needs practice. Doing that, she precisely hits a target that she can hardly recognize, with the first shot.

If you know other variations of this absurd novel, like the transformation of Orion after a deadly sting from a scorpion, then this is also correct. Correct, however, only in the sense that there are other variations. Otherwise, this makes absolutely no difference, because all the stories are poppycock.

I have already refrained from details about the pornographic description of the 'creation' of Aphrodite ('the one born in the foam'). I have to do the same in the case of the 'creation' of Orion, out of concern for juvenile readers. In one version, Orion even has three fathers. How Poseidon, Zeus and Hermes have managed to mix it all together and the coarseness associated with it, can under no circumstances be written down here.

The Sumerians have seen a sheep in this constellation, which is perhaps the most beautiful, visible from Earth. The Germanics – with a more hands-on character – have seen a plow, the Egyptians their god Osiris and the Vikings their god Thor. For the Chinese, it is one of their signs of the zodiac.

The Chinese have twelve signs of the zodiac. When Buddha left the Earth, he invited all animals, but only the rat, the buffalo, the tiger, the hare (rabbit), the dragon, the snake, the horse, the sheep, the monkey, the rooster, the dog and the pig came to the farewell party.

One cycle of the zodiac consists of twelve astrological ages (one year each) in the order of the appearance of the 'party guests'. Thereafter, it repeats itself. The buffalo had actually arrived first, but the rat sat on his back and jumped off, shortly before the arrival. Therefore, the cycles always start with the rat.

The statue of the Artemis in the temple of Ephesus, one of the Seven Wonders of the World, is covered with something thought to resemble breasts, as she is also personifying the breadwinner for all living things, even if she has occasionally sent the Caledonian boar – very counterproductive to this responsibility – to destroy growing fields.

Since the year 1895, Austrian archaeologists have dug time and again at the temple site. They had once looked at the statue of the Artemis with precise scrutiny: There are quite definitely no breasts covering the Artemis, but bull testicles. The chaste goddess Artemis has been so richly provided with them, to demonstrate fertility.

THE 17,000-DOLLAR RING

Byron Ferguson from Hartselle, Alabama, USA, is among the best archery trick shooters ever and one of the most famous since Howard Hill. His stunts and tricks have made him a cult figure. His 'incredible shots', shown in live shows, regular TV appearances and immortalized on DVD video, are fascinating again and again.

When he increases the difficulty of his shots, he explains that he wants to show that his shots are not just 'unbelievable shots', but 'incredible shots'. Does anybody know the difference? Etymologically speaking, the words 'unbelievable' and 'incredible' should be synonymous, except that incredible is a more sophisticated, Latin based *(credere, to believe)* way of saying that something is unbelievable. However, deep down in Alabama, they must have their very own reason for such a differentiation.

When his talents became boring to him, Byron Ferguson deviated from hitting small coins and Aspirin tablets in midair (at one event, he repeated that eight times in a row). Tired of his perfected skills, he asked his wife Wanda to toss only the smaller Baby Aspirin tablets into the air, which he also successfully splits into pieces. He enjoys telling the audiences at each such occasion that she is still his first wife, especially when she winces a bit as the targets splinter right in front of her eyes.

With the arrows shot from his longbow, he strikes the symbols on playing cards, extinguishes candles and opens Coke bottles. Ramps redirect his arrows right into the target when he shoots at balloons. He draws the bow with his feet; he shoots backwards or takes aim by looking into a mirror.

He shoots while seated on the loading platform of a moving truck or imitates famous rifle- or pistol trick shots and repeats those with his longbow, sometimes combined with other stunts.

Byron Ferguson makes no secret about his technique. He describes his successful method as: 'Become the arrow'. That is instinctive shooting in its purest form. Unlike the archers who use aiming equipment on modern bows, the instinctive archer has to develop that sixth sense and gut feeling, so that the arrows fly to their target automatically, like a spoon finds the mouth when someone is eating his soup. This is accuracy without the help of an aiming device, as it comes automatically for a roofer when he hits the nails or for a baseball pitcher when he is throwing a strike.

Byron tells of one of his most difficult shots, performed in Tokyo in the well famous Japanese TV Show 'Super People'. The cunning Japanese did not give him any advance warning or the possibility of special practice when he was asked to shoot an arrow at 25 yards (22.9 meters) through a wedding ring at a live show.

A diamond was mounted in the ring. Moreover, the nervous bride and her future husband sat in the audience. Byron settled for one attempt. He later asked – with an anxious voice – what the value of the ring was and got the answer: *"seventeen thousand"*. When Byron heard that, he was a bit shocked. As hard as a diamond is, when an arrow hits it, it will burst into pieces.

From this day on, whenever this fabulous shot is mentioned, people usually refer to the 17,000 Dollar ring, although the most important thing was undoubtedly to shoot an arrow through such a small opening at a distance of 25 yards (22.9 meters), without knowing about the trick to perform, unprepared and in a live show. However, the excitement may have been unnecessary. He was in Japan and – perhaps – they meant 17,000 Yen. At the prevailing exchange rate at that point of time, that was somewhat below 200 Dollars.

THE ROYAL COMPANY OF ARCHERS

Scotland, that is whisky, haggis (a savory pudding containing sheep's pluck), friendly people, beautiful landscapes and wonderful coastlines of the Highlands and Lowlands, the islands, Loch Ness and the monster Nessie, sheep, rugby, golf, the adopted shenanigans of left-hand driving, kilts and bagpipes.

Neil Armstrong, the first man on the moon, is of Scottish descent. The Armstrong clan was among the worst of the 'Border Reivers' – bandits, who committed their evil deeds along the Anglo-Scottish border from the late 13th to the early 17th century.

Other famous Scotsmen: Adam Smith – a pioneer of political economy, Alexander Graham Bell – one of the inventors of the first practical telephone, John Logie Baird – a pioneer in the area of television, just to name of few.

From the dark side of life we have the scary stories around Bible John, Robert Black, Ian Brady, Robert Knox, Peter Manual and Dennis Nilsen, well know mass murderers.

Naming famous Scots, we should not forget Alexander Selkirk, alias Robinson Crusoe from Lower Largo, Fife, Scotland. Quarrelsome and disobedient in his youth, followed by excessive alcohol consumption and subsequent brawls in his adult life, he was brought off the rails and in companionship with the English. He finally landed on a deserted island where he had to live alone for several years, but *without* cannibals around or a companion called 'Friday, as later stories want to make us believe.

Scots can often be found straddling the fence at a particular conflict. Edinburgh is the only city outside of the United States with a monument to Abraham Lincoln, which may lead to the swift conclusion that the Scots sided with the Union of the North. In fact, they were simultaneously great supporters who favored the South.

 When the subject of the Scottish Independence rears its ugly head, the Scots have ready thoughts as to the separation within the United Kingdom.

Realize that they want to send away the Trident submarines of the Royal Navy or function without subsidy from the remainder of the UK and everything else they can dispose of, and are even prepared to take all the organizational hassle and then – they do want to hold on to the Queen and her Royal Teutonic clan!

Frankly speaking, that is like playing Rugby with the head of Mary Stuart. If you could tell that story to Braveheart (provided that he is not predominantly a product of wild Hollywood fantasies), it would make him turn in his grave so intensely that one could produce enough energy to have the electricity for all street lights in Scotland, from the Scottish Borders in the South, up to Dunnet Head, the most northern place of the country.

When I, as already mentioned, made the German translation of the book 'The Witchery of Archery', the literary mother of modern archery, written by the American novelist Maurice Thompson in the year 1878/79, I came across a chapter dealing with the Royal Company of Archers, an old traditional Scottish archery club.

Despite so many battles between Scotland and England, I got the impression that one – to some extent – can forget Braveheart, the Highlander and everything we have learned from the Hollywood movies. Compared to some later developments in Scotland, the image one can perceive is as real as Nessie coming out of Lake Loch Ness to beg for 'fish and chips' from Japanese tourists.

Forget your general picture of Scotland, at least what concerns the city of Edinburgh, if that has been mainly influenced by Hollywood movies.

The English monarch finds a very safe place around the Scottish capital – thanks to the Royal Company of Archers, an archery club founded in the year 1676.

From the time of a visit by King George IV in the year 1822 they act as the personal bodyguard of the British monarch whenever he or she comes to Scotland, or better yet, to Scotland near Edinburgh. The Royal Company of Archers – armed to the teeth with bow and arrow – is located in the Scottish capital of Edinburgh, or Edinborough as it is locally pronounced or Dùn Èideann in Scottish Gaelic.

Edinburgh is a beautiful and impressive city, often called the Athens of the North, a term created by the German poet Theodor Fontane. It was the hometown of Dr. Jekyll and Mr. Hyde and – perhaps not just by coincidence – the birthplace of Tony Blair, the sixth Scottish-born among the eleven British Prime Ministers who came into the world outside England.

Only Scots can become members of the Royal Company of Archers, with the exception of those who have a strong connection to Scotland. If that would be a frequently reappearing tourist, a lover of Scotch whisky or someone of higher rank, is not clearly defined. Under that generous scheme, perhaps, the back door is left ajar to sneak in some English archers.

The traveling British monarch of today would better rely on the official secret service for adequate protection. I assume that the MI5 or the MI6 are the right units for the traveling monarch. The MI6, for example, is the home of the agent 007 – James Bond. As the MI5 operates primarily on a domestic level and the MI6 abroad, it is not sure who is taking responsibility in the case of the monarch's trip to Scotland.

No matter if MI5 or MI6 or other sections, the circumstances have made the original duties of the Royal Company of Archers more or less obsolete and their activities are strongly reduced to rather ceremonial performances, nevertheless carried out in a very serious fashion. For centuries, the Company, come what may, held up the flag of tradition – uninterruptedly, loyal and unwavering. This staunchness alone demands our highest respect.

Britain has plenty of security organizations, ranging from rather odd activities to more sensible divisions. High on the list are the many MI (military intelligence) units, numbered from M1 to M19:

MI1 – code-breaking, MI2 – spying on Russia and Scandinavia, Middle- and Far East, Central and South America and the USA (!), MI3 – Eastern Europe, Baltic states, MI4 – aerial reconnaissance, MI5 – FBI imitation, protect national security, MI6 – CIA imitation, harm international security, MI7 – extraterrestrial matters, MI8 – Internet hacking, communication interception, MI9 – undercover operations, MI10 – technical intelligence, industrial spying, MI11 – military security, MI12 – censorship, sports and betting (they were also involved in manipulations and twisting of rules at the 1908 Olympic Games in London), MI13 – their operations are basically classified, but some activities have been disclosed in the comic book series 'The Scarifyers', MI14 and M15 (both!) – spying on Germany, MI16 – Royal secret service, MI17 – pre-retirement sanctuary for MI-figureheads, MI18 – degenerated art and pornography, MI19 – POW briefing, at its heydays with no less than nine 'cages' from southern England to Scotland.

Rumors that the 'MI19-London Cage', located in a fashionable part of the city, had been converted into a private club, called 'Mistress Camilla's Mansion', must be dismissed as absurd.

The MI7, dealing with extraterrestrial matters, relies more or less on science fiction literature from the USA. Furthermore, they evaluate data provided by India's spy satellites.

The MI16 is claimed as the Royal Secret service that frequently spies within the Windsor family. They had been the first to discover that Lady Di was not driving a Vauxhall, but relied on a BMW instead. That is when she became a target.

I always wondered why the Brits need the additional family-internal spies. As the whole bunch of the Windsors is more or less of German descent, including the married-in 'Batterbergs', better known under the *Englishized* name 'Mountbatten', this could well be handled by the MI14 and MI15, the two spying divisions that exclusively deal with Germany.

Evil practices came into focus lately, connected to the inglorious GCHQ – the UK Government Communications Headquarters, the center of Her Majesty's Signal Intelligence (SIGINT). If you use a telephone or computer in Continental Europe for an intimate conversation or a delicate Internet connection via a transatlantic cable, you might become part of 'Her Majesty's Peep Show', as these guys will tap into the traffic to monitor and store whatever they can get.

This is not only one of the most reprehensible forms of eavesdropping, but also an ideal working place for peeping Tom.

The GCHQ is presumably also a major player in industrial spying. You must simply become inventive when easy stealing from the colonies is no longer possible.

The Brits certainly cling to their archaic traditions. Numerous 'ushers' (escorts and guides) or personal assistants follow the Queen in antique clothes. They look after the Queens horses, her dogs, her money, her Rolls Royces and her guests (in that order).

A special guide accompanies the Queen on the short land trip to the banks of the Thames river whenever she intends to take a boat ride. The expenses for the court household also include a royal 'swany', a special usher who looks after the Queen's swans.

Whenever the Queen will be shown on new stamps, the royal helpers dig through old photographs, taken in her early youth. They draft her speeches or authorize flowers to be named after her Majesty. The 'Queen Elizabeth Rose' with its noble blossoms in subtle pink, introduced in 1954 to honor her coronation, still sells.

With so many antique uniforms, often passed on from generation to generation, one does not have to wonder that over 2400 different species of moths are recorded on the British Isles.

I spare myself to list all the other 'intelligence' sections, from ticket control in London to the sheep spotters on the Falklands, but will go into a little more detail about the Royal Company of Archers; after all, they still do their job with bow and arrow.

As said before, the Royal Company of Archers does not have the responsibility for the monarch's security in all of Scotland. The alarm is only triggered when the monarch comes within five miles of the City of Edinburgh.

The highlight of obligation for the archers is the annual Royal visit to Scotland, her Majesty's yearly garden party, the attendance outside St. Giles' Cathedral at the service of installation of Knights of the Thistle (the thistle is Scotland's state flower), the Investitures at the Palace of Holyroodhouse and the Presentation of New Colors to Scottish regiments.

At the 'Holyroodhouse' (the monarch's official residence in Scotland), they provide the corridor guard of honor. I cannot fathom what might happen if William Wallace (better known as Braveheart) and his men would be standing in the corridors at Holyroodhouse.

But I think these are just fantasies. In reality, it was just Mel Gibson and some extras hanging around at 'Hollywood house' for the Braveheart movie. And I can very well understand that Rowan Atkinson (Mr. Bean) has refused the role as leading actor with the words: *"too unrealistic!"*

The uniforms of the Royal Company of Archers are unique and vary for different people and special occasions. What they, however, all have in common, is their extremely fancy look (they themselves call it distinctive).

The appearance of their outfits resembles the clothing of the guard of a Polynesian king in the South Sea or the plumage of Papageno in Mozart's opera 'the magic flute', and their feathered headgear could indeed look very smashing, if worn at the horse race at Ascot.

The Royal Company of Archers hung always proudly and firmly onto their duties and did not even quit the job when King Edward VIII. was urged to step down in the year 1936, only because he wanted to get married to a twice-divorced American woman. By all means, that has proven to be a minor incident compared to the future development.

"Sound, sound the music, sound it, let hills and dales (valleys) rebound it, let hills and dales rebound it, in praise of archery" are the first lines of text of their own march, appropriately called the 'archers march', and the music to it cannot be overheard when played by their pipes and drums band.

But wait, there is more! The Royal Company of Archers has a real 'Gold Stick'.

Traditional longbows are made from sticks, technically referred to as 'stave'. But this one it is not for the manufacture of a bow from precious materials. The name comes from a thing made from wood with just a golden or perhaps gilded head and it is not long enough that one could eventually make a functional bow from it.

So, what is it and what's the use of this Gold Stick from the Royal Company of Archers? It is more complicated: The Gold Stick of the Royal Company of Archers is not just a stick, it is a real person – their captain.

A real person as a Gold stick? Yes, a Gold Stick is someone having the honor of being a servant at the court of the King. This function emanated at the time of the Tudors when two officers were made personal bodyguard of the King and they have borne this title ever since. Their name comes from that Gold Stick, a gilded rod that they hold as their regalia (it can also be used as a truncheon, in case of need).

The honored persons are not called 'Holder of the Gold Stick', as one could expect, but simply Gold Stick. We can also find this kind of 'concentrated definition' in more modern times. Frank Sinatra, the little Italian-American from Hoboken, New Jersey, member of the 'rat-pack' and perhaps the Cosa Nostra, was not called the man with the (good ?) voice, but just 'The Voice'.

Today, there are more than the original two Gold Sticks and they share the duty in a monthly cycle. The Gold Stick who is active at a given time, is called 'Gold-Stick-in-Waiting'. He does not have the title 'Gold-Stick-on-Duty', because 'waiting' is a more characteristic term that describes his duties.

The Gold Sticks are present at many ceremonial acts like 'Trooping the Color' on the monarch's official birthday (always in June, because of the bad London weather). This should not be mixed up with 'coloring the troops' in coloring books given to the British kindergartens by Princess Anne around Christmas time.

Several people can become a Gold Stick or automatically have the honor of this function. One Gold Stick comes from (and serves in) Scotland and it is – you know it now – nobody less than the captain of the Royal Company of Archers in Edinburgh.

There are also 'Silver Sticks'. These are no fancy toothpicks of the rich, but real people as well. The Silver Stick is the deputy to the Gold-Stick or rather the Silver-Stick-in-Waiting is the deputy to the Gold-Stick-in-Waiting. He is mostly involved in ceremonial events of lesser importance, except when he is summoned for duty at the arrival of foreign Heads of State.

As the function of the Silver Stick in England is always connected to the Commander of the Household Cavalry, he is practically alone and therefore always 'in waiting'. Yes, the Scots also have their own Silver Stick. You can guess where he resides – in the clubhouse of the Royal Company of Archers of course

Speaking of silver, the Royal Company of Archers has a lot of silver and silver arrows among their annual prizes. Listing all of them throughout the history of the Company would be a little too extensive.

Very famous is their annual competition for the 'Prize of the Goose'. It once involved a live goose and just its head was sticking out from the mark. The winner had to kill the goose by shooting through the head. This was not that easy as the rest of the goose was protected. The winner was then called 'Captain of the Goose'.

In the long run, and under these conditions, that could not have been a well-respected title, considering the brutal and utterly idiotic setup of a target and a voluntary participation in such a giant act of stupidity. Subsequently, the goose, or rather its head, was replaced by a small glass globe, thus leaving a destructive effect.

The beginning of the goose-head shooting of the Royal Company of Archers was in the year 1703. As golf was already known in Scotland as of the 15th century, they could have easily used a discarded hardwood golf ball from their golf-playing friends on the neighboring course or even an old 'featherie ball', a round leather pouch, stuffed with chicken- or goose feathers.

Today, it could certainly be a particular thrill when using a Gold Stick as a target instead. I by no means refer to the captain, but the golden head of his regalia. If made from pure gold, it could easily take a few scratches, if not – send the pieces back to London.

GERMANY – NAMED AFTER CAESAR'S SISTER

Dear readers and friends of archery, we must move on through the mud of shoddy literature. Among the most horrible things ever put on paper, you will find the German folktales, collected by the Grimm brothers, Jacob and Wilhelm Grimm – and bow and arrow are often right in the middle of the action.

Without being too critical, I like to give you an idea how the Grimms even destroyed their own reputation through greed for literary fame after once being among the front-runners setting the standards of the German language.

Germany, before it became a nation in the year 1871, was split up into several states, larger and smaller. The language evolved quite differently from region to region. Therefore, it was highly essential to have as many literary documents as possible to come to a common standard. The most important contribution with regard to the consolidation of the language was the translation of the Bible by the Reformer Dr. Martin Luther from Latin into German, with a first edition of the New Testament published in the year 1522 and a complete German Bible (New and Old Testament combined) in the year 1534.

The effect was enormous as Johannes Gutenberg (c. 1398 - 1468) from Mainz, Germany, the inventor of the European letterpress, had laid the grounds for a printing technique and made a mass production of books possible at affordable prices. A few years after the printing of Luther's complete Bible, Roger Ascham published his book 'Toxophilius' in the year 1545, the first book on archery written in English.

The Grimm brothers almost had it all. Their wonderful collection of fairy tales was – and still is – something unique in this world. Rapunzel, Hansel and Gretel, Cinderella, Little Red Riding Hood, Rumpelstiltskin, Little Snow White, Hans in Luck, The Two Kings' Children, The Clever Little Taylor, The Star Money or Snow White and Red Rose; altogether two hundred and ten (!) fairy tales, which have been part of childhoods everywhere, as well as having been transformed into plays, ballet- and opera productions for adults.

The Grimm brothers are considered to be co-founders of the German linguistic sciences. Their research, studies and communication of the language are widely known and immensely appreciated.

If they would not have added their horrifying collection of German folktales or would at least have exercised wisdom and forethought when selecting their material, their star would shine more clearly and brilliantly. But back then, the Grimms wanted quantity, not quality and even gave up the work on their German dictionary, where they ended after completing the letter 'D'.

The brothers knew exactly what their plan should be when they decided to pursue their new focus. The method was simple: Try at first to collect *all* the German folktales, regardless of the content. When the first book had been completed, they issued a second volume, fairly certain that they now had everything under control.

At this point, the Grimm's told their readers in the preface of the second book that they now wanted to evaluate the material collected so far, before they would issue a third book – probably a revised version after discarding the 'worst of the bad'. A third book was (fortunately) never published, also because the public had not very well received the first two volumes. In the end, all efforts had merely resulted in a most wild and bizarre collection of folktales, some of them just a few sentences long.

Richard Wagner, on the other hand, took 'the best of the bad' as an inspirational source for some of his operas, like Tannhauser or Lohengrin and not to forget the Ring of the Nibelungen. The latter, with its four parts – Rhinegold, Valkyrie, Siegfried and Twilight of the Gods – belongs to the most exhausting works of classical music and demands an incomparable amount of patience and stamina from the audience.

Germany had to honor the brothers in one way or the other and someone came up with the suggestion to put their portraits on the 1000-Deutschmark bills. Intentionally done or not, this had put them in a secure hiding place. In better times, when Germany still had a decent currency in circulation instead of the awful operetta-currency Euro, these large bills were ideal for dubious transactions on a cash basis, and – aside from used car traffickers and pimps from the East Bloc – the public seldom set eyes on such a banknote.

I spared no effort to go through all 585 (!) of their gruesome concoctions to search for stories that involve bow and arrow. What follows is a good example, how useless and nerve-racking the stories are: If you believe the Grimm brothers, the words 'German' and 'Germany' derive from the name of the sister of the Roman Emperor Caesar, and only because a swan has led the way and escaped twice not being shot dead with bow and arrow. One arrow missed and another was not shot, which saved the life of the animal.

What name would Germany have if an arrow *had* killed this swan? Germany, in this case, would be called 'Tongeren' and not Germany. If you do not believe it, ask for the second volume of 'Deutsche Sagen' (German folktales) and look for folktale number 539, 'Karl Ynach, Salvius Brabon and Mrs. Schwan'.

Internationally, there are different words for Germany and its people, which do not originate from the word 'Germania'. The

French call Germany 'Allemagne', derivative of the 'Allemanni'. In many East European states, the name for Germany is based on the word 'nemec', which means 'mute' or 'speechless', because the Germans had been blamed for rebuffing to learn or speak Slavic languages.

Come on! Why should the Germans drop their studies of the English or Italian language and would then attend someone's birthday party, not singing 'Happy Birthday to you' or 'Tanti Auguri a te', but come up with a Polish song instead. You have to drink a few beers too many to do that.

In Poland, Germany is called 'Niemcy', in the Czech language 'Nemecko', and in the Ukraine 'Nimetschtschynain'. Only the Russians understand that the Germans prefer to learn other languages and call the country 'Germanija'.

Germany has a Slavic minority, called the Sorbs, who live in the country with a population of about sixty thousand. The Sorbs have serious problems with the Slavic base of their language when they have to name their own homeland, but they found a solution: They call it 'Bawory' instead of Germany, which is the name for Bavaria.

That is like giving the USA the name of Texas, when immigrants with strange languages have no specific name for their new homeland.

The Italians use the word 'Germania' for Germany and 'Tedesci' for Germans, the latter deriving from the old German word 'Diotisk'.

There are many variations of the word 'Deutschland' according to the ability of people to pronounce a single word correctly. In Norway and Sweden, they come close with the term 'Tyksland', the Dutch almost have it with 'Duitsland' and the Japanese practice hard with 'Doitsu'.

Only the Chinese know what is important: They call Germany 'Déguó', which means something like 'Land of Virtue'.

Now back to the dreadful German folktales. The Grimm brothers would have been better off to collect and record their wonderful fairy tales, but having reached expertise on this 'genre', they found their own style when they wrote down the folktales.

Gottfried, with the byname Karl (Charles), was the King of Tongeren. He lived near the river Meuse in the Castle of Megen (now called Nijmegen, a city in the Netherlands). His son Charles Ynach (sometimes spelled Inach) had been banned from the country, because he came a bit too close to a virgin girl.

He fled to Rome into the house of his uncle Cloadich. Thereafter, he had spent some time with a Senator called Octavius, but he soon had to flee again, together with the Senator and his family, from the cruelties of Sylla, a Roman dictator, and came to the Greek region of Arcadia.

He found a place to stay in the house of the Proconsul Lucius Julius, who had two daughters, Juila and Germana. Charles fell in love with Germana and revealed to her that he was the son of a King.

You can probably guess what comes next: He fled again. This time he took Germana with him. But before leaving, they grabbed all the cash and valuables they could find and disappeared.

Their way led them to Venice, Milan, Savoy and Burgundy in France, and they arrived after four days in Cambray.

If the Grimm brothers had bothered to take a quick look at the map, they would have recognized that such a trip – back then – could not have been completed in four days.

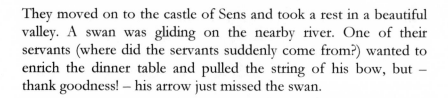

They moved on to the castle of Sens and took a rest in a beautiful valley. A swan was gliding on the nearby river. One of their servants (where did the servants suddenly come from?) wanted to enrich the dinner table and pulled the string of his bow, but – thank goodness! – his arrow just missed the swan.

The bird was scared. It flew up and landed in the lap of Germana. The new name for Germany was saved for the time being, because the swan was still needed.

Very pleased with the good outcome, in particular as the swan was a good bird, she asked Charles about the German name for a swan. Charles, who meanwhile became her husband, told her that the word was Swana (modern German: Schwan). Germana replied that she wanted to be called 'Swana' from now on. She was afraid that one day someone would recognize her by her real name. Germana, now Swana, took the swan with her and fed him.

Their travels continued to the castle of Florimont near Brussels, where Charles got the message that his father had died and he immediately returned to Tongeren. When he had arrived in his hometown, he was received with jubilation as the new King. The country had lived in peace for a while and Charles and Germana (Swana), had two children, a son and a daughter. They named their son Octavian and the daughter Swana, after her mother.

Charles later joined hands with Ariovist and fought against the Romans, but died in the battle of Besoncon. Germana (Swana), his widow, was in hiding with her children and the swan in the castle of Megen at the Meuse River. She feared that her brother – no one less than Caesar, the great Emperor of Rome – would be looking for her.

Can you still follow? Germana's (Swana's) father had two children, herself and her sisters Julia, and now she is afraid of her *brother*...

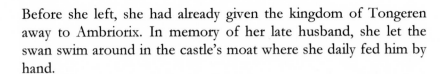

Before she left, she had already given the kingdom of Tongeren away to Ambriorix. In memory of her late husband, she let the swan swim around in the castle's moat where she daily fed him by hand.

Salvius Brabon was a very special warrior in the army of Caesar. He came from the Greek region of Arcadia. At that time, Caesar and his troops were on company holiday and stayed at the castle of Kleve. Salvius got bored, took his bow and shot around some arrows in the countryside. He thought about his past life, and an important dream he once had came to his mind.

When he sat on the banks of the Rhine River, not far away from the castle of Kleve, he meditated again and saw a beautiful white swan. The bird nibbled at a rowboat so as to try to get attention.

Salvius was mesmerized and when he connected the appearance of the bird with his important dream, he jumped into the rowboat. The swan, without fear, flew ahead of Salvius, after he took the oars to follow him.

The swan led the way along the Rhine River and Salvius anxiously waited for something to happen. He kept on rowing until the swan saw the castle of Megen where its mistress lived.

The swan was full of joy to be home again and immediately flew to the castle's moat to look for its mistress. Salvius was disappointed and a little angry, because he felt so abruptly abandoned by his guide after so many miles of hard sculling on the Rhine river – downstream at least – and he came ashore.

He kept his bow ready to shoot the swan if he would find him. He finally saw the bird swimming in the moat, put an arrow on the string and was about to shoot, but just in time, Germana (Swana) came to the window.

Totally scared, when she saw that her beloved swan was about to be shot, she instinctively fell back into her mother tongue and cried out loud in the Greek language: *"My knight, I adjure you, do not kill this swan!"*

Salvius was surprised to hear these words in his own language and put away his bow.

Two (deadly) arrows for a swan, one of them missed – badly aimed by a dumb servant – and the other was not shot at all. Whatever, this had ensured Germany – sorry Tongeren – the name of Germany, as we will learn from the following pages.

Do not laugh, this is serious content of German folktales by the Grimm brothers!

Salvius asked the woman, who – after her outcry in his own language – was obviously a compatriot of him, what she was doing in this foreign land.

She was not afraid anymore when Salvius approached her in their common language and asked him to come inside the castle where she could give him all the information in a discrete way. Salvius accepted with pleasure and full of curiosity. Once within the walls, he had many questions.

Germana (Swana) was already aware of the fact that Caesar was resting in Kleve. Since she knew that Salvius was a knight and that he came from Arcadia, she asked him to take an oath and to promise that he would help her as this should always be done for widows and orphans.

She then told him the full story. Swana asked Salvius for his mediation to reconcile with her brother Caesar. She gave him a distinctive mark in the form of a golden idol, a present that Caesar had once given her.

Salvius promised to act in her best interest and returned to Kleve. Having arrived there, he greeted his master Julius Caesar and showed him the idol. Caesar recognized it straight away and asked Salvius where he found it.

Salvius told the story and asked for forgiveness in the name of Caesar's sister. Caesar immediately burst into tears and regretted the death of his brother-in-law. He wanted to rush out to see his sister again and also his niece and nephew.

Salvius guided Caesar to the castle of Megen and asked for Caesar's blessing to marry the daughter of the widow, the little Swana, a wish that was promptly fulfilled. They got married in Leuven and Caesar was reconciled with his sister. He gave Salvius and his niece a good piece of land as their dukedom and his nephew Octavian got the Kingdom of Agrippina (today the city of Cologne) on the Rhine River.

I think you have waited long enough for the solution: Caesar renamed Tongeren into Germania, after the name of his sister Germana. Caesar gave his nephew the byname 'Germanicus' and since then, the Germans are Germans, living in Germany.

My God! Put a ten-year-old child on a roller coaster, securely fastened, and let it have half a gallon of 'Alco pops' and something to sniff. Then give him a pen and a piece of paper and allow him three consecutive rides during which he should write a story about the origin of the name of Mexico.

The result of its elaboration could not be far off, what concerns time, geography, history and other fundamentals, from what has been produced in this absurd product of a folktale.

LEUPICHIS ON THE RUN

Here is another folktale, collected by the Grimm brothers, where you have to ask yourself how anyone can come up with such drivel, again casting bow and arrow into a miserable role.

Leupichis, one of five brothers, was frequently dragged around during his time in captivity. All the others had already died and he desperately wanted to escape the Huns and return home to the countryside of Friuli in Italy.

Friuli? Yes: *"Hints of tropical fruit on the nose, leeches, melon, dry on the palate with well-adjusted acidity and fine fruit, balanced flavor with a long finish."* Correct, this happens to be the Pinot Grigio, my favorite white wine, which is produced in that region!

One day, Leupichis implemented his escape plan. He took his bow, a few arrows, some food and ran away.

He did not know which way to go – neither did the Grimm brothers and the storyteller did not have any useful hints either. Most likely, the Grimms, as usual in a big hurry to write down all this trash, must have come up with the idea to copy the story with the swan that had led Salvius to Caesar's sister Germana, the name giver of Germany.

But, instead of rowing along the Rhine River, Leupichis marched through valleys and wilderness, and a wolf, instead of a swan, became his guide.

Like the swan, the wolf frequently stopped along the way and Leupichis regarded this all as a divine message.

After a while, Leupichis had eaten all the bread that he had taken with him. Driven by his hunger, he took his bow and shot at the wolf to kill and eat him.

As usual, also this meager story is not very logically constructed when the existence of the wolf and its directives had been a divine providence. The wolf evaded the arrow and disappeared.

The ancestors of the archers – are they just incompetent idiots? Once again, this is a tale where an arrow has missed. Fortunately, this is all gobbledygook, as the archers would otherwise be the dimwits of our history.

In all those tales of the past, featuring sporty achievements, the heroes jump high enough, run fast enough, throw wide enough, drill deep enough or even fly through the air, and when it comes to the archers, arrows miss, bounce off, do no harm, up to the 'mother of all misses', when Cupid hit himself with an arrow.

Whatever, Leupichis no longer knew which way he should take as the wolf was gone. He was exhausted, slumped down and fell asleep. A man appeared in his dreams and spoke to him: *"Get up, the one who is sleeping, and take the route in the direction where your feet are lying, and there you find Italy!"*

When I had read these lines for the first time, I thought that the Grimm brothers or their storyteller will now twist the story in such a way that Italy, from that moment on, got its typical shape of a boot, but they made it a size smaller.

Leupichis got up and walked into the direction his feet were pointing and came to the home of the Slavs, where an old women gave him shelter and food in her home.

He then continued on his way and came to Lombardy – according to the Grimm brothers, the place where he came from.

We should not blame the Grimm brothers too much for their inaccurate geographical descriptions, mistakenly making Leupichis' home region Friuli a part of the Lombardy. In the end, they more or less just hastily wrote down what others had told them. At all cost, they wanted to have the book of German folktales published before someone else took the stories. That is no different from some of the news articles or TV reports today.

Also for another reason, we should generously oversee some of their mistakes. Within a volume of 585 folktales (in words: five hundred and eighty-five), it is more than likely that one or the other mix-up has slipped through, although the overall assessment should be more critical.

Let us go on with the story! He found the house of his parents in shambles. The roof was gone, but the walls were still standing. Everything was overgrown with brambles and thistles. He found a great elm tree between the walls, where he hung up his bow. He carefully cleaned up the place and when he had finally finished his work and all repairs were made, he took a wife and got married. Well, in the old days, people still followed the right order in life.

He fathered a son named Archis; Archis fathered a son named Warnefried and Warnefried fathered a son named Paul.

That is the end of the story. Where is the sense, what is the message?

I think that the Grimm brothers have written down the folktale in such a hurry that they even forgot about a meaningful end. It became a pointless shaggy-dog story; no wonder, it was already number 407 of their overzealous 'safeguarding' of German folktales, and they had another 178 to go.

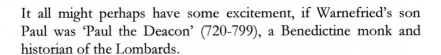

It all might perhaps have some excitement, if Warnefried's son Paul was 'Paul the Deacon' (720-799), a Benedictine monk and historian of the Lombards.

If the origin of Paul the Deacon – again depended on a missed arrow shot – was not the (forgotten) background of the story, then someone could at least have sucked some honey from the elm tree, especially as it is the tree of intuition. It is also the patron of merchants and thieves – what a perfect combination!

Even an average scriptwriter could have made something out of this. Instead, this meager story was left incomplete and open to speculation. Nonetheless, it was lifted to the ranks of a distinguished German folktale.

I have the strong suspicion that the Grimm brothers had just been taken for a ride, something that applies to many of their folktales.

We know from various sources that the storyteller had even informed the Grimms that Leupichis was his own remote ancestor. I have no doubt that a serious writer would have put aside his quill and emptied the inkpot over the head of this buffoon. Alternatively, he could have been referred as a new patient to the next nuthouse, instead of writing down this bullshit.

It is difficult to assess how many Germans have given away their passport after reading the folktales of the Grimm brothers. Nevertheless, there are signs, time and again, that the unhindered and uncensored distribution of these folktales is partly to blame for the emigration of some irritated individuals.

Some years ago, there was a broadcast by 'RTS 2', the second program of the State Television of Senegal – 'Radiodiffusion-Télévision Sénégalaise (RTS)', which was part of the weekly show 'Nos Immigrants' (our immigrants).

A German who, at the time, owned a car repair shop in the city of M'bour, in the district of Thies on the beautiful 'Petite Côte' (little coast), was asked about the reasons for coming to Senegal and stated the following: *"It was not about taxes, not the uncertainties in the rental system, not the health care reform and not the premature and stupid abandonment of the Deutschmark in favor of the rotten Euro. It was because of the folktale number 514 of the Grimm brothers, which has led me to go to Africa."*

This folktale is indeed a reason to run away from civilization. But what kind of civilization do we have when such wild stories – and for that matter also the Greek and Roman myths and most of our legends – are not censored and withheld from the public?

No. 514 of the Grimms' folktales explains to us the origination of Switzerland: Hunger and distress forced the Swedes and Frisians (an old tribe that today primarily lives in or around the northern part of Germany) to send away some of their people. They met every month to draw lots and determined who of them would have to leave the country.

This went on for some time, but it was not enough. The meetings and the cruel lottery soon took place each week and every tenth person was selected. In the end, some six thousand Swedes and twelve thousand Frisians trekked over the Alps. Their leaders were called 'Switer' and when all had settled down, they named the country 'Switzerland', derived from the name of their leaders.

In summary: Typical examples of folktales by the Grimm brothers, carelessly and thoughtlessly written down. The latter even tries to make us believe that nobody was living in Switzerland before the start of the lottery of the Swedes and Frisians.

When God was raining brains, did the Grimm brothers hold umbrellas?

HOW BAMBERG GOT ITS NAME

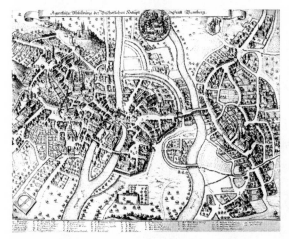

I would now like to use the occasion to demonstrate that one can easily write his own folktale at the same intellectual level, characteristic for all these literary outpourings, ranging from the Greek myths to the folktales.

At first, you have to decide what kind of story you want to create. Something like a Greek myth, a legend or a folktale? I suggest making it a German folktale.

The next thing to choose is the type of the story. I would say we go with a popular pattern: 'where does the name come from?'

Finally, we need a geographical location: As I was born in Upper Franconia, the northern part of Bavaria, I am fairly well acquainted with the region and its history. This should already give me a decisive advantage over the Grimm brothers.

I will then combine this with the best basis you can have for a successful mystery story with 'historical' background: superficial knowledge. Dan Brown and his 'Illuminati' or 'the Da Vinci Code', are examples of errors, mistakes, as well as mixing and twisting of facts, presented in an enthralling way.

The origin of the name of the city of Bamberg is still disputed among experts, and therefore, I have the excellent occasion to stir around in the fog of mystery and come up with an explanation.

Bamberg is located in Upper Franconia. Its old town has the largest and fully intact historical city core in Germany, which is in the World Heritage list of the UNESCO since the year 1993.

But even more important: The city of Bamberg is widely renowned for its beer production. It is often called 'the true capital of beer', looking back to almost 1000 years of beer making and a rich historic- and cultural heritage of brewing tradition. The river Regnitz flows through the center of the cathedral city, like the golden thread of the history of beer brewing.

It is not the brewing alone, but also the craftsmanship around the beer trade: Coopers produce barrels, coppersmiths make brewing equipment and farmers grow natural ingredients. Many prestigious public building projects have been realized thanks to beer-taxes in the old days – a levy that could easily be forgotten over pleasurable hours in the many pubs and beer cellars all over the town.

What a city! It is high time for a proper legend explaining the origin of its name and, of course, we want bow and arrow to play a leading role. Our hero will securely hit his targets, unlike Cupid and many other archers of the past, whose *misses* made history.

'Sigismund' would be a nice name for a main character in a German folktale. And the title? When you read the story, you should agree with me on: 'How Bamberg got its name'.

In that sense, let us get to work: It was around the year 1000 when the scholars Bastian, Dieterich and Gottfridus have met in a valley in Upper Franconia. They wanted to find a name for a new town. Emperor Otto II. had given a nice piece of land in the valley of the river Regnitz to his cousin Heinrich I, who did not know what to do with it and passed it on to his son Heinrich II. He and his wife Kunigunde then decided to establish a new town on this land.

Three scholars were sent into the valley to select a city name right on the spot. There were seven hills around them and all these little mountains already had a name: Altenburger Berg, Domberg, Michaelsberg, Abtsberg, Jacobsberg, Kaulberg and Stephansberg. The word 'Berg' means mountain in German and 'berg' at the end of a city name sounds rather nice.

They definitely wanted to have a name for the town ending with 'berg', because this has additional advantages. You never know if some nobles pick up the family name from the name of the new town, and someday they become part of the British Royal family. It is then easy to change that into English, as it was done with Battenberg, which was converted to Mountbatten. But what word standing before 'mountain' should they choose?

There is already a famous city with seven hills around the town, among which it was founded. The name chosen was Rome, the Eternal City, named after Romulus. He was the twin brother of Remus and central character of Rome's creation.

The hallucinated anecdote of this foundation is typical for Roman myths, although this one has not been pilfered from a Greek story. In the end, the twin brothers quarrel, and Remus is killed. No, we want a straightforward German folktale and a city name with 'berg' at the end!

We continue with the story and let the archer Sigismund walk by, just about to go up on the Altenburger Mountain, where he used

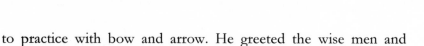

to practice with bow and arrow. He greeted the wise men and asked for the reason of their intense discussion.

"We are trying to find a name for a new city, which will be founded here. Do you have any idea, archer?" they responded.

Sigismund shook his head. *"No, but if something comes to my mind, I will let you know",* he replied and moved on until he came to a small hut of a peasant woman. She had just done the dishes and he saw a copper pot, pans and all sorts of cooking devices, hanging nicely lined up on a rope.

Sigismund, who always enjoyed a bit of fun in life, could not resist and drew his bow. The woman rushed into the hut and barricaded the windows, while Sigismund shot one arrow after another at the kitchen utensils.

One could hear a loud *'Bam!'* when the frying pan was hit. *'Bam!'* and *'Bam!'* again when he struck the copper pot and it fell to the ground. *'Bam!', 'Bam!', 'Bam!'.* Silence came back when the last arrow was shot.

The scholars were frightened and dazed from the noise. After they were under control again and had collected their thoughts, one of them looked up to the mountain and said: *"I have it; damn I have it, that's it! We are naming the new city Bam-berg!"*

Do you think this is a stupid story? Right you are! But then, you must apply the same criteria to the intellectual level of most other myths, legends and folktales.

Believe me, if I would have given this tale to the Grimm brothers, no doubt, it would play an important role in one of their books, even if I had relocated the Gulf Stream or the pyramids into this region!

COUNT DRACULA AND HIS DAUGHTER

 Vlad III., later known as count Dracula, did really exist – both of them! In this chapter, we want to break the myth that arrows killed Dracula and his daughter.

Vlad III. was supposedly a bloodthirsty Transylvanian ruler, who brutally and ruthlessly tortured and killed his enemies and unloved contemporaries. He was given the byname 'Tepes' (the Impaler) for his alleged predilection for his method of killing people.

Well, he certainly was a little bloodthirsty and cruel, but it was only after he and his family had to suffer much themselves. Vlad III. reacted to the cruelties of the Ottoman enemies committed against his people, thereby just repeating their atrocities.

But he was also responsible for cruel deeds when he fought against inside enemies and opponents. He was adverse to thievery, fraud or profiteering and simply exercised his own style to cope with these offenses.

The peasants, however, thought of him as a benevolent ruler, who protected his subjects and as a tough advocate representing their cause. Until today, the Romanians see him as a fair adversary against corruption. We know from reliable sources that he was persistent in his efforts to promote honesty and to reduce crime.

The Romanians still have a saying in relation to the forceful actions of Vlad III: *"Unde esti tu, Tepes Doamne?"* (where are you, Master Impaler) when they are denouncing the chaotic state of affairs, corruption or perpetual laziness.

During the election campaign in the year 2004, one of the candidates held a speech about the corruption in his county and mentioned Vlad III. and his consistent interventions against this unacceptable pattern.

Romania was on the threshold of a membership in the European Union, and had Vlad III.'s actions been reprehensible in any way, then certainly no such mention would have been made.

The dictator Nicolae Ceauşescu, who was overthrown in the year 1989, had developed a special adoration for Dracula and ordered a monumental film with the intention to suggest to the audience that Vlad Tepes was his spiritual ancestor.

Everyone was laughing, but not the political class in the former 'DDR' (East Germany). In socialist solidarity, they had used this rare opportunity to entertain and educate the masses and gave the movie a new title: 'The real life of count Dracula'.

Ceauşescu tried to tell his people – under a very dubious linguistic point of view – that the name Dracula was a derivative of the Slavic word root 'drag', which means something like 'sweetheart', and ridiculed the image of Count Dracula even further.

In reality, his name derives neither from 'sweetheart' nor from 'drac' (devil), but from 'Drăculea' (son of the dragon), because his father was a member of the 'Order of the Dragon'.

All of that had posthumously harmed Vlad III.

When the actions of the insane Ceauşescu and his secret police, called 'Securitate', became unbearable, all of it was wrongly associated with the weird and exaggerated stories and the falsified picture of Vlad III. and Count Dracula and seen as the typical bad behavior of Romanian rulers; but bitter revenge was coming soon.

When the Ceauşescu couple escaped from Bucharest during the revolution in the year 1989, they initially traveled to the small village of Snagov, where the tomb of Vlad III. is located. They were finally captured in Targoviste, the place where Vlad III. once held court. After a short trial, they were executed by a firing squad.

Vlad III. was born in the year 1431 as the second son of Vlad II. Dracul and the Princess Cneajna from the principality of Moldavia. His home country was originally the Walachia, but he lived in Transylvania, after his family was exiled. His sometimes dubious fame comes mainly from manipulated stories about him as Vlad III., many untrue Dracula novels and from the numerous grotesque horror movies.

During his reign, he is said to have killed 20000 to 40000 European people with his favorite method, the impaling. In his fight against the Ottoman Muslims, even 100000 of them are said to have met their death that way. In reality, he was much more peaceful and – measured against the habits of his time – almost harmless.

All these figures must be regarded as highly overstated. We can rather believe an episode that describes the impaling of 600 merchants in Brasov and according to a document produced by his rival Dan III., this event has only cost the lives of 41 profiteering traders.

Dracula felt committed to defend his country against evil and predatory internal and foreign aggressors. He consequently fought against Bojaric oppressors and greedy merchants. His enemies and adversaries, led by the lobby of the wheeler-dealers, had solely invented most of the scary stories. They outbid themselves in deceitful descriptions of alleged atrocities. Most of these statements, often from Saxon sources, are strongly exaggerated or even outright lies and often politically and religiously motivated.

Especially the merchants, mostly Saxons living in Transylvania, have promoted their propagandist lies. They were considered by the people to be exploitative parasites and have acted out of concern for their profitable transactions – and most likely also because of personal fears.

The gruesome descriptions surpassed everything thus far. Methods of torture, drowning and roasting of the victims – no imaginable manner of death was omitted, and in the end, Vlad III. and his men even feasted on the remains. The group of alleged victims had consistently expanded, until all of any religious and social strata, men and women, infants, children and older people, were affected. Finally, they came up with the superlative: *"He* (Vlad III.) *caused more pain and suffering, then even the most bloodthirsty tormentors of Christianity, Herod, Nero, Diocletian and all heathens together."*

In contrast, there is neither evidence, nor any remotely substantial document of that magnitude coming from Russian or Rumanian sources. Yet, even there, one cannot be certain. The most widely used word in Romanian descriptions (also in daily use) is 'probabil' (probably).

Vlad III. was 'probabil' beheaded at the end of the year 1476 or early in 1477, but the case was not yet closed for all times. His head was pickled in a honey pot and taken to Constantinople. The rest of his body was buried in the monastery of Snagov. Thereafter, Vlad III. has spent several centuries as the undead Vampire Dracula. During this period – and it should be noted by virtue of fairness – there have been a few cruel 'derailments', but that was not the Vlad III. anymore who could have been called to come before the jury.

When the Vatican was fed up (according to the official propaganda version), they have put the monster- and ghost hunter Van Helsing on the case with a secret mission. Equipped with garlic, a silver stake and a crossbow, from which he could shoot seven arrows without reloading, he embarked on a journey to Transylvania.

After many adventures and struggles, Van Helsing, who meanwhile had become a werewolf, kills Dracula with a bite in his throat. Van Hesling takes the shape of a human again and goes back to Rome to receive new orders. This is as far as the real story goes. No silver stake or a silver arrow has killed Dracula; he was simply bitten to death.

The life and loving attention of Vlad III. for his people can easily be analyzed under historical aspects, free of prejudice and in a transparent fashion.

Even without digging in the Vatican's secret archive, we have very clear contours regarding the life he had to live after he was beheaded, as the undead vampire Dracula. Nevertheless, we commonly know Dracula only from third-rate horror movies.

In the Dracula movie by the Universal Studios of Hollywood, produced in the year 1931 – the first screen adaptation authorized by Bram Stoker, author of the novel of the same title – the action was simply transferred to London.

This junk version of the Dracula story begins with a brief intermezzo in Transylvania with Renfield, a British real estate agent, who was asked to find a dilapidated property in London. The Count moves to London and roams the upper class of this time-honored city.

It was at least Van Helsing who was allowed to kill Dracula in this movie version, but – not authentic – with a wooden peg, which he rammed into his breast.

And what about Dracula's daughter, who was supposed to be killed by a wooden arrow that had penetrated her heart? This again is just sheer nonsense; a further continuation of the weird horror movies produced in Hollywood.

They gave the audience five years to digest the nuisance, fabricated in the year 1931, before they came up in 1936 with the sequel, called 'Dracula's daughter'. They finally invented a female variant as an expected 'enrichment' of the vampire myth, encouraged by the success of another craziness put on celluloid, 'Frankenstein's bride', shown in the cinemas the year before.

The new movie was again produced in the Hollywood Studios. Gloria Holden played Dracula's daughter and the advertising slogan of the film was *"She gives you that weird feeling."*

The film has a strong erotic component. Moreover, it clearly leans to the template of the novel 'Le Fanu' by Joseph Sheridan, one of the most sinister narrators of the Victorian era, and to the figure of the Countess 'Mircalla von Karnstein', better known as the first female and the first lesbian vampire 'Carmilla'.

The second version of this trashy film starts at the end of the first. Two police officers enter the tomb of the vampire and find the dead body of Dracula and, standing next to him, a well-known Vampire Slayer. No, not Buffy, she was born in New York City only 41 years after this movie.

It was Van Helsing, who immediately admits that he had rammed the pole into the heart of the Count and explained that this was not an act of murder, as the victim had already been dead for 500 years.

No wonder that he was taken away by Scotland Yard and considered to be mentally ill. But after a while, they began to believe him, especially as the body of Count Dracula had miraculously disappeared from the pathological department.

Then she appeared in London's society, Dracula's daughter, in the shape of the Hungarian Countess 'Marya Zaleska'.

She had stolen the body of her father and burned it, in the hope that she would be liberated of his curse.

In order not to test the patience for too long, here is the end, short and sweet: The Countess collapsed and died, hit by an arrow that was shot directly into her heart by her jealous servant. Van Helsing finally manages to convince the London police chief of his innocence.

But there was hope for the better at last: For a change, this sordid concoction, called a movie, did not become a blockbuster. Even Hollywood, which too often feeds us historical nonsense in shiny packages, can't polish a turd.

We put on record that Count Dracula, in his first life as Vlad III. Tepes, was beheaded and as the vampire Count Dracula, he was bitten to death and not killed by an arrow or a pole.

There also was never an arrow shot at his daughter, as such a person – contrary to Vlad III. and Count Dracula – never existed.

But there is something I must personally add: When I recently visited my dentist for a check-up, I made my usual Vampire jokes (like having problems with the canine teeth around midnight).

After the extensive research for this book, I was certainly well prepared to speak a little about Count Dracula.

I wanted to impress my dentist (her) and stated that Count Dracula was actually Vlad III. with the byname 'Tepes' (Impaler). I pronounced the word as it is written. Her face became unusually serious, and she replied: *"You are saying it wrong. 'Tzepesh' is the way you have to pronounce it."*

I countered: *"I know that it is spelled T-e-p-e-s."*

"No!" was her emphatic response, *"the T is not a regular T. Under the T you have a 'virgulina', which looks like a small comma and this is also below the ş at the end."*

"Has she studied dental medicine or the vampire-diaries?" I murmured to myself.

She slowly and methodically continued: *"The T is then pronounced 'tz', as in quartz and the ş at the end, sounds like the s in sugar – Ttz-e-p-e-sh."*

The situation became a little scary. I wondered about her knowledge in such detail. Does she have a patient file with that name? Is there someone who has his canine teeth periodically sharpened? Perhaps in the same chair as I am sitting now? Is *he* perhaps still alive? But 'probabil' these are just extrasensory perceptions.

(Off the record: She was born in the same country as Vlad III.).

'ALL INTO THE GOLD!' – A GOOD LUCK WISH?

Some archers, mainly in the German speaking countries, wish themselves *"All into the Gold!"* (Alle ins Gold!), at least those, aiming at targets with colorful rings. They refer to the *bull's eye*, the inner one of the two yellow rings in the center of the target. Most archers are unaware that this is not such a good wish after all.

At first, we have to distinguish between two types of wishes: Those, which are meant positively like *"make a good catch!"*, among the anglers or *"good luck!"*, in a general sense. Then, there are those wishes with negative connotations like *"break a leg!"*, a well-known idiom used among actors or musicians in the theater.

Yet, even most negative expressions can have a positive intention. Superstitious people believe that the malicious powers of destiny like to reverse good wishes to the opposite and therefore, the wishes are at first expressed the other way around in order to outsmart the gods.

Do the archers belong to the first group when they wish good luck in a competition? No, that is far from it! They really think of the worst, and thereby they do not even belong to the second group, where people do that just to mislead the powers of destiny. But as I said before, most archers are not aware of this.

It was in the year 1199 when David, the Earl of Huntington and his faithful wife Maud (Matilda) Kevelioc Meschines of Chester, sat on the grandstand and watched a tournament with jousting knights and archers shooting their arrows. The Maud of Chester (from Chester, North England), as she commonly became known, wore a lot of precious jewelry in celebration of this particular day, especially a heavy golden necklace. It was a present given to her by her husband on the occasion of the recent birth of their daughter Isobella le Scot.

The archers had their turn. In those days, one did not worry too much about having sufficient clearance to the spectators. They stood, closely packed, to the left and right of the line of fire, which gave this sport a special 'kick'. One injured person more or less was not important compared to the excitement to see the arrows fly a path close to their heads. If one would introduce today's regulatory distances of the archery competitions in rally racing, most people would not attend these motors sports events anymore, although we would then have a lot fewer accidents and victims among the spectators.

William Dalgleish, an accomplished archer, drew his bow to secure his almost certain victory with the last arrow. He set his sight to the target and thought of his triumph in the tournament, when suddenly he was distracted by a fidgety horse behind him. William was startled and bent to the side, but unfortunately, he also let his arrow fly.

Its path was not towards the straw doll, as desired, or at least into the cheap standing places of the craftsmen and farmers, but into the distinguished visitor's gallery, directly into the bosom of the Maud of Chester. It had hit in the middle of her golden necklace, which had saved her life. Nevertheless, she suffered some painful injuries.

William continued to watch the rest of the tournament from above, frequently cursed by the Maud of Chester. The guards had put him in a cage that they had hung up high, visible from afar. He lost all his land and was banned for many years. From that time on, it was a customary practice among the archers to unnerve themselves in archery tournaments and to wish the opponent *"all into the gold!"* – a tradition that has remained until today.

By the way: John Dalgleish, a distant relative of the William Dalgleish, was less fortunate and was hanged in Edinburgh in the Year 1723. He was once an executioner himself (the hangman of Edinburgh) and had replaced a certain Mr. Sutherland, but he did not keep the post for very long. At a particular occasion, he even bungled the execution of Maggie Dickson, who had survived with a lot of luck.

Back then, it was common practice that the condemned persons were allowed to speak their last words. When John Dalgleish was about to be hanged himself, a certain Mr. Alexander Pennecuick had the vicious idea to pre-formulate the last words of the widely unpopular and hated Dalgleish and penned them as mockery verses. They were published, in a ridiculous manner, in one of the folding books which had been very popular at that time, thereby listing all the misdeeds of John Dalgleish.

The beginning and the end of these verses are quite famous: *"When Hangie saw Death drawing near..."* (Hangie, nickname for a person about to be hanged). At the end of this maliciously formulated farewell speech, Dalgleish hopes to have himself the luck of Maggie Dickson: *"And spare my life, as I did to ill hanged Megg!"*

The curse came also upon the Pennecuicks. Like many Scottish families, they lived beyond their means, and hence their patrimony, including the estate near Edinburgh, passed from them. Alexander Pennecuick is said to have died of starvation in the streets.

THE GOLDEN BOW

Some people say that they had never cried so hard until they saw the Las Vegas show 'The Singing Cupid'.

Towards the end of the performance, a winged archer – impersonated by a swivel hipped singer – strides down the stairs in his glittering suit. He points at a picture of a little boy (no real little boy on stage is allowed at a late night show, according to Nevada State law), plucks his golden bow and starts singing:

"Oh Lord, let me shoot an angel for his dad,
His mom just ran away,
I know, she really was all they ever had,
Oh Lord, let my arrow not go astray."

We can certainly say that the picture of Nixon and Elvis holding a golden bow in the Oval Office is a fake (based on the popular picture) and it was probably not even the 'Idol of Swivel and Sway' who impersonated Cupid in that show. Moreover, there is plausible proof that Elvis did not – repeat *not* – give away a golden bow to President Nixon.

But where is it, that precious souvenir? It is said to be made of rare and expensive woods with a nickel-free 24-carat gold plating, which makes it kind to the skin. It cannot be used like a normal

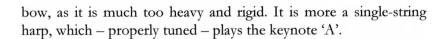

bow, as it is much too heavy and rigid. It is more a single-string harp, which – properly tuned – plays the keynote 'A'.

But what has caused all the excitement about Elvis giving away a golden bow?

It all began at the Northwest gate of the White House when Elvis Presley personally delivered a letter, wherein he requested a meeting with President Nixon. The surprised guard at the gate must have fainted. Just imagine, you are sitting in the gatehouse and suddenly Elvis comes around and hands you a letter for the boss. Hallelujah!

The six-page letter was written during an American Airlines Flight on their stationary. How on earth did Elvis come up with the idea to write a letter to the President of the United States, saying that he has a gift for him and asking for the credentials of a Federal Agent-at-Large in the war on drugs? On top of it, he personally delivered the document at the Northwest gate of the White House. If you and I had done that, would we not have taken the risk that people would assume that we are *on* drugs and not *against* drugs?

The meeting really took place on December 21, 1970. Elvis brought a pistol (repeat again: not a bow!) into the White House and gave it to Nixon. He again brought forward his request to become an official Agent-at-Large. Nixon's advisors thought it could eventually be a good idea to have someone at a *higher level* in show business watching the drug scene and told him: *"Let's hear what he has to say!"* Perhaps, the advisors were primarily keen on meeting the King themselves and after a few autographs from him.

Hold on to your socks, this is *not* a joke! The #1 of the U.S. archives' greatest hits, based on all the requests made each year to the National Archives for reproductions of photographs and documents, is an item that has been requested more than any other, more than the Bill of Rights or even the Constitution of the

United States: It is the photograph of Elvis Presley and Richard M. Nixon when they shake hands at the occasion of Presley's visit to the White House. Also high in popularity: The handwritten letter of Elvis and some internal White House documents pertaining to this visit.

This is the downside of any Democracy, like the one we have it in the USA. If you write a crazy letter to the President, it becomes part of the official National Archives. After a while, it is available to everyone and people would ask questions as to your mental state at the time – even if temporary – when a weird idea hit you. But things are even worse: Every handwritten remark on that letter and all internal documents referring to a possibly wacky idea are easily available for public information. According to the internal memorandums, Nixon had repeatedly asked about the credibility of Elvis. Honestly, this must be considered as one of the greatest acts of blasphemy in human history.

Elvis and Nixon – both men are great and self-made achievers, but Elvis will be *the* King forever, a cultural icon known the world over. Egil 'Bud' Krogh was a Nixon aide and present at the meeting in the White House, where he received a call from Dwight Chapin. It was December 21, 1970, when the voice on the phone said: *"The King is here."* Krogh looked at Nixon's agenda and said: *"King who? There aren't any kings on the President's schedule."* He got the answer: *"No, not just any two-bit king, the r-e-a-l King – Elvis!"*

After all, should we, ourselves, not be deeply impressed that *the* King wanted to serve his country as a simple Agent-at-Large in the fight against drugs (and Communism!)?

The King and his bodyguards had shown a very human side at their visit in the White House: According to a small book written by Krogh with the title 'When Elvis met Nixon', Elvis and his buddies virtually looted Nixon's desk for souvenirs and gifts – but certainly left no golden bow.

The following is a summary of all six pages of the letter. The distorted handwriting on the original papers strongly suggests, that this was not just caused by a bumpy ride on the plane.

Dear Mr. President,

First I would like to introduce myself. I am Elvis Presley and admire you and have great respect for your office. I talked to Vice President Agnew in Palm Springs a week ago and expressed my concern for our country. The drug culture, the hippie elements, the SDS, Black Panthers, etc. do not consider me as their enemy or as they call it the establishment. I call it American and I love it. Sir, I can and will be of any service that I can to help the country out. I have no concerns or motives other than helping the country out. So I wish not to be given a title or an appointed position. I can and will do more good if I were made a Federal Agent at Large, and I will help out by doing it my way through my communications with people of all ages. First and foremost I am an entertainer, but all I need is the Federal credentials. I am on the plane with Sen. George Murphy and we have been discussing the problems that our country is faced with.

Sir I am staying at the Washington Hotel Room 505-506-507. I have two men who work with me by the name of Jerry Schilling and Sonny West. I am registered under the name of Jon Burrows. I will be here for as long as it takes to get the credentials of a Federal Agent. I have done in-depth study of drug abuse and Communist brainwashing techniques and I am right in the middle of the whole thing where I can and will do the most good. I am glad to help just so long as it is kept very private. You can have your staff or whomever call me anytime today, tonight, or tomorrow. I was nominated this coming year one of America's Ten Most Outstanding Young Men. That will be in January 18 in my home town of Memphis, Tennessee. I am sending you the short autobiography about myself so you can better understand this approach. I would love to meet you just to say hello if you're not too busy. Respectfully, Elvis Presley

P.S. I believe that you, Sir, were one of the Top Ten Outstanding Men of America also.

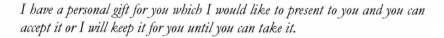

I have a personal gift for you which I would like to present to you and you can accept it or I will keep it for you until you can take it.

WASHINGTON HOTEL, PHONE ME-85900 RM 505-506 UNDER THE NAME OF JON BURROWS ... PRIVATE AND CONFIDENTIAL

Attn. President Nixon, via Sen. George Murphy, From Elvis Presley

Isn't this all not very impressive? Elvis thought that not only he, but also the President of the United States was among the Top Ten Men in the country. *Wow!* I did not know that this position was so high up in national ranking.

But wait! The King would keep the *gift* until Nixon can take it? The president of the United States can take anything as long it is legal. And what? The President of the United States, on his way out of office, makes a stop in Memphis to pick up a gun from Elvis? Even the old Greeks could not drink and sniff enough to come up with such a story in their warped myths, but this one is for real – golden bow or gun.

Whatever, Elvis reached out his helping hand to the President of the USA in deep concern about the safety of America. Nixon became the first and only President who was given not only the temporary telephone number of Elvis in Washington, D.C., but also all his other numbers in Memphis, Beverly Hills, Palm Springs, where he could be reached directly or via his staff.

The King even considered the Beatles to be a threat to the country. Quoted from a memorandum by Bud Krogh to the President's file, meeting with Elvis Presley, Monday, December 21, 1970, we will find the remarks of the King about the mop-top heads from Liverpool: *"The Beatles came to this country, made their money, and then returned to England where they promoted an anti-American theme."*

Nixon nodded to this statement. I always said it, and I will not get tired to repeat: Nixon, for certain, had also a pronounced serious and honest side, and Elvis had shown a profound understanding of real values.

And what concerns the stage appearance of the Elvis: He made the Beatles look like tax advisors in a karaoke bar or a Chinese factory orchestra shortly before the end of their working day.

The King's elaborate costumes and his physical play on stage had expressed professionalism and great respect for a paying audience. The Beatles, on the contrary, with their unostentatious apparel and timid movements, always gave me the impression that their choreography was limited to the range of motion of a bored group of commuters hanging around at a bus station.

Pistol or bow? The faked image is no evidence if it was just produced to stir up the discussion again. I guess we have to dig a little deeper. The following written expression of thanks from President Nixon to Elvis should give us proof: Elvis did not give him a golden bow – it was a pistol, Colt 45!

But we know Nixon and his darker sides. Did he lie about the gift in conspiracy with Elvis? The following text is quoted from a carbon copy of this letter.

December 31, 1970 – Dear Mr. Presley, It was a pleasure to meet you in my office recently, and I want you to know once again how much I appreciate your thoughtfulness in giving me the commemorative World War II Colt 45 pistol, encased in the handsome wooden chest. You were particularly kind to remember me with this impressive gift, as well as your family photographs, and I am delighted to have them for my collection of special mementos. With my best wishes to you, Mrs. Presley, and to your daughter, Lisa, for a happy and peaceful 1971, Sincerely, (Name stamp on the copy: Richard Nixon)

The supporters of the theory that Elvis had taken the golden bow from Las Vegas to give it to Nixon, come up with the argument that Elvis could never have brought a gun into the White House, and by no means would he have been allowed to carry it around in his hand, given the environment and especially not in front of the President. It could have been loaded and what if he would have used it in anger if he was not made a Federal Agent? What impression does it make to the public if Nixon accepts it as a gift?

I think this is a bit farfetched and the official documents leave little doubt. The gift of Elvis, a commemorative gun, is now on display at the Nixon Library in Yorba Linda, California, and this is, in my humble opinion, not just another trick to distract people from the disappearance of the golden bow.

But where is the golden bow? It is not in Las Vegas, not in Graceland or anywhere else that we know. If you want to do some research yourself, I can only recommend you to go to the National Archives in College Park, Maryland. In the Nixon Library, you can find all relevant documents in the White House Central Files, within the health (HE) section, folder title EX HE 5-1 1/1/72-1/31/72, and let them hand you box number 19.

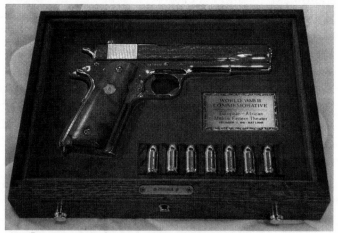

Image taken from the Nixon Library and Museum

182

THE ORIGIN OF THE LONGBOW AND THE WELSH

Welsh made stories try to make us believe that not only the English longbow itself originates from Wales to some extend, but moreover, we are being led to believe that the Welsh archers had been the major force within the English army.

The stories about the longbow archers in the Battle of Crecy in the year 1346 are mostly used to pull the wool over the eyes of people, what concerns the importance of this 'terrifying' weapon. An accumulation of these bows in warlike actions is often described as 'the atomic bomb of the Middle Ages'. In reality, this is all more like a set of firecrackers and has been critically evaluated in a later chapter, dealing separately with the English longbows (page 249).

Bad arguments do not get better by constant repeating, so we can also forget the battles of Poitiers and Agincourt in the years 1356 and 1415. The Hundred-Years War was lost in the end, a lot of money defenestrated, a lot of arrows wasted – for nothing! Whilst the French were concluding – 'you can loose a few battles, if you win the war', the English found their happiness in – 'you can loose the war, if you beat the French in some battles'.

There had been indeed Welsh archers in the armies of Edward III. and Henry V., but that has not increased overall effectiveness. Anyhow, besides talking about the archers here, we want to see what the English longbow has to do with Wales.

The Welsh in general, when they are not singing at every possible occasion, have a strong thirst for scuffles and are wild fighters, regardless if the matter is worth a serious dispute or not. This would make them ideal mercenaries for every occasion, if they wouldn't be so volatile, unreliable and lacking in loyalties. Thus, the number of Welsh archers in the English armies of the Hundred-Years War has steadily declined from battle to battle.

That the Welsh have sucked a lot of honey for their legends from Shakespeare's works, is a sure indicator for falsehood. It is known to any literally educated person, but unfortunately too often left unspoken, that Shakespeare's works are of highly doubtful quality and practically everything has been massively pilfered from others. So, for that matter, any 'evidence' taken from that source is for the trash can.

The English longbow got its name from the impressive size. That this device is not simply called 'bow', like in any other county, is due to the fact, that the English bows had been somewhat shorter before.

Instead of developing something more effectively at a given size, like the Mongols with their composite bows, the English added to the length, but also the basic wood material had been changed.

Descriptions of English bows before 1300 speak of a size of around 5 foot in length. The necessity to have a more lethal weapon at longer distances and with better accuracy, triggered the development of a longer bow and the wood from yew provided the ideal material. As the yew was a rare tree and stealing from the colonies was not yet a source of supply yet, the English had to import this wood from other countries. The type of yew found in England was mostly not suitable for bow making (read more in the chapter about the almost eradicated yew (page 206).

As supplies still proved to be insufficient, every ship coming to an English port had to bring 4 bow staves for every turn (a stave is a piece of wood a bow is made from). The number of such staves had later even been increased to 10.

The Welsh have a single source what concerns their bows and archers in the middle of the 12th to the early 13th century. 'Gerald of Wales' was an all-round talent in his time, but that doesn't mean much in his case. In these days, it was generally easy to become an all-round-talent. Whatever talent you wanted to develop, most things were still on a very low level, practical as well as theoretical, with an extremely short and flat learning curve.

Of course, this is not valid for mathematicians and alike, but looking at the activities of Gerald of Wales, it didn't take much to put together a collection of professions. He was, amongst other things, an archdeacon (assistant to the bishop), astrologer (not to be mixed up with astronomer – a serious endeavor), diplomat, church-politician, historian, folklorist, recruiter for the crusades and above all – important for the Welsh's collection of historical facts – a fanciful writer and poet. His numerous attempts to get a decent job, the position of the bishop of St. Davis, had always failed.

Geralds 'reports' of wide spread archery in the South of Wales. The bows, rather small and highly ineffective at longer distances, were not made of yew, like the English longbows, but the wood came from the wych elm trees. It was however a good bow for the Welch and their fighting tactics – a quick and not too long charge, followed by an even quicker retreat into the hiding.

The wych elm became famous in later times outside Wales. Numerous graffiti appeared in the early 1940s throughout the West Midlands with the words 'Who put Bella in the Wych Elm', in connection with an unsolved murder. The skeletonized body of a woman was found in a hollowed out trunk of a wych elm near

Wychbury Hill at Stourbridge, Worcestershire (where they still make that fantastic seasoning sauce). The crime is still unsolved, but many wild theories rank around the victim, from a Birmingham prostitute to a Nazi-spy.

Back to the longbow: Gerald's description of the bow's power was good indication of the inferior quality of Welsh door-making. He stated that the arrows, shot from Welsh bows, penetrated the door 'a hand's width deep'.

Whatever, up to now, we have no evidence of anything which could have been seen as a predecessor of the English longbow in Wales.

As bows and arrows were wide spread throughout Europe, perhaps someone could have brought in this weapon into the country. Strangely enough, bow and arrow were not used by the close neighbors from Ireland, Scotland and not even by the Celts of North Wales, they all had more fun fighting man-to-man.

The Vikings had effective bows as well as the Normans, but how could such a bow come into Wales? No-one so far had the desire to conquer even a square foot of Wales until the Anglo-Normans came along in 1136. They had quite a friendly reception in South Wales. The Welsh from the South soon sided with the Normans against the Welsh in the North. A Welsh nationhood was far away and if you like to quarrel with everyone around you, including friends and family, how can you imagine a unified country?

The Anglo-Normans should have done it all alone. With such 'allies' on their side, it could hardly be a surprise that they did not advance even into Mid Wales, not to speak of the North.

Welsh archers later joined the Normans during their invasion of Ireland. A pimped-up tale by Gerald of Wales wants to make us believe that 300 Welsh archers made all the difference. To come to a fair judgement, one must know that the Irish tribes, protected by little or no armor, where mainly fighting with stones and spears.

In the mid of the 13th century, we finally saw a little flame of Welsh nationalism, but things went in typical Welsh fashion. Llewelyn, King of the North claimed all of Wales for himself, but words and deeds did not go hand in hand. He did nothing to occupy the South. His grandson, Llewelyn ap Gruffydd, had chosen another approach. He went into English politics and persuaded Henry III. to make him 'Prince of all Wales', but again, he made absolutely no efforts to take over the South.

So things went on and on until King Edward I. had enough of this. In 1277, his English army, supported by South Wales and in an alliance with Mid Wales, occupied the North. Llewelyn was put under domiciliary arrest, after he was forced to sign a treaty.

This again did not last for long. In 1282, Dafydd from Mid Wales changed sides, causing Llewelyn to make trouble again. Instead of three armies, consisting of English, South Wales and Mid Mid Wales forces, Edward came with three genuine English troop-units and put a lid on the pot. Llewelyn was defeated and killed.

There was yet another revolution in the year 1295. It was rather small, involving only the North. Madog ap Llewelyn was quickly defeated by the English army, which had brought along a good number of archers.

Therefore, must the importance of Wales in connection with the English longbow rather be seen in providing moving targets and practice for the English archers?

The two campaigns of the Welsh Wars by Edward I., in 1277 and 1282/1283 had also been excellent opportunities to try out new tactics and techniques.

The archers from the famous 'Macclesfield 100', were mainly serving as King's bodyguard. The other archers, a meanwhile obsolescent model of war within the troops, had only 16.000 arrows for 3.600 of them - it was the time for trying out something new.

A little over 100 crossbowmen brought along 170.000 arrows, or bolts, as the shorter version for use in the crossbows are called. More powerful, more accurate, but heavier and more difficult to handle. Especially the loading of the weapon requires some time and effort. Whilst the string of a light crossbow can be drawn by hand, the heavier types need the help of mechanical devices. Therefore, this new weapon, with it's advantages and disadvantages, included the need for new tactics of war.

After Edward had sorted out the Welsh problem, he turned his attention to the Scotland, which turned out to be a harder to swallow affair, especially as William Wallace (later made famous worldwide by Mel Gibson, playing his character in the Hollywood movie 'Braveheart') was at first inflicting a devastating defeat on the English troops, but the Scots lost in the end.

As we have already come to the stage now where the crossbow had replaced the longbow, I must say that I cannot find any significant evidence of a Welsh share in the making of this weapon.

In the chapter 'TRANSITION' at the beginning of the book, I have said that 'England is important for us archers. It is the home country of the longbow and added: 'with some credit we can give to the Welsh'.

This is an often heard statement and some people even call it 'a Welsh longbow', but you can make your own judgement now.

KYUDO ARCHERS

 **I** sincerely hope the small Kyudo community will forgive me when I say that Kyudo is not the type of archery which can be taken seriously.

It is more like eating soup with a fork, for an alleged strengthening of patience, spirit, dexterity and character.

Some of you might already have seen it, this bizarre construct of a bow with a length of approximately 90 inches (228.6 cm) where the arrow is asymmetrically positioned on the string, which is drawn in the area of the lower half of the bow.

This weapon has also disappeared in the 16th century in favor of the firearms, but has survived in the sphere of the Japanese aristocracy, especially at courtly celebrations and even survived into our times.

Some Kyudo disciples cling to this obscure device, which is not a sensible shooting gear, but more the requisite for a mental exercise – a bizarre version of Zen. Nevertheless, the perpetual conjuration of the spirit of the Samurai shows that the Kyudo archer also wants to feel a bit like a warrior.

The verbal component 'do' in Kyudo is based on the Chinese term 'dao', which we find again in the word 'Daoism', describing a Chinese philosophy and religion. Dao means – in the literal translation – way, street, path. In earlier times, Dao was designated to mean 'the method', 'the principle' or 'the right way'. Kyudo is nothing more than 'the way of the bow', perhaps a matter of simple instructions.

In ancient China, also the Daoists shot with bow and arrow as a spiritual enrichment. They were not necessarily interested to hit a target with precision, but used this equipment more for their gymnastic exercises.

Confucius says: *"You can perceive moral and acting of a man, the way he is handling his bow."* Is he telling us that mimic and gestures with a bow in your hand, to express who you are, is hence more important than shooting well?

The Kyudo archers wear traditional garments, half-naked upper body and a long skirt. It does not allow sporty exercises, but only slow and ceremonial movements. Also the Scots wear skirts (called a Kilt), but they are shorter, more comfortable and above all, more practical. The fine sandals of the Kyudo archers might be good for the dance floor, but they are highly impractical as sporty footwear.

Occasionally, one can see extravagant Shintoism headpieces. They make the creations gracing the heads of ladies of High Society, as they wear them in the annual hat show at the Ascot horse race, look like run-of-the-mill items from the bargain basement of a thrift store.

We are not quite sure why someone had developed such a bow in the first place. Some believe that this bow, which cannot be shot while standing up with an arrow correctly placed in the middle, was designed for archers on horses, but that contradicts with the fact that this bow had already been brought into play before the warriors came along on horsebacks. Others believe that the bamboo, available back then on a large scale in Japan, could not support a powerful draw in the center of the bow.

There are other explanations with regard to the origination of this weird shooting gear. Historical narratives may lead to believe that this bow was once created as a stage property in a peasant theater and served the sole purpose of mocking the big warriors.

Many anecdotes or stories are connected with this topic. One version explains that a bow maker had made such a bow just for fun under the influence of too much rice wine and the droll bow was preserved as an early fashionable phenomenon.

In the context of this bow, as a weapon of war, another theory illustrates that upon the emerging of the infantry in the armies of war, the archers were kneeling down to expose less of the body as a strike area and therefore the bow had to be drawn somewhere around its lower third.

In yet a further interpretation, which I personally favor most, the inventor of this comical shooting device was a little man, just 4 feet and 6 inches (137 centimeters) tall. The folks in his village called him 'chippoke dansei' (tiny man). He wanted to shoot an impressive bow and look like an important archer. He had developed the Kyudo bow for himself and made his 'weapon' much longer than necessary, with an asymmetrical draw, far down in the lower part.

What's more, he could not handle a large draw weight and made it relatively weak – still today characteristic of Kyudo bows. He thus constructed a bow that he could draw freely and easily, but at the same time, it had an impressive appearance through its size. Many little warriors wanted to have such an arrow-launcher and that is why the wondrous Kyudo bow started its own 'triumphal march' on the grounds of archery.

Of course, there had been many Japanese archers who were able to shoot and hit well and had the appropriate skills and strength. They used small and symmetric bows ('Hankyu'), which were also known in similar versions in our hemisphere, but the fancy Kyudo archers called everyone using an effective bow a robber or assassin. He, who could draw a real strong bow, was immediately ill-reputed as a rough-hewn peasant.

When the Kyudo bow found its way into the environment of the noble courtiers, it was shielded from the common people and made an object of meditational rituals.

Over time, the Kyudo archers strayed with their minds, looking for positive aspects of shooting with this ludicrous bow, and the ceremonies became increasingly strange.

The Kyudo bow is difficult to shoot, as it has virtually no value as a shooting device. In addition, the bows often have no significant strength (from 12 pounds upwards), something we otherwise only know from bows for children in amusement parks. For that reason, the string of a Kyudo bow is drawn with the thumb, all the way behind the ears, to get at least some force on the twine.

The archers shoot at the 'Mato', placed closely over the ground. It has a height of 14.2 inches (36 centimeters) and simulates an enemy archer who is reloading in a ducked posture. The 'Kyudinos' are therefore shooting – in a fictitious fight – at a defenseless, kneeling opponent. Very noble indeed!

Officially, the Mato is exactly 3.5 inches (8.9 centimeters) above the ground, with a center, called 'Hoshimato'. It has a diameter of 4.7 inches (12 centimeters), representing the unarmored spot under the outstretched arm of a warrior.

Taking the 14.2 inches (36 centimeters) total height of the target, the middle at 7.1 inches (18 centimeters) and the 3.5 inches (8.9 centimeters) distance above ground, then the center is at a height of 10.6 inches (26.9 centimeters).

If the Mato, according to the Kyudo community, corresponds with the part of the body which is less protected by armor, I agree even more with the theory that the bow was invented by the 'chippoke dansei' (tiny man).

The beginners first shoot from a distance of a little more than 6 feet (1.2 meters) at the 'Makiwara' (rice-wisp). The Makiwara has a diameter of 30 centimeters (11.8 inches). The thickness of this straw bundle is approximately 85 centimeters (33.5 inches).

This depth is totally unnecessary just to stop the arrows. We can only assume that the Kyudo archers want to mentally convince themselves that their hands are holding a 'powerful' weapon.

The tyro is spending up to six months shooting in that fashion, until the distance gets longer to about 20 to 35 feet (7.6 to 10.7 meters). This is unsurprising, because in the beginning, one could not even hit the fattest Sumo wrestler standing 10 feet (3 meters) away, with that strangely constructed thing of a bow. Officially, one needs the time at the onset of mastering this 'art' to become thoroughly familiar with the motion sequence.

Caught in an ideological rigidity and uncompromising, the Kyudo archers stick to all these absurdities, as they feel obliged to protect the traditions of their ancestors – utterly stupid or not.

The archers know the paradox of the arrow, in particular that, at first, it bends its center towards the bow, caused by sudden pressure of the forward-moving string. The arrow then begins to oscillate (alternating deflections of the shaft) and winds itself around the bow. It flies on this way, with steadily decreasing bends, until it finally straightens out and starts to turn with the help of the feathers or the plastic vanes at the end of the shaft.

It is important that a right-handed archer (right hand pulls the string) puts the arrow to the left of the bow and a left-handed archer (left hand pulls the string) to the right of it. The Kyudo archer of today deliberately places the arrow on the wrong side, a

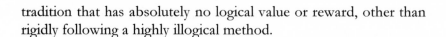

tradition that has absolutely no logical value or reward, other than rigidly following a highly illogical method.

Common sense and the brain's logic are not allowed among these cross-dressed archers, and the arrow will inevitably try to break away. In order to compensate for this, the Kyudo archer makes a sudden movement of the wrist and twists the bow, within fractions of a second, on the launching of the arrow ('tsunomi no hataraki').

This bizarre behavior can be compared to hitting with a hammer next to the nails and then, with a sudden twist of the wrist, they are hit on the head, just before the hammer misses. As a result, simple nailing is brought to a higher level as a meditative ritual.

Instead of trying out a reasonable use of their bow or – much better – replacing this crap with ordinary equipment, the Kyudo archers are sinking deeper and deeper into their bizarre world and become exotic individualists, who do not care about the world around them.

In one respect, however, this eccentric passion is ahead of any self-praise, as we commonly know it today: The propaganda slogans are unsurpassable.

Original soundtrack of the Kyudo community: *"The one practicing Kyudo is performing a ceremony, which is soothing the spirit, and at its end, the world, created by the spirit, is disappearing and the true ego is emerging. His character is developed and his personality and the truthfulness in his spirit are cultivated. All qualities like truth, strength of mind, modesty, harmony, honesty and self-control are improved."*

This slogan really supersedes even the flowery and ornamental character descriptions of some wines like *"incredible pure plum and silken opulent texture, bright and fresh with beautiful aromas of honeysuckle blossoms and white peach".*

On top of it all, we have the masters of Kyudo playing the psalms of revelation on the hurdy-gurdy of infatuation. They even believe that Kyudo is *more* than normal archery – a highly refined method, so to speak. Replace the word 'refined' with 'messed up', and the sentence is correct.

To imitate Kyudo archery in the real world, you could try to play tennis in a raincoat, rubber boots on your feet and a frying pan in your hand. Balls must be hit *under* the net, which has been slightly lifted.

This sport will then become so complicated that spirit and character are inevitably strengthened. The sheer impossibility to score points in a sensible manner will foster patience, peace of mind and modesty.

The following statement, created by the Kyudo community, blatantly contradicts with the safety regulations of the archery sport: *"Heart and spirit are clean and calm and the archer is so much absorbed in his thoughts ('muga muchu') that he becomes unaware of everything around him."*

I hope that the Kyudo archers are not driving their cars in that fashion and steer with their feet, while their hands operate the gas pedal, clutch and brake – unaware of anything around them. Regular driving lessons probably contradict with their tradition.

They say, a good shot should not just be stubbornly repeated, but every arrow ought to fly better than the previous one; Kyudo is an endless effort. How bad must this bow be that improvements of shooting are infinite?

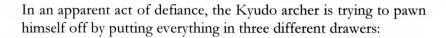

In an apparent act of defiance, the Kyudo archer is trying to pawn himself off by putting everything in three different drawers:

1. 'Toteki' – hitting the target without observing a specific form. This is the method of the sports archer.

2. 'Kanteki' – the target is 'killed' and penetrated. This is the style of the warrior.

3. 'Zaiteki' – the arrow already sticks firmly in the target *before* it has left the bow. The archer is filled with spirit and energy; heart and spirit are clean. This is supposed to be the right way of shooting with bow and arrow, and that is Kyudo.

We can certainly leave these eccentric characters with their own opinion and reluctant to accept an attitude adjustment, but to describe Kyudo – in comparison to other forms of shooting with bow and arrow – as 'the only true and proper way of archery', is a bit rich as a statement, based on a ritually cultivated loss of reality.

Harmony, politeness, respect and thoughtfulness are very important for the Kyudo archers and preconditions to successful practice Kyudo within a community. But let us be honest, we should not behave differently, when playing Scrabble or Ludo.

ARROWS – SLOWER THAN THE SHADOW ON A SUNDIAL?

Once upon a time, there was a heartless and bloodthirsty princess 'Turandot', the daughter of the Emperor of China.

She was very much distraught by the fact that all women in Asia were forced into slavery after they got married to – as she believed – power-obsessed, chauvinist idiots (men).

She wanted to escape this fate and asked every suitor to solve three riddles before he was allowed to ask for her hand. When the suitor was not able to come up with all proper answers, he was simply beheaded.

Friedrich Schiller used this theme for his play 'Turandot, the princess of China'. As the audience in the theater was eagerly trying to find the answers, the riddles were an additional attraction of the stage play and even became the icing on the cake.

It was therefore difficult to create interest for a second performance after the solutions were known. Schiller was forced to invent and implement new questions. Even Goethe was helping him out with one riddle.

Fifteen riddles had been created, three for each one of the five performances, on January 30, February 2 and April 24, in the year 1802 and March 9 and January 11, in the year 1804.

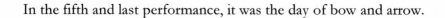

In the fifth and last performance, it was the day of bow and arrow.

The particular question was:

"I am turning on a disc,
I am wandering around ceaselessly and untiringly,
Small is the field, which I am circling,
You can cover it with both of your hands,
But I need thousands of miles,
Until I have crossed this little field,
I am flying off with the speed of the storm,
And faster than the arrow shot from a bow."

...and the answer is: the shadow on a sundial. What, an arrow flies slower than the shadow on a sundial? No way!

How did Schiller get that idea? When he thought of speed as a measure, did he not think of the shadow as it appears and moves on the sundial, but brought it into relation with the speed of the Earth's rotation?

The Earth turns around its axis once every 24 hours and, depending on where you are, more or less rapidly. At the poles, it spins very slowly in a small circle. However, at the equator, the circumference is 40075 kilometers (24901 miles), which results in a speed of about 1670 km/h (1038 mph), in fact faster than an arrow. The farther we move away from the equator, the slower the movement.

Let us take the city of Weimar in Germany, for example, the location of the five performances of Turandot. Here, the Earth is still turning with a speed of 900 km/h (559 mph). Indeed, still faster than an arrow. A longbow, at Schiller's time, had an initial velocity far below 150 fps (164.6 km/h), the acceleration of a top compound bow is somewhat below 400 fps (438.9 km/h), and even an arrow shot from a crossbow would not be fast enough.

If Schiller had in mind the shadow on a sundial in Weimar, related to the spin of the Earth, then it indeed speeds around the axis of the Earth at 900 km/h (559 mph). However, this velocity is also given to every bow, quiver and arrow, hanging around somewhere on a wall – or to snails crawling over a lettuce leaf in that location.

But the question was explicitly about the shadow on the sundial and its movement (*"I am turning on a disc"*).

Did Schiller think of a shadow that dashed through space? But then, it is not the shadow that has traveled the long way, but the light that came from the sun. That is why we call that 'speed of light' and not 'speed of shadow'. Only the interruption by the pointer of the sundial produces the – slowly moving – shadow.

Sit down Schiller that does not make the grade!

Turandot is the last opera by Giacomo Puccini, which was actually completed after his death. The libretto is based on the stage play of Carlo Cozzi, which was also the basis for a free interpretation and the drama by Schiller.

In the opera, unlike in the play by Schiller, the three riddles always remain the same:

1. *"What is born each night and dies at dawn?"* The answer is: *"Hope"*.
2. *"What flickers red and warm like a flame, yet is not fire?"* The answer is: *"Blood"*.
3. *"What is like ice, yet burns?"* The answer is: *"Turandot"*.

Calaf, the suitor, has all the right answers, but Turandot does not give up.

Prince Calaf wanted to appease Turandot and gave her a riddle of his own. If the answer is correct, he dies. If the answer is incorrect, she has to marry him.

TURANDOT

MUSICA DI **G. PUCCINI** G. ADAMI e R. SIMONI
LIBRETTO DI
— EDIZIONI RICORDI —

She accepts the new deal. The riddle he asks: 'What is his name?' She has until dawn.

Turandot immediately issues a decree that no one in Peking is allowed to sleep before Turandot knows the name of her suitor. If she fails, everyone in the city will be killed.

In the end and after much excitement, Turandot – very impressed by her first kiss – and Calaf come together. His name? The answer is: *"Love"*.

Calaf sings the famous aria 'Nessun Dorma' (nobody shall sleep), the number one song at opera highlight-events. It was the favorite theme song of the 'Three Tenors'– Placido Domingo, Luciano Pavarotti and José Carreras – whenever they made some extra money for charity.

It is pretty safe to say that everyone in the modern world is familiar with this aria, but thanks to Luciano Pavarotti's performance of the aria at the opening of the FIFA soccer (football) world championship in Italy in 1990, watched by over one billion people, it got an extra boost.

The final words of the aria are: *"All' alba vincerò, vincerò, vinceeeeeeeeeròòòòòòòòò!"* (At dawn I will win, I will win, I will win).

It was already after dawn when the world championship was decided in the final match, and Germany won the cup.

THE VICTORY SALUTE OF WINSTON CHURCHILL

Winston Churchill has led Britain into and through (mainly into) two world wars, on whose behalf, we can only guess.

At this point, we do not know if he really accepted 150,000 pounds from the Rothschild bankers to bring Britain into war.

Whatever, his money pot was depleted when he died, mainly due to his extravagant living style and extensive alcohol drinking. Any money he owned had largely gone away. His widow was not left with comfortable means and ended up selling their paintings, silver and furniture to make ends meet.

Winston Churchill was a controversial character. Some name him Britain's greatest Englishman, others a Judas, a Zionist puppet, a 33rd degree mason, a racist, a Druid priest, a fringe spiritualist and member of the golden dawn, an Illuminati, an anti-Christian, Shithouse (from his initials WC), you name it.

Churchill had a strong interest in the occult and put together the 'black team' of wartime astrologers, dowsers and ritual magicians, under the stewardship of Louis de Whol, a German-born astrologer. He contributed much to his distorted and mysterious image himself, saying that he escaped capture in the Boer war by his psychic ability to choose which door to knock that would give him shelter.

That is, however, only part of the truth, as Churchill was captured in 1899 by nobody less than General Louis Botha, who was to become the first Prime Minister of the South African Union. Churchill was hiding in a gully – without a door to knock on. It would have been easy for Botha to pull the trigger on his Mauser rifle, but he didn't. Later, Churchill fled from the POW camp and wrote two books about his adventures in Africa.

Winston Churchill was a heavy drinker, a fact that was particularly recognized by Lady Astor: *"You, Mr. Churchill, are drunk."* Churchill replied: *"And you, Lady Astor, are ugly. But I shall be sober in the morning."*

If 'WC' was really sober the next morning, we do not know, but we must have our sincere doubts. We do know, however, that he started to cut back on alcohol (at least expressed the intention) at the age of 76: *"I am trying to cut down on alcohol. I have knocked off Brandy and take Cointreau instead."*

Nevertheless, in the last ten years of his retirement, he drank more than ever and frequently came into conflict with Lady Astor:

LA: *"If I would be your wife Mr. Churchill, I would poison your wine."* WC: *"If you would be my wife, I would drink it."*

We don't know if these stories were just made up, because when 'WC' was sitting at a dinner table, he was either already sauced or achieved that state shortly thereafter, most likely unable to come up with such brilliant witticism.

There is a wartime episode about King George V., who gave up alcohol to set an example to the troops. Churchill openly declared this idea as absurd and stated that he would not give up his beloved tipple, just because the King did.

Churchill drank to the point where people accepted his state as being normal. They certainly had no comparison otherwise. At the same time, raised as an aristocrat, he was able to keep control of himself and even felt that drunkenness (the visible type) was contemptible and disgusting. Therefore, the continuity of his imbibing alcohol was in good order – British upper class standards applied.

The rather mediocre student Winston Churchill had an easy way ahead concerning his later advancement. Although he had to repeat several years in school and twice failed the entrance examination to the military, his family of the English high nobility and the money of his American mother Jennie Jerome secured his career.

He was not interested in his hereditary right of a peerage (member of the Upper House with inherited title) and rejected the honor. Instead, he rather wanted to be an American Indian and used the origin of his mother for the legend that he is a descendant from the Iroquois Indians.

Winston Churchill changed sides in his political career four times, and his skills were on offer on several occasions for the right price. In the House of Commons, he became known as 'the Shithouse', perfectly matching his initials 'WC'.

203

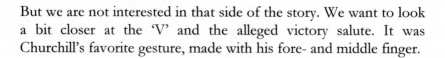

But we are not interested in that side of the story. We want to look a bit closer at the 'V' and the alleged victory salute. It was Churchill's favorite gesture, made with his fore- and middle finger.

He flashed the V-sign at every chance he got – preferably with photographers around – and whenever he did not have his hand on a glass of whisky or a cigar.

Some even believe that he held cigars for too long and could not close these two fingers anymore. Whisky and a cigar had already been a fundamental part of his breakfast.

For us archers, the V-salute refers to something totally different: It is neither a sign of the Illuminati and the symbol of worship of the devil, the suggested motivation for WC to move his arm and hands other than reaching for a cigar or a glass of something high-proof, nor the victory sign, what the Americans have made of it.

While the 'V' is the first letter of the word 'victory', that is not the original meaning of this gesture.

We do not want to leave the interpretation of this important sign from the history of archery and brave men to the appearance of a steadily intoxicated Prime Minister or to the belief of some uneducated GI's and therefore, we put the right facts on the records once and for all:

The victory salute was invented by the English longbow archers during the long lasting wars against France.

When the French had captured an English archer, they usually let him run away, so they did not have another mouth to feed. But before allowing him freedom, they had cut off his fore- and middle finger, which he needed to draw his bow. This made him incapacitated as an archer in war.

The English archers showed those two fingers to the French before the battle, in defiance and as a threat: *"Look here, I still have my fingers, I can still draw my strong longbow!"*

At the end of a victorious battle, it was a sign of triumph, joy and relief that they still had all their fingers, which would remain there on that particular day.

The American GI's in World War II misunderstood this gesture – most likely also misunderstood by Churchill – and have boosted its popularity as the sign of victory. Since that time, it has been used around the world as celebration to alert and reinforce successes.

The 'V'-sign has also other meanings, depending on the country and in what connection it is used.

With the palm of the hand facing to the outside, it is mostly the peace symbol, or it simply can mean the number two or a quantity of two. In Italy, this is the sign of two horns for a 'cornuto' (a man who was given horns by his cheating wife).

With the palm of the hand to the inside, it can be used as an insult or an obscene gesture. The latter is even legally scorned in Australia, Ireland, New Zealand, South Africa and Great Britain.

In order to avoid possible confusion in a particular situation, you should also verbally express your intentions, especially when conveying to the barkeeper that you want another couple of beers.

And last, but not least, it is a gesture occasionally made, when a picture is taken of a person and someone gives him a pair of rabbit ears behind his head.

THE YEW – ALMOST ERADICATED BY THE ARCHERS?

The 'taxus baccata' is a conifer native to most central and southern regions in Europe, the north of Africa and Southwest Asia.

Yew is a general term for this tree, but as other related trees became known, we are talking more specifically about the 'English yew' or the 'European yew' in this chapter.

The Greek terms 'toxotes' (archer) and 'toxin' (bow) derive from the word 'taxus' (Greek toxos), as the bows were made from yew wood. Its hardiness and elasticity are unique for making it the best bow wood of all others, but good pieces of yew suitable for bow making, have become extremely rare.

Also the word toxic (poisonous) comes from the word toxos, as the highly poisonous berries of the tree have been used to make poison – and arrows that were meant to be fatal.

The typical shape of yews, especially the twisted type in England, gives them a mystical look. They appear in many legends and folktales, described as expelling demons and lining the way to the underworld. For the Celts, it was the tree of the Druids. The yews are often found in or around cemeteries.

In the Germanic provinces, the yew was considered able to repel magic. Branches of the yew, when laid down crosswise, were thought to be protecting against demons and dwarfs steeling in the house.

The yews, as we know them today ('taxus baccata'), are more like bushes than trees, especially the ones we often find in the gardens of town houses. Many of the old yews, those giant and straight trees, have substantially diminished.

The wood of the yew was in particular demand in England, especially for their famous longbows. Every ship that came to the English harbors to trade merchandise, had to carry wood from the yew for the manufacture of bows.

Just as they robbed their colonies, the Brits did not take most of the wood from their own forests. This was not only in line with their widely known behavior of appropriating goods for themselves, but mainly because their own yews were often not suitable for bow making. Damp winds caused the yews to grow twisted and crippled.

Judgment treads upon the heels of wickedness: As the world champions of colonialism have shown the same behavior with their superabundant tea imports, they have been punished for life with a daily teatime.

The wood was mainly imported from Spain, Portugal, France, Austria, Germany and the Baltic states and has caused the woods to be nearly pillaged in those countries. But also merchants from Nuremberg and Bamberg, Bavaria, situated along the old trade routes on the way to the river ports, cut into the flow of goods and wood from the yew that came from Austria and Bavaria. They took their slice of the enormous profits and participated in this robbery. More than 500000 yew trees were cut between the years 1531 and 1590 and transported via these trading towns to Cologne on the Rhine river and then on to England.

In the south of Germany, 10000 yews were cut annually for military purposes. This has naturally led to overexploitation and destruction of many timber stands. But this is only part of the truth. Many other countries were keen on obtaining the precious wood and its excessive use as raw material did not begin with the boom of the longbows. Our early ancestors had already used the wood for the manufacture of hunting weapons.

On April 1, 1948, a spear was found near the city of Lehringen, in Lower Saxony, Germany, seven feet and ten inches long (2.4 meters) and made from the wood of a yew. It was implanted in the chest of a forest elephant and attributed to the Neanderthals. They must have worked hard to cut the steaks from the large animal, as 28 flint knives have been found near the spear and the skeleton of the animal, killed some 150000 years ago. One of the oldest wooden artifacts is a yew spear, uncovered at Clacton-on-Sea in the UK, with an estimated age of 450000 years.

There have been repeated discoveries of coffins, made from the wood of the yew, in ancient Egyptian tombs. Pile-dwelling villages near the Mondsee (Moon Sea) in Upper Austria are signs of an early appreciation for this type of wood, since the Bronze Age.

Later on, the yew was used by the lathe operators for carvings, as construction timber (especially water engineering) and by the carriage builders.

Wood from the yew was also present, when delicate fingers took the lute and made the strings sound. This highly elastic wood was chosen for the curved body of the instrument.

4000-year-old flutes, made from the wood of the yew, were found in Ireland and still function. Nonetheless, the common use of yew for most old flutes in Ireland is not responsible for making Irish folk music sound so unique and makes people say: *"If you've heard one song, you've heard 'em all."*

The yew is the last tree in the 'Tree Ogham', a medieval alphabet used to write early Irish and a Celtic coding-system of the Druids.

Until the 20th century, the browsing by the grazing livestock and wild animals was largely tolerated and has caused substantial damage to the yew tree population. Horse owners and wagoners had systematically torn out the trees, because of their toxicity.

Today, we find many old yews near English churches. Anyone in the country was permitted to cut trees for crafting bows wherever they could find them, except in churchyards.

Yews can live well over 1000 years. Some trees, like the Fortingall Yew in Perthshire, Scotland, may well be older than 2000 years and might even have reached an age between 2000 and 5000 years. The yew grows very slowly and, therefore, any exploitation can only be compensated with immense difficulties and over an enormous time span. These beautiful coniferous trees are by nature the longest living plants in Europe, but 'thanks' to the longbow and other needs, they are on the Red List of threatened and protected species.

Meanwhile, a new enemy has appeared in the form of stem canker, which is probably the result of a fungal infection.

Every component of the yew is extremely poisonous, wood, bark, needles and seed, except the fleshy aril around the seed. Birds provide the best way to reproduce the yew by ingestion and subsequent excretion of the berries. Their beaks and digestive system do not break down the seed's coating.

Traditionally, the poison of the yew was used for murderous plans. Soon, also the folk medicine made use of it as an ingredient in remedies against rabies and snakebites. In homeopathic medicine, it helps against gout, bladder trouble and liver- and skin diseases.

Pharmaceutical companies are searching all over the planet for yew forests, even with the help of satellites. It is a good thing that this possibility was not available in Colonial times.

MONGOLIAN ARCHERS

 **A**rchery is a national sport in Mongolia and one of the three sporting events at the National Festival, besides wrestling and horseback riding.

In modern archery, the country has no presence on the world stage accompanied by great success, and they prefer to exercise this sport in their own traditional way.

One the other hand, the Mongols are among the front-runners when it comes to beat and scuffle. They pick up their many medals in wrestling, boxing and judo, as well as sport shooting.

The Mongols had always been good horsemen and excellent archers with a superb weapon, their composite reflex bow. It is an advanced type of bow used by the Scythians and the Huns. Its penetrating power was even superior to the average English longbow.

They also used another type of bow, which had been developed by the Tungus, somewhat different in shape and material.

Every Mongol warrior carried two of those bows with him and a few hundred arrows, made in different versions according to the intended use. They were either very heavy, with a massive tip for shooting at short distances or lighter in weight and used for longer ranges. Some even had a poisoned tip.

The fletching, often made from the tail feathers of an eagle, was highly developed at the time and could not only stabilize an arrow, but even influence its flight path.

When the Mongols pulled the string of the bow, they did not use the three fingers in the middle of the hand, but their thumb, which was protected by a thumb ring. As they constantly adopted new techniques of warfare from their enemies, they began to use other ways of drawing the bow – even alternating – which gave the thumb or other fingers a rest during a longer lasting exchange of arrows in a battle.

Typical for nomads, they carried along everything they needed at all times, including things outside the direct warfare. In fact, they transported an entire city on their horses and thus have been much more flexible than their opponents, who were more tied to specific locations.

However, if we want to come closer to the truth, we must mention that all those factors were only of minor importance to their overall success.

At the outset of their conquests, the Mongols fought together, but always separated into different tribes, and within these groups, they had the usual, often ineffective hierarchies.

This was similar to what we know from the noble environments of past days in Europe. Not always stood the best and most capable person at the top, but the order within the noble families defined the rank. The incompetent son, the lazy brother-in-law, the consumptive child of the mistress or the boozing cousin, they all could take a leading role. Some of the nobles even ended in high military ranks owing to their gambling addiction, which forced them to escape from their creditors.

In the end, after the downfall of the first Mongolian Empire, the tribes lived in constant conflict with each other, which at least gave their neighbors some rest.

The hunt for booty was the driving force for these riding scoundrels, which was, however, not shared according to ex-ante rules, but everyone had to look after himself to get a piece of the cake.

Fundamental changes in the following period largely increased the effectiveness of the Mongols in the battles and the success in wars.

This was, however, not at all due to any extraordinary capabilities of their archers that would have superseded those of their enemies. It was much more the radical change of the social system, implemented by 'Genghis Khan', which took place around the year 1190, initially accompanied by severe disputes and confrontations with the representatives of the noble class.

And honestly, the tricks performed by the Mongols on their horses and when shooting with bow and arrow, were not any more exciting than something one can see today in any halfway decent circus. They would also not surpass the stunts of some teenagers on their skateboards in the middle of street traffic.

From then on, the fighting was not mainly for the plunder, but for a higher goal: total victory over the enemy. As the bloodthirsty Mongols did not have enough aggressive enemies, they simply created them by attacking anyone around.

The confiscated goods now belonged to Genghis Khan, who shared them with the other tribes, independent from ancestry or the ranking of the nobles and only according to the military achievements.

What's more, the affiliation to a specific tribe or clan was not the basis for the designation of military ranks. Solid trust was a prerequisite that a leader was still able to surround himself with his own people and primarily the military achievements determined the ranks in the army.

This system had put an end to selfishness and intrigues by the clans. It allowed a clear battle order and facilitated the integration of other nations. Many people in leading positions or even some of the best military leaders have been of humble origin or came from the subdued countries of former opponents. The only exception was made for the family of Genghis Khan that had maintained its structure according to its original hierarchy.

In the new order, state and military were together as one. To be a Mongol was not dependent on his descent, but on his membership in the army. Equal opportunities for advancement without nepotism, fair sharing of the robbed goods, rigid discipline and strictly enforced rules, made the Mongolian army a successful model with rapid growth.

Just imagine, one could transfer this model to the hopelessly ineffective European administration in Brussels or could at least send to them Genghis Khan and a few men to straighten out this bunch of bureaucrats and Euro-whackos. A triumphant march back to Mongolia through the streets of Europe could be assured. But I am afraid that even the bravest warriors of Genghis Khan would shy away from even coming near to the Euro-swamp, after the horror stories from the Euro zone had reached Mongolia.

The decimal system determined the structure of the army. The 'Tumen' (unit of ten thousand men) was divided into the 'Minghan' (unit of one thousand men). These, in turn, were split into the 'Zuut' or 'Jagun' (unit of one hundred men) and finally into the 'Arban' (unit of ten men). All had a leader on top that could meet the respective responsibilities.

The units of ten thousand men and the units of a thousand men were composed as efficient as possible and without considering any affiliations. Only within the smaller units of one hundred men, the tribes that had already been fighting for a long time on the side of Genghis Khan, were allowed to stay together.

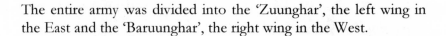

The entire army was divided into the 'Zuunghar', the left wing in the East and the 'Baruunghar', the right wing in the West.

At a later stage, the right wing developed into the army of the 'Khanat', the notorious 'Golden Horde'.

Between them, there was the elite, the Army of the Center, called 'Khol', which in turn was mainly composed of the guard of Genghis Khan, the 'Keshig'.

The 'Keshig' was a frightening unit of one thousand men, which was led into battle by Genghis Khan himself.

This central part of the troops finally grew to a unit of ten thousand. The sons of the leaders of the one-hundred-men units and the one-thousand-men units had to join this guard. Genghis Khan thereby secured himself a strong commitment of his troops on the wings and simultaneously trained his own and loyal new generation.

Sons of the tribal leaders of the allies fought in the middle, and this clever move ensured the reliability and the loyalty of other parts of the troops.

There have been some smaller elite units, whose function could never be determined with certainty and thus remained a mystery until today. Secret service, sabotage units, special assignments, the ear of Genghis Khan at the grassroots level and in the tents of the leaders or perhaps only personal bodyguards of the Great Khan for private adventures and pleasure trips? Nobody knows for sure.

This structure of the army, as described, was kept intact for a long time and occasionally only slightly modified with the integration of other people.

It seems to be a law of nature that such kind of effectiveness will soon reach its limits on our planet. After having conquered almost all of the land around, they did not have enough enemies to keep the system alive.

This shows the weakness that is part of all large systems, whether of a political, social or commercial nature. If they are frail and ineffective, they sooner or later run out by themselves. When they are working properly, but the growth rates are slowing down or the main purpose has been achieved, then even in such schemes, the end is foreseeable too.

On September 3, 1260, the tide had turned. The Mongols had suffered their first defeat in the battle against the Mameluks. The Empire began to fall apart and simultaneously the social- and military order.

The system of ranks according to personal origin was implemented again, the clan families became more important and the subjugated countries and their people went back to their original forms of organization. The army of the Mongols lost their uniqueness and fell to the level of nomadic gangs.

We do not have to shed any tears over the end of this period of terror. The number of people murdered by the Mongolian bandits during their raids is enormous. However, a count in excess of one million is somewhat exaggerated.

Soon, an efficient control was no longer possible – especially when considering the large number of occupied territories. The magnitude of the acts of war and the growing number of conflicts had surpassed the manageable limits, and the Mongols were forced to give up their simple and courageous way of fighting in favor of intimidating maneuvering.

Many of their opponents were massacred as an act of deterrence and people have been murdered, deliberately and systematically, with the intention to conceal the budding weakness of the Mongols.

Waning success at the front line was followed by vulgar deception and cunning, and the self-confidence of the troops had disappeared. Once, the Mongols had taunted the enemy and attacked with a numerically inferior, but better equipped and motivated force. Now, they had put straw dolls on their spare horses instead, to fake a larger strength of troops. They spread rumors to unsettle the enemy and deployed spies and agents.

To sum it up: The archers of the Mongols have not been superior to their enemies through their special mastery of bow and arrow. They had simply been part of a very well organized and motivated troop of warriors that was itself part of a sophisticated, equitably organized and very effective social system.

The Mongols were not special as individual artists with bow and arrow, but only collectively better organized and motivated.

Bloodthirstiness and greed for booty had shifted large parts of the nation's gross national product to state organized robbery and murder, to the detriment of their neighbors. When this all collapsed, hardly anything expandable was left to restructure the 'economy'.

Today, Mongolia – which should not be mixed up with the Inner Mongolia, an officially autonomous region in China – has a population of about 3 million. Mongolia has the lowest per capita density in the world, as it is also the second largest landlocked country on the planet. Such a small population, within such a large country, shows one thing very clearly: No one around wants to have a piece of it.

One third of the population lives in poverty. This has not changed much since 1992 when a gradually developed market economy has replaced socialist planning. This is all a good learning example for the economists: You can neither plan anything, nor let a free market economy take its course, if people constantly move around. The condition of the soil and the climate make Mongolia unsuitable for agriculture and they can no longer raid their neighbors.

They just cannot sit still and the nomadism is breaking through again and again, but they have so much time now and especially a lot of space to keep moving about with their cattle. Honestly, I too would roam a lot, not knowing where to put my grill for the next barbecue, if my backyard would have the size of Texas.

To the surprise of all and not too long ago, it was discovered by accident that the Mongols are sitting on the largest untapped coking and thermal coal deposit in the world. Shortly before the end of nowhere, one has to turn sharp left to the Tavan Tolgoi ('Five Hill') where the deposit is located, in the south of Mongolia.

However, we have to be afraid that this will not change much in Mongolia. In a part of the world where living was once mainly secured from robbing the neighbors, combined with a mentality that lazing around has to be preferred to any kind of work in general, one does not have to wonder when the steps of the nomads are getting ever slower, the closer they come to Tavan Tolgi for a possible exploitation of the coal, connected to settling down for serious work.

And, presumably, it was just laziness that had for a long time prevented the country from discovering more valuable things in their soil, like these large deposits of copper and gold in their Gobi desert, which might – or might not – boost prosperity.

MONGOLIAN WOMEN

Mongolian women still have to take on the bulk of the agricultural work and are responsible for the education of the children.

The men, work-shy in general, prefer to shoot around with bow and arrow or follow other favorite pastimes, if they should ever be in the mood to do anything at all.

Girls milk the sheep and goats, while their brothers ride through the countryside with their fathers to tend their slowly moving cattle.

The Franciscan monk 'Plano de Carpini' visited the Mongols by order of the Pope in the years between 1245 and 1247 and he reported about the life of the Mongolian women: *"They are carrying bows and arrows with them. They are riding and galloping like men; they have shorter stirrups, handle horses very well and mind all the property. They drive carts and repair them; they load camels, and are quick and vigorous in their tasks. They all wear trousers and some of them shoot like men."*

And what concerns the Mongolian men, the monk said: *"The men do nothing at all, they are occupied with their horses, look after the herds once in a while and otherwise they are practicing with bow and arrow or go hunting."*

During periods of the many armed conflicts, when the men were away from home, the women had to take on additional duties of importance.

They guarded the livestock, and the young warriors were not only coddled, but also educated. The women enjoyed great freedom, great responsibility and even greater power to make decisions.

Especially the mothers among the Mongols have a rather well respected position. Illegitimate children are no mishap, but proof of the fruitfulness of the wife, filling the husband with immense pride. Mongolian men often brag just in front of the particular neighbor who is responsible for the offspring.

A good example of the wisdom of the Mongolian women is 'Go'a', the ancestress of the Genghisids. She pointed out very early – long before the time of Genghis Khan – the importance of a unified nation.

One day, she gave each of her sons an arrow and asked them to break it apart, which they did. Then she gave them a bundle of five arrows. Again, she asked to break them apart, but no one of the sons was able to do it.

She said to her sons: *"You all have been born from my womb. If everyone stays on its own, you will be broken. But if you stay together, what can anyone do to you so easily?"*

At that very moment, the eldest daughter Kokachin came in, took a bundle of five arrows from one of her brothers and broke it apart with ease. She did not grab the arrows in the middle, but at the end and with a short jerk, they broke apart.

Then she said to her brothers: *"Do not hang around all day in the tents with petty chatter, you better do something for your education, otherwise an enemy will come along some day that will defeat you merely by his higher intelligence!"*

The Mongols believe that it is advantageous if a man's wife is somewhat older than her husband. This makes her wiser and capable to guide him in important matters.

When a Mongolian wife appears to be obviously smarter than her 'hubby' – which is practically always the case, independent from her age – he can come up with the excuse that she is merely older.

What concerns physical work (which is also true for the intellectual capabilities), nothing much has changed since the old days. The men ride from yurt to yurt to chat and drink tea; they are still lazing in their tents and when the boredom becomes too great, they grab their bow and a quiver full of arrows and go out shooting.

The wise Princess Manduchai had once rescued the cohesion of the Empire by getting married to a seven-year-old boy. She told the other women: *"He already has the brain of an adult man, the rest will grow."*

GAU – A MONSTROUS WORD?

When you participate in the official archery championships in Germany, you start at *district* level; the next step is the *regional* event, followed by the *state-* and then the *national* championship.

The regions are traditionally called 'Gau', but in some states, the championship is not called 'Gaumeisterschaft' (regional championship), but 'Bezirksmeisterschaft' instead. Some people do not like the word Gau, as it reminds them of fateful times.

Try to pronounce the word 'Bezirksmeisterschaft'! As a non-German speaker, you will probably be reminded of the 'Khoisan click-sound language' of some African tribes.

While 'Gau' is an ancient German territorial- and administrative division, the word Gau was unfortunately used during a short, yet adverse time under the Nazi-Regime. Little 'Fuehrers' in each region have, for instance, been titled 'Gau-Leiter' (regional leader).

Can you ban a word from a language, just because it was used as a prefix by bad people during a blemished time of history? The same people had used toilet paper and drank coffee or tea during that period (the latter was – and still is – a favorite pastime of the colonial masters). Must that all be banned?

Stalin had a predilection for music and literature, Mussolini played the violin quite well and Emperor Nero has sung ballads to the harp. The alleged cannibal Idi Amin, British lieutenant of the King's African rifles and African dictator, admired the Scottish resistance to the English, and we have nothing better to do than to ask for the ban of the word 'Gau'?

What has the word done wrong that violins or harps haven't? Do the Scots have to be ashamed, because Idi Amin was one of their admirers?

Tony Blair, this sneaky warmonger, who should be standing trial instead of striking it rich with his 'advisory' company, tells everyone that he owns and occasionally strums a Fender guitar. Nevertheless, Fender Musical Instruments Corporation has never considered a stop to the manufacturing of its world-famous Fender Stratocaster Guitar, because Blair has one. And honestly, if we want to get rid of everything Blair has or had, we could not buy shoes without checking his footwear preferences.

Adolf with the mustache was called 'Fuehrer' (leader). How come that the many 'Weltmarktfuehrers' (world market leaders) in the various industrial sectors have no problem with that word? It is very simple: The word has done nothing wrong.

Another victim of idiocy is the German Shepherd. A bitch of their breed, named 'Blondi', was roaming around on the Obersalzberg (mountain) in Berchtesgaden and was caressed by the crackpot with the mustache for propaganda photos.

Many breeders deeply regret that he had chosen a German Shepherd and that the dog therefore inherited a bad reputation.

Eva Brown, his mistress, had preferred the Scottish terrier, a breed George W. Bush – after all a two-term President of the United States – was not afraid to choose for himself.

The archers should not take part in such stupid baubles. If one puts the German Shepherd and the word Gau into the same context, then the following should lead to some enlightenment:

The German Shepherd is the most popular dog in the world. First and foremost, this dog is a search and rescue dog, most loyal and fearless. And believe it or not, it is also very popular in Israel – no, not only *very popular*, it is the *most popular* dog there. Today, the national race, the Canaan dog, only occupies the 5th position on the canine popularity scale in Israel.

In the year 2009, a Jewish woman from Israel fetched the title 'Best in Breed' in the world-championship for her German shepherd dog named 'Sam Beit Haboxer Mehagiva'. That must have been a hard setback for the misguided promoters of the elimination of the word Gau.

The audience cordially applauded when she left a German breeder in second place at a competition that took place right in the middle of Germany, where 27,000 (!) enthusiastic spectators followed the event in the Grotenburg-Stadium in Krefeld.

In light of these facts, which crazy guy still wants to ban the word 'Gaumeisterschaften' in favor of 'Bezirksmeisterschaften', a word no one outside Germany can pronounce?

The word Gau is an old word of the German language, originally describing a fertile landscape with lots of fresh water. The Gau regions are often named after rivers, like the Jagstgau, the Maingau and of course the Rheingau, one of the locations of wine grapes for England's favorite German wine. The world-famous 'Liebfraumilch' (milk of our beloved Lady), composed of diverse grapes from different regions, is the oldest trademark wine in Germany and mainly exported. It acquired its name from the Gothic 'Church of Our beloved Lady' (Liebfraukirche).

The names also refer to a direction, like Sundgau (South) or the word was integrated in city names like Breisgau, Oberammergau, Saulgau or Gau-Algesheim. Some designations emerged from old Roman settlements. In Franconia, the Gau regions are identical with the old Germanic areas.

Most people do not know that the word Gau is closely related to the comparable term in the Chinese language and known in connection with archery, where the particulars can be followed back to the Shang dynasty 1766-1027 BC.

In connection with regional events, one knows the word 'Gao', which means something like 'feudal province'. 'Gao-Xian' (picture above), for example, is a county in the province of Sichuan, the home of the roasted Sichuan- or Szechuan duck.

One of the five standard books of Confucius, the book of the rites and customs ('li-chi') has a full chapter just on archery. There is a 'jinbiao' (championship) and the one who emerged victoriously, was called 'bashi' (champion).

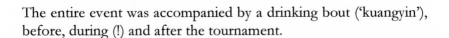

The entire event was accompanied by a drinking bout ('kuangyin'), before, during (!) and after the tournament.

The word Gao was combined with the word 'jinbiao' to become 'gao-jinbiao' (provincial championship) or with the word 'bashi', which describes the provincial champion ('gao-bashi').

The WA – World Archery Association (formerly FITA), has broken with the old Chinese traditions. According to its regulations, smoking is strictly forbidden in the competition area and there is a limit of 0.1 per mil on the maximum alcohol level.

Alcohol may not be consumed during the competition, and in some countries, the consumption of alcohol is even considered to be doping in connection with this sport.

Fortunately, there are no restrictions concerning the time after the event and the 'gao-kuangyin' (the regional drinking binge) can be postponed until the end of the tournament.

'Cheers' or 'Gan-bei!'

And finally a good hint, not only for archers: If you are proposing a toast to Chinese friends or business partners, never say 'Kanpai' like the President of Coca-Cola at a dinner in Washington D.C., in the presence of the President of China, Hu Jintao.

This can result in worse reactions than just loud laughter. 'Kanpei' is Japanese.

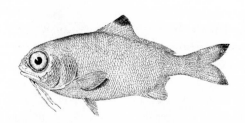

BOW FISHING

Bow and arrow can also be used for fishing – yet most countries do not allow this method. It is, however, very popular – where else – in the USA. The principle is very simple: Tie a long piece of string to an arrow and shoot at the fish.

The water radically reduces the speed of the arrow and the fish is not a hard target, so one can re-use the arrow over and over, even when a shot has missed, unless it strikes a rock. The fish is pulled in with the string, which can be a lot stronger than those used on a fishing rod. The points of the arrow are fitted with barbs, which are either permanent or expanding when the arrow is pulled. The most effective way to shoot is in shallow water and from a short distance. It is difficult to calculate the path of the arrow due to distorted perspectives and light refractions in the water. The fish is not where one sees them and they look larger than they really are.

Bow fishing already existed in the Stone Age, but enthusiastic bow fishers believe that they have developed a method to kill even 'hook-shy' or 'lethargic' fish. I find these terms rather ignorant. Why should a fish not develop a natural instinct against the risks of being caught and becomes reluctant to bite the bait? To the contrary, I think that this is a sign of advanced intelligence, possibly superior to the cerebral function of people exercising this sport just for the fun of it.

Fishing with explosives is a – mostly illegal – method applied worldwide, especially in Russia, where they use old stock of hand grenades from the former Soviet army (often with bad surprises when they sit in a rubber boat). This brings not only fish to the surface with ruptured swim bladders, but also the bodies of other

226

edible or inedible creatures. Following the aforementioned logic concerning hook-shy fish, this method is even more intelligent and effective than fishing with a rod or with bow and arrow.

The 'amusement' of sending barbed arrows into fishes has been discovered in the USA as a new TV format, and some people claim that it is the fastest growing archery 'sport'. According to the DNR (Department of Natural Resources), bow fishing helps the USA to fight invasive species from waterways and supports the efforts to better the environment.

Unfortunately, many of the bow fishers can hardly distinguish the different species, and if they could, they would not restrict themselves to the invasive kind. Too often, they kill harmless aquatic creatures which cannot be eaten anyway. Perhaps the DNR should occasionally look at some bow fishing videos on YouTube. Invasive species? You can watch uncouth people, bawling like drunken passengers on the roller coaster and shooting their arrows not at an individual fish, but right into a school of salmon, from a boat or from ashore, at a place where the salmon gather before they jump a barrier in an attempt to swim upstream.

Lots of women are in the front line of bow-fishing, perhaps because this sport offers the possibility to wear the skimpiest bikinis, ensuring appropriate attention on the Internet, especially with so many 'smartphone-photographers' around.

To put things straight: If you are fishing for food, according to the principle *"eat your game or sell it!"*, then bow fishing might be acceptable and away from mad-brained leisure activities and hence, it can be either a halfway decent sport or a very special form of crazy behavior.

BOW HUNTING FOR BULLFROGS

Bow hunting is allowed in certain parts of the world. In most other places, like in many European countries, it is illegal, and this is also the case in Germany. However, for a certain period in the recent past, this was not entirely true anymore.

One species of animals was free to be hunted with bow and arrow in special regions of Germany, and you will not guess what it was: the American bullfrog 'lithobates catesbeianus'.

This giant among the frogs is neither native to Germany – nor has it been invited into this region of the world map.

The careless abandonment of some species was responsible for the problem that the bullfrog became a massive plague. The lack of natural enemies made it possible that this class of frog was able to proliferate without inhibition.

The skin of their offspring appears to have a natural antigen that keeps large fish, like the carp, from eating the tadpoles of the frog. Only in their inborn environment in the USA, some fish and snakes decimate the offspring of the frogs.

In order to cope with the proportion of this plague, tests have been performed with predatory wide head eels. But, together with the giant baby tadpoles in the same body of water, the eels lost their appetite and did not eat anything for days, neither the baby tadpoles, nor any other grub on their usual menu.

The insatiable appetite of the 'lithobates catesbeianus' urges it to eat smaller local relatives, fledglings of water birds and – as an occasional change of variety on its menu – its own species.

In addition, this menacing frog will devour fish, fully-grown birds, mice, rats and other rodents, crustaceans, snakes and bats.

The predator's ferocious appetite will often cause it to choke on some thoughtlessly swallowed bite. Occasionally, one can even see the beak of a kingfisher sticking out of its belly. It is said that there are specimen of the bullfrog in Canada that have attacked dogs and cats and even jumped at humans.

Nevertheless, some of these stories seem to be exaggerated, like the occasionally mentioned body size of 12 inches (30.5 centimeters) of an adult specimen, whereas 8 inches (20.3 centimeters) come closer to the truth. More than 2 pounds of body weight are normal for a large frog, and females have been found with a weight of almost four and a half pounds.

In this special case, we can dispel the often expressed opinion that these creatures are originating from the CIA labs, like so many other obscure objects on this planet. It is a fact that the bullfrog from the Antilles, for example, has already separated from its relatives on the continent some 23 to 24 million years ago.

The 'Pavarotti of the frogs', which also has a strong and impressive voice, came to Germany, presumably through the zoo trade and pet shops and had escaped from garden ponds and aquariums.

Many owners simply dumped them into nearby waters when the fellows had grown too big or when their croaking – "*croak, croak, croak*" – had become unbearable.

The region around the city of Karlsruhe was hit hardest by the bullfrog plague. According to officials, there had been a pet shop

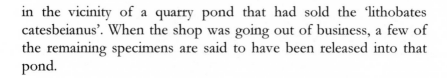

in the vicinity of a quarry pond that had sold the 'lithobates catesbeianus'. When the shop was going out of business, a few of the remaining specimens are said to have been released into that pond.

Close to the little village of Eggenstein is a water area, about the size of fifty acres, which was massively infested. The nightly croaking of the bullfrogs should have already been noticed in the year 1996 or earlier. Yet, nobody has taken any serious action, not even the local fishing association, when two thousand hand-sized tadpoles had been fished out of the waters.

It was only after a diver reported in the year 2001 that a giant, strange frog was wreaking havoc, when people suddenly became alarmed. Shortly thereafter, 'bow hunting for bullfrogs' became allowed in this region.

This turned out to be a lame-brained method, often accompanied by foolish arguments, which did not allow admitting that the hunting was just for the fun of it. Certainly, a more practical approach would have been to catch the tadpoles, thereby effectively interrupting the chain of reproduction, rather than aiming with bow and arrow at live balloons.

Female frogs spawn with some fifteen- to twenty-five thousand eggs, any many of them mature freely due to lack of any natural enemies. If the new females can reproduce at the same levels, the use of bow and arrow – to shoot at individual animals – can hardly be an effective method. On top of it, this all becomes very expensive, considering the many arrows that are shredded and lost.

Fences protected the waters, including rivers and ponds of Boeblingen and the neighboring city of Meckenheim. The Sea of Meckenheim, however, fell prey to the infestation and had to be drained and dried out to a large extend, after more than twenty thousand tadpoles had been caught over the years.

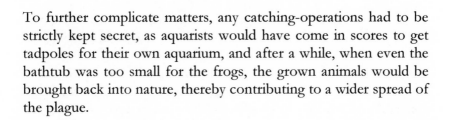

To further complicate matters, any catching-operations had to be strictly kept secret, as aquarists would have come in scores to get tadpoles for their own aquarium, and after a while, when even the bathtub was too small for the frogs, the grown animals would be brought back into nature, thereby contributing to a wider spread of the plague.

Many owners of garden ponds are of the opinion that the oversized tadpoles would effectively take care of grubs of the mosquitoes.

Not so quick! In this early stage of development, the giant frogs are still vegetarians and just eat the plants. Only after the tadpoles have transformed into frogs, they get an 'appetite for meat' and occasionally even attack the owners and their pets.

Close to one of the affected ponds, there is a little creek with a direct connection to the Rhine River. That is a gate to the largest river in Germany. Some specimens are said to have been seen in its tributaries.

The first bullfrogs came to Germany in the year 1934. Five breeding pairs had been imported from Philadelphia, USA, to provide the basis for a frog's leg production, but shortly after the mass production had started, some citizens became scared and the plant was closed soon thereafter.

Coincidence of history: 1934 was the year, when bow hunting in Germany was no longer allowed. This was included in the legislation, which later became part of the state hunting laws.

There are continuous attempts to legally permit bow hunting in Germany again. The 'Deutscher Bogenjagd Verband' (German Bow hunting Association), founded in the year 1999, is working hard towards this goal.

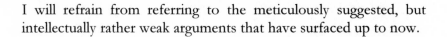

I will refrain from referring to the meticulously suggested, but intellectually rather weak arguments that have surfaced up to now.

The promoters of bow hunting have gone so far as to say that bow and arrow would be a safe and unspectacular alternative to conventional hunting in peripheral areas like parks and – brace yourself! – in cemeteries.

Preservation of peace in graveyards through bow hunting? I am neither a physician nor a psychiatrist, but I ask myself if there is a special diagnosis for such a statement? In any case, I doubt very much that there is a sufficiently strong remedy.

Logic is not always a blessing bestowed on the Bow Hunter Federation Austria – BFA. They underline the long tradition of hunting with bow and arrow and state that 'Oetzi' ('Frozen Fritz', the mummy they have found in the Alps a few years ago) was not killed with a 'Steyr Mannlicher' (Austrian cult brand for hunting rifles), but with bow and arrow.

I fully agree that no rifle had been used 5000 years ago, but I am also absolutely sure that 'Oetzi' was not shot with a compound bow, which is the equipment predominantly used and promoted for bow hunting. Holles Wilbur Allen Jr., from Kansas, USA, the inventor of this bow, applied for a patent on June 23, 1966, which was granted in December 1969. There is a separate chapter on this bow in this book (page 264).

Moreover, did anyone tell the Bow Hunter Federation Austria that the efforts for legalizing the bow hunt aim at hunting for game and not murdering humans crossing the Alps?

There must be a long – widely unknown – tradition of the English language in Lower Austria, the seat of the Federation, which would be the reason that this organization is not called 'Oesterreichische Bogenjaeger Vereinigung', but 'Bow Hunter Federation Austria'.

Perhaps, when choosing an English name for their association, they mainly had in mind that they have to go abroad for their bow hunting hobby and any hotel reservation under the Austrian tongue-twisting name would harbor a too great risk of misspelling.

So, the bullfrog has revived hunting with bow and arrow in Germany – at least temporarily and to a small degree. But some thoughts are reaching further. The City of Berlin thinks about tackling the plague of wild boars with bow and arrow.

The bullfrog is merely a part of an overall threat that some people want to limit with bow and arrow. There are many illegally imported species of animals and their offspring out in nature, which are a dangerous threat to the local flora and fauna.

Animals often escape or are abandoned because turtles soon grow too big or a snake will get sick. Some zoological gardens are confronted with the unsolvable situation to accommodate thousands of such creatures year after year.

But can you tackle these problems with bow and arrow?

On the other side of the Rhine River, in France, one turns the handicap into an advantage.

The country has a well-known passion for eating strange things like frogs and frog's legs, bull testicles, pig's feet, rooster's comb, cow brains or snails.

In the case of a bullfrog, one leg is already sufficient for a (French) meal.

In this country, characterized by culinary peculiarities, one is *catching* the frogs and deals with the problem in the following way:

-   Take the frog leg, coat it lightly with flour, and melt some butter in a pan at moderate heat.

-   Mix it with olive oil, put the leg into the pan, and fry it until it is golden brown from both sides.

-   Season it with pepper and salt during the roasting and gradually add further small pieces of butter.

-   Take out the leg and arrange it on a preheated plate.

-   Drain the fried butter, save it, add white wine to the roast clause and half of the parsley, and steam everything for a few seconds.

-   Mix in the rest of the butter, pour it over the leg and add the other half of the parsley.

'Bon appétit!'

ARROWS – ONLY MADE FOR SHOOTING?

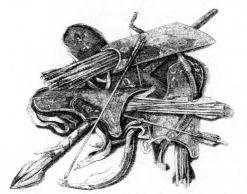 **N**ot always! Arrows have for instance been used as items for gaming and lotteries, already at a very early stage. When the arrows are in a quiver, one cannot see the complete shaft, and someone, someday, must have come up with the idea to letter the arrows and use them as lots!

Perhaps, this was already invented during the early Stone Age, as a way of passing time while waiting during a hunting trip. Whenever this practice may have begun, it soon became a widespread habit, which is occasionally still followed today.

Even the Quran refers to gambling with arrows and warns of the 'Maysir', an Arab arrow lottery as a work of the devil. The Maysir can become very addictive, and one can easily and quickly ruin oneself and the entire family.

A camel is slaughtered for the Maysir lottery and, according to the number of participants, lettered arrows are put into a quiver, which are then drawn by the players. The arrows are labeled differently, and the markings refer to a specific quantity of the meat, which is then given to the player who has picked out this particular arrow.

The sum of all marked arrows equals one hundred percent. One arrow is left blank and the player who draws it receives nothing. Now it becomes a lot worse: This player has to pay for the entire camel.

So, if someone participates in the Maysir and draws the right arrow, he goes home with more or less of the meat without paying for any of it. However, one can also be unlucky and lose a lot of money for nothing. If there are one hundred players, there is a risk ratio of 1:99, which can be rather tempting for some optimistic people. How about, if we try something like that at the next barbecue of the archery club?

Arrows have often been used in oracles. The quiver was turned upside down and the positions of the arrows, which had fallen out, had been interpreted to forecast a person's destiny or to make predictions about the fortune in the hunt that followed.

In pre-Islamic times, gods were asked for their approval before important undertakings. There were three arrows in the quiver. One was labeled with approval, another one was for refusal and one arrow was left blank. The oracle was questioned according to a fixed ritual, until a distinct decision came up.

In early Islamic traditions, bow and arrow played a central role. Adam, as the first human being, is said to have received a bow and arrows as a gift from God, and an archangel has taught him how to use these weapons.

The prophet Muhammad himself had six bows. He once said: *"The angels do not carry out any sport of the humans, except archery."*

It is said that Muhammad himself had the idea to enter the area of practice only barefoot, so that the arrows which have missed the target, are detected and not crushed with the soles of the shoes.

Now I know where the suggestion comes from to walk barefoot across the lawn, when all attempts to find lost arrows have failed.

I assume that works equally well, both on grass and in the sand.

HERACLES AND BOW AND ARROW

Here is another – and last one – of the lunatic Greek myths. It tells us that bow and arrow can be less effective when it comes to kill a monster than strangling it with bare hands. If you already know this story, but with another main character, then you think of the Roman version, where Heracles is called Hercules.

At the beginning of the myth, which was most likely written again under the heavy influence of opiates, we have the godfather Zeus, cavorting around in his usual fashion. This time, the ancient sex addict, whose actions were mainly controlled from an organ three feet below his brain, fell in love with Alcmene.

As we are just about to leave the madhouse of Greek mythology, let us go back once more into early history, where the biggest chunk of Greek myths begins. In one of the many variations of the 'big bang', the order was the following: At the beginning was chaos, a gaping abyss without beginning and end. The misty fog around already contained the primary components of all life: Earth, water, fire and air. The primordial gods came up and Gaia (Earth) was followed by Erebos (darkness), Nyx (night), Tartaros (underworld) and Eros or Cupid (god of love).

Gaia gave birth to Uranus (Sky) and Pontos (Sea) in asexual reproduction. Gaia wanted to speed up things and 'teamed up' with her son Uranus. They had many children, among which six brothers and sisters, who became married to each other and were themselves blessed with large offspring in one form or another.

Cronus, one of the sons of Gaia and Uranus, had six children with his sister Rhea: Hestia, Hades, Demeter, Poseidon, Hera and Zeus. Soon, a large number of divine and half-divine powers populated the world and – no wonder in this depraved breeding environment – many Titans, Cyclopes, Giants and creatures, with a hundred arms and several heads, frolicked on Earth.

Cronos had learned from his mother Gaia that he was destined to be overcome by one of his children as he had overthrown his own father Uranus. Cronos then decided to eat all of his offspring. Zeus, the last child, was saved as Rhea gave Cronos a stone instead, wrapped in swaddling clothes. He ate it with good appetite, and Zeus was secretly born in Crete.

Zeus married Hera, one of his sisters who had been eaten by Cronos and they had several children together.

Wait a second! How can Zeus marry his sister Hera, when her father had eaten her? The old Greeks found a solution: Cronos had to throw up and the stone, given to him instead of Zeus, came out, as well as all the already swallowed children. But perhaps it was just a stomach upset after he had read a Greek fantasy story.

Amphitryon, the husband of Alcmene, fled from Mycenae after he had slain his father-in-law Electryon. Zeus took advantage of the situation and transformed himself into Amphitryon. She was totally unsuspecting and so he could father a son with her, named Heracles.

At the beginning of the story, Zeus has the ability to take the shape of Amphitryon, but then, the pen-pusher of this horrible tale did not have the imagination to come up with new effects; perhaps the sway of the drugs began to wane. Oh my! As the nonsensical story continues, the whole plot was exposed when Amphitryon returned. Zeus was miraculously deprived of his miracle powers and completely helpless.

Come on! Every vacuum cleaner representative can cope with such a situation and hides for a while in the bedroom closet.

The husband had forgiven his wife and instantly fathered a son with her, called Iphicles. As also Heracles had just been fathered, both Heracles and Iphicles were born together and therefore, they are officially twins.

I was always curious to know what happens when fraternal twins are produced, especially when they often look so different. One reason is the production of high levels of estrogen, which stimulates the ovaries to produce more than one egg at a time. Fraternal twins can have more than one father (which is not so seldom the case), a phenomenon that is known as 'superfetation'. Prominent examples of different looking fraternal twins (regardless of one or two fathers) are: Robin and Maurice Gibb, Arnold Schwarzenegger and Danny de Vito or Jenna and Barbara Bush.

Hera, sister-wife of Zeus, discovered the whole process and became – as usual on such occasions – furiously jealous and was about to make life difficult for Heracles. When the birth of the 'twin half-brothers' came near, Zeus had decreed that the firstborn child would become Master of Mycenae. Zeus, first in the action, was convinced that this would be Heracles. However, there was another child due to be born in the house of the Perseus family, namely Eurystheus, son of Sthenelus, an uncle of Amphitryon. Hera delayed the contradictions of Alcmene, and Heracles and his twin-half-brother Iphicles were born after Eurystheus.

Alcmene, in fear of Hera, abandoned her son Heracles outside the city walls of Thebes. His elder half-sister Athena (daughter of Zeus and Metis) found him and took the child – of all things – into the house of Hera. She was unaware and even nursed him out of pity. Heracles was sucking so hard for the milk that Hera pushed him away. The milk squirted all over and a portion of it reached the sky and formed the Milky Way, still visible today.

Yes, dear reader, this is the ancient Greek explanation for the Milky Way! An impressive act in every respect. The name Heracles means: 'The one who gained fame on Hera'.

Athena finally brought the kid back to his real mother Alcmene, where Heracles grew up with his brother. When he was just eight years old, Hera sent two giant snakes into the chamber of the children. Iphicles was afraid and crying, but Heracles grabbed the snakes and strangled them. Thereupon, the prophet Teiresias predicted a great future for Heracles and told him that he would defeat and kill many monsters.

Heracles learned to handle a chariot, the fistfight, singing and playing the lyre, but had some major problems with the latter. His teacher Ismenios wanted to improve his technique. When he refused, Ismenios beat him, whereupon Heracles took the lyre, smashed it on the teacher's head and killed him. Heracles was acquitted at subsequent court proceedings, but was banished to a farm until the age of eighteen.

Nevertheless, the rampage of Heracles continued. He destroyed a city that was at war with Thebes. Hera liked the dwellers of this town and punished Heracles with mental illness. Strength combined with mental illness – that is an extremely dangerous mix. Heracles killed the sons of his twin brother Iphicles and six of his friends, because he thought they were enemies.

When he was clear-headed again, he consulted the oracle of Delphi to find out how things will go on. The oracle told him to go to Tyrins. There he should meet Eurystheus, serve him and fulfill every one of his commands. His reward would be an elevation to the rank of a god. Heracles immediately went away to Tyrins. After his arrival, he was directly confronted with his primary assignment. As the first of his twelve tasks, he was asked to kill the oversized Nemean lion. This was a difficult mission, as the fur from this monster could easily resist iron, bronze or stones.

According to the Greek scribbles, this big lion had either fallen from the moon or it was a descendant of Typhon and Echidna. I think it has most likely fallen from the moon, as the alleged parents Typhon and Echidna have been monsters with a highly unpleasant look. As a product of such horrible creatures, no offspring could look like a lion.

Typhon was a monster with a hundred dragon- and snakeheads, which were able to speak the different languages of the gods and the animals. Echidna, his mother, half girl, half ugly looking serpent, had also been the mother of other horror figures, which all had a look closer to the one of their producers Typhon and Echidna, like the two-headed Orthos or the three-headed hell-hound Cerberus.

Finally, we have bow and arrow in the story, but *not* to the honor of this weapon. Heracles took his bow and a few arrows and looked for the monster lion. When he finally had found him and stood in its way, he shot all his arrows at the beast, but they just bounced off without doing any harm. He threw away his useless bow and hit the lion with his sword – just bending it. He tore out an olive tree, broke off a branch and used it as a club. The lion only shook its head, not because it hurt, but only as the rumble in the skull annoyed it.

Heracles remembered what he had done in a similar situation when he was eight years old. He forgot about the ineffective archery weapons, the sword or the club. He just walked over and strangled the lion with his bare hands.

Using the claws of the dead monster, he cut open its fur, from which he made his famous cape. It became his trademark, besides bow and a quiver filled with arrows, which he kept as symbols despite the poor performance. Later, the Nemean lion was sent up by Hera as a constellation in the sky.

 As we now have finished the last chapter with antique Greek rubbish, I shall not withhold some essential information about an important document. It is a scrap of papyrus with a poem about Heracles, called 'The Heracles (Hercules) Papyrus'. It is kept at the Sackler Library of the University of Oxford and has a size of 235 by 106 millimeters (9.25 by 4.2 inches). The 106 millimeters (4.2 inches) are – more or less – the width of toilet paper.

If this is, what I presume, a fraction of a longer piece, it could confirm another suspicion: The Greek myths have been written to kill time and to be read while the Hellenes sat on the loo.

The width of toilet paper in most European countries is 96 mm and in the USA 4.5" (114.3 mm). The regular left-hand roll in the UK also has a size of 4.5" (114.3 mm) and the smaller version, called 'the cheater roll', also has the standard European size.

The standard length of toilet paper in Europe is about 115 to 125 mm, while the 4.5" measurement in the USA and the UK is square size, so the old Greek certainly had a good length per sheet.

Don't worry, your hands are not getting bigger! The size of toilet tissue has been reduced in the last decades as manufacturers try to trim cost by trimming sheet size.

RATI AND KAMA

From the antique Greek myths, we know the god of love Eros (Cupid). The Indian myths present us with two different gods of similar function, Rati and Kama. They have more abstract and subtle contours, if one can at all use sophisticated adjectives in connection with these wild fantasies.

Before you get confused with similar stories: There are so many variations of the Indian myths, that you cannot come up with a universal version.

Rati is the daughter of Daksa, one of the ten Prajapatis. She is the Hindu goddess of love, carnal desire, lust, passion and sexual pleasure. As a means of transport, she rides on a goose, composed of five female figures, ready to shoot fire arrows from a sugar cane bow. Many sculptures stress her beauty, which inspires such awe that she can even enchant the god of love Kama – the second god created by the Indians who takes responsibility for love affairs. He, like Cupid, circulates his arrows to spread love throughout, and Rati became a constant companion of Kama in many legends.

Kama is described as a handsome young man who carries around a bow, also made from sugar cane, and arrows of flowers to spread love.

What makes him a little different from Cupid is the fact that he has green skin (which might or might not contradict with the term handsome) and that he is sitting on a bird, although he is mostly shown with his own wings.

243

Rati and Kama got married and had two children, Harsha ('Joy') and Yashas ('Grace'). When the god Shiva, one of the highest Gods in the various Indian traditions, burned Kama to ashes, Rati begged for his resurrection, which frequently occurs when Kama is reborn again as Pradyumna, the son of Krishna (he was the one who stole the butter).

Pradyumna (ex-Kama) was separated at birth from his parents, Krishna and Rukmini. Rati – now under the name of Mayavati – plays an important role in the childcare. She acted as his nanny, and when that became a little boring, she became his lover – after all, she was once his spouse. Later on, Pradyumma accepts nanny Mayavati as his wife, thereby uniting Rati and Kama again.

In order to streamline the hodgepodge of different versions within the Indian myths, I have chosen some more popular interpretations to bring the story to its end in a halfway understandable fashion.

In the beginning, the Chief-Executive-Creator Brahma created the ten Prajapatis. They were needed to assist him in various tasks related to cosmic matters, laws of nature or in arranging of the course our planet should take. One of the Prajapatis wanted to present a wife to Kama. Shortly before, Kama wanted to come up with something funny and shot his arrows of love at Brahma and his entire staff. Immediately all the Prajapatis were attracted to Brahma's daughter Sarasvati, including Brahma himself.

Shiva just happened to walk by and found that all very funny and laughed. Nevertheless, Brahma and his Prajapatis became afraid of Shiva and started to shiver and perspire. This indicates that Shiva must have been at a somewhat higher level on the Board of Management of Indian gods; why else would Chief-Executive-Creator Brahma and his team of Assistant-Creators shiver? Whatever, Rati – a beautiful woman – rose from the sweat of the Prajapati. He presented her to Kama and they got married.

And what concerns the birth of Kama (also called Kamadeva): He was born from the mind of Brahma. Right after his birth, he stood in front of his creator and asked *"kam darpayani?"* (whom shall I please?). The answer came promptly: *"Move around in this world and engage yourself in the eternal work of creation with your five arrows of flowers and thus multiply the population."*

Only *five* arrows to shoot, and Kama hit Brahma and all his *ten* Prajapatis? It took many years to repeat such a 'stunt', when Rambo always shot *five* arrows out of a supply of *four*, as you will find out in a later chapter of this book about the compound bow.

I find it hard to believe that this story, as well as the yarn fabricated by the Greeks with Eros (Cupid), their god of love, has been independently developed. This is also valid for many Greek myths and all the incestuous relationships, up and down, sideways and then again crisscrossed within the family or the weird constructions within the group of the gods and the numerous variations of this outlandish crap. It is more likely that travelers, back in those times, have picked up all this drivel and it was then copied over and over.

Many Indian myths, especially the stories surrounding Rati, belong to the most obscene smut in the world of literature and make 'Lady Chatterley's lovers', 'Madam Bovary' or the 'Last Exit to Brooklyn' look like episodes of a Mickey Mouse magazine. But the Indians are able to top even the worst.

Chinnamasta, a goddess, had accidentally stepped on Rati and Kama, who just happened to be engaged in a sexual encounter in the viparita-rate position (Rati on top) – suggesting female dominance.

My goodness, what a mess! Where and on what occasion can you accidentally step on an intertwined couple, if you do not happen to be at the Woodstock Festival?

Instead of just stepping down and walking away, she took her scimitar and cut off her own head which she then held in her hand. She remained standing on the couple, but turned her eyes – or better the head in her hand – away, in order not to look too closely at the couple under her feet and to demonstrate self-control over her sexual desires. Blood pours out of her neck and on Rati and Kama, but they do not interrupt the action.

Two women accompany Chinnamasta, and they all wear a chain of severed male heads around their neck. These strange necklaces demonstrate that they have their own way to cope with the desires of men.

To top the old Greeks and their bizarre fantasies is not so easy. Ordinary people cannot come even close to producing such animalistic junk, no matter what they smoke, unless they pass across a special plant, called Cannabis ('Cannabis sativa'). The plant grows wild in particular locations in India and becomes the basis for the most potent form of drugs you can get, made from natural ingredients.

Excessive use of Cannabis could be the reason for the weird content of some Indian myths and I have to stress that we talk about are the Indians from India here and not the Indians of America, who have their own problems with their folk stories.

Honestly, this Indian confusion gets to my nerves. When Columbus discovered America, he thought that he had found a new way to India. When he first met the Native Americans, he erroneously named them 'Indians', and we still don't have a specific name for them, more than 500 years after this mishap.

LUMBAGO

Not far back in our history, people believed that lumbago is something that has been caused by a jinxed arrow. There are two different variations as to who has sent that unfriendly missile: a magician or a witch.

When triggered by 'magic', according to this foolish assumption, the magician throws a spiked arrow at his victim, which decomposes after the impact, resulting in severe pain.

This spell works on the astral body of vertebrates and derived intelligent species like humans, elves, dwarfs or halflings and all ghosts coming from these groups. Vampires and the 'undead' are not affected by this spell.

In the German speaking countries, lumbago is still called a 'Hexenschuss' (a shot coming from a witch). This term originates from the Middle Ages, blaming witches and their arrows for the pain.

During the persecution of heretics and witches by the Roman Church, called the Inquisition, thousands of women had been burned at the stake, because they were accused to be witches. The favorite accusation brought forward by the papal inquisitors – undoubtedly caused by a malfunction of their brain combined with religious delusions – was 'harmful magic'.

In medieval presentations, one often sees witches equipped with bow and arrow, demonstrating the 'long distance effect' of their harmful magic. The arrow thereby represents the malady.

It took some time, even for the scientists, to discount this theory and to recognize its invalid interpretation. Under medical aspects, this ailment is triggered by other causes.

I therefore want to leave a message for the Inquisition department of the Vatican in Rome, which is furthermore an urgent request to incorporate the following text passage into the next update of the operating instructions of their field service:

Lumbago' is a sudden and sharp pain in the sensitive lumbar spine, caused by the self-innervation (the nerves that supply the spinal cord itself). Lumbago is not a disease pattern, but only a collective term for sudden pain in this area, which leaves a lot of room for speculations, but it is *not* – repeat *not* – caused by witches and their arrows.

Maniera di bruciare quelli che furono condannati dalla Inquisizione.

'Maniera di bruciare quelli che furono condannati dall'Inquisizione'
(The way to burn those who were condemned by the Inquisition)

ENGLISH LONGBOWS – THE 'ATOMIC BOMB OF THE MIDDLE AGES'?

Bow and arrow have always encouraged story writing, yet no other bow has inspired more legends and myths than the English longbow. In their time, these bows were surely impressive military equipment – but within obvious limits.

The successes of the English longbow archers – in some battles against numerically far superior armies of the French – are among the most frequently cited of the great events of the military history of the Middle Ages.

The first major appearance of the longbow archers was mainly due to empty state coffers. King Edward had financially overstretched himself when he recruited his mercenaries and soon had to do without their services, as far as possible. In the end, he had to hire the lower paid archers, who had to plunder through Normandy to earn their pay. The French, obviously, did not like that the English could not pay regular salaries to their military, but allowed them to rob in French territory instead.

When the French finally put together an impressive army, Edward ran away with bag and baggage to Flanders. The French followed and soon, the pursuers came closer.

It was in the year 1346 when Edward had chosen a suitable defense on a hill at Crécy. The French considered this just a routine matter, which would quickly pass. However, neither were their Genoese crossbowmen utilized in a sensible way, nor was the army effectively organized. Arrogantly and prematurely, the French attacked, directly out of the deployment of the troops.

According to the stories told, the French were always pounded with arrows from the English longbow archers and at the end, the battlefield was covered with more than a thousand French knights, while the English suffered barely any losses.

Now, the point is: The longbow archers, originally hired due to a lack of money, had done no more as to help to beat an enemy that simply acted in an imprudent, arrogant and above all, unorganized way. Be that as it may, the legend was born.

The English had a similar success in two other battles, which took place 10 years later in 1356 and – another 59 years later – in 1415, but in the end, the Hundred Years War was lost. Subsequently, the Kings of England were not able to assert their claim to the French throne, which was held by the House of the Valois, but this was only of marginal interest in the many legends.

In contrast to the historical reality, the miracle stories of the legendary longbow escalated into the supernatural. The historians have cleverly condensed three major battles won by the English – in 100 (!) years.

The longbow was definitively no wonder weapon. Early in the 14th century, the arrows could indeed penetrate a coat of chain mail, but which type? A well-equipped knight or nobleman usually had a very good and impenetrable armor, while the common soldier had to be satisfied with inferior models.

Good armor was often tested with arrows, which were even shot at from a stronger crossbow and resisted without any problem. In other words, inferior equipment of some of the French opponents further contributed to the 'phenomenal' success of the longbow.

And, dealing with the Hundred Years' War, we should not forget to mention Joan of Arc. She was largely responsible for the victory of the French, when she and her men broke the siege of Orleans in the year 1428. She did not happily live thereafter, as the Bishop of Beauvais, Pierre Cauchons, a vassal of the English, took care that she was burned at the stake. Joan was sainted in later times.

In summary: Neither the outstanding characteristics of the English longbow, nor any unusual capabilities of the longbow archers have been the main reason for the success on the English side in some battles of this long lasting war. It was, to a far larger extend, mainly due to some poor equipment of the enemy and, moreover, the ignorance and arrogance of the French nobility, who preferred to jump into the turmoil of a battle without tactics and discipline.

Whatever, the warfare in those days had soon reached a complexity that made it necessary to have a coordinated and well-exercised acting of all military units and the different types of weapons. When the French had learned their lessons – most of them the hard way – the 'magic' of the longbow was soon over. In the year 1450 at Formigny, the French lured the English archers out of their hiding and just rode them down with their horses. In this battle, the French had lost just 200 of their men, although they were confronted with 3000 English archers on the other side, who perished without any fanfare.

If one glances at the first great battle of Crecy in more detail, the success of the longbows should be critically reviewed for another reason. 6000 longbow archers, who were allegedly able to fire 12 arrows per minute, stood behind a hedge. The French attacked on foot and had sent two groups of 200 horsemen ahead. At the end, there was this hedge, impenetrable for the horses and a small path in-between, just wide enough to allow five of their horses to get through at a time. How could the French, as reported, have run up fifteen times or more against the English *with all their men*, when their troops had been hindered this way from advancing?

Often, the arrows did not penetrate any iron plates or leather saddle pads which protected the attackers, but shattered or bounced off from other obstacles and the pieces flew back between friends and enemies. In the end, the battle was not decided by the longbows, as longbow fans believe (I am one of them), but only when the English horsemen entered the battle.

An honest evaluation of the facts comes from the English themselves and their historian Jonathan Sumption, one of the most renowned experts in this field, said: *"The longbow had a comparatively small role in the victories of the English in the 14th century. It was fit for limited duties against the French cavalry, by wounding the horses on their unprotected flank, whereby the horseman remained lying on the ground with his heavy suit of armor. They have been much more effective against the men on foot."*

And what concerns the victorious battle of Auray in the year 1365, Sumption noted: *"The English archers, although largely represented, contributed almost nothing to the outcome of the battle. The French were better in combat on foot and pushed forward under a roof of shields they had held up. After the English longbow men saw that they had achieved nothing, they threw away their bows and entered the fray with cutting and stabbing arms."*

There are other reports on these battles telling us that bowmen had been executed for running away from hand-to-hand combat that had followed later in the action.

Therefore, one does certainly not meet the truth in the belief that the longbow archers hunted their opponents like rabbits. The bombardment with arrows was just one of their tasks, thereafter they were sent to the slaughter as a light cavalry.

However, leadership and tactics improved over time. By then, combined with a lot of luck – especially when they fought against a careless enemy – the archers had also gained some self-confidence and earned a bit of fame, yet of somewhat limited dimension.

When the English and the French finally arrived at peace, the longbow archers had lost their job. They traveled through Europe with other unemployed mercenaries, just to face a nasty surprise.

When they were hired in Italy, they did not meet ignorant French feudal horsemen, but professional and combat-tested soldiers and were handed a solid beating.

The Italian chronicler Filippo Villani mainly praised the heavy armament of the mercenaries that they brought along from France. And what about the 'famous' archers? He just noted condescendingly: *"They were better during nightly raids and were more up to stealing than to fight well in the field. Their success was more due to the cowardice of our people than to the bravery of the archers."*

Charles the Bold of Burgundy recruited thousands of English longbow archers. In the years 1476 and 1477, near Nancy, his armies were simply overrun by the Swiss infantry. The Swiss mercenary was less protected than a French knight in heavy armor, but much more mobile and, above all, far more disciplined.

When Henry VIII. wanted to come back to previous glory and invaded France, he soon had to realize – greatly downcast – that there would be no more harvesting with his 'famous' archers and was bound to recruit other mercenaries. His daughter Elizabeth I., who succeeded him on the throne, accepted the consequences and decreed that the longbow men were excluded from the recruitment.

It is a well-known fact that Henry VIII. was mentally disturbed. His six marriages, the fate of the beheaded and divorced women and the ongoing quarrels with the Pope, are part of world history and interesting themes for movies and dramas. England, the USA and Canada teamed up for the historical television series 'The Tudors', produced for the American premium cable television channel Showtime, whilst Ireland provided most of the scenery.

Not all the wives of Henry VIII. landed on the scaffold, as widely assumed. The English remember their individual fate with the words *"divorced, beheaded, died, divorced, beheaded, survived"*.

In fact, his last wife, Catherine Parr, had survived her husband Henry VIII. and was the only English Queen who was married four times. She had already twice become a widow – in suspiciously rapid succession – before she wedded Henry VIII., and when she got married to the monster, she had already previously secured her fourth husband, Thomas Seymour.

Despite all those definite facts, modern historians and longbow freaks do not get tired to work on the longbow legends. I am a longbow archer myself, but if I would play golf, I would not promote legends telling people that in the old days some Scottish golfers were able to hit their balls behind the moon.

The original longbows were hard to handle and often had draw weights of up to 150 pounds or more. Sports archers, today, come closer to 35 to 40 pounds and traditional archers shoot recurve- and longbows, where the draw weight goes up to 50 or 60 pounds, of course with state-of-the-art material and constructions.

Hard training was necessary to draw and effectively shoot the old longbows and one had to start practicing early in his youth. If a peasant had several sons, it was common practice that his eldest son inherited the farm and the others were often skilled to become longbow archers and sent away to the military.

Penetrating power and range of shooting were more important than accuracy, which had to be classified as rather poor. This is why all the rubbish about Robin Hood and his famous shots makes no sense at all.

It was Napoleon III., who spread around the nonsense that the *average (!)* English longbow archer was able to shoot 12 arrows per minute, thereby missing the target at 200 meters (218.7 yards) only once. An English 'historian' excitedly picked up this exaggerated statement. He increased the enthusiasm when he said that the English longbow archers could have prevented the defeat of Napoleon Bonaparte (Napoleon I.) at Waterloo in the year 1815 and would have caused a bloodbath among his opponents.

He was probably still very impressed that two years earlier, archers contributed to another solid defeat of Napoleon I. However, the Bashkir and Tatar horsemen and their archers in the Battle of Nations against Napoleon in the year 1813 (see the chapter 'The last battle with bow and arrow', page 281) did not have a decisive influence on the outcome of the battle and they also did not shoot with a longbow, but with a more effective composite bow. Besides their brave employment, it was also the surprising effect of the archer's appearance, as the enemy soldiers believed they had been drawn into a time tunnel and were involved in the wrong war.

Why was the longbow – this alleged wonder weapon – so swiftly abandoned at a certain point of time, apart from the invention of the crossbow and the gunpowder? Why do we know so little about the longbows, apart from the exaggerated legends around the Hundred Years' War, while the other longbow stories are usually just cheap legends, dealing more with bandits and raids?

Did they run out of men who were able to draw such a strong bow? Was it the lack of old yew, the classic wood for those bows, which was overexploited in Europe at some stage?

It seems to come closer to the truth that the longbow has never been a major weapon overall. The myths and legends that deal with the importance of the longbows during the Crusades, had been just wishful thinking. The major use of the English longbow began, when the Crusades were a thing of the past (1291). Richard the Lionheart even came back from a Crusade as an ardent proponent of the crossbow.

The longbows have mainly been a supplement to the range of weapons in the armies and have forced the enemy to tactical changes or kept them at a distance for a while. They came back to proper honor much later and into our time, as hunting- and sporting gear, especially when (but not only) the Americans had begun to improve the old equipment, notwithstanding the fact that parallel to this development, other and more modern types of bows have been developed.

Modern longbows (better referred to as flatbows) are not made of a single piece of wood (a stave), but of bonded layers of different kinds of wood, as well as glass material or carbon fiber. They usually have a slight deflex-reflex shape, which is more pronounced on the recurve bows. In addition, modern synthetic material for the strings provides for greater dynamic.

The old English longbow has maintained its charm – with or without untrue legends – up to the present time. For the fans of the Middle Ages who live out their passion during the LARP (Live Action Role Play) events, it is essential props, like woolen socks or the scratchy linen shirt. From time to time, I also shoot such a 'dinosaur of archery', with a much lower draw weight of course.

Whatever, the English longbow was never – or at least not for long – the decisive weapon of war. If one takes explosive power as a yardstick, it was rather a firecracker, instead of the 'atomic bomb of the middle ages', as some people put it.

I habitually use a modern flatbow, made in Scotland, when I let the arrows fly. When I participated in a traditional Scottish 'Bow Fest' near Kelso, I brought the bow along and back to where it was manufactured, right into the Border Region, once inhabited by the Border Reivers – feared raiders along the Anglo-Scottish border.

I returned safely, with the bow – *and* the victory in my division. *Yaldi!* (untranslatable Scottish outcry of extreme joy).

A BLACK KITE WAS IN THE WAY

The Mongols believe that the sun is rising and setting, just because a bird got in the way of an arrow shot.

My goodness! In the Mongolian steppes, they must also have produced some strong stuff that clouded the mind of their poets so much that the writers came up with folktales and legends, high up on the Richter-scale for literary bullshit.

The Arkhi, a schnapps made from kefir, is more comparable to wine as it reaches only an alcoholic strength by volume of 10% due to the lack of temperature control. It tastes a bit 'cheesy' with a rancid note. Beware of the Arkhi from the third distillation phase! This particular product tastes like a herd of goats had marched through.

Different from other uncontrolled fruit or wine brandies, the brewing of the Mongol-plonk contains no methanol risk.

The harmful methyl alcohol (or wood spirit) comes from the fermentation of the cellular material and poses the danger of serious effects. As the Arkhi is exclusively made from milk products, without any herbal ingredients, the fermentation cannot produce any methyl alcohol and thus not influence story writing beyond a mental disorder following a conventional binge drinking.

Nevertheless, a lot of weird stories and obscure fantasies have been developed in the yurts of the Mongols during cold winter days. They are not much different from the Greek twaddle or some legends that have been produced in our part of the world.

As we can, most likely, exclude the Arkhi, the favorite drink of the Mongols, is must have been something stronger that the poet had sniffed or drunk when he came up with the following story. Perhaps it was just the immense boredom in his yurt during cold winter nights that drove him nuts.

Once there were seven suns and they stood fixed in the sky. The Mongol people wanted to get rid of them because the never-ending light was too strong and too bright.

After much debate, they asked the archer Erkhii Mergen to use his arrows and shoot at them. They had probably not realized that seven suns were a little too much, but no sun at all would have been the imminent end of all life on Earth.

The famous master archer shot down six of the seven suns and had already sent up another arrow to get the last one down, when a bird suddenly crossed its flight path. The arrow hit the bird's tail, was deflected and missed. The last sun took cover and disappeared in the West.

We do not know why the seventh sun – and for that matter all the other suns – had not immediately gone into hiding after the suns were shot down one after another. Did they all wait to see which one of their colleagues would be next, until the last sun realized that it is the only remaining target left for the archer?

Anyway, the next morning, the sun came back up from the East, and shyly looked around. At night, she sought cover again in the West and then came back again in the morning from the East. She has done that every day since then.

What a 'brilliant' piece of a legend! On top of it, we have another one of the many examples that the course of the human race was decided by an arrow shot which had *missed*.

The bird that had flown in the way of the arrow was a black kite. To this day, they all have split tail feathers or – more precisely described – a tail with a few feathers missing in the middle. That happens to be the only part of a bird that one can hit without seriously injuring it.

The bird was extremely lucky (and for that matter, the human race as well). Just imagine what damage an arrow, capable of shooting down a sun from the sky, could have done to the poor animal. Fortunately, just a few feathers were lost from its tail.

In the early days, folktales and legends mainly survived by the tradition of storytelling. This implies the problem that the stories are not only frequently falsified, but moreover, they are constantly embellished. This was especially the case in Mongolia, where the storytelling was often the only entertainment during the long nights in the yurts. As a consequence, the Mongols have a saying: *"There are as many different versions of a story, as there are people telling it."*

It was not until the 20th century, when the Mongols began to collect their folktales and wrote them down. Good for the Mongols, as otherwise their legends would soon be forgotten. Nowadays, they rather hang around in their tents and watch Mongolian pop songs on their solar powered TV – despite the fact that most of them (the songs) are worse than the Arkhi from the third distillation phase.

We know a similar story from Chinese sources. If there is anything that can be copied or plagiarized, the Chinese are after it. Pinching other people's products is not regarded as a crime in China, but as a form of art. In this case, however, it seems that the Chinese had the story first and the Mongols had copied it with some variations. The Chinese even had ten suns bothering the humans, as we will learn in the next chapter. In their story, it was not a black kite that rescued the world, but a Chinese Emperor, who stopped the archer before he could put all of us in the dark.

THE IMMORTAL ARCHER HOU YI

Although he had achieved much fame and honor, the Chinese master archer Hou Yi was not happy with his life.

Hou Yi – or simply Yi – was a mythological Chinese figure. He is sometimes described as the god of archery, sent from heaven to aid the humans, and he was the one who had shot down nine of the ten suns from the sky.

According to the wild Chinese fantasies, these ten suns were three-legged sunbirds, all offspring of Dijun, who has the byname 'Jade Emperor'. He is not just a regular Emperor, but also the god of the Eastern part of heaven.

The sunbirds all sat in a mulberry tree in the eastern sky and every day, one of them traveled around the world on a carriage, pulled by their mother Xihe (a Chinese sun goddess).

The sunbirds finally grew tired of this routine and decided that they would all travel together at the same time. This had caused the heat on Earth to become unbearable. As a result, crops shriveled in the fields and the lakes and ponds dried up. Humans and animals sought shelter and suffered from the heat. When the situation became intolerable, they decided to take action.

Dijun, displeased with the behavior of his 'sunbird-sons', called the archer Hou Yi to introduce reason by frightening his sons with his arrows.

When Hou Yi saw what the sunbirds had done to the Earth, he decided that he would not only scare them away, but to shoot them down one by one. Another version tells us that Hou Yi just got mad when the sunbirds laughed and insulted him, as they could not believe that their father would allow anyone to kill them.

After he had shot down the ninth sunbird, Dijun came just in time to stop Hou Yi, who was about to kill his last child. More important: Bringing down the tenth sunbird would have caused the world to remain in total darkness forever.

The old Chinese had been very afraid of a solar eclipse and still are very superstitious when it happens. Special astrologers at the court had to predict the time of a coming event of this type. One day, such an incident occurred without warning. The ones who had been responsible for this work, Xi and He (the names most likely derive from Xihe, the sun goddess), had earlier been found drunk, whereupon Emperor Zhong Kang ordered to execute them.

Despite the fact that Hou Yi had disobeyed orders and had almost totally screwed up, he was hailed a hero of humanity. One could say that he was only over-anxious and his mind was carried away, but I think that Hou Yi was simply stupid.

Hou Yi was married to Chang'e, the goddess of the moon. Both were immortal and lived in heaven.

Emperor Dijun was of course extremely mad at the master archer Hou Yi, after he had killed nine of his children and banished him and his wife to live as mere mortals on Earth.

Huo Yi was shocked, but soon he was out to seek immortality for him and his wife again. He wanted to live forever and simply spend more time with his wife. As a mortal human with a regular job, where he slew monsters and demons, he was away most of the time and often left his wife alone and bored.

He tried to find a solution and went to the Kunlun Mountains to look for Xi Wang Mu, a goddess and the mother of the West.

Xi Wang Mu was aware of his intent to become immortal again and agreed to give him an elixir of immortality, but only under the condition that he would build a new palace for her; Hou Yi was also a famous architect. It took several months of hard labor before the work was finished.

Upon completion, he received two bottles of the elixir that could confer immortality. Xi Wang Mu warned him that these were the last two bottles of its kind. Before he was allowed to drink them, he had to spend one full year of fasting to mentally and physically prepare himself.

Hou Yi was happy, thanked Xi Wang Mu for the gift and returned home to surprise his wife. When he arrived, important work waited for him. Emperor Yao, who was in office for 99 years (!), from 2333 to 2234 BC, wanted him to engage in an extermination battle against a plague of monsters, which had created chaos in the kingdom.

Of course, Hou Yi put his duties first and hid the bottles with the elixir in the rafters of his house, waiting for him until he and his wife would have time for the lengthy preparations before they could drink the elixir, as requested by Xi Wang Mu.

He told his wife about the bottles, but not about the place where he kept them hidden, as he was afraid that, during his absence, his wife could drink the bottles with one of her secret lovers and disappear.

Hou Yi and his arrows killed all the monsters, one after another, like Chiseltooth, the giant with the huge incisor protruding from the top of his mouth, Bashe – a monstrous water serpent, the giant Peng Bird – which was able to cause a storm, just by flapping its wings, malevolent boars and other monsters. This earned him the title 'Pacifier of the Country'.

Shortly before he returned home, his wife had found the bottles with the elixir of immortality and immediately drank *both* of them.

She did not want to live forever with a husband who, in the meantime, had become a real tyrant and despotic ruler, because Hou Yi had shown a strange behavior of late, and his obsession to become immortal again had caused him to be erratic and unpredictable.

He often had the idea to steal the bottles from Xi Wang Mu, especially when he became impatient during the construction of her new palace. He had even tried to make his own pills of immortality and grinded the bodies of adolescent boys for a hundred nights in a row.

Hou Yi came back, just at the moment when his overdosed wife floated out of the window.

He tried to grab her, but could not reach her anymore and she drifted away to the moon. We do not know if Chang'e was immortal again. Perhaps, the overdose compensated for the missed time of fasting and preparation.

In the end, we again have a legend featuring a dumb archer, despite his brilliant shooting capabilities.

THE COMPOUND BOW – SOUNDLESS WEAPON OF THE MILITARY?

As soon as someone had started with this nonsense, the Internet – in its early days – was full of shrewd explanations, telling us that the compound bow was developed by the US military as a soundless weapon.

This bow was indeed invented in the USA, already in the late sixties of the last century, but mainly with the aim to produce a more effective weapon for bow hunting.

After some initial difficulties, this bow became a big success, at first in the USA and later on around the world. Fortunately, it is also used in pure sporting events.

It does not look like a real bow, and many found it rather unattractive. Others thought that it is not an improvement, but rather a step backward in comparison to rifles. Its effectiveness as a bow, however, is beyond any doubt.

The type of archer who shoots with this bow has changed dramatically. No longer is it the camouflaged hunter or the Rambo type with headband, sunglasses, military boots and a survival knife.

Besides the bow's use for hunting by an army of bow hunters, mainly in the USA, it is nowadays also part of sports archery and regular tournaments, with an ever-growing community across all genders and ages. It is the top of the flagpole pertaining to the technical development of bows.

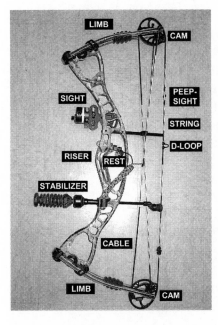

Although this is not a bow for everyone, it must be mentioned that even the traditional archers use modern materials and technologies, such as bow limbs with carbon layers and new arrow shaft materials, made from aluminum or carbon.

The existing bows could only accelerate an arrow up to a certain limit. The noise of the string upon release startles the game. A deer can react so fast that one can often not hit it from 25 yards (22.9 meters) away.

The hunt with bow and arrow was – and still is – very popular in the USA. It is a curious phenomenon that there have been ongoing efforts to improve the speed of the arrows and the penetrating power, while rifles are freely available at many stores around the corner.

Hollis Wilbur Allen, the inventor of the compound bow, woke up with the idea to draw the string by using some type of pulley. When he finally had a working bow, he discovered another effect: He had to pull the full weight of the bow just at the beginning. Thereafter, at a certain point and due to the bow's construction, a substantial let-off made it possible to hold the string with ease. This again allowed higher draw weights, which in turn can produce a significantly faster acceleration, and the limbs of the bow became much shorter.

After some further improvements, he received the patent for this bow in December 1969, but initially, he could not find anyone who wanted to manufacture it. Unattractive, machine like – nobody wanted it. Several states in the USA had even banned mechanical equipment for hunting and the WA – the World Archery Association (formerly FITA) – had declined the request to admit such a bow into their tournaments.

The inventor did not give up and went on with improvements of the bow. He solved some remaining problems, but despite all his efforts, it looked like the bow would never be produced on a commercial scale.

One day, he sent a prototype to Tom Jennings, the technical editor of the Archery World magazine. Tom Jennings was a famous archer and bow maker himself. He tested the bow and wrote a report titled: 'Bow with compound interest'. 'Compound interest' is normally a term used in the financial world and means interest on interest on an investment.

In a figurative sense, he had meant the additional benefit of easily holding the pulled string of a bow with a large draw weight, thanks to the pulley construction. He probably played with the word 'compound' as well and its meaning of 'reinforce' or 'put together'. It was certainly not his intention to create a name for the bow, but soon, it became known as 'compound bow' and kept that name.

This report aroused positive interest. Extensive tests followed with the help of experienced archers, who were all excited about the results, but the bow still had this 'ugly' look...

The breakthrough had not been made yet and the ban by the licensing authority and the archery associations was still not lifted. Tom Jennings took the risk. Instead of producing his recurve bows, he focused solely on the production of the compound bow.

The big step forward came in the year 1970. Through ongoing persuasion by Jennings and Allen, the ban on the bow's use was

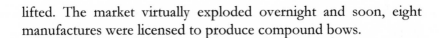

lifted. The market virtually exploded overnight and soon, eight manufactures were licensed to produce compound bows.

In the meantime, many changes and improvements have been made, but the basic principle has not changed much. The group of archers engaged in this type of archery has steadily expanded, not only in the field of hunting or sport shooting, but also in regard to the type of people who use this bow.

But where does the popular belief come from that this bow had been developed as a soundless weapon for the military? The answer is – as often: from the Hollywood movies.

When this bow was not yet widely known, especially in Europe, many people saw it for the first time in the Rambo movies part two and three, Rambo – First Blood Part II and Rambo III.

At the same time, the excitement for the Rambo-knife was born. Many enthusiasts use it at their breakfast table and cut through their rolls after they have checked and made certain – with the compass on the handle – that the butter is in the right place.

A demountable version of the compound bow had also been developed, which had become very popular among the Rambo fans. Normally – in contrast to all other bows – the compound bow must permanently remain strung.

Rambo's bow had impressed the audience so much that they did not even notice that suddenly different tanks moved over the screen. The production of the film started in Israel, but had to be relocated to the United States for safety reasons. Seized tanks of Soviet origin, that were available in large numbers in Israel, had to be replaced, like many other weapons, with modified products from US manufacturers.

The movie was full of horrible directing- and editing errors. In one scene, Rambo jumps out like a feather from a boat, but due to the bad cutting of the film material, one can still see the springboard from which he had bounced off.

Rambo always carried around a case that contained *four* arrows with explosive heads, but he shoots *five* of 'them' at all times.

A Russian helicopter – actually of French production – fires rockets on him, but has neither rockets nor firing tanks. Rambo hijacks the helicopter and when he sits in the cockpit, the firing tanks are suddenly there – filled with rockets.

He shot at a helicopter which flew in front of him, and he takes it down with a M72A2 (light anti-tank weapon). At that moment, he is in the middle of the backblast area and much too close to it. He would have normally been atomized according to the rules of physics – but not so according to the natural laws of Hollywood.

Then, he conquered another helicopter with a hole in the windshield. When he flew back, the hole was missing and after he landed, the hole reappeared.

Rambo rescues a prisoner of war from the North Vietnamese. The 'Charlies' (from 'C' for 'Communists', like 'T' for 'Tango') followed him through a deep swamp. When they all came out, Rambo's pants are muddy and dirty, the pants of the Vietnamese were only wet, but squeaky clean.

Sylvester Stallone, the principal actor in the various movies, whose face was not always copied in time over the head of the stuntman, shoots so well with his wonder bow – always with 'five arrows out of a supply of four' – that the legend of the compound bow as a soundless weapon for the military was born, and it remains a persistent rumor to the present days.

ANCIENT WISDOM

The legend of 'Apostle John and the Partridge' tells us that the Apostle John often took a rest and played with a tamed partridge.

One day, a hunter came by and watched the Apostle. He was surprised to see such a great man who occupied his time with his feathered friend.

The hunter asked him: *"Honorable John, why are you wasting your time playing with a partridge?"*

John looked at the hunter, pointed to his bow and said: *Why is your bow not strung?*

The hunter replied: *"It is not strung, because I am not using it. When I leave it strung all the time, it loses its elasticity and the arrows would not fly so well."*

"You see", said the Apostle. *"It is the same with us humans. Like your bow, which needs to be relaxed from time to time, also you have to relax, otherwise you will not have the strength, when you need it."*

Many, many years later and not so long ago, John (Apostles are probably immortal) played again with a partridge.

An archer approached him; he was also surprised to see how the Apostle spent his time.

The same questions and answers were exchanged, but this time the archer replied: *"Dear John, I have a modern compound bow. The string is not removed anymore; the bow has to be strung all the time."*

"Well", said the Apostle John, *"I haven't heard of such a bow before"*.

The archer added: *"John, stop playing with the partridge, otherwise you will lose your tension. In these days, you must always be under stress. You can only keep pace, when you are constantly energized. Action, action, action, also in your spare time, is a must!"*

John was impressed. He let the partridge fly and went away to tell it to the other Apostles.

THE BATTLE OF LITTLE BIG HORN

The famous Battle of Little Big Horn became part of world history. It was a last major uprising of the Indians against the white invaders, who had robbed their land, pushed them into reservations, destroyed their culture and abandoned them in places and situations where they often faced extinction.

But the white man wanted more and grossly disregarded a contract that guaranteed the Indians of the Sioux tribe the western part of South Dakota as a reservation for their exclusive use: *"No white person is permitted to acquire any land in this territory, to settle in this region or to pass through, without the permission of the Indians."* This was a binding agreement.

For the Sioux, the sacred 'Paha Sapa' (the black hills) are the spiritual center of their world where they communicate with the supernatural world. The white man wanted to build a fort on these hills and for that reason, General Sheridan sent off a combat patrol. This unit was led by George Armstrong Custer.

In reality, the soldiers looked for gold. When they actually found it, the news quickly spread. Thousands of gold seekers overran the country, obliterated villages, harvested the forests and polluted the rivers.

When the military – more or less half-hearted – wanted to drive them back again, the invading soldiers of fortune resisted with success.

The unified tribes of the Sioux threatened with war. The US government in Washington tried to find a compromise and proposed to purchase the land from the Indians. The Sioux finally brought their concerns before a special commission.

 The reaction of the Sioux was very clear: *"You have driven out the game from our territory and everything securing our living and now we have nothing left of value except our mountains, and those you also demand from us. The soil is full of minerals of all kinds and the ground is covered with powerful pine trees, and when we leave this to the Great Father, we know that we are giving up the last thing which is valuable to us and to the whites as well."* Note: The term 'Great (White) Father' was introduced by the representatives of the US government to the indigenous Americans, invoking the President's authority over the natives.

Chief 'Sitting Bull' (picture above) himself was not present, but he had sent a message: *"We do not want whites here. The black hills belong to us. When the whites are trying to take them away from us, we will fight."*

Chief 'Red Cloud', who tried to mediate, demanded 600 million Dollars. The government offered a paltry 6 million. Regardless of this disgraceful and slippery offer, the Indians were not interested in the money.

President Grant ordered that all hostile groups of the Sioux should gather at the agencies (the connection point of the government with the Indians) and otherwise threatened with force.

Ulysses S. Grant (18th Great White Father) was the 'ideal' appointment to the job. He was known to be a drunkard, accompanied by corruption. He had left the army hastily before he was court-martialed for alcoholism. Thereafter, he worked with little success in different positions and eventually helped out in his father's companies.

If some of that sounds familiar to you, relating to later appointments, you might not be so wrong at all.

Corruption scandals of previously unimaginable dimensions came up in his immediate vicinity, like machinations in connection with gold speculations, the tax scandal around the 'Whisky Ring', the tax affair of his finance minister and the corruption affair of his Vice President, however, without any evidence against President Grant himself.

The preparations for the celebrations of the 100th anniversary of the United States had just begun, when General Sheridan worked out his plans for an expedition.

With his three armies, he wanted to force the Sioux to the agencies. On the other side, the Indians mobilized the different tribes.

Hundreds of warriors who had already gone to the agencies left again and went back to the Indian territories.

One of the biggest shames in human history took its course. The most disgraceful and unjustified campaign against the Indians began in March 1876.

It was high time again for a warlike conflict for another reason, besides stealing gold: The military already sat around and they had twiddled their thumbs for over ten years, after the end of the US Civil War in 1865.

The Sioux and other tribes camped along the rivers 'Little Big Horn' and 'Rosebud Creek'. From the West, East and South, US military forces marched up with 3000 soldiers, and among them, the 7th cavalry regiment of Lieutenant-Colonel Custer.

The Indians, under the leadership of 'Crazy Horse', forced General Crook (the name says it all) to break off the attack and to return to the base camp. The troops of General Crook were badly missed during the later development of the battle. According to the plan, they had to participate in the siege of the Sioux.

Crazy Horse went to an Indian village near the river Little Big Horn. Custer and his 660 soldiers and some Indian scouts had orders to prevent the escape of the Sioux to the East.

General Alfred Terry and Colonel John Gibbon and their men came from the North. They all thought that General Crook, who was already driven back with his men into the camp, would arrive from the South to pinch and trap the Sioux from the North and South.

The scouts of Custer had located the Indian village. He divided his soldiers into three units. Major Reno was to attack the village from the West and Captain Benteen was ordered to intercept the Indians who wanted to escape to the South. Custer himself wanted to attack with the main unit of 225 men from the North.

But the Indians wanted no escape. Nobody would have liked to miss such a rare opportunity to work over a bunch of criminals and uniformed bandits.

Custer (picture on the left) had previously received strictest orders not to try anything on his own and above all, he was ordered not to attack the Indians alone. Under the influence of a severe loss of reality and driven by the greed for fame, he had ignored the orders.

One thing was for sure now: Custer would never again harvest any fame, because the last moments in the life of this military bonehead, who largely overestimated his capabilities, had come.

The attack of Reno failed completely and he fled with his men over the river from the attack of the Hunkpapa and their Chief Gall. Custer and his men fell into a trap. He dodged the attack and wanted to reach a ridge of hills to barricade with his men.

One of the hills had later been called 'Custer Hill'. What seems inexplicable to me that this was done to the 'honor' of this uniformed buffoon and not as a monument of shame. A total mess, created by an undisciplined leader and a tactical fool in a criminal war, this is indeed something 'monumental'.

Crazy Horse appeared on top of the hill and with him more than 1000 Oglala warriors, and from below, the Hunkpapa, under the leadership of Chief Gall, who had earlier already kicked the ass of Reno and his armed dudes, stormed up.

It did not even need half an hour before Custer and all of his 225 men were dead.

A hail of arrows came over Custer and his soldiers. Again and again, the Indians rode up with their ponies. Even after all the soldiers were already dead, they did not stop to shoot their arrows.

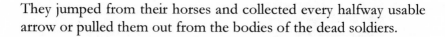

They jumped from their horses and collected every halfway usable arrow or pulled them out from the bodies of the dead soldiers.

When their quivers were filled up, they jumped on their horses, rode in a circle and came back again. They were not only driven by their justified revenge, but moreover by the knowledge that bow and arrow would today go to the happy hunting grounds of archery history.

They were proud to stand at the end of the historical road of bow and arrow as a weapon of war. It was a long way that stretched from the first humans who have created bow and arrow, to these hills in the Southeast of Montana.

The Indians knew that they had indeed won this battle, but already lost the war a long time ago. The white man would come back with a superior force.

It was no longer a matter of return of their land or defending their last bastions of freedom, not to speak of their old, traditional ways of life. These hopes had long been abandoned.

It makes the heart skip a beat, the heart of a man, convinced of justice, but in particular that of an enthusiastic archer. In our minds, we ride with the Indians and see the arrows stuck in the bodies of Custer and his men, making them look like porcupines.

The ancestors and all the great warriors who had gone so far are here with them now. They want to watch the action, before the final curtain would go down on the story of bow and arrow as a weapon of war.

The ponies were hardly able to walk among the dead men who lay around on the ground and scattered arrow shafts broke under their hoofs, but the Indians did not stop to fire the arrows from their bows.

And now, once again, free of enemy fire, they presented their best tricks. They stood on their little horses, hung sideways, rode backwards, changed horses during the gallop and sometimes shot two or three arrows at once, which they skillfully held on the string between their fingers.

He, who reads or hears the story of The Battle of Little Big Horn, can really feel the heavy breathing of a long history that is now ending.

One can envision – high up in the sky – the first hunters who provided food for themselves and their families, the early humans who fought against wild animals, the first warriors who had shot with this weapon in armed conflicts.

Here they are all together now: The great conquerors, the many heroes and archery legends, the archers, who have bravely fought and lost their lives in battles and even the robbers and highwaymen who have used bow and arrow for their misdeeds.

In our fantasy, they now all push forward to secure a good observation position in the stands, high up in the happy hunting grounds.

They all line up: Robin Hood, the English longbow men, Frozen Fritz, Rati and Kama, Crusaders, Samurai, the old Greek and Romans. Zeus, the philandering father of the Gods in the middle of the Amazons, Teutons, Vikings, African hunters, Cupid, Diana, Elves, William Tell, famous Chinese archers and many others who had fought with bow and arrow.

Genghis Khan, the warriors of the notorious 'Golden Horde' and the rest of the Mongolian army loutishly work their way through the crowd and between the many legs, tiny Kyudo archers push forward to catch a glimpse of the action.

Below them, the last arrows fly through the air as part of a warlike struggle in human history. It all began in the Stone Age and will end here, when the sun has disappeared below the horizon.

The Indians called the women and children from their camps. This is something they would never see again. None of the young warriors will ever be able to tell their children any new stories about the heroic deeds of archers with their bows and arrows. This time had faded away and will end here forever in Montana, in the hills near the river Little Big Horn.

Even after all of Custer's men have been scalped, some Indians still rode around to let their last arrows fly for the entertainment of the spectators. They continued to shoot until the twilight had approached and gave them no clear target anymore.

It was all quiet, when Crazy Horse (picture on the left) rode up, slowly and majestically. He sat upright on the blanket on his pony's back and his hand tightly gripped a bow.

Only one arrow was left in his quiver, but it was a very special one. His father, who already got it from his own father, gave it to him. It was a beautiful specimen, which had never been shot before. It represented the veneration of bow and arrow, as the weapon of defense against the enemies and their long arm when they went hunting to feed their families.

It always had a special place of honor in the wigwam of the Chief, but now, it had lost its symbolic meaning for the future, on this summer day in Montana, but there was one last and good use.

They pulled the lifeless body of Custer before the pony of Crazy Horse. He did not hesitate and shot the arrow, with a contemptuous look, into the middle of the chest of this evildoer, right between two brass buttons on his bloodstained blue jacket.

The dead men of Custer were badly mauled. He himself is said to have been the last one killed. This, however, is an untrue statement and was produced by the chroniclers. They needed Custer alive and standing, fighting to the very end in the middle of his dead men, as a motive for the many heroic paintings.

Custer was the only one who kept his scalp. This is true and it was not a last homage to a brave enemy, but simply because they had nothing catchable to hold up his head, as Custer had only very sparse scalp hair, despite the curly locks on the back of his head.

It was just on the 4th of July, when the news of the defeat reached the US capital and spoiled the celebrations of the National Holiday, and on top of everything, the 100th anniversary.

If you are an enthusiastic archer, you might now be tempted to get a beer, a glass of wine, whisky, champagne or perhaps some sake or plum wine. You will then make yourself comfortable in your seat, put your bow and the quiver with a few arrows on your lap and read this chapter all over again with pleasure and excitement.

Sorry dear archers – and all the others, excited by this story: I have bad news for you! The latter part of this narrative, following the defeat of the white soldiers, is of course just a product of pure fantasy, which I made up to show you how quickly and easily one can be tricked by the writers of legends.

When the battle took place in the year 1876, bow and arrow hung on the walls of the wigwams since a long time as sports equipment. The majority of the Indians had the latest brand of modern repeating rifles, 'Spencer', 'Henry' and 'Winchester'.

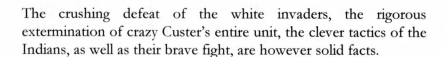

The crushing defeat of the white invaders, the rigorous extermination of crazy Custer's entire unit, the clever tactics of the Indians, as well as their brave fight, are however solid facts.

The pale faces now wanted revenge. The Cheyenne surrendered. The camp of Sitting Bull was closed and many of the Indians went to the agencies, where they were threatened that food rations would be withheld if they would not immediately give up the Paha Sapa, the black hills.

The army destroyed food, blankets and supplies and many were forced to admit defeat. The others succumbed of hunger and the cold.

Sitting Bull had escaped and brought himself and many of his men to safety across the border to Canada.

The last of the free Sioux surrendered in a proud procession of two miles in length. As the Indians approached Fort Robinson, they began to sing their war songs. An army officer remarked: *"This is not surrender, this is a triumphal march."*

Crazy horse was killed in the camp by soldiers. Severely wounded, he said his last words: *"Let me go, friends, you have caused me enough pain!"*

He died the same night at the age of 35.

THE LAST BATTLE WITH BOW AND ARROW

For a long time, bow and arrow have not been used anymore as weapons of war – but when did this period end?

They survived much longer in the military environment than generally assumed, not only in skirmishes between native tribes, but also in major conflicts.

If it was not the 'Battle of Little Big Horn' in the year 1876, when and where was the last notable use of bow and arrow in a military confrontation?

It all took place some decades before the Battle of Little big Horn, but nevertheless not that long ago and not in some remote place on our planet, but right in the middle of Europe, precisely near the city of Leipzig, Saxony, Germany. Bashkir and Tatar horsemen and archers took part in this last act of war when bow and arrow played a significant role, and this was not merely a minor event, but something of a larger magnitude.

The Battle of Nations, October 16 to 19, 1813, was the decisive battle of the liberation wars against the rule of Napoleon Bonaparte. With over half a million soldiers on both sides, it was one of the greatest battles in world history.

The allied forces of Austria, Prussia, the Russian empire and Sweden fought against Napoleon's troops and his allies and finished the long nightmare, caused by the war-horny and crazy little Corsican.

The Bashkir- and Tatar archers were not only there, but also right in the middle of the action with their leather-wrapped Turkish composite bows, made from cherry wood, horn and tendons. Their feathered arrows had a length of about 35 inches (88.9 centimeters) and were equipped with iron tips. They had two leather quivers – one for the arrows and one for the bow – which hung on their back and on the waist belt.

The Bashkir- and Tartar soldiers were regarded as true birds of paradise within the uniformed army of the allies. Every one of them was responsible for his own clothing and they rummaged to find whatever they could. Most came dressed in colorful pants and leather boots. Their heads were usually covered with a leather cap trimmed with fur and occasionally they wore medieval chain hoods and armor of iron and thick leather. This colorful and individual appearance looked perfectly well with these warriors.

According to common sense, they should not have been in Leipzig at this point in history. Nevertheless, they were very effective. They shot ten arrows per minute with their horses in full gallop, while the riflemen could only fire three salvos in the same period.

A French colonel, who was wounded, looked at the arrow that stuck in his body and was so surprised and shocked by the projectile from another time, that he and his men just panicked and ran away.

Who exactly rode around in this battle with these archaic weapons? The Bashkirs and Tartars were part of the unofficial Russian cavalry and were assigned as independent units to the Russians and Prussians. Their ancestors have been Turks or Mongols, and the warriors of the latter group often had a line of ancestry that reached back to the soldiers of the legendary Golden Horde of Genghis Khan.

After the allied forces finally shifted the acts of war to the home country of Napoleon, the Bashkirs and Tartars ended up in Paris. When they arrived, they had come a long way with their horses, almost 2500 miles (4023 kilometers) from the southern Russian steppes.

Once the French saw the Bashkir archers for the first time, they called them 'les amours' and referred to Cupid, the archer and god of love, perhaps under the assumption that they just hallucinated what they saw.

Even Goethe was very much impressed by the commitment of the archers in this battle near Leipzig. In the year 1814, he received a bow as a gift from a Bashkir commander who had spent the night at his house in Weimar.

Johann Peter Eckermann, a poet and friend of Goethe, reported that Goethe had once brought a bow, which he had kept in a hut in his garden. *"Here, take it!"*, said Goethe, *"I see it is still in the same condition as it has been, when I got it from a Bashkir chief in the year 1814."*

Goethe shot some arrows and Eckermann did the same. The latter shot an arrow into a window shutter of Goethe's study. It was so deep into the wood that they could not pull it out.

"Leave it there", said Goethe, *"it can serve me a few days as a reminder of our jokes!"* (quoted from Eckermann's conversations with Goethe).

Eckermann had tried to make the archery sport popular in Germany, but without success at that point of time.

The Battle of Nations Monument is one of the landmarks of the city of Leipzig and also partly a salute to the archers and their brave fights over many centuries.

Initially, the citizens of Leipzig (the second largest city in the state of Saxony – following Dresden, the capital) were not very happy about the monument. The Saxons fought on the wrong side as allies of Napoleon and were punished with territorial losses.

It took 100 years before it was inaugurated in the year 1913 and just in time for the 100th anniversary of the Battle of Nations. With a height of 91 meters (almost 300 feet), it belongs to the largest monuments in Europe.

THE TRAGEDY OF RAMSTEIN

What on Earth is that story doing in *this* book?

Is it because the aerobatic squadron of the Italian Air Force, which was involved in that tragic accident, is called the 'Frecce Tricolori' (the three-colored arrows)? No, there is more than just the name that relates to archery! After initial hesitation and long reflection, I have decided to include this horrible incident, and the circumstances surrounding it, as a mysterious story – in the twilight of truth.

At first, we have two things coming together: The most modern version of the long distance effect through the use of missiles, originally established by bow and arrow and the jet planes, which make humans themselves become part of the flight of an arrow. On top of that, a wrong target was hit (you remember, that had also happened to Cupid quite often), and we have tragic consequences and mysterious circumstances – the Greek mythology is full of that.

Take NATO for the Oracle, the French for unpredictable forces, the Italians for life on other worlds, the Americans for the Roman Empire and Gaddafi for a bad ghost. Imagine the location in the Mediterranean Sea, where Odysseus once hopelessly navigated around. Then we have Germany, the mysterious country behind the Black Forest (at least from a Roman point of view) and an incident in front of a crowd that was bigger than the one in the Colosseum in Rome.

If you got all that, you are ready to cope with the following:

The 'Frecce Tricolori' is the world-famous aerobatic squadron of the Italian Air Force. The three colors, green, white and red, represent those of the Italian flag. Created in 1961 in the present form, their roots go back to the year 1920. Their full name is '313. Gruppo Addestramento Acrobatico – Pattuglia Acrobatica Nazionale (PAN)'. The 313th squadron is stationed at the airport 'Mario Visintine', in Rivolto, close to Udine. When the pilots demonstrate their formation flights in their jets, they make the spectators hold their breath. 350000 people watched the air show on August 28, 1988, when the Italians showed their tricks at the US airbase in Ramstein, Germany. There had never been an event of this magnitude with such a large crowd.

Shortly before the end of the show, three jets collided in the air at an altitude of 50 meters (164 feet) and crashed to the ground – one of them directly into the audience. This accident, with seventy people dead and about one thousand injured – many critically – was among the greatest catastrophes at an air show. The military immediately took over the command and by doing that, caused further damage. Stubborn regulations followed by further administrative gaffe, lead to downright disaster. More people died and suffered because of these blunders.

It gets worse: There are – believe it or not – 350000 people crowded together in one place. Over their heads, in a distance of a few feet, airplanes – single or in squadrons – perform risky maneuvers and the organizers have no more preparations for any calamities then villagers presenting a country fair.

There was only *one* helicopter available, prepared to aid and assist for the purpose of rescue and moreover, it was shattered by scattering parts from the crashing planes. The pilot was critically wounded and later died in a hospital in Texas. Any coordination with the German rescue stations or with the surrounding hospitals was practically not existent within the medical support units.

Hypodermic needles and infusion bags used by Americans were not compatible with German dimensions and methods. The telephone network, lesser developed at the time, had collapsed completely. Mobile phones had not yet made their appearance and a few amateur radio operators sent messages to recruit blood donations – hoping to be heard.

The military protocol was inflexible and produced unbelievable scenes. Busses, that had transported extremely critical patients, could not find the hospitals, because the drivers were not familiar with the area and unable to speak German. The disorganized rescue operation, which followed the military handbook, became an orgy of gigantic mishaps.

Security policy dictated that the military did not immediately allow the rescue personnel to enter the premises of the airport. Others, like the THW (Technisches Hilfswerk – technical assistance organization), were not even called upon and had remained at their bases. I now wonder, if that is such a secret place, why do they allow 350000 civilian visitors on the premises?

The military did not report their own casualties. To this day, they have kept the number of their own victims a secret. The tragedy of the Ramstein air show went down in history, not at least because of the confusion and the following escalation of events during and after this calamity.

The compensation granted to the bereaved was highly unsatisfactory. The Governments of Germany, Italy and the USA contributed to a fund, from which 21 million Deutschmarks (at the time about 12 million US Dollars) were paid out. That is a fraction of the compensation that might be paid to Michael Jackson for a botched nose job and less than the annual bonus, some investment banks had paid to their junior stock traders. In any case, most of the money was allocated to health insurance and the social security system and did not go directly to the individual victims.

Not a Cent was available for psychological harm of the victims or their relatives. Moreover, fire fighters, police officers or spectators had problems for years to cope with the aftereffects of their experience.

The regional court of Koblenz denied respective petitions. In its explanatory statement, they even overstepped some of the nonsense in the military handbooks. A diagnosis of Post-Traumatic Stress Disorder (PTSD) was not known at the time of the accident. However, if you open the window of your car and call someone an idiot or show him your middle finger, then the German judicial system interprets this as an extraordinary emotional distress for the recipient of your greetings and will include severe penalties. The ruling took place in the year 2003, 15 years (!) after the incident. Good thing the country is a lot faster in manufacturing cars, as otherwise it would only have jobs – outside the legal system – for waiters at the Oktoberfest in Munich or for part-time ghosts, hired to scare tourists in its ornate castles. And there was this statement, most favored by the 'overburdened' courts, 15 years after the accident: *"Moreover, the claims are anyhow statute-barred."* And they went on: *"Neither the exact course of the tragedy, nor the liability-issues are unequivocal."*

The American military was of the opinion that this was *not* a private event. In that case, a different law would have to be applied. It prevented the Americans to become liable as the organizers, because their legal system certainly includes mental harm – and not just coming from insults in road traffic. The American legal system always tries to cleverly *lure* a case into a government- or military public entity domain in order to avoid lawsuits and the assumption of responsibility. American law does not allow the military, federal government and various public- and state entities to be sued. The plaintiff has to ask 'permission' from the government or military to allow a suit to be filed against them, which is usually denied.

This is called 'Veil of Immunity'. But that is not so special after all. The Camorra has its 'omertà' (code of silence) and even kids in the school playground have their way to deal with a 'snitch'.

The show was then officially made a NATO maneuver. Strange, no one of the 350000 spectators could remember that they had been invited to a NATO maneuver.

Under the impression of this disaster, some necessary consequences had been drawn concerning the rescue system, the disaster control and matters of cooperation between the military and the civil installations. Nevertheless, the traditional air shows (NATO maneuvers?) at the Ramstein airbase came to an end forever.

Besides the administrative obstructions concerning adequate compensation following the very tragic side of this disaster, the matter 'stunk to high heaven', and not only conspiracy theories soon found their breeding ground.

A particular event was brought back into the limelight: 'The plane crash of Ustica', an incident that had occurred a few years before. Another lawyer and expert on aviation law, who represented victims of the Ramstein tragedy, also made comments in this direction. The facts that have been collected in the years following this disaster at Ramstein air base, have cast doubt on the 'official' version that a mistake of the Pilot Nutarelli had caused the accident. Bit by bit, other important elements came to light, which had so far been suppressed by written agreements of confidentiality.

A firefighter who was standing about 65 yards (59 meters) away from the location of the impact and had remained unhurt, said: *"The Americans had just one thing in mind: Put everything away, remove everything without consideration for losses. No doctor was able to look after the injured right on the spot. Everything on the trucks was the issue."*

Two of the pilots of the Frecce Tricolori, killed in the Ramstein accident, Ico Nutarelli and Mario Naldini, had played an important role in the so called 'Ustica-complex', a dark chapter in the history of NATO, and were to appear before the fact-finding committee, just a week after this disaster. In the years before, there had been a large number of unnatural causes of death among the members of the military around the Ustica plane crash. What has happened?

On the evening of June 27, 1980, a Douglas DC-9 of the Italian Airline Itavia crashed into the sea near the island of Ustica. This flight number 870 from Bologna to Palermo in Sicily was delayed for two hours. All 81 people on the plane died. This catastrophe was given the name 'Strage di Ustica' (bloodbath of Ustica). It is almost certain today, after all the years of covering up and hiding behind smoke screens, that an air-to-air missile hit the plane, which plunged into the sea. At first, there were speculations that the plane broke apart in the air, caused by fatigue of material or that it was blown apart by a bomb.

The recovery of the wreck in the year 1987, from a depth of over 3475 meters (11400 feet) by a French submarine of the semi state-controlled company Ifremer, had given some better explanations. The plane was only discovered thanks to the persistence of some bereaved that persevered. The missing black box had been found in the year 1991. Then, when traces of the military explosive T4 were discovered in the remnants of the plane, the military- and secret service circles came into a tight squeeze. A substantial amount of time had passed, while the incident remained largely unsolved: Metal fatigue, maybe a bomb, the plane shot down by a missile, intentionally or by accident?

1989: It was the general believe that the plane was accidentally shot down by a missile, as confirmed by the state investigative commission in the same year. The possibility of a bomb was eliminated. The cause for the disaster was deemed a ground-to-air missile. ━━━━━━━━━━━➤ 1990: A group of experts, still in the minority, maintained the view that there had been a bomb, but the majority of thoughts led to a ground-to-air missile. In the interim, the investigative commission of the Italian parliament complains about false statements and the withholding of information by government bodies. ➤ 1994: A majority of experts now found reason to believe that a bomb was the culprit, while a minority still supported the ground-to-air missile theory. In the same year, a second investigation confirms with absolute certainty – contrary to all prior statements – that military planes held exercises in the area leading to apparent operations by NATO planes. Radar data showed nine combat aircraft. If correct, this would be an indication that the plane had been shot down by an air-to-air missile. ➤ 1999: An investigative report was made public in which the sitting judge Rosario Priore drew the following conclusion: *"L'incidente al DC-9 è occorso a seguito di azione militare di intercettamento, il DC-9 è stato abbattuto"* (the crash of the DC-9 took place after a military interception, the DC-9 was shot down).

One question – and a crucial one – that remained open, was about the identity of the attacking aircraft and its nationality. This was followed by several court actions trying to determine some sort of responsibility. Nine officers of the Italian Air Force and the secret service were charged with holding back information and making false statements, as well as other allegations, even including high treason, because the incident had been claimed as 'atto di guerra', an act of war against the Republic of Italy. In the meantime, it was found to be proven beyond doubt: an air-to-air missile shot down The DC-9.

Furthermore, it is now clear that there had been an aerial combat on the evening of June 27, 1980, over the Tyrrhenian Sea, between two MIGs of the Libyan air force and a group of NATO-jets.

On July 18, 1980, a Libyan MIG-23 that was involved in the aerial combat was found in Calabria in the South of Italy. Forensics made it possible to establish the time of death of the pilot and to connect him and the crashed jet with the June 27 incident.

The same evening of June 27, 1980, Muammar al Gaddafi was on his way to Poland and presumably sat on an identical plane like the one of the Itavia Airline, and both flew in the same air space. Several interceptor fighters had taken off from a stationary base or from an aircraft carrier, with the intention to shoot down Gaddafi. As there always had been good connections between Italy and their former colony Libya, Gaddafi had most likely received secret information from Rome, and his plane was subsequently redirected to Malta. In addition, Libyan jets were sent into Italian airspace.

During an aerial combat with the MIGs, the DC-9 of ITAVIA got in the way of the skirmish. It was mistakenly thought to be the plane of Gaddafi, especially as the DC-9 was not taken into account, due to its delay of two hours.

Another presumption: The two MIG-23s were on their way to former Yugoslavia for a routine inspection and had tried to take a shortcut over Italian territory. To avoid possible conflicts, the Libyan MIGs attempted to come close to the ITAVIA plane where they could temporarily get into its radar shadow. Then, a missile shot from an interceptor and intended for the MIGs, had accidentally hit the ITAVIA DC-9. No, the supposed shortcut appears little convincing. Why should Libyan planes try to save a few gallons of fuel, when Gaddafi had enough oil and often did not know how to spend the many petrodollars.

Lastly, there is another theory that probably contains the most reasonable facts. This time, the MIGs were on their way back from the former Yugoslavia. When they had reached the Adriatic Sea, after a low-altitude flight under the radar, they had hidden behind the DC-9 of ITAVIA to continue their flight in its radar shadow. In the air over the Tuscany, they had been discovered by two F-104 Star fighters of the Italian air force. The pilots, Ico Nutarelli and Mario Naldini, whom we already know as pilots and victims of the Ramstein disaster, triggered the air-raid alarm. This would explain why it was prompted twice and parallel. As Italy normally tolerates such flyovers by military planes from Libya, its former colony, one did not make a big deal out of it.

Just at this very moment, a Boeing E-3 Sentry, better known as AWACS-aircraft – Airborne Early Warning and Control System – of the US Air Force, had evidently been in the area. In addition, the French aircraft carrier 'Clemenceau' and a convoy of ships cruised in the Mediterranean Sea – however, without any official proof of an aircraft carrier in the area.

Is it not somewhat strange? You can see and record with spy satellites when someone brings his trash to the can before the house and on the other hand, a French aircraft carrier and his convoying ships cannot be spotted? The French themselves did not come up with an answer. Their log books are perhaps just very sporadically completed and with great 'nonchalance'. The entire crew possibly sat in the on-board theater and enjoyed an old movie with the comedian Louis de Funès, while the carrier drifted aimlessly through the Mediterranean Sea.

Come on! A French aircraft carrier would make a fool of the 'Marine Nationale Française' (the French naval forces), not able to determine its own position of yesterday? Yes, and Santa Clause runs for President together with Elvis. Who are you kidding?

The story was a different one: The AWACS aircraft or the aircraft carrier or both have located the MIGs and have sent up QRA aircrafts – (Quick Reaction Alert). In the course of the fight, the ITAVIA plane was presumably hit. Despite the slow pace investigations, which had lasted for several years and slipshod cooperation of NATO, only one thing is for sure: There had been an aerial combat, involving two Libyan jets, and one of them crashed in Calabria.

This was followed by a series of strange cases of death involving officers of the Italian air force.

August 1980: Colonel Giorgi Teodoli died in a car accident. He was the successor of the commander of the airbase of Poggio Ballone near Grosseto where the two pilots, Ivo Nutarelli and Mario Naldini, had landed after they had triggered the air-raid alarm. ⟶ May 9, 1981: Captain Maurizio Gari died at the age of 37 – heart failure. He was commander of the radar station of Poggio Ballone near Grosseto and one of the officers present during the night of June 27 to June 28, 1980. ⟶ March 30, 1987: Sergeant Alberto Dettori hung himself. He was one of the men on duty on the same night in the radar station of Poggio Ballonde. ⟶ August 28, 1988: The pilots Ico Nutarelli and Mario Naldini die in the tragic accident at Ramstein. As already mentioned, this was one week before they had to testify before the investigating committee in the Ustica plane crash. ⟶ February 1, 1991: Air Force Sergeant Antonio Muzio was shot. He was connected with the radar station of Lamezia Terme. ⟶ February 2, 1992: Air Force Sergeant Antonio Pagliare died in a car accident. He was working at the radar station of Otranto. ⟶ December 21, 1995: Franco Parisi hung himself. He was stationed in 1980 in the radar station of Otranto and a few days earlier, he had received a subpoena to testify in court. ⟶ April 4, 2002: Michele Landi hung himself. He was an IT-consultant for the same prosecuting authorities that had investigated the ITAVIA flight 870. He died a few days after he had told colleagues that he obtained new information about the Ustica case.

Additional cases of unusual death, which had occurred within the ranks of the 'Aeronautica Militare', were associated with the events of June 27, 1980. The strangely deceased people had all received secret facts concerning the Ustica case.

Whilst the Italians will probably rack their brains and speculate forever about the many mysteries of the Ustica case, we have to note the following:

Men have always improved the long-range effect created by bow and arrow. Today, missiles guide themselves into predetermined targets; they can carry devastating explosive forces and can even fight against each other, missile against missile – a long distance effect against another long-distance effect, so to speak. But in the end, all depends on humans, who are – and will remain – the permanent element of uncertainty.

This is perhaps the reason, why the Vikings preferred to fight head-on and more seldom at distance with bow and arrow. They wanted to see their 'target' face to face, before they struck with their axes.

P.S. The Gaddafi problem has meanwhile been solved. I am relieved, because at one time, I drove a car similar to the one he once had. A French fighter jet, with a pilot unaware of its exact position and guided by Italian radar, could very well have erroneously fired its 'arrows' at my vehicle on the way to my vacation resort in the Tuscany.

YABUSAME ARCHERS

Yabusame is another Japanese ceremonial art of archery for men in fancy clothing, besides Kyudo and according to the motto: If you make a fool of yourself, why not in archery.

Both types of archers use the same long and asymmetric bow. A distinguishing feature is the hat they wear. The poofy headgear of the Kyudo archer is too large to be worn on a horse, especially when someone has to ride around with it. The 'Yabusames' prefer something more practical, a thing of woven reed that looks like a badly designed cowboy hat of the gauchos in South America. It is held by several straps, firmly attached around the head and neck.

On the back of their nags, the archers approach the targets at a speed going up to 40 mph (64 km/h) and let their arrows fly with a deep shout *"In-Yo-In-Yo"* (darkness and light), in a broader sense similar to the Chinese terms of Yin and Yang.

Darkness or light refers to the coming shot in terms of 'miss or hit' and the fortune depending on it. Thus, Yabusame was introduced as a way to please the myriads of gods who watch over Japan and to obtain their blessings. 'Darkness' should better refer to the stupidity that someone still practices this nonsense; 'light' would then represent the hope to come back to normal archery some day. But this is difficult, and the 'Yabusames' securely hide behind their folkloristic practices.

Their performances, however, seem to move in the right direction: The Japanese have already dropped one of their traditions as part of Yabusame archery – the shooting at dogs called 'Inuoumono'.

In the old days, dogs were put into a small circular enclosure and these gaga-archers, dressed in colorful garments, rode around and shot arrows at the most pitiable animals.

The hour of mental illness had commenced. As all of their archery gimmicks are closely related to the noble Zen culture, it is a shame that Buddhist priests had to ask the archers to pad their arrows, so that the dogs were only annoyed and bruised rather than killed.

Besides, people shooting arrows to influence the powers of destiny and occasionally even aim at confined and helpless dogs, need not wonder about the occurrence of the next 'jishin' (earthquake).

During the Kamakura Period (1192-1334), mounted archery was used in military training. If an archer did not meet his degree of competence when trying to hit the target, he was commanded to commit 'seppuku', a ritualistic act of suicide, better known in the Western world as 'Harakiri'.

That part of the rules I can accept, even applaud, as it took – at least partially – care of an otherwise serious problem.

If all of today's Yabusame archers would be asked to commit seppuku, independent of their results, it would certainly speed up the abolition of this strange behavior, and it would perhaps give them something to think about, with the possible outcome that they eventually decide to buy a decent bow and join the civilized world (of archery).

Some arrows used for the Yabusame shenanigans are blunt and round shaped in order not to penetrate the wooden target and thus create a louder sound. Experienced archers are allowed to use sharp points, and when the arrow strikes the board, it will splinter and confetti falls to the ground. So, it's 'boom-boom' for the newbies and confetti for the masters.

This style of archery has its roots at the beginning of the Kamakura period. The Emperor 'Minamoto no Yorimoto' was dissatisfied with the lack of archery skills of his Samurai and organized Yabusame as a form of practice.

Yabusame is not an exact term for horseback archery and, more precisely, the word means 'mounted archery'. Today, this is an even more suitable phrase for a simple reason: The archer is not always 'mounted' on a real horse. In Japan, especially in big cities, it is very expensive to rent horses, not to speak of keeping them. Yabusame hobby archers, without own horses or paddocks, can only practice in halls, mounted on wooden training-nags.

The masters of Yabusame usually accept only members of their own family as new disciples. It is estimated that there are only 50 good Yabusame archers remaining. This means that there are 50 to go, in addition to the not-so-good Yabusame archers, before this abnormal behavior ends.

The most famous and celebrated event of mounted archery occurred during the Genpei War (1180-1185) and had a major impact on Japanese culture, society and politics.

It was the struggle for power between the Heike and the Genji clans. In the battle of Ichi no Tani, the Heike were defeated and wanted to flee to Yashima, a large island, and jumped into their waiting boats. The Genji pursued them, mounted on their horses, but were stopped by the sea.

The Heike were held up from sailing away as they had to wait for the right wind. For the fun of it, they put up a fan on the mast of a ship, as a target for the Genji archers to shoot. This was also seen as a gesture of chivalrous rivalry between the enemies.

'Nasu no Yoichi', one of the Genji warriors, accepted the challenge. He rode his horse into the sea as far as he could and hit the fan with his first shot. Nasu no Yoichi won much fame and he is still celebrated to this day.

Every second Saturday of the month, the public indoor swimming pool of the little town of Utashinai, on the Island of Hokkaido, is reserved from 10 a.m. until 3 p.m. for the Yabusame archers.

They put a plastic horse into the shallow water in the non-swimmer area and the archers then try to repeat the shot of Nasu no Yoichi and shoot at a fan that hangs from the upper springboard.

The Yabusame devotees even try to promote their sport outside of Japan and have not shied away to perform at special ceremonies, such as entertaining foreign dignitaries and heads of state.

We cannot be surprised that the Yabusame archers had chosen Prince Charles as a victim to watch a special performance (his mother refused to come, because of the abuse of horses). The Prince of Wales – or 'Prince of Wiles', as he is occasionally called – was extremely fascinated and pleased with the performance at Hyde Park in London, in May 2001. The fearless Samurai warriors did refrain, however, from performing 'Inuoumono' and shooting at the Queen's Welsh Corgis – her beloved dogs.

After they had entertained the Prince of Wales with this idiocy, George W. Bush also had the pleasure and fascinating experience to watch Yabusame on the occasion of his official visit to Japan, in February 2002.

Modern Japanese, fed up with traditional Punch and Judy shows, have long ago turned to more modern up-to-date entertainment.

Tokyo Disneyland is one of the most visited parks in the world. Instead of Kyudo, Yabusame, Inuoumono, Gagaku music, Odori- or Mai dancing, Nogaku musicals or Sumo wrestling, the Japanese now get the occasion at Tokyo Disneyland to enjoy something more solid and suitable for the 21st century: Adventureland, Westernland, Fantasyland and Tomorrowland-World Bazaar.

This is supplemented by Tokyo Disney Sea with another seven exciting topics: Mediterranean Harbor, American Waterfront, Mysterious Island, Mermaid Lagoon, Arabian Coast, Lost River Delta and Port Discovery.

If you are prepared to try local food in Japan, don't behave like an American tourist and ask for jellyfish, puffer fish, raw sea cucumbers, cooked chicken eyes, snake on the spit, skewered scorpions, stinky tofu or crunchy insects. This will all be served during the next stop on your Asia-in-a-week trip – in China.

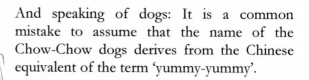

And speaking of dogs: It is a common mistake to assume that the name of the Chow-Chow dogs derives from the Chinese equivalent of the term 'yummy-yummy'.

In fact, the name comes from the Pidgin English, which was the common language among the traders in East Asia. Several curiosities on the menu, suspected to contain dog meat, were given the name chow-chow.

If you are cautious about what you eat abroad, do not restrict this attitude only to Asian countries. In some areas of Switzerland, for example, dog *and* cat meat are still on the menu.

ARCHERY AND THE OLYMPIC GAMES

The Magyar Posta (Hungarian postal service) had issued a nice stamp on the occasion of the 17th Olympic Games in Rome in the year 1960. It shows an antique archer and reminds us of the ancient Games.

There is just a minor problem: At the Olympic Games in Rome, there had been no archery competition at all.

It was only in the year 1972 at the Olympic Games in Munich, Bavaria, that archery was finally back in the program, after a long sabbatical from this platform.

Ninety-five archers, men and women, took part in the competitions and until today, archery has maintained its status as an Olympic event. The bows became very technical, with a lot of extra equipment, like a bow sight or a stabilizer. The material continuously improved, not only for the bow itself, but also for the components of the arrows or the string.

However, this reappearance was not merely a kind gesture to the archers. It is of utmost importance to remember something that places archery on top of every other sport at the Olympic Games: The first sporting activity – ever – in the history of the Games was an arrow shot, made by an archer at the advent of the antique Games in the year 776 BC.

In this connection, we should not forget the Games in Barcelona in 1992, where this tradition was revived at the opening ceremony. People were watching – with great pleasure – when an archer lit the Olympic flame with a burning arrow.

Even more nervous than the archer himself, who had long practiced this shot, was the man with his thumb on the button, responsible for the timely and synchronous electronic ignition of the flame.

The preservation of the Spanish national pride was at his fingertips. The archer had to merely shoot high enough into the dark sky to avoid that the arrow would fly underneath the bowl, with a miracle ignition above.

The flow of the gas had to be controlled in a timely fashion to eliminate the risk of a small explosion caused by the flaming arrow. What, at the end of the day (or rather night), has ignited the flame, remains a secret that is hidden in the dark sky of Barcelona.

Now one step after another: Following the qualification round, 64 men and 64 women compete against each other in a final round, with direct elimination, until they come to the deciding matches, determining the winners of the Olympic archery medals.

Unfortunately, the spectators are too far away to clearly see the target area, which makes it virtually impossible to follow the ongoing competition.

Technical improvements, such as large screens, which allow the crowd to get a better view or electronic scoreboards, have in the meantime improved the situation, at least at the very top level of archery tournaments. At lower levels of competitions, this is practically impossible to implement and not feasible from a financial point of view.

Changes of the rules or procedures are often subject to discussion, with the aim to make the sport more attractive for the spectators and more suitable for television.

In that regard, one could use the – rather rare – occasion to learn something from the Mongols. In Mongolia, where once Genghis Khan and his horde had spread terror with their bows and arrows, archery is one of the three most popular kinds of sport, besides wrestling and horseback riding.

The girls and women are closely involved, at least in archery and horseback riding. At the Mongolian National Day 'Eriin Gurwan Naadam' (the masculine games), the main events naturally include wrestling matches, horse races and archery competitions.

Things are little different from our Western archery habits in the Mongol steppes. First of all, they do not shoot at regular targets or target faces with colorful rings. Their targets are placed at a distance of approximately 75 meters (82 yards), have the size of a Coke can, are made from leather and lie on the ground.

The spectators are afforded with a special bonus, as the referees stand very close to the target, and their courage and trust in the archer's accuracy of shooting are tested.

One can clearly see if the target was hit – or the referee. If the latter was not hit, but rather the target, they signal a hit by dancing and singing ('Uuhailah'). Different dance movements tell the archers and spectators 'well done!' or 'the arrow has arrived and has hit the target'. The beginning of the shooting is not indicated by the blow of a whistle or the sound of a horn, but by a dance by the referees: 'We are ready!'

All archers can win the title in a tournament. In the year 1919, 120 out of 122 archers were named champion. But there is also something to achieve for the losers: They go home with an honoring like 'wonderful archer', 'courageous archer' or 'reliable archer'.

Following the Mongol example in our part of the world, some rookie in archery could participate in tournaments at a much earlier stage. With an average of nine of out of ten arrows missing the target completely and much time needed to find them again, he could still go home with the title 'courageous shooter with great perseverance'.

Today's very technical archery, with high-tech material, steadily keeps its status as an Olympic discipline. However, during the time before, the fight for the Olympic recognition seemed never-ending.

With the creation of the FITA (now WA – World Archery Federation) in the year 1931, the foundation stone was laid to establish archery at the Olympic Games yet again. This international association was founded through the initiative of Poland, France, Belgium, Sweden and Czechoslovakia. As of August 2013, 156 nations are under its umbrella.

The Frenchman Pierre de Coubertin brought the modern Olympic Games to life in Athens in the year 1896. Archery was unfortunately not a part of the event, but was included four years later, at the Games in the year 1900 in Paris.

One of the archery competitions was called 'Sur la perche à la herse' (mast shooting). The targets had been a rooster on the top of a mast, 10 meters (33 feet) above the ground, two chickens on two crossbars below and underneath them, eight fledglings on another crossbar; fortunately, all of them were just wooden figures.

At that time, the shooting was done with the traditional longbow and the crossbow.

Archery was also present in the year 1904 in St. Louis and 1908 in London.

The Games became more and more professional, starting with the Olympic Games in Stockholm in the year 1912. They have paved the way towards a perfect organizational process. This time, after the chaotic circumstances in the years before, the hosts provided for a smooth course of the events and athletes from all five continents participated.

For the first time, electronic timing was used, as well as devices for a photo finish. The latter, for instance, decided on the silver- and bronze medal in the 1500-meters run.

In addition, the Games became much more attractive, because for the first time, women participated in the swimming competitions – still dressed with ankle-length bathing suits.

There have been gold medals even for artistic achievements. At the Games in the year 1912, such medals were awarded for urban planning, sculpture and plastic art, painting/graphic, literature and poetry of every kind and music, with the distinction between music in general, song-, instrumental- and orchestral compositions.

The Games elevated to become more professional, yet they had their scandals and difficulties: The gold medal for the art of literature, division poetry of every kind, was given to the work 'Ode to Sport' by the poets 'Georg Hohrod' and 'Martin Eschbach', who were never seen in person.

It was later discovered that these names had been pseudonyms, and – hiding behind them – was no one less than the founder of the new Olympic Games, Baron Pierre de Coubertin himself.

The question whether he just wanted to be judged in an anonymous and unbiased way or whether this was the first big Olympic manipulation scandal, should be left open in the light of his initiative to revive the Olympic idea, with the implementation of the Olympiad of modern times.

On a political level, it was not at all easy in the year 1912. For the first time, the planned marching-in of the teams behind signboards with printed country names has led to protests.

Russia griped about the separate participation of the Grand Duchy of Finland, which, in those days, had belonged to the Russian Empire.

Austria had criticized the participation of Bohemia – until 1918 part of the Austrian monarchy – with a separate team. A compromise was finally found by way of letting the provincial representatives march in with smaller signs and no flags. At the presentation ceremonies, a small pennant was allowed to be pulled up simultaneously under the flags of Russia or Austria.

That is all quite interesting, but what about archery in the year 1912? A dead loss, but a 'pulling-the-rope competition' was in the program instead!

Likewise, in the year 1916 in Berlin, there had been no archery competitions. In fact, there had been no competitions at all. The event was canceled due to World War I.

Archery was found again among the Olympic competitions in the year 1920 in Antwerp and then even twice: For the first and for the last time. It took solid fifty-two year before archery came back to the games. It was a crucial factor that one did not have – different from the pulling-the-rope competition – international rules and the shootings could only be performed according to the particular regulations of the respective host country.

All attempts to make this sport an Olympic discipline again had failed time after time because of the refusal by the IOC. In the year 1960, the International Olympic Committee allowed archery to be included in the supporting program of the Games. However, this was merely an evasive maneuver to calm down urging archers.

Subsequently, there was no archery competition at the Games in the year 1964 in Tokyo, due to the lack of a national association, which could have arranged such a tournament.

That was probably not a big loss after all. The archers would have been forced to follow the regulations of the host country, according to the rules of those days. In this case, one must openly say: Better no competition than some comical form of Asian archery.

Solid rules and meaningful competitions are good for everyone – as the success-story of the South Korean archers with the Olympic bow clearly demonstrates.

The fact that no decent archery competition could be organized, led to the refusal by the IOC to admit archery to the Games of the year 1968 in Mexico City.

In the times before, also Pierre de Coubertain, the initiator of the modern Olympic Games, was not very keen to bring back archery to the competitions, not least because of the bad habits of the archers in the antiquity. In those days, they did indeed shoot at living pigs as targets.

The archers were again themselves responsible that they failed to participate in later years. In the year 1900, at the Games in Paris, they utterly insulted the spectators, when they had shot in a specific competition at live doves.

Matters became even worse: In the years 1904 and 1908, they allowed women to take part in the archery competitions. It came, as it had to be expected, in line with the attitude of the time concerning women and sports. Archery was thrown out again in 1912. Although the archers had shot only at regular targets and small dummy birds, the Olympic lights of archery were shot out for a while.

After that one-time comeback of archery as an Olympic discipline in the year 1920, it became darkest night – in an Olympic sense – for this sport, for the mentioned period of 52 years.

Through perseverance, the long run-up since the foundation of the FITA (now WA), has finally led to permanent success: In the year 1972 in Munich, on 'Bavarian lawn', the archers had arrived on target. Archery was again back to the Olympic Games.

The competitions took place in the 'English Garden', one of the largest inner city parks in the world, right in the middle of the city of Munich, at the west bank of the river Isar.

The English Garden is very famous – but not for the Olympic revival of archery. It is known around the world for its nudists who, whenever the weather allows, lie around on the many lawns.

When the world appeared to be a little more prudent, it was an insiders' tip in special travel guides. Visitors from many countries around the world came to Munich, especially to see this attraction. One could even book a hotel room with a view of the naked.

Before it is totally forgotten, the Olympic archery highlights of 1972: John Williams, USA (gold medal men) reached 2528 points and a new world record. Doreen Wilber, USA (gold medal women) collected 2424 points and had also set a new world record.

It is difficult to compare world records in archery history, because the equipment, the distance, the targets and the rules have changed quite often in the past.

THE ARROW IN THE WEATHERCOCK

Books have proved to be an excellent basis to standardize language, especially after the invention of the printing press around the year 1450 by 'Johannes Gensfleisch' from Mainz, Germany, better known as Johannes Gutenberg.

It was hence possible to provide relatively inexpensive mass production of printed material. Gutenberg printed the first Bible between the years 1452 and 1454 – still in Latin. The real breakthrough in Germany came from the translation of the Bible into the German Language by Dr. Martin Luther and the following mass printing (1522 first edition of the New Testament and 1534 both volumes combined, New and Old Testament).

Very soon, one third of the population able to read owned such a Bible. The language, at that time diverted into many dialects and spellings, began to take shape and changed into a more regulated version. The content as such was not that important. Whether the Bible, or something of different genre, witty or basic, it was mainly important to form a baseline against which spelling and grammar could be compared.

Books in general, with more or less valuable content, did not only help to regulate the orthography, they also compressed and standardized folktales, which were before fragmented into numerous versions. The race began and the one who came first set the standard of a more or less common story. It is like spreading a rumor – the first version heard is usually the best and most trusted.

But that phenomenon soon reversed itself: After some folktales had been 'trimmed' into a unique version, clever writers used this occasion to modify these tales again into new fables of their own and distributed them among the people.

Among many others, there is one basic story which came back in numerous individual and regional versions. Wherever some rocks reach above ground, many storytellers declare that as the work of the devil. What all of these pilfered tales have in common: At the end, the devil took the bow and shot an arrow into a cock's butt.

Inspired by these folktales, people soon came up with the idea to put a weathercock on the roof of their house. Today, most of the weathercocks *stand* on the arrow pointing in the direction the wind comes from, which became a better indicator.

Let us first take an original, standardized folktale, 'Die Teufelsmauer' (the devil's wall), as it appears in the first volume of the German folktales of the Grimm Brothers, numbered 189.

A mountain range was created by the devil, called the Harz Mountains, when he furiously threw around some building material. He had asked God to give him a piece of the Earth and he agreed. God, however, wanted to limit this area and told the devil that he can have as much as he would be able to surround with a stone wall and before the cock's crow in the morning.

The devil began his work, and just before he was about to set the last stone, he heard the cock's crow. The devil, very angry, tore the wall apart and threw everything into piles. Until today, he haunts the region.

What follows is one of the modified versions, a folktale called 'Die Teufelsmauer und der Hahn von St. Johann (the devil's wall and the cock of St. John's), putting the action into Austria:

The devil wanted to erect a wall and redirect the Danube River to flood a small church. He didn't like that so many pilgrims came to worship in this place because of the wonders of the Holy Albinus, who preached in this little church of St. John im Mauerthale (Mauertal valley), in Lower Austria.

Also here, he had to finish his work before the cock started to crow. The devil – aware of his past problems when he tried to get a piece of the Earth – had taken precautions and had purchased all the cocks in the area.

Only a single countrywoman did not want to sell her cock and sent the devil away. The bird sat on the church steeple and began to crow too early. The devil shot an arrow at him and still today, the cock sits on the top of that church, with an arrow in its butt, but has meanwhile been replaced by a metal version.

In another adaption of this 'masterpiece of archery legends', the devil wanted to redirect the Danube in even larger dimensions. Two men, one of them lived in Aggstein and the other one in Hinterhaus, had asked for the hand of the daughter of the Knight of Aggstein. The matter was decided in a tournament and the unsuccessful contestant from Hinterhaus – full of grief – wanted to throw himself into the Danube. The devil offered him to dam the water high up to the Aggstein castle to drown his opponent. He wanted to build a wall before the cock was crowing. Here too, the cock crowed too early and got an arrow into his butt, before the devil returned to hell.

The knight from Hinterhaus regretted his collaboration with the devil and set off on a pilgrimage into the Holy Land. Later, he entered the monastery of Aggstein and lived a long life as a pious monk.

In conclusion: Primitive tomfoolery, couched in folktale and most of it just shoddy imitations.

311

SHAOHAO – THE CHINESE COUNTERFEITER

The Chinese claim that they have their history precisely recorded and under control like no other culture. Their records can be followed back and deep into the past, based on the periods in which certain families and Emperors ruled.

Well, that is a bit exaggerated, as it seems that the Chinese are not able to go back in history beyond the year 2852 BC. Before that, they just gave three Emperors an 'extended term': Nuwa was a goddess and the first Emperor. She created Earth and repaired the wall of heaven. She ruled for 180000 years. Then we have the time of Youchao, with a term of 110000 years, followed by Suiren, with the longest 'years of reign' – for 456000 years. From then on, we have more realistic numbers:

During the period 2852 - 2737 BC, we have the first mythical Emperor, named 'Fuxi'. At the same time, the manufacture of pottery started in China. The Chinese should have immediately started to make enough large pots, to dump and hide the widespread hogwash contained in their myths, on whatever material it was written upon. The paper was invented 105 AD.

2737 - 2699 BC – the Yan Emperor or Shennong.

2699 - 2588 BC – the Yellow Emperor or Gonsung Xuanyuan. He is the father of Chinese civilization. Some 50 years earlier (2650), the Egyptians had already finished their first pyramid.

2587 - 2491 BC – Shaohao or Jin Tian. The Chinese claim that he has invented bow and arrow.

As we know that the Chinese mimics had already started to copy anything in sight since man was created, it should not make us wonder that Shaohao claims to have 'invented' bow and arrow.

But there is certainly *"sum ting wong"* (something wrong) here! In the Oetztal Alps, between Austria and Italy, they have found a mummy named 'Oetzi' or 'Frozen Fritz', who fell over with an arrow in his shoulder, shot from a bow some 5000 years ago. That would have been around 3000 years BC and approximately 400 to 500 years before bow and arrow have been 'invented' by the Chinese. Therefore, even the idea of this 'first machine' was stolen.

2490 - 2413 BC – Zhuanxu or Gaoyang.

2412 - 2343 BC – Ku or Gaoxin.

2343 - 2333 BC – Zhi or Qingyang-shi.

2333 - 2234 BC – the 99 (!) years of Yao or Yaotang-shi.

2233 – 2184 BC – Shun or Youyu-shi

I think we can stop here. Whatever the Chinese might really have invented, papermaking, gunpowder, printing or the compass – it was certainly not bow and arrow.

The only obligation that remains for the chronicler is to mention the last period of the historical order. After 1949 AD, starting with Mao Zedong, the rulers were called Chairman of the Communist party and not Emperor anymore.

New 'inventions' have followed, like toxic painting on toys, Adidas- and Nike shoes, Fruit of the Loom underwear, Watermark pens, Rolex watches, Lacoste shirts, Black Forest clocks and many other brand-name products.

THE AMAZONS

Oh yes, the Amazons at last! The legends around them must be among the weirdest ever written.

Dead wrong! - the Amazons really existed!

First of all: Why are the Amazons called Amazons?

The dumbest explanation is that the Amazons are said to have burned the right breast of their daughters, so they could handle a bow without hindrance. Therefore, the Greek name 'Amazon' is often attributed to 'a-mazos' (breast less).

Stupid ramblings! In reality, the female warriors wore only a leather triangle, which protected the breast from the forward slap of the string. This kind of protection is even common in modern archery and is also worn by men. Furthermore: Why only the right breast? In that case, all the Amazons would have been left-handed, according to the correct way a bow is drawn.

In all antique Greek presentations – which are authentic for a change – the Amazons are displayed with two breasts. The origin of the term Amazons from the words 'a-mazos' is therefore flatly refused by serious researchers.

Another, no less absurd interpretation, derives the name from the word 'zone' (belt). An Amazon would therefore be 'well-belted', as if the name of a warrior woman would come from fashion accessories. Others suggest that the name is based on the Indo-Iranian word 'Hamazan' (fighter).

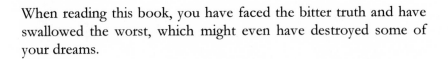

When reading this book, you have faced the bitter truth and have swallowed the worst, which might even have destroyed some of your dreams.

Therefore, shortly before turning over the last pages, you certainly want to know where the name for the 'Amazons' *really* comes from. After all, they are the main characters in stories that are *not* legends. Correct, they are *not* legends!

Beyond the slightest doubt, the name derives from the Greek word for bread 'maz**as**' (and not maz**os**!) and 'a-maz**as**' means *bread*-less.

We know that the Amazons considered the consumption of bread to be 'sissy'. Their male slaves – only occasionally needed for certain 'services' – were mostly nourished on bread, while the female warriors fed themselves on protein- and vitamin-rich food, such as meat, fish and fruit.

Homer, one of the writers of the wildest Greek fantasy stories, such as the Odyssey, from which we know the archery trick shot through the holes of twelve axes, mentions the Amazons in another one of his concoctions called 'the Iliad'.

Homer does not just mention the 'Amazons', but includes these factual female warriors as an important part of his antique cock-and-bull story, under the name 'Antianeirai' (men-hating).

Whoever raises the objection now – especially after having read this book – that these Amazons could not have existed if someone like Homer mentions them in one of his bizarre stories, must learn this last lesson about lies and twisted stories, called myths, folktales or legends (or many other stories for that matter).

Homer assumes that his readers know the essentials about the existence and the life of the Amazons. He has cleverly added these well-known and true facts with the intention to distract the reader from the principal- but untrue content of his literary outpourings.

We know such 'jokes' from the Internet, called 'hoaxes', which are constructed in this way. Emails with false stories, cleverly mixed with factual, but in substance meaningless elements, are spread around. When friends and colleagues are then misled by the cleverly added 'ingredients' and subsequently believe that the main story is true, the hoax usually finds a rapid and wide distribution.

This Iliad-hoax of Homer, with its devious integration of these female warriors into an otherwise untrue story, confirms to us, in Homer's very own way, the existence of the Amazons – free of any doubt.

The Amazons had been excellent archers and audacious riders. They were honorable, courageous and dignified and were never described as treacherous or cowardly.

On top of it all, there was the erotic aspect. The often only sparsely clothed Amazons have stimulated the imagination of men up to the present time and are the most popular subject in comic strips.

Even the Spanish conquerors were so much impressed by the stories and the erotic perceptions around the Amazons that their mind became twisted and distorted.

During their conquests in the years 1541 and 1542, under the leadership of 'Francisco de Orellana', the Spanish, after a long solitude and abstinence on their seemingly endless journey, moved up-stream in South America.

They noticed a number of attractive and well-armed female warriors on the banks of the river, who fearlessly shot arrows at their ships. With the Amazons in mind, they immediately called the river 'Amazon'. That had later proved to be very embarrassing for the conceited Spanish 'hombres' as it turned out that their 'Amazons' were in reality men with long, black hair.

As there is no doubt that the Amazons really existed, it leaves people arguing about their place of primary origin. Today, we can more or less locate that in the north of the present day Turkey and at the mouth of the River Thermodon (today Terme Çay), which leads into the Black Sea.

Despite these undisputable facts, the Ukraine claims to be the homeland of the Amazons. In the city of 'Lviv', in the Western Ukraine, they do not think that the Amazons are just a myth. Moreover, they are convinced that they are part of Ukrainian history.

The sports scientist and radical feminist, promoter of Amazon-myths and girl gangs, Kateryna Tarnovska, has founded a school where young women are taught to be modern Amazons. They practice martial arts and follow a unique philosophy. Convinced, that the women in the country have Amazon blood, the girls exercise self-defense and female martial art, called 'Asgarda', the knight arts for Ukrainian women. In several hours of training sessions, they are trained in combat and the use of ancient Ukrainian weapons, like sickles, sticks and chains.

They acquire philosophical, psychological and naturopathic knowledge, and to assure perfectionism for Ukrainian Amazons, there are courses that teach them strategies for a more hands-on use. In this category, they practice many things like good conversational culture, how to start a family and to raise children, perfect housekeeping, entrepreneurship, assertiveness, cooking, good eating habits, knitting, painting and involve in embroidery.

All of that makes the Ukrainian 'Amazons' fit for modern life.

After Russia, the Ukraine is the second largest country – by area – in Europe and is located from time immemorial between two worlds in the East and the West. Situated near the Amazon country, it is quite possible that Amazons had once passed through, but to place the land of the Amazons exclusively on the banks of the 'Azov Sea' in the district of 'Oblast Donek' and thereby identifying them completely with the Ukraine, is not just wishful thinking, but highly embarrassing.

We do not have any original Amazons anymore, because they had subsequently integrated with the Scythians and at some point, abandoned their peculiar method of securing the survival of their species with men held in slavery.

Today, they live on as erotic fighting machines and superheroes in comic books and computer games. Nowadays, they seldom use bow and arrow, and when they do not travel with old instruments of war, they pull the trigger of high-tech shooting devices.

There are numerous Hollywood movies, based on comic book templates that tell stories about the heroic deeds of these fighting women.

We know Jennifer Garner as 'Electra' or Charlize Theron as 'Aeon Flux'.

In the eponymous film adaptation of the video game 'Blood Rayne', we meet 'Rayne', who is played by Kristanna Loken in the first part and Natassia Malthe in the second part.

In the 'X-men' movies, the heroine 'Storm' is played by Halle Berry, who we also know from the movie 'Cat Woman'. Pamela Anderson left David Hasselhoff alone on the beach with the rest of the pinkish-red Baywatch bathing suits and appeared on the movie screen as 'Barb Wire' with her famous saying: *"Don't call me babe!"*

One movie, however, was a flop: It was the horrible filming of 'Red Sonja', and definitely not only because the Dutch have tried to participate in a US production (with a Danish actress).

The great – but not tall – movie director Dino de Laurentis, who is, among other things, responsible for the world-famous monumental film 'War and Peace', desperately sought a leading actress that matched his picture of an Amazon. Dino, son of an Italian pasta maker and once a traveling salesman for pasta products, had finally found what he wanted, eight weeks before the shooting began.

Dino, standing 5 feet 4 tall in his elevated Bugarri shoes, had seen Brigitte Nielsen, looking down on him from the cover of a fashion magazine: athletic, 6 feet tall and blond. Shortly thereafter, Brigitte Nielsen, who had a modeling job in Milan, flew to Rome for a screen test.

Dino was probably not able to concentrate on the job anymore. The movie was a total disaster and the ticket sales did merely come close to recoup half of the production cost.

At the 'Golden Raspberry Awards', the price for very poor performance and the counterpart of the 'Oscar', the movie was in the front line of the 'honors'. Worst actress: Brigitte Nielsen (nominated). Worst supporting actress: Sandahl Bergman (nominated). Poor Sandahl Bergmann! She must have had a premonition when she rejected the leading role of 'Sonja'.

Thereafter, Brigitte Nielsen acted in several other movies at the lower end of the artistic scale, with varying degree of success. Her supporting role in Rocky IV and the close cooperation with Silvester Stallone ended in a short marriage with the 'Italian Stallion'.

Things had come out a lot better for Brigitte Nielsen in the film 'Conan the Barbarian' on the side of the 'Styrian Oak' Arnold Schwarzenegger. They did not only nominate her for the Golden Globe award as best supporting actress in her role as 'Valeria', she had even won it.

This film, however, became a big problem for 'Conan' alias Arnold Schwarzenegger, after he took office as 'Gofferner' (Austrian English for Governor) of California.

There had been many jokes about him and his leading role in this movie. He took it with humor: *"That was my worst movie. Whenever my children are behaving badly, I send them to their room and let them see 'Red Sonja' ten times in a row. I have little trouble with them."*

The superlatives that are usually attributed to the new Amazons are hard to beat: 'Most beautiful woman in the world', 'most beautiful woman of all time', 'most attractive woman in the world' or 'sexiest woman alive', are common attributes for the female fighting machines, who incidentally collect Oscars and Golden Globes like the tooth fairy hoards baby teeth.

We should not forget Angelina Jolie in her role as 'Lara Croft' or – many years ago – Jane Fonda as Barbarella.

Tony Guard invented the character of Lara Croft as a hero for a computer game. He initially wanted a male hero, but then he thought it would be ridiculous and inappropriate to provide his main character with such acrobatic features, and the figure became female.

Lara Croft is one of the bestselling computer games. There is no other video game surrounded by so many merchandising articles. While predominantly male beings spent their time playing on the computer, Lara Croft has a high percentage of female players. The Amazons must be – here and there – still within.

Two movies followed, 'Lara Croft – Tomb Raider' and 'Lara Croft – The Cradle of Life'. In addition, there are many comics with stories of Lara Croft.

The beautiful Charlize Theron (Aeon Flux), who grew up in Johannesburg, South Africa, even descends from a real Amazon.

Her abusive father, a Huguenot contractor, pulled a gun on her mother and physically attacked her after he came home drunk.

Without further ado, her German born mother took the gun away and shot him dead. The shooting was legally adjudged to have been self-defense and her mother faced no charges.

Charlize was 15 years old when she watched that – and she and her mother have remained very close.

It would be too much to list all female superheroes. There are hundreds with the initial letters of their names spread across the alphabet: Aeon Flux, Alice, Atom Eve, Batgirl, Batwoman, Barb Wire, Catwoman, Domino, Doll Girl. Dawn, Elastigirl, Electra, Fallen Angel, Ganymede, Hellcat, Icemaden, Jayna, Katana, Layla, Maxima, Monstress, Nightcat, Nightveil, Owlwoman, Poison Ivy, Power Girl, Queen of Swords, Rayne, Red Sonja, Sabra, Scarlet Witch, Shanna the She Devil, Spidergirl, Spiderwoman, She-Ra, Supergirl, Tank Girl, Thor Girl, Valda the Iron Maiden, Vampirella, Vixen, White Witch, Witchblade, Wonder Girl, Xena, Gertrude Yorkes, Zatanna or Princess Zelda.

The only letter that cannot be found is the 'U'. I don't see this just as a coincidence. For me, it is a clear sign and an outcry of the Amazons: We are not from the U-kraine!

A FAIRY TALE – THE NAUGHTY BOY

Most fairy tales are wholesome and good. The package contains the ingredients listed.

We enjoy fairy tales – well, at least the major part of them – and as an adult, we read the story, knowing that it is not true – it is only a fairy tale.

Children can safely be left in the belief that there is a man in the moon or a Santa Claus, and it was the Tooth Fairy that picked up their many lost baby teeth under the pillow and left something as a consolation. This is all harmless.

These tales often have good educational components; they teach children in a simple, memorable way and stimulate the imagination.

But there are other examples as well, not suitable for children, even in the 21st century. They contain bestiality, cruelty, harsh punishment, incest, torture, rape, cannibalism, infanticide or necrophilia.

Let us finish the chapters of this book with a fairy tale by Hans Christian Andersen. After all, he is someone who correctly calls his stories fairy tales.

A lovely tale comes to mind, naturally with bow and arrow. As a bonus, this special fable makes fun of the Greek mythology.

An old poet sat at home in front of the oven in his little living room and some apples were roasting in front of it. He was not only a good poet, but also a good man and he felt pity for the people who were still outside, as the weather was terrible.

Suddenly, there was a knock on the door: *"Please open, I am freezing and I am all wet!"* he heard a child whining. The poet hastily opened the door and saw a little boy that stood there, completely naked. He shivered from the cold. The water ran through his curly blond hair.

"You poor boy!" said the poet. He took his hand and pulled him inside. *"Come to me, I will warm you and you can have some wine and an apple, you are a gorgeous boy!"*

The boy was gorgeous indeed. His eyes sparkled like bright stars. He looked like a real angel, but he was pale and cold. In his hand, he carried a beautiful bow. It seemed a little damaged by the rain. Besides, the arrows had been affected and the colors on the shafts faded into one another, dissolved from the water.

The poet sat down at the stove with the little boy on his lap. He dried his curly hair, warmed his hands in his and heated up some mulled wine. The boy quickly recovered. He had red cheeks again and soon he jumped up and danced around the room.

"You are a funny boy", said the poet, *"what's your name?"* The boy answered: *"My name is Cupid, don't you know me?"* and he continued: *"There lies my bow, believe me, I can shoot with it!"*

"See, now the weather is fine again out there, the moon shines", said the boy after a while. *"But your bow has been damaged"*, argued the poet, when the boy was about to leave.

"That would be bad", said the boy. *"No, it has dried up again; it has not suffered any damage. The string is sitting tight and I will try it out now."*

The boy put an arrow on the string, drew the bow and shot the good old poet right in the middle of his heart. *"See, my bow is not damaged!"* he said and went away laughing.

What a naughty boy! How could he shoot at the good old poet who let him in and was so friendly and kind? He even gave him apples and some of his best wine.

The poet lay on the floor and wept, he had indeed just been shot into the heart (perhaps he should not have given some of the wine to a little child, especially as the boy was armed).

"How outrageous, what a naughty boy this Cupid", he said. *"I will tell that to all children, so that they become wary and never play with him, because he will certainly harm them."*

All good children, girls and boys who had been told this story, are now aware of the evil Cupid. But he gets them all. He comes to the students, when they return from their lectures and walks by their side. He follows young girls, when they are going to church and watches for an opportunity; he is always waylaying people.

In the theater, he sits in the chandelier, fully ablaze; men fancy it a lamp, but they are soon undeceived. He wanders around in the Royal gardens and public walks, making mischief everywhere.

He even shot your mother and your father straight into their heart. Just ask them, they will confirm it. They will even tell you that he once shot at your grandmother and grandfather.

Yes, this boy is bad. You don't want to have anything to do with him; he tries to shoot everybody.

Ugh! This Cupid is wicked, but you know him now. Beware of him, beware of him, dear child!

APODOSIS

If something you had believed in is perhaps no longer the way it used to be, think about it: the way it was before, was not the way it was at all!